Praise for THINGS THEY LOST

'Dazzling… In giddily exuberant prose, Oduor gradually reveals a terrifying story of generations of maternal abuse and dysfunction.'

Financial Times

'Oduor's magical, beguiling debut novel carries echoes of Toni Morrison's *Beloved*… Her ability to tap into a depth and range of feeling, while accessing unexpected humour, is uncanny. Throughout the novel, Oduor skilfully balances whimsy with satirical, devastating realism… The result is a surreal novel that is beautifully written, compelling, ominous and mysterious, with a strong, young, female Kenyan voice at the centre.'

Guardian

'An extraordinary tale about love, longing, and the bond between mothers and daughters.'

Vogue

'A tale steeped in the acrid surrealism of childhood, populated by wicked wraiths and held together by the vicious spell mothers can cast on their daughters.'

Leila Aboulela, author of *Bird Summons*

'The supernatural runs amok, for good and ill, in this boisterous and bittersweet saga tracking four generations of women from a cursed family in a fictional East African town… Oduor's freewheeling invention [is] an undeniable strength.'

Daily Mail

'Some novels demand you read every word with great care, making the experience one of cumulative intensity. *Things They Lost*, the astonishing debut from the Kenyan writer Okwiri Oduor, is such a novel. Oduor has produced page after page of gorgeous, elegiac prose. Dense and rich as a black Christmas cake and alternately whimsical, sweet and dark, *Things They Lost* is a complex work, brimming with uncompromisingly African magical realism, about the ambiguity of toxic mother-daughter relationships and the urgently restorative nature of friends!

'*Things They Lost*, written by Caine Prize-winning Kenyan author Oduor, defies categorisation... The writing is mesmeric, at times as warm and rhythmic as a lullaby, and filled with gentle, keen observations of the natural world. A book with a big heart that feels like a hug.'

New Internationalist

'An original and dazzling debut novel… A haunting, magical union of Kenyan folklore and the sometimes fragile union between mother and daughter.'

New African

'A soaring debut. *Things They Lost* is an exhilarating read. I could not put it down.'

Peace Adzo Medie, author of *His Only Wife*

'From the start, Oduor – a winner of the Caine Prize for African Writing, among other honors – broadcasts her tremendous talents... Come for the beguiling narrative, and stay for the rich, evocative language.'

Vulture, Most Anticipated Books of 2022

'What a singular and palpable world, teeming with life and wonder. In exuberant prose, at once witty and poetic, Okwiri Oduor threads a wondrous tale of girlhood, longing, and community with the ghosts that both love and hurt us. I read this book with gratefulness and awe! We will be reading Ms. Oduor for years to come.'

Novuyo Rosa Tshuma, author of *House of Stone*

'In this debut set in late 1980s Kenya, spirits benevolent and malicious rattle in attics and lead people's lives astray. Twelve-year-old Ayosa remembers things from long before her birth when she was just "a wriggling thing". Abandoned by her flighty mother for months at a time, she lives on handouts from neighbours and interprets violent intrusions from the natural world as desire... Rich with myth and the natural landscape of Kenya, this novel is entertaining and innovative.'

The Irish Times

'Kaleidoscopic in depth and breadth, this extraordinary debut is a magical and evocative story of mothers and daughters, longing and love.'

Ms. Magazine

'It is a story about mothers and daughters, of daughters who become mothers to daughters who become mothers, and a story of girls who are abandoned and alone, of girls who find family in other lonesome girls. It is also the story of how death permeates our lives... *Things They Lost* wrestles with how these changes are processed collectively, a complex combination of celebratory remembering and wilful forgetting.'

Guernica Magazine

'In this enchanting debut novel, Kenyan-born writer Oduor spins the magical tale of lonely young Ayosa... [and] explores generational abuse and violence with a gentle touch, managing to elicit compassion rather than judgment for these withholding mothers and daughters. From the novel's dazzling first sentence to its gratifying conclusion, readers will be mesmerized by Oduor's linguistic skills.'

Library Journal (starred review)

'Okwiri Oduor's penchant for magic emerges from her attention to ordinary things: she can make a teacup seem like the most interesting thing in the world... Her work does this thing where it makes me feel satisfied, like I have eaten exactly the right amount of my favourite food, but I am also ready to eat more until I am uncomfortably full and bursting at the seams with story and enchantment.'

Johannesburg Review of Books

'Rich, delicious and dark... The prose is beautiful and sensuous, filled with the wonder of the natural world, sealed with the supernatural. It slides and surprises, conjures up imagery with words that bewitchingly suit the scene, and remains utterly magical.'

The Book Satchel

'Meet Ayosa, the wonder of her world, the trauma, all captured by the most expressive and poetic writing. They say have your own style; does this whole book launch a new narrative fiction genre?'

Nataka Books

'This rich, delicious & dark family saga is titillating and unsettling, which creates such a beautiful picture of intergenerational trauma... It absolutely takes your breath away.'

Introverted Black Reader

THINGS THEY LOST

OKWIRI ODUOR

ONEWORLD

A Oneworld Book

First published in the United Kingdom, Ireland and Australia
by Oneworld Publications, 2022
This paperback edition published 2023

ISBN 978-0-86154-491-2
eISBN 978-0-86154-388-5

Interior design by Wendy Blum
Printed and bound in Great Britain by Clays Ltd, Elcograf S.p.A

Oneworld Publications
10 Bloomsbury Street
London WC1B 3SR
England

For Aya

December staggered in like a weary mud-encrusted vagabond who had been on her way to someplace else but whose legs had buckled and now she was here. On the second, which in Mapeli Town was known as Epitaph Day, the townspeople awoke while the sky was still silver, still tinged with ruffles of pink and blue. They gargled salt water. They greased their elbows. They tucked a flower in their hair or pinned it on their lapel. They marched to the schoolhouse, where the flag flapped at half-mast for all those who had drowned in the river or choked on a fishbone or stepped on a puff adder while walking to the marketplace. With eyes bleary and heads bowed, the townspeople thought of all the ones they had ever lost. They sang Luwere-luwere-luwere until their voices crackled. They murmured, Go well, Opembe, or, Greet our people, Makokha.

Then Mama Chibwire opened her shack and the townspeople gathered inside. They sat on the wooden benches with strings of sunlight spilling through holes in the tin roof and burning their eyes. They hunched over their knees and exchanged spittle on the unwashed mouths of their brew mugs. They called all their dead ones by name.

There was Netia, who had sometimes chewed on shards of broken glass as though these shards were roasted groundnuts. There was Dora Petronilla, who had never bought any salt of her own, who always knocked on neighbors' doors and said, Abane! I forgot again! Will you help me with some? There was Mwatha, who, after a treacherous pregnancy, birthed a reticulated python. There was Sagana, whose mouth had only wanted to eat wild, wood-rotting fungi. There was Halima, who had sold fried termites by the roadside, and Wambua, who had been born with a patch of gangrene on his calf, and Njambi, who had liked to stain her teeth red with henna.

The townspeople shook their heads, their hearts hurting afresh. Akh! they said. Death is tart, and death is cloying! And they sobbed into their brew mugs. And their hands sought out other fingers to clasp. And their arms sought out other arms to cling to. They had Lost. Later, when all the dead ones had been thought of in turn, and when all the brew in Mama Chibwire's barrels was gone, Sospeter Were brought out his PA system and radio cassette player, and the townspeople tied cardigans round their waists and writhed to *It's Disco Time with Samba Mapangala & Orchestre Virunga*. In that moment, with the ground throbbing beneath the soles of their feet, and with sweat trickling down the vales of their backs, the townspeople thought to themselves that they too could not wait to die, could not wait to leave behind people who would gather each Epitaph Day and think of them like this.

Some townspeople did not observe Epitaph Day. They had not lost anyone that year, or the ones they had lost were not worth remembering at all, or they had little inclination to share in the town's collective memory and rituals of grief. These people sat groggily on the edges of their beds. They stretched to thaw the cluster of knots in their shoulders. They tugged at their bedspreads and wriggled out of their sleeping clothes. They listened to the morning news—about Benazir Bhutto being sworn in as prime minister of Pakistan, and about the nuclear tests in French Polynesia. They listened to news about the flooding at the Nyando River in Kisumu, about the landslides in Marsabit, about the submerged maize crops in the Kericho Highlands. The radioman said that 1988 was the wettest year the country had seen in more than two decades.

Mako! the townspeople murmured to themselves, their mouths wide with dismay. They wondered which petty godhead had been offended and was now throwing childish tantrums like this. Shaking their heads, they gargled salt water. They greased their elbows. They stood at their kitchen sinks and soaked yellow scones in sweet black tea. They breathed in the tripe that was trapped in the lace edges of their drapes. In one tenement, Nyokabi sat on a footstool in her little kitchen, her wrapper mottled with clods of soil, a newspaper sheet on the floor before her. She bent over it, flaking yams, splitting them, tossing them into a basin of water. In another tenement, Subira, a housemaid, put on her madam's best frock and stuffed her madam's sleeping infant inside a duffel bag, then walked to the end of the street and took the bus to Kaloleni. Born-Free Opondo, whose flat was filled with cats and roosters and dusty bric-a-brac, rummaged through the papers stacked on his sitting room sofa, searching for his copy of *Mabepari wa Venisi*. Silas Hosanna—the lorry driver—rammed into a cow. With his hat folded beneath his arm, and with his face rumpled with sorrow, he dragged the cow's carcass to Mutheu Must Go Café. He knocked on the door, and when Sindano, the proprietor, came out, he said to her, Tell your mama I will buy her a new cow. Sindano smacked her lips

3

and said, You can tell her yourself. She is buried in the old cemetery, behind the abandoned posho mill. Didn't you hear the old bird ate a razor in her bread and kicked the bucket?

Incense curled in the air and its gray ash collapsed in heaps on window ledges. Fingers spread cold pomade on scalps. Clay mugs clinked against the stone receptacles of kitchen cabinets. The day crickets shrieked. And the wind, it rasped against the backs of spittlebugs, and it yanked bloomers off the wash lines and flung them across the sky. The clouds swayed. The string of alleys and thoroughfares twisted and tangled, so that people walking out in the street arrived to find that their legs were at home but their torsos still out in the marketplace. In the haze, a cat was not a cat but a length of twine twirled around a spool. A bird was not a bird but a cavernous bird-shaped room where chords of surging sound hung on painted walls. The town was not a town but a blood lily, shuddering, furling and unfurling, and then wilting, clenching into itself.

The townspeople unrolled reed mats on their verandas and sprawled themselves out. The red wind howled in their ears and lulled them. In their sleep, they left themselves and went elsewhere—they were on the road to Lungalunga, or inside the underwear drawers of old women's cupboards, or crouched on curtain boxes, beside dead geckos and cotton balls and browning birthday cards. The bodies they left behind on the reed mats were stiff and soggy, and mongrels came and licked the salt that clung to their temples. Aphids and katydids and lacewings hopped about. Weeping willows swayed, sprinkling fresh dew on the verandas. Nectar dripped from the orange tubes of lion's ear flowers. Ibises reeled through the air, gripping squirming fish between their beaks.

4

A whirlwind sprouted from the ground. It flung gravel at the slumbering townspeople to see if they would stir, and when they did not, it skipped from door to door, flinging open kitchen cabinets, pilfering measuring jugs and soup ladles and bread pans. Beyond the tin houses that crinkled in the heat, beyond the fields of bristle grass and juniper bushes and sunflowers bobbing drowsily, beyond the grebes and albatrosses wading in the roiling mud of the riverbank, beyond the papyrus reeds and sycamores and wattle trees, beyond the hill that sometimes shifted, as though from one aching foot to another, beyond all of that, was something else.

A ruin. Once a staggering mansion, now only a resting ground for weary shadows. The red wind rattled the chain-link, and the faint, rusted sign that read *Manor Mabel Brown* shook. The manor itself emerged piecemeal from the trees: a rickety gate flanked by stone angels with severed heads, and then a yard full of tangled balls of thorn trees and wildflowers and barbed wire and stiff yellow grass, and then an awning, double doors, a chimney. Another awning, double doors, and chimney. It parted in the middle, gave way to a drawbridge, and the drawbridge climbed over a bog.

In the early 1900s, an Englishwoman named Mabel Brown had chosen this hill to settle on, and the town had sprouted at her feet. First, the stonemasons had come. Next, the carpenters and the bricklayers and the roofers and the plumbers had followed, until the manor—fashioned after aristocratic Tuscany country homes—loomed through the woods. The entire town had burgeoned like that—at first, to build the Englishwoman her lurid and vulgar home, and later, to furnish it, and later yet, to attend to her every desire. For instance, when Mabel Brown grew fond of raspberry ice cream, someone moved into the town who could nurture raspberry bushes. Or when Mabel Brown developed a liking for plume hats, someone moved into the town who could fold an entire ostrich like origami and place it gently upon the woman's head. When Mabel Brown needed to attend a masquerade ball at the residence of one of her Happy Valley acquaintances, someone moved into the town, straight pins, thimble, and bobbins between the teeth, who could weave the most magnificent basque gown that anyone had ever seen.

The town was named after her, the Englishwoman. Yet, somewhere along the line, as though in a game of broken telephone, the name had transformed. Mabel Town had turned to Mapeli Town. It was not so much a deformation as an emancipation, for the name had softened, and could wedge itself better in the townspeople's mouths. Mabel Town had belonged to the Englishwoman, but Mapeli Town was *theirs*. They said "Mapeli" with such resolute pride, and no longer thought of the Englishwoman—the muskets she fired at the backs of fleeing children, the wildlife that she hauled from her hunting expeditions, the affairs that she had with her gardeners and cooks and drivers, the rents that she charged the townspeople for land that was more theirs than hers. But Mabel Brown was long gone, and now, sitting on a groaning staircase inside the decaying manor, was the loneliest girl in the world.

The Fatumas wanted her, or maybe they just wanted to knock against her shinbones to see if her shinbones were the types of shinbones that would cry ngo-ngo-ngo when you knocked on them with your knuckles, and now she herself wanted to know this, so she squatted down and knocked on her shinbones and they did not cry ngo-ngo-ngo because only oak doors and things like oak doors cry like that when you knock on them.

Her shinbones were made of paper. Different people's shinbones were made of different things. Some people's shinbones were made of bamboo flutes, and some people's shinbones were made of copper wire, and some people's shinbones were made of lemongrass stalks. She knew that her shinbones were made of paper because she knew the story of herself. Back in the Yonder Days, she was wriggling in the sky, and then her mama looked up with tears in her eyes, and her mama said, Please-please-please-I-need-you. That is how to summon wriggling things to yourself. And after you have said, Please-please-please-I-need-you, you close your eyes and think of what type of arm bones and collarbones and shinbones you want the wriggling thing to have when it comes to you.

Her mama was distracted the day she summoned Ayosa to herself. It was a hot damp day, and blowflies buzzed in her mama's ears and nostrils and on the corners of her mouth. Her mama rolled up a newspaper and swatted at the blowflies, and she summoned the wriggling thing from the sky and swatted at the blowflies, and when Ayosa came to her, she was still thinking of the blowflies, still swatting at them with the newspaper. That was how come Ayosa's shinbones were made up of newspaper. Ayosa was lucky that her shinbones were not made of flies at all.

Her mama had never told her this story. Ayosa just knew it by herself. She had been there, and had seen it all unfold. She remembered many details about the day—her mama's worn-out, bruised face, and her palms crinkled by the green river water, and her bloodied dress, and the sun dangling down from the sky, as though from a string, all loose and cold and gray. Earlier that day, the logger-man had held a knife to her mama's throat, tearing it open. He'd said, Don't think you can just contradict me as you like, Nabumbo Promise Brown. And when he'd set off walking down the road, her mama had jumped into her jalopy and run him over. Snapped his legs like sugarcane stalks. Said to him, I have finished two other people like this. Say ng'we and I will finish you too!

They had always loved each other like that, the two of them. Loved with that love that whirred and maimed like a chain saw.

Ayosa had many such memories, of the Yonder Days, before she'd turned into a girl. She had been a wriggling thing, unbound, light as a Sunday morning thought. She'd drifted on by, watching people. Well, watching mostly her mama. She had watched her mama for years before that day when her mama felt her close by and said, Please-please-please I need you. Most people did not have these sorts of memories. Ayosa knew that it was rather unusual to possess them. She constantly had to watch her mouth lest she unnerve her mama with the knowledge of something that had taken place long before she was born. Something that she was not supposed to know. For example, she could not just blurt out, Remember, Mama, when you were six and you drowned your brother in the well? Remember, Mama, what happened after? How your mother didn't feel like being your mother anymore, so she sent you off to the orphanage? Or, Remember that time you fell deep inside yourself, Mama, and you found another life waiting in there? A separate life? In that life you were someone else, living in another country. Remember? And later, when you came back, you said, My God, who knew that lives sometimes are nestled inside each other like babushka dolls?

Ayosa took out her notebook and wrote all this down. Someday she would confess to her mama. Tell her that she *knew* all the things. Tell her that she had followed her all those years. She wondered how her mama would take the news. Probably she would pack up her bags and leave. No doubt, Ayosa thought. Her mama would *definitely* leave her. But what difference did it make? Her mama was always leaving her.

What are you writing? the Fatumas asked.

Notes, she said.

The Fatumas studied her. About your mama? You have that look that comes on your face when you're thinking of her.

Ayosa shrugged. She put the notebook away. She squatted, rested her chin on the crack between her knobbly knees. The Fatumas moved to the double-hung window, transistor radio in their hands. The breeze slid in through cracks held down by old Scotch tape, and it ruffled their hair and muslin frocks. The Fatumas were creatures of the attic, half girl and half reverie. There were two of them. They both had gaunt, gauzy bodies. Their hair was made of cobwebs. Their eyes were bay windows, and when you looked into them, you saw fruit bats and toad-stools and tadpoles dangling from gnarled fig branches.

Four hundred years ago, a fisherman had pulled the Fatumas out of the Indian Ocean and into his dhow. That's all the Fatumas knew—that they had come from the depths of the water, somewhere between the Comoros and Zanzibar. They had spent centuries in indentured servitude, first on Kiwayu Island, next in Pemba, and after, traded off for petty items like tobacco and palm wine. That's how they had ended up so far in the hinterland, in the hands of an old hag called Nyang'au. Nyang'au had found work in Mabel Brown's household as a cook. The truth, however, was that she had known nothing at all about the al-chemy of fat and salt, nor about the gas range and masonry oven and electric griddle. She had kept the Fatumas stuffed inside a coffee tin on the mantelpiece, and for thirty-two years, had made them cook the cui-sine for which Nyang'au's name was famed across the entire province. Truffles. Foie gras. Caviar. Gourmet cheeses. Mead from comb honey, and wine from rhubarb or parsnip or beetroot. When Nyang'au took ill and died, the Fatumas found themselves suddenly unencumbered. They longed terribly to return to the vast sea but did not know how to get there. In desperation, they climbed up to the attic and hid. That's where, decades later, the little Ayosa had discovered them.

Ayosa had learned their faces long before she grew aware of her own. As a child, she had been fussy and full of rage, always squalling, and her mama often carried her to the attic and left her there to weep herself hoarse. The Fatumas had soothed her, had sung lala kitoto to her in their soft echoey voices. She had stared into their bay window eyes and been enchanted by things she saw—wasps circling the sta-mens of nightshades, or elfin skippers swaying in their hammocklike cocoons, or flap-necked chameleons walking that walk that was not a walk but a stutter.

Hush! the Fatumas hissed at Ayosa.

I didn't say a thing.

You're *thinking*. Don't think. The death news is starting.

They adjusted the knob on the transistor radio. Raised the volume. The radioman said:

> *The death is announced of Samson Mungwana, who taught home economics at Masaku Secondary School. Samson was bitten by a rabid dog on Saturday night. He is survived by no one—he was a childless widower.*

The Fatumas turned away from the window, their eyes brimming. The radioman said:

> *The death is announced of Paul Njaramba, who walked out in the rain without a jacket on and caught pneumonia. He is survived by a dog and a cat and a wife and a baby.*

The Fatumas let out a gasp, their breaths swirling out of their gray lips in thin rinds, turning to mist on the windowpanes.

The radioman said:

> *The death is announced of Zainabu Wamukoya, who stepped on a live wire by accident while jumping over a puddle in the street. Zainabu is survived by her mama, Mkanda Wamukoya.*

This was how the Fatumas spent their days, standing at those broken windows, their foreheads pressed to the panes. They listened to the death news, grief-stricken by the things they heard had happened to those strangers. Then they hurled themselves down and curled up in balls and wailed, slamming their fists on the warped parquet floor. When they did this, the whole house shook from side to side and hemmed and hawed and made such turmoil that rooms sometimes slid across entire hallways. Ayosa pressed her hands over her ears. She squeezed her eyes shut and waited for their grief to subside.

There was a girl at the window, standing so still you would think she was only a crease in the drapes. Ayosa had first noticed her months ago, although she suspected that the girl had stood there much longer than that. Watching, just watching. And blinking. Unflinching. If flies came and buzzed around her face, she did not swat at them. Sometimes a cat came and sat on her shoulder and she did not shoo it away. The girl at the window came on some mornings and did not on others.

Ayosa once went down to Jentrix the apothecary's place to fetch chili seedlings for her mama, and she saw the girl there too, standing at the apothecary's window, watching the apothecary turn a footling breech baby down the right way inside a woman's belly. Ayosa knew then that this girl had a timetable of sorts, one that told her which window to watch on which day. Later, when the apothecary was done with the pregnant woman, she gave Ayosa a bowl of gruel and Ayosa pointed at the window and said, Who's that?

Just a throwaway girl, Jentrix the apothecary said.

What's that mean?

Means someone left her in the gutter, like litter. Don't mind her, she means no harm.

The girl spent an hour or two at a time at the window. It did not matter if there was something interesting to look at or not. Sometimes she would just study the cobwebs that fluttered when the air startled. Or she would watch the way the shadows skittered across the floor, like a brood of boisterous kittens. Or she would watch the dirty dishes in the sink, stacked so high that some plates and bowls touched the ceiling. Or she would watch Ayosa sitting there, peeling a pear with a paring knife, or scraping candle wax off the table, or winding one of her mama's cassette tapes back with a ballpoint pen before shoving it into the radio.

Ayosa had a great fear now—that one day something would happen, and the throwaway girl would not come to the window anymore. Maybe the people who had left her in the gutter like litter would return for her. Or maybe she would feel too grown to while the time away like this, with her forehead pressed to strangers' windowpanes. And then what? Ayosa's heart sank whenever she thought of it. Truth was, there was something about the throwaway girl. A sweetness. A gentleness. They said nothing out loud to each other, yet their silence was a type of language. When they looked at each other, they spoke multitudes with their eyes.

They said: Poor thing, your mama isn't back yet? She left you alone for so long . . . If I didn't know better, I would think you were a throwaway girl too.

And: You're getting awfully skinny, you want some oxtail? I've got some oxtail. My mama made some soup and froze it, can't remember when exactly, but I guess it's still good to eat.

And: Listen to me, you've got to watch out for the busboys and preacher-men. And if you watch out and still get dirtied anyway, you've got to run to the Marie Stopes clinic—they will know what to do.

Today, the girl at the window had hurried off early. To catch some fish, she'd said with her eyes. She'd said that she had stolen a fishing line and that she had a pocketful of squirming bait and she supposed that she and her cat would have smoked trout for supper. Now Ayosa sat on the porch steps, sad and alone, and watched as the milkman rode up the hill. As he steadied his bicycle against an avocado tree. As he unstrapped a canister from the carrier and placed it on the step.

Hello, Mr. Milkman, Ayosa said.

The milkman said nothing.

Mr. Milkman, I said: Hello, Mr. Milkman.

The milkman turned away. He climbed onto his bicycle, jingled the bell, and rode down the hill. Ayosa picked up a rock and hurled it after him. The rock fell on a rosebush, upsetting a cloud of gnats. It happened every day—the milkman came and left without saying a thing to her, without even raising his eyes from the ground, and she picked up a rock and hurled it at him. Sometimes the rock hit him on the shoulder or the neck, and sometimes it did not.

Ayosa dragged the canister inside. She stood on a footstool and reached into the cabinet for a drinking jar. She filled it with milk and sipped on it. The milk was warm and frothy. It tasted like the cow's moldy tits. Outside, the clouds twirled and the world became paisley prints and palm oil stains and hot breaths on necks and grass tickling the backs of thighs. Ayosa trailed away from the house. She walked through the woods, past the cow barn that her mama had turned into a studio, past the wattle trees and sycamores, all the way down to the river. She hoped to see the throwaway girl fishing for trout with her cat. But she did not, so she sat with her feet in the water. A fisherman bobbed by on his boat, his bare back rippling with sweat. From that distance, he could not tell if Ayosa was really a girl or if she was a spirit child, and he did not mean to take any chances, and so he tipped his sunhat, reached into his net, and tossed her an offering of the thing he had just caught.

It was a lungfish. It writhed in Ayosa's lap and then slithered into the mud. Ayosa watched it crawl away. She wiped her hands against her frock. She watched as a monitor lizard emerged from a canopy of thistles and poppies, watched it forage about the riverbank. Ayosa took off her shoes and walked barefoot on the rocks. The water wanted her. It foamed in the spaces between her toes, tickling the soles of her feet. It brought her a red ribbon to tie her braids with, and a little child's rain poncho, and a biro pen cap, and the rubber wristband of a Casio watch, and a fish with a hook inside its mouth. She clutched these things to her chest and closed her eyes. She took a record of herself— the humming in her ears, and the silverfish glistening inside her eyelids, and the way her heart fluttered and then stilled. She memorized this, stored it elsewhere inside herself, so that someday, when she was all alone and nothing in the world thought of her, she would come back to this moment, would examine it and remember what it had felt like to be wanted.

She dug in the wet sand and when the hole was large enough, she put the things that the river had brought her inside it. She sang Luwere-luwere-luwere, and her voice crackled because "Luwere" was the type of song that finished all the sound inside a person's throat. It was the type of song that finished the breath inside a person's nostrils. She stopped singing it, lest it kill her. Now she tossed rocks into blackberry bushes. She climbed the wattle trees and when she got blisters on her palms, she burst them with a thorn. She poked twigs into the crests of anthills. Gnats and dragonflies and grasshoppers and bees spun maddeningly over her head, round and round, like a ceiling fan. She swatted at them and they scattered, but then a moment later, they all returned, darting about in round formation. The insects wanted her. She stopped swatting at them, and when they perched on her nose and ears and neck, her toes curled. She searched herself for the place where the feeling of being wanted percolated. It was in different places each time. Sometimes it was a throbbing in the back of her ears. Sometimes it was a soft tickling on the soles of her feet.

Ayosa broke off a stick. Waving it above her head, she walked through the fields of sunflowers and bristle grass, to the edge of the valley. A murram road marked the start of Mapeli Town. She stood there for a long while, watching as traders sold used brassieres and chewing clay and bucketfuls of little dried sardines. Omena! they called. Omena! Five shillings for one gorogoro!

Her mama had forbidden her from ever crossing the murram road, from ever venturing into the town on her own. Her mama said that the townspeople were dirty. That their mouths were full of mud. That they were uncouth, the crassest type of people there ever had been. Who knows what they will do to a sweet girl like you, her mama always said.

Ayosa looked about her, hoping to see the dirty people with the mouths that were full of mud. Across the street stood a decrepit shack. The sign above the door read *Mutheu Must Go Café*. The shack was a lonely, abandoned thing. Ayosa could tell by the way the tin eaves trembled pitifully in the breeze, and by the way the door hung on one rusted hinge, and by the way knotweed sprung through crevices in the flea-chewed walls, its white tassels draping over the windows, its hedgerow clamping over the entire shack. Ayosa stared at the shack for a long while, deliberating. She thought to herself that going there was not really disobeying her mama. She thought: a place that stood off on its own like that was not really part of anyone's town. That shack was its own separate town. Her mama had not forbidden her from visiting *other* towns.

So Ayosa started toward the shack. She forgot to look left and right first as her mama had taught her, and a bicycle almost ran her over. The bicyclist reached into his pocket, took out an egg, and hurled it at her. Yolk splattered all over her shoe.

You have the face of a warthog! the bicyclist called, holding one middle finger up.

Ayosa picked up a fistful of gravel and hurled it at the bicyclist. You have the face of an octopus, she called, holding two middle fingers up.

The bicyclist disappeared down the road. Ayosa watched egg yolk seep into her canvas shoe. Her toes were slimy and warm. She wiggled them to unstick them. Then she walked to the shack and stood in the doorway.

Above the window, a little brass bell hung by string from the rafter. Ayosa touched it, turning it over, examining the inscription on the tarnished lip. It read *Mutheu's Bell*.

A woman was stacking mugs on a tray at the counter.

Who is Mutheu? Ayosa said.

The woman looked up, wiping her brow with the back of her hand.

My mama's cow, she said, ripping open a paper bag and pouring sugar into a row of china bowls.

What type of cow?

A zebu cow, the woman said. Her face was the color of chickpeas that had been soaking overnight. Her wide-set eyes sloped downward. She had the type of beauty that spread itself patiently. One had to stare at her face intently in order to see the things sprouting in it—the dainty crow's-feet trickling out like tributaries into her temples, and the smattering of dimples that crimpled her cheeks, and the way her chin folded when she smiled.

Will you show me Mutheu the zebu cow? Ayosa said to her.

No, my dear, the woman said.

Because why?

Because this morning that blasted cow was crossing the road to graze on the other side and a lorry ran it over. The lorry-man came here dragging the dead cow behind him. He said to me, Tell your mama I will buy her another cow. And me, I said to him, Silas Hosanna, if you dare buy my mama another cow, I will be the one dragging your carcass across the town.

Did you not like Mutheu?

Lord, no. I hated the cow.

Because why did you hate it?

Just see! the woman said. She lifted her blouse, showing Ayosa a midsection riddled with scars, each of which was shaped like a door-knob. All these are hoof marks from Mutheu. That cow liked to chase me across the town and kick me.

Ayosa's fingers ached with desire to touch the scars. She tucked her hands beneath her armpits to stop herself from reaching over. The woman walked round the counter and busied herself with things Ayosa could not see.

Will you stand just nde'e over there all day?

Ayosa shrugged. I should go, I suppose.

Because why?

Because I saw your café from across the street and your café is called Mutheu Must Go Café so I came over here to ask who Mutheu is and why she must go but I suppose I know now so maybe you don't want me over here anymore.

I don't want you over here anymore? What type of mud is that you are starting to speak now? If I don't want you I will say, Look, I don't want you. But you haven't heard me say that, have you?

No.

Well then, sit. I will get you some chai.

Ayosa slid into a nearby chair.

Madam, where are the people?

What people?

Ayosa nodded at the empty tables around her. The customers, she said. Don't they come in here to drink your chai?

The woman let out a dry laugh. My dear, you are the first person who has stepped inside this door in ten years. People in this town would never drink any chai that I made.

Because why?

Because they are afraid of me.

Because why are they afraid of you?

The woman dug a hand inside the pocket of her apron. She was silent for a long moment, her eyes on a cleft in the wood of the window ledge.

Well, I killed ten men.

Ayosa's eyes widened. You strangled them?

No.

You struck them on the head with an axe?

No.

You pushed them down a flight of stairs?

No, my dear.

Did you drive a knife through their bellies?

Jesus, child, how do you know so many ways to kill a man?

The death news, Ayosa said.

The woman gave her head a sorrowful shake. Well, this is what happened. You see, ten different times I tried to get married. But always something killed the man on the morning of our wedding. One swallowed his tongue, another one was struck by lightning. One got lockjaw from being pricked by a thorn, and another one swallowed a mothball. Like that, like that. Ten whole men, not even half ones! So now no one wants a thing to do with me. That's why no one ever comes here to drink my chai.

Then why do you keep the café open if no one will come?

What else am I supposed to do now? I have a café. Shall I close it only because no one wants to drink my chai?

I suppose not, Ayosa said. She looked toward the window. Why do you have that bell over there? she said, pointing.

Oh, that? I hung it up this morning because I was so happy that the cow was dead. Every time the wind blows in and the bell tinkles, I cross myself and say, Wajamani-that-cow-is-dead.

The woman brought a metal teapot to Ayosa's table. How many sugars?

Twenty-six, Ayosa said.

Atse! Twenty-six whole sugars?

People can't have twenty-six sugars?

Of course not! People can only have two sugars.

So why did you ask me if you knew already?

The woman clicked her tongue. Now, child, you better not be impertinent or I will name this café Ayosa Must Go. You hear?

Sorry-sorry, Ayosa said, scrunching her forehead. She stared into the woman's sun-scorched face. How did you know my name? I didn't tell it to you.

Everyone knows your name! Everyone knows you, and they know your mama. Knew your grandmama too, and her mama before her.

Well, it's not fair that you know me but me I don't know you.

Sindano, the woman said. That's what my people call me.

How many people do you have?

Oh, just one. My mama.

And she calls you Sindano, like a needle for sewing dresses?

Yes, like a needle for sewing dresses. And *called*. The old toad croaked a month ago.

Why did your mama give you a name like that one?

Sindano lowered the kettle over another mug. Well, my mama named me after a song. The one about camels going through the eyes of needles.

Sing for me I hear.

Sindano placed the kettle down. She sang:

> *Ngamia ni rahisi sana*
> *Kuingia tundu la sindano*
> *Kuliko mtu mwenye mali*
> *Kuingia mbinguni kwa Baba*

Ayosa sipped her chai. It was tepid and tasted faintly of ghee. She wondered if it had been brewed with milk from Mutheu the dead cow, wondered if maybe Sindano had stood over its carcass and twisted its limp udder until it was all wrung out.

Sindano? Ayosa said.

Yes, my name?

Will you make me wash the dishes?

Because why?

Because I have no money. My mama told me that when you go to a restaurant and order things without any money to pay for them, then they will make you go to the kitchen and wash the dishes.

Sindano shrugged. Drink all the chai you want, you hear? You will not wash any dishes here. I'm just glad someone wants to drink my chai.

Ayosa pushed open the window. A gust of wind tore at the curtains and tablecloths. The brass bell tinkled. Sindano crossed herself and murmured, Wajamani-that-cow-is-dead. Then she looked at Ayosa and added, How is she, your mama?

Ayosa shrugged. Fine, I imagine.

Sindano knew not to probe. She got up and walked to the counter. She said, It's four o'clock. Ms. Temperance is about to come on.

Ms. Temperance was a caramel-tongued poet. Each day, after the noontime news, she read to the people a piece that she had composed. One time, she did not read to the people because she was ill, and the people stormed out of their houses and threw a Molotov cocktail into the radio station. The people could not go a day without her poetry.

Ms. Temperance had a poem for Epitaph Day. She said:

> Do you remember those crisp mornings waiting for
> > the world
> to end waiting for the second coming of cargo trains
> and tenacity and Auma of the thistles who cut her
> arm off to feed the greedy baby doll? Do you
> remember how blue tasted bent over the creek that
> > swallowed
> Auma of the thistles who fed her toes to the
> starving porcelain child? And red when we lay our
> > heads
> down as the day grew tart? The boy we drowned
> yesterday is waiting at the station with lilies in his
> arms, saying, What in the world took you so long?

Sindano gave Ayosa a glazed doughnut and Ayosa finished the doughnut in two bites and her toes curled and her eyes welled and Sindano gave her another glazed doughnut and another glazed doughnut and another glazed doughnut and Sindano said, Jesus, child, when was the last time you ate anything?

When she staggered into the kitchen, Ayosa found a bunch of white daisies on the table. The flowers were wrapped in newspaper, their stems bound together with sisal string. Ayosa ran up the stairs and looked through an east-facing window. She saw the shiny-eyed, snot-faced girl, Temerity, just marching through the sugarcane field.

Temerity lived at the edge of the property. Her grandmother, Jentrix, was the apothecary. Every few days, Jentrix sent Temerity over with some cooked food and a bunch of something—flowers, or carrots, or herbs. Sometimes Temerity brought Ayosa a glass marble too, or a bent hanger that she had found. Sometimes she brought Ayosa a crow's beak, wrapped neatly in tissue paper. Sometimes she brought Ayosa a little rodent with its neck broken between the clasps of a mousetrap.

Ayosa slid the window up. She leaned out and yelled, Temerity! Temerity!

Temerity stopped. She turned, saw Ayosa, and waved both her hands above her head. Ayosa! she squealed.

Don't go! Ayosa called.

Because why?

Because please stay!

Okay, Temerity said. For a little while.

Temerity skipped back up the path, and Ayosa ran down the stairs to meet her. They stood in the middle of the kitchen, silently watching each other. The refrigerator heaved heavily in the corner. On the window ledge, a basil plant leaned over its ceramic pot, following a trickle of light. A stick of incense burned itself to gray ash, smoke rising in thin whorls above it. A regiment of ants marched toward a dollop of butter melting on the countertop.

We had a spelling test today, Temerity announced. I got seven words wrong.

Like what?

Like "discombobulated."

Ayosa reached inside the pocket of her frock for her pen and notebook. She wrote the word down on a clean page, tore it out, and handed it to Temerity.

Temerity stared at it for a long while.

Will you never return to the schoolhouse?

Never, for as long as I live.

But you're the smartest of all the girls, Temerity said, puzzled by this.

And of all the boys, Ayosa added.

True-true, Temerity said. So why won't you come back to the schoolhouse?

I don't like the teacher.

We have a new teacher this term. Miss Jalisa Shinobi went away.

Where did she go?

Don't know. Maybe she died.

I didn't hear her name on the death news.

Well, maybe she got kidnapped. In any case, we have a new teacher now. Miss Rahel Waiyaki Barnabas. She gives us Goody Goody if we can spell things right. If you came back to the schoolhouse, you would get all the Goody Goody, Ayosa.

Ayosa shrugged. I don't like any of the teachers. Even the nice ones.

Ayosa's mama had gotten her a library card from the community hall. Ayosa borrowed storybooks there—*Tom Sawyer, Huckleberry*

Finn, Charlotte's Web, The Secret Garden, Little House on the Prairie. The librarian would not let her touch *Things Fall Apart* or *Devil on the Cross*. The librarian said that those books were not suitable for bushy-tailed young girls. Or for anyone, really.

Here, she would say, and shove a Pippi Longstocking title into Ayosa's hands.

Ayosa had read all the Pippi Longstocking books in the library. In the stories, Pippi Longstocking's father was king of all the Negroes. Which made Pippi princess of all the Negroes. Pippi was mighty proud of this fact. One time, Pippi was talking to the children next door—Tommy and Annika—telling them that in Kenya, there was not a single person who could tell the truth. Pippi said that if she ever were caught lying, then it was only because of this—that she had spent too much time in Kenya.

After reading this, Ayosa wrote a vexed letter to the author, Astrid Lindgren. Saying how wrong her assessment was, and that all the people she knew would never lie to you. They told you the truth even when you ought not to hear it. They told you if your mouth smelled like sewage, or if your head had too many corners, or if you were the type of girl they wished had never been born. If anything, that was the problem with Kenyans. They did not *know* how to hold back with the truth. They brutalized you with the truth. Astrid Lindgren never responded to Ayosa.

Nevertheless, Ayosa preferred to study her lessons this way—by going to the library and borrowing books. One could learn all the arithmetic and science and geography that one required through stories. She would *never* return to the schoolhouse. Her mama did not know about this, though. She did not know that Ayosa had not sat in a classroom for nearly a year. Ayosa was glad for Temerity's loyalty. Temerity would never tell on her to her mama.

Rajabi broke her nose, Temerity said.

How did Rajabi break her nose?

Mutisya slammed a swing in her face. Also Genesis started a fire in the teachers' staff room. He threw a hot coal into Bwana Kombo's filing cabinet.

Because why did Genesis do that?

Because he did not want to take the end-term test, so he burned all the question papers. His mama wants him sent to an approved school. Genesis is too much for his mama. His mama is always being called to the principal's office for something Genesis did. Drowning the school pig in the pit latrine. Sawing off all the ducks' legs in the school farm. Shooting the head boy with a tranquilizer arrow from his slingshot. His mama says, Boys like Genesis come straight from the devil's musty loins.

Okay, Ayosa said, wary already. This was part of the reason why she had stopped going to school—children really did not know how to act.

Got to run, Temerity said.

Where do you got to run?

Schoolhouse. I only came home to eat lunch. Then my grand-mother made me bring you things.

Sorry for the inconvenience, Ayosa said. Temerity shrugged and started toward the door.

Bye-bye, Temerity, Ayosa called, waving her handkerchief at the disappearing figure.

Ayosa opened the steel tiffin that the apothecary had sent Temer-ity to bring. Inside it was some rice and chickpeas, fried in onion and garlic and herbs. Ayosa hated chickpeas. She set the tiffin down. She moved away from the table, dragging a footstool across the terrazzo floor to the pantry. She climbed onto the footstool and reached for a can of cream of mushroom soup. Then she pried the lid open, leaned on the doorpost with the jamb poking into her spine, and drank the soup in two gulps. After, she stuffed a handful of tamarind pods in her pocket.

Her mama had brought the tamarind from a place called Takaungu. Her mama had shown her the photographs she had taken at that place—a green mamba twisted in a heat-induced stupor on the tarmac, a barn owl glaring from a thatched roof, mangroves, palm trees, and then the ocean so blue, stretching out as far as the eye could see, turning into air, into sky. Her mama said there was something about Takaungu.

What? Ayosa had asked, but her mama never had told her.

Was it that people mostly walked backward? Or that the ocean sometimes grew weary of just lying down, so it roused itself and sat cross-legged on the coral reef? Was it that women lived on one side of the town and men on the other, and they spoke to each other only when the moon was full? Ayosa reckoned that one day she would have to go there and see for herself.

In the distance, the muezzin chanted in the minaret. The cargo train slithered by, making the windows rattle. The gossamer curtains slid in and out the window. A cricket screeched from the lemongrass bushes on the veranda. A jewel beetle leapt out of a basket of garlic. Ayosa trapped it in her palm and then crushed it. She wanted to see if her wrist would take on the same iridescence of its exoskeleton. It did not. She scattered the beetle's shreds on the floor.

The girl at the window came and watched even though there was nothing to see, just Ayosa turning the calendar, marking down the days gone by since her mama left, and then scooping out some Vaseline and greasing her ashen elbows and knees and ankles.

Where are your people? Ayosa said with her eyes.

Inside the windows. That's why I look into them.

Meaning, *I'm* your person too?

Wouldn't you like to know? the girl said. Then she laughed and skipped away.

One day, at two o'clock, Ayosa startled, and found that she had fallen asleep in the pantry, standing against a shelf of pickled carrots and radishes. She rubbed her eyes, disoriented because she did not remember going to the pantry in the first place. One foot was atop a soda crate. She stepped away from it and stretched. Then she heard noises in the kitchen and startled a second time. Pots banging. Cabinet doors creaking. And a voice, lumpy as gruel, singing, *The past is gone but let's cast spells and bewitch tomorrow.*

Ayosa stood in the doorway and watched. Before her was a . . . what was that . . . a woman? A thing pretending to be a woman? The thing—the woman—noticed her there. And she stopped what she had been doing—squeezing juice out of a grapefruit—and smiled. If that isn't Ayosa Ataraxis Brown! she said.

Ayosa did not respond. She just watched, openmouthed. The woman looked just like her mama. Yet, at the same time, there was something otherworldly about her. She looked like a wraith, clothed in limpid, waxen flesh. Her dress was dainty as a tea doily. Her limbs were thin as knitting needles. Her eyes were broken shards of glass.

Buttercup, it's me. Your mama. Aren't you pleased to see me?

The woman took a step forward. Or rather, she billowed, and Ayosa could tell quite distinctly that she was more of a thing pretending to be her mama than her actual mama. A wraith, no doubt.

You're not my mama, Ayosa said.

I am your mama, silly, the wraith said, laughing its laughter that sounded like tinkling wind chimes.

Ayosa crossed her arms over her chest. She was not one to be fooled so easily. She said, Prove it.

Prove what?

That you're my mama.

I don't have to prove a thing to you, missy, the wraith said.

Now girl and wraith looked at each other, somewhat bewildered. They had not counted on locking horns like this.

Ayosa stood still, thinking of a way to verify whether this was her mama or whether it was a wraith. And she thought of her mama. Her *real* mama, not the wraith. She thought of how sometimes her mama positively repulsed her. How her kisses felt like roaches crawling across

Ayosa's face. How her caresses scorched the small of Ayosa's back. How her curdled breath made Ayosa's eyes water. And her gaze, her serrated quartz gaze, it scraped ravines across Ayosa's knees. Whenever this happened, Ayosa reacted by turning away, by withdrawing her affections. She did something nasty—poured bleach into her mama's linens, or put grass snakes in her mama's bed, or telephoned the radio station to say, Nabumbo Promise Brown is a diabolical bitch. And her mama, she packed her things and jumped into her jalopy and drove off. She always was gone for weeks at a time, or for months, and once, for a whole year and a half. She left Ayosa all alone, as punishment for her misbehavior. At least that's what it felt like to Ayosa, although her mama disputed this.

Her mama would say, I don't go away to *punish* you, Buttercup. I must, for work purposes. You know that I would never leave you alone if I did not have to. I only go away because I've got to put food on the table.

And Ayosa always wondered what food her mama meant. Ayosa scrounged for her own food. She foraged about in the garden for vegetables or in the supermarket dumpster for canned foods too dinged up to sell. Oftentimes, Jentrix the apothecary took pity on her and sent Temerity over with a Tupperware of soup.

Sometimes, during her mama's unceremonious absences, Ayosa would come home to find a woman brewing coffee or folding laundry or answering the telephone. A woman who looked just like her mama, except that when you touched her, her flesh was all empty, wispy as smoke. A wraith. Just like this one here in front of her.

Ayosa stood still, watching as the woman who looked like her mama but was *not* her mama picked seeds out of her glass of fresh grapefruit juice. Ayosa said to herself, Yes-yes, I am right to be suspicious of this here woman.

The region had recently become infested with wraiths. She had read the stories in the newspaper, had heard them told on the radio too. About people who trusted too easily and got snatched. The trees and lampposts all over town were teeming with posters for missing persons.

She said to the woman, Come on, I've got to show you something.

Ayosa opened the door and went out into the blinding daylight, and the sun on her skin stung like the lash of a leather belt. This stinging sensation reminded Ayosa of another thing. It reminded her of how, whenever she was being naughty, her mama took out her braided cow-skin belt and whipped her. And in recompense, Ayosa bit and scratched and spat at her. Then they both had dreadful welts and bruises, which they wore like medals received for service on a battlefield.

Ayosa and her mama loved each other deeply. Ayosa's mama said that was what made their love affair murky. She said that true love was just like this—sweet in some parts, and sour in others. She said that deep love was vast and pure, but that it also got hateful in some of its corners where the sunlight did not touch. She said that you could not love so deep without hating. And that you most certainly could not hate a person without loving them first. Whenever Ayosa and her mama were far from each other, their hearts swelled anew, and they fell in love all over again. They wrote treacly, perfumed letters to each other, taping dried lavender and wormwood between the paragraphs. Saying, *I am aching to hold you in my arms again.* Saying, *You visit me in my dreams each night, and clutch my midnight sorrows to your bosom.* Saying, *I want to dive in the sea that's roiling in my beloved's eyes.*

She said to the woman, What did my mama write me in the last letter that she sent me?

She wrote that it was the last letter she's ever writing you.

Ayosa stopped short. How did you know that?

Because I'm the one that wrote the letter.

Ayosa pursed her lips, skeptical still. She continued walking.

Where are you taking me?

Not far, Ayosa said, and then she saw that they were close enough now, that they did not need to walk all the way across the yard. That they did not need to go past the tangled balls of thorn trees and wildflowers and barbed wire and stiff yellow grass, and past the awning and double doors and chimney and drawbridge. She stopped. She said, Look!

The woman looked. She placed her hand on Ayosa's shoulder. The hand was not wispy at all, but solid, heavy as a fig branch. Fuck-toad! Ayosa thought. This was no wraith. It *was* her mama after all.

She said, Nabumbo Promise?

Yes, my name?

Are you taking your iron pills?

Her mama pulled her hand away, tucked it beneath her armpit. She said, I forgot that you're like this. Mean mouthed. Needle tongued. See if I don't smack the sass off those yellow teeth of yours.

Ayosa frowned. She was thinking of her teeth now, wondering if they were as yellow as her mama was making them out to be. And if so, yellow like marigolds? Like butter beans? Like those washed-out fever dreams you got when you were yearning sorely for someone?

Ayosa said, Never mind me, Nabumbo Promise. I was alone for so long I forgot to be polite. But your fingers feel like ice lollies, so maybe don't smack me about *that*.

Like ice lollies?

Cold. And clammy, Ayosa said. She squinted toward the far-off yard, the one that stretched beyond the bog and drawbridge. There, where a choir of crickets sang a sorrowful elegy. She felt stupid for bringing her mama out here. She had only meant to test her, to say, What's that over there? Only my *real* mama would know.

Her mama now said, Buttercup, you wanted to show me something?

That, Ayosa said, and pointed once more. It was the place where her mama's own mother was buried. Her mama fell silent. She looked as though someone had ripped her belly open with a carving fork.

Sorry, Mama. I didn't mean to hurt you, Ayosa said.

Her mama shook her head. I'm not hurt. Not at all. Are those . . . cabbage roses? And . . . lacecap hydrangeas?

Yes, Mama.

You planted them yourself?

Uh-huh. The apothecary gave me seeds.

Her mama lowered her head. Dimples twitched in her chin. Her nostrils flared. Her pink lips parted to show glistening, not-yellow teeth. Cowrie-shell teeth.

She said, I suppose you wanted to show me the grave because last week was Epitaph Day.

Sure. Uh-huh.

I suppose we should recite a prayer for *her*.

Yes, Mama.

Her mama tipped her head and tried. She tried hard and good, invoking devotions that refused to budge, stubborn as donkeys. She gave up. Bit her lip. She turned away from the grave and said, Ayosa Ataraxis Brown, I have a question for you.

Oh?

Will you be more than just a daughter to me?

You mean a friend?

Will you be more than just a friend to me?

What could I be that's more than a daughter and more than a friend?

A sister, her mama said, reaching over to touch Ayosa's chin. Will you be my sister?

Sister? Ayosa asked. Is that possible?

Anything is possible under this vicious yellow sun. You and I, we could be sisters all right.

Ayosa was silent, contemplating the strangeness of it all. She had never heard of such a thing. She wondered if maybe her mama had spent too much time in the sun. If maybe parts of her brain had melted into slop. Sisters! Ayosa whispered, turning the word slowly in her mouth.

Look, her mama said. We could have a ceremony. A sister-making ceremony.

There's no such thing.

The priest could do it. It's like a wedding ceremony, except afterward you're not man and wife at all. You're fastened to each other tighter than man and wife could ever be. Fastened to each other tighter than born-sisters could ever be, because born-sisters can't help their sistership while made-sisters choose it for themselves.

Ayosa stood there, openmouthed, trying to decide if her mama was being ludicrous or shrewd. Probably both, she thought, tugging at a string that was hanging off her hem. She broke the string off and chewed on it.

I know what you're thinking, Ayosa Ataraxis Brown. You're thinking, Because why does my mama want me for a sister? Well, because the first go-around with my born-sister things were dreadful and maybe this second go-around with my made-sister things will be divine. You love me something fiery, don't you?

Yes, Mama. I love you something fiery.

Her mama smiled at the thought of Ayosa's fiery love. And then she thought of something else, and the smile fell clean off her face. But *why* do you love me something fiery? she said, as though only a deranged person would do such a thing. Me myself, I don't love *you* something fiery. My love for you is deep, but even then, it's not always so. Sometimes my love for you is lukewarm at best. And sometimes I feel nothing for you. Nothing at all. I search inside myself for that hot, scalding love and it's not there anymore. I don't know where it goes. So *why* do you love me something fiery?

I guess because we are stuck with each other, Mama. Here we are. Just the two of us.

You're right, her mama sighed. That must count for something.

Ayosa imagined their sister-making ceremony. She imagined she and her mama standing barefoot in the yard, in cream-colored linen smocks, with baby's breath threaded through their hair. The priest would say, Speak now or forever hold your peace, and nobody would speak because there simply was nobody else. Then her mama would take out the tripod and set the camera timer and they would grin with tears trembling in their eyes. And later, when the photograph came out, her mama would write on the back of it:

> *Honey waffles and*
> *silver sister bands*
> *and Billie Holiday.*

You could leave, her mama said. God knows I've done enough leaving for the both of us. But why don't *you*?

Because.

Because why?

Because I don't want to, Ayosa said, now close to tears. It felt a little like her mama did not want to be sisters with *her*.

I bet you will, her mama said. One of these days. I will call your name and you won't come to me because you will be gone-*gone*!

I bet I won't, Ayosa said, chewing on a stalk of grass. She wiped the wetness of her eyes with the back of her arm. She stared at this sweet mama of hers. Her mama whom she loved with that fiery love. Her mama whom she sometimes abhorred. Whom she sometimes bloodied with her fingernails. Whom she sometimes hid from and wished death upon.

I hope you *die*, she said to her mama when she was upset.

To which her mama said, Wishing death on your mama is the same as wishing death on yourself.

To which Ayosa said, One day I will put hemlock in your soup. I swear to God I will.

Now Nabumbo Promise touched her with her icy hands. Pulled her close. Ayosa was tall enough to graze her shoulder. Soon enough, they would be equal amounts of tall. Which meant: Tall enough to pilfer secrets from each other's eyes. Tall enough to bite off each other's noses in anger. But also, tall enough to braid hemp and tinsel and strings of sunlight into each other's hair. Saying, Bas now, I've got you, dear girl. I've got your back and your shoulders. I've got your neck too and your hands and your feet. All of you fits on me, see?

Her mama was a tumbleweed—she'd come rolling from far-off places and was full of knots and shingles and thorns. You're smothering me, Ayosa giggled, clawing herself out of a tangled mess of hair and lace and clavicle. Her mama refused to let her go. She held Ayosa tighter, lifting her and twisting her so that Ayosa was straddled on her back. Carrying Ayosa, her mama turned, ambled toward their big house that was full of shadows.

You should not have bothered yourself, her mama said.

About what?

About planting the flowers. My dead mother doesn't give a damn about them.

It was no bother at all, Ayosa said. Didn't do them for *her*.

Who then?

You, who else?

They fell silent. All the way home, Ayosa thought of her mama's dead mother. The thin-lipped woman. Lola Freedom. Lying facedown, mouth agape, as though she were screaming into the earth's crust. Screaming not from anguish but from bitterness. Lola Freedom was sick of lying facedown and wanted to be turned over.

Someone turn me, she screamed at the worms and the ticks and the cigarette butts.

Ayosa might have dug her out and turned her over herself, but she knew that the woman did not deserve that sort of mercy. Ayosa left her corpse alone because Lola Freedom did not deserve to watch the birds huddling above like pilgrims at a shrine. The birds biting rosary beads between their beaks. Saying, Hail-Mary-Full-of-Grace, at the waning scarlet sun. It was a glorious sight indeed, and that bitter woman inside the ground did not deserve to see any of it.

When they got back to the house, Nabumbo Promise deposited her on the porch step. Above them was a hornets' nest, and they stood awhile with their heads raised, watching that enormous papery capsule writhing above them, full of murder and full of nectar. Still watching the wasps, Ayosa said, Why won't you write me any more letters?

Because I will never leave you again.

Ayosa fell silent.

What? her mama said.

Ayosa said nothing, because what could she say? She had heard her mama speak such words before. *Tell you what, I'm never leaving you again.* Or, *May the good Lord strike me down if I dare walk away from you.* It happened each time her mama returned. Her mama was always contrite. But then she did it over and over.

Ayosa was almost thirteen—old enough to know that people had their ways. What was the point of denying it? Of lying and pretending? Of hoping against hope? She thought to herself, Can't teach an old dog new tricks.

Nabumbo Promise looked at her with sad eyes. Listen! she said, I'm never leaving you again.

Ayosa shrugged.

You don't believe me?

Doesn't matter.

Nabumbo Promise grabbed Ayosa by the elbows. She said, Why don't you believe me? Tell me! Open those yellow teeth and tell me.

She shook Ayosa hard, shook her and shook her, until Ayosa's bones and teeth and skull rattled, until blood gathered in the back of her throat, until her lips split open and smarted from the salt in her tears.

Now speaking to the wasps and the eaves and the birds in the sky, her mama said, I swear to God I'm never leaving you again, Ayosa Ataraxis Brown. First thing tomorrow morning, I will telephone the priest and ask him which Saturday he's got free for our sister-making ceremony.

The girl at the window sucked on jaggery and watched as Ayosa read her book. Ayosa kept losing her place in the page and having to start over. It was difficult to pay attention to Anne's attack on Gilbert Blythe when someone was watching her, watching the way she turned the pages and licked the corner of her mouth and scratched her elbow and made the chair beneath her squeak. Ayosa lowered her book and raised her eyes. She and the girl at the window stared at each other. Ayosa wondered why they never talked to each other at all. Or at least, why they never talked with their mouths. Someday it would have to happen, wouldn't it? They would have to break the speech barrier. But for now, they continued to talk with their eyes.

What are you reading? the girl at the window said.

Anne of Green Gables. Do you also like to read?

Not at all.

Because why?

Because back in the days when I went to the schoolhouse, Miss Patti said I was thick in the head.

Because why did Miss Patti say that?

Because I couldn't read. Then I called Miss Patti "Miss Fatty" and she broke my knuckles with a blackboard ruler. But my mama said I wasn't thick in the head. She took me to the eye doctor and the eye doctor said my eye holes are shaped funny. He said the words on the page look like snuff powder to me, that's why I can't read them. So I got fitted for spectacles. But me and my mama, we didn't get to fetch my spectacles from the eye doctor.

Because why?

Because . . . I don't have to tell you everything! The girl at the window shrugged. Got to go, she said, and skipped away.

The townspeople gargled salt water. They greased their elbows. They tucked flowers in their hair or pinned it on their lapels. They marched to Our Lady of Lourdes Church, where the drums throbbed and the pews wailed an endless dirge, a requiem for the souls of the damned. The air was heavy with novenas, and these hung low, churning over the townspeople's heads, and when you looked at them you could see the sorts of things that they had wished for the Lord to grant them.

They wished for the seamstress to finish sewing their shirts before Christmas Day, and for the bean crop not to be destroyed by weevils, and for sons held in police custody to be returned to them whole. They wished that no one they knew would be in the bus that hurtled into the Rift Valley tomorrow morning. They wished that another building in Kona Mbaya would collapse so that they might get casual work sifting through the rubble. They wished that the rain would fall and appease the howling red air.

In the front pew sat a beady-eyed woman, her hat embellished with fowl feathers. She wore a handful of overripe blackberries on her breast, like a brooch. She carried a silver speculum in her hand. She had the type of throat that sometimes caved in on itself, like an old coal mine, suffocating her. She used the speculum for this—to prop those limp walls of her pharynx up again. Her name was Dorcas Munyonyi. She was the priest's favorite faithful—the things she wanted were different, less provincial. Nothing to do with seamstresses or bean crops or policemen. Dorcas Munyonyi desired eternal rest for the departed faithful, and the collapse of the Soviet Union, and the end of the Cold War. Dorcas Munyonyi watched as Father Jude Thaddeus, in his sweeping yellow feast day vestments, followed the liturgical dancers to the altar. The church was a living, heaving thing, with pigeons cawing overhead, and women piercing the stuffy air with their ululations.

Father Jude Thaddeus stood facing the faithful. A somber, gnawing calm fell over the church, and even the flames of the candles stopped dancing. The faithful murmured together: *I confess to almighty God, and to you my brothers and sisters, that I have sinned through my own faults, in my thoughts and in my words, in what I have done and in what I have failed to do, and I ask Blessed Mary ever virgin, all the angels and saints, and you, my brothers and sisters, to pray for me to the Lord our God.*

The choir sang "Iende Mbele Injili," and Dorcas Munyonyi glided forward to the pulpit. She was no longer Dorcas Munyonyi. She was the Handmaid of the Lord. She looked just like the curly-haired, red-faced, fat-limbed saints painted on the walls of the church, people who, in death, had been infantilized—they wore terry-cloth nappies and played the harp on fluffy clouds. The Handmaid of the Lord began the first reading. Halfway through the passage, she stumbled upon a word. She broke it between her teeth, and she placed the pieces in the hot, wet space between her tongue and the roof of her mouth, and she chewed the pieces and soaked them in saliva and swished them round and round her cheeks. The priest tipped his head back. In his lap, he clawed at the knuckles of one hand with the nails of the other. He could hardly stand it. He was fondest of her, of Dorcas Munyonyi, when she stuttered like this.

Ayosa awoke at half eight. Something was wrong. She did not know what exactly, but knew that this *wrongness* was what had startled her in her sleep. She lay still for a moment, disoriented. Then she kicked off the covers, crawled out of bed, and stood in the middle of the room. She looked about her, searching for it, the wrongness.

Everything was motionless. There were no sugar ants stumbling over each other on the windowsill, no barn mice or teal-faced lizards burrowing about in the thatch, no bee-eaters or barbets flurrying and whistling in the frangipani branches. She looked through the window, into the foggy backyard. The sky hung low, swaying like a windswept tarpaulin.

Something darted in the corner of her eye. The wrongness, it was not outside at all, but right here in the room with her, just a hair's breadth away, curdling the air with its fetid heat. And she *knew* what it was. Her Jinamizi. It was a dark, horrible thing that visited her sometimes, bringing her memories that were not hers, that had never been hers. She said, Please don't touch me, as though Jinamizis were things that one could reason with. She pressed her eyes tight and braced herself for that moment when the Jinamizi would knock her over. She did not feel it—neither the nauseating giddiness of her body twisting in on itself, nor the dreadful clanging and shattering of objects inside herself as her legs crumpled beneath her body.

In the memories that the Jinamizi brought, she was no longer Ayosa. She was neon-colored coral polyps pulsating in a far-off sea, full of plankton. And then she was the first woman—the Mother Woman—shivering, writhing alone inside a muddy trench, bearing a litter of doe-eyed, jaundiced babies. And then she was a persecuted man with a bullet boring through his cranium, shredding it to sawdust. Nearby, in a watchtower, a soldier smoked tobacco in a sheet of paper torn from a Bible. He had just pulled the trigger, and now he watched as the persecuted man's blood spread pretty and dainty upon the white snow, like a yard of silky rayon velvet. Beneath the watchtower, another thing smoked. An incinerator, charring the remains of nameless, faceless, disposable people.

Stop! Ayosa begged the Jinamizi, gnashing her teeth.

The Jinamizi did not stop. Now she was the Mother Woman once more, still swollen from her recent parturition, shielding her wretched litter from a pack of wolves. Saying, in her crude prehistoric language,

> *These babies are sure cursed*
> *but rather I take them out*
> *with my own hand than watch*
> *a wolf do the job for me.*

And the Mother Woman ate her own babies so that the wolf would not touch them. She ate them so she could wear their bones inside her own, like gemstones. So she could whisper tender words to them when they had their horrible death nightmares. *Hush now, the bogeyman can't kill you because you're already dead!*

The Jinamizi went away as suddenly as it had come, and Ayosa returned home to herself, shaking, hollow inside, full of desire for unknowable things. She picked herself up and held on to the bedpost to steady her legs. She breathed in. Breathed out. Said to herself, Ayosa Ataraxis Brown, you are *you* and not any of those dreadful things.

She switched on the clock radio on her bedside table. She greased her elbows with Vaseline. She dislodged crusts out of her eyes with her index finger. She stuffed her notebook and pencil inside the pocket of her frock. She tugged at the drapes. She smoothened the coverlet. She fumbled into her shoes. She tied her tresses with a ribbon. She curtsied. She said, How do you do, madam, to herself, like she did each morning.

She listened to the wail of the telephone. It stopped, unanswered. Now she listened for the crash of aluminum pots in a cabinet, and when she did not hear this at all, her heart sank. She thought, My mama probably left in the night. She thought, I don't care, anyway.

She walked out of the bedroom, down the groaning staircase, and through the corridor. She made her way to the kitchen. Her mama was there all right, sitting at the table. She was hunched forward, chin to palm, staring at the wall. She wore the same cream-colored, doily-textured dress from yesterday. She had slept in it, and it was crinkled and stained with toothpaste. Her hair was in her face, and the same toothpaste that had stained her dress was encrusted on her cheeks and forehead.

She looks like a child, Ayosa thought. Like a little girl dazed by the coming of the morning light. Like a little girl who has not yet figured out how to Girl in a manner that is satisfactory. Brush hair. Remove dregs of sleep from face. Take care of elbow ash. The bare *minimum*.

Ayosa felt immense sympathy for her mama. She herself had many such days, where no matter how much she tried, she could not quite fathom that Night had dissipated and that Day was here. Day could be so frightful—long and bright and empty. What to do with Day on days like those—like these?

Ayosa's answer was always this: Swimming in the creek. Or breaking into the sacristy at the Catholic church and stealing communion wafers to later eat dipped in strawberry jam. Or, sometimes, roaming the wilderness, gathering in the scoop of her frock things that people had lost—scraps of browning paper, and hibiscus flowers, and a stranger's secrets, and jars full of pectin and zest and tangerine peels.

She thought to herself, Yes-yes, we ought to get out of this big house of shadows. Aloud, she said, Mama? Let's go outside. Sun's shining. The radio said it might rain later.

Her mama did not turn away from the wall. She did not stir. In a moment of utter panic, Ayosa wondered if perhaps her mama had left after all. If perhaps the woman before her was only a wraith. She moved closer to her, took ahold of the woman's wrist, and almost wept with relief when she found that the bone within it bulged so far out you could use it as a knocker for an oak door. A solid wrist. The woman *was* her mama. Sitting motionless. There, but not *there*. Eyes looking, but not seeing.

Oh! she said.

She'd forgotten that her mama got like this. That sometimes she stumbled inside herself—went into the land down under. It had first happened when her mama was nineteen years old. Back then, Ayosa was not a girl, was only a thing wriggling by her mama's side. She had seen it all transpire. Her mama contracted sepsis from a bone fracture and then lay comatose for a week. She was locked inside herself, where she wandered about, and discovered that there was another life unfolding in there. Another world.

Her mama had an outside life and an inside life. In the outside life, she was Nabumbo Promise Brown. Daughter of Lola Freedom. Sister of Rosette Brown. Granddaughter of Mabel Brown. But in the inside life, she was none of those things. She was Another Person. She lived in a tree hollow, inside a red city. She was a beggar and a thief. She robbed and plundered and murdered.

When the sepsis wore off and she awoke from the coma, Nabumbo Promise sat reeling in bed. She told her sister, Rosette, about her discovery, about the lives nestled inside each other like babushka dolls. Her sister told her to hush, that it was only the morphine speaking. Nabumbo Promise believed this until the episodes began. She would be driving down the open country on assignment when the rift inside her opened and she fell into the land down under. Or she would be going over condition reports for photos returned to her from an exhibition. Or she would be in a lunch meeting with the managing editor of the newspaper, discussing features and angles and deadlines. Without warning, she would find herself gone. Descended into that red city.

Ayosa turned away from her mama. There was nothing more to do but to wait. She opened the window to let some air in. She filled a glass with water and set it on the table. Then she opened the kitchen door and made her way across the yard, which was overgrown with tangled balls of thorn trees and wildflowers and barbed wire and stiff yellow grass.

Ayosa half walked and half ran to Mutheu Must Go Café. She found Sindano still in her church clothes—maxi wax-print dress, with a pattern of a pair of hummingbirds hovering over a nectarine. She wore a head wrap of the same fabric. She bustled about, arranging cutlery that she had painstakingly polished so that the pieces shone on the tables like fairy lights. She had baked a dozen tortes, each of which was filled with treacly chocolate lava. Sindano went round the tables, placing down plates and apportioning sticky, decadent pieces.

Do you plan to stand at the door all day? Sindano said.

Ayosa sheepishly sidled into a chair. Sindano walked to the counter and returned with mugs that she filled from a thermos flask.

Is there a party? Ayosa said.

What do you mean? Sindano asked.

Did the town forgive you for killing those ten men on your wedding day? Is everyone coming over for tea?

Sindano laughed. No, not at all. It's Sunday. I do this every Sunday.

And no one comes?

You know how it is here, Sindano said, shrugging. Still I bake on Sundays and hope that someone will come.

The wind tinkled the bell in the window. Sindano crossed herself. Ayosa did too. In unison, they said, Wajamani-that-cow-is-dead.

Then Sindano lowered her thermos flask. She said, Child, you look like you're chewing on some words. Go on, spit them out.

Oh, nothing, Ayosa said.

You heard from your mama?

Ayosa nodded.

Is her heart beating?

Ayosa nodded again.

What's that long face, then? Sounds like you've got yourself a whole mama, not a half one.

She's in the kitchen. But she's not in the kitchen at all. She's turned all inside out. She's fallen into herself.

How long has she been gone?

Two or three hours, I think.

Don't you worry yourself. She will be back soon. Otherwise, smelling salts ought to do the trick. The apothecary can administer some.

I'm not worried.

What then, what's that long face for?

I want to prepare a feast for my mama. I was wondering if you could maybe help me? Problem is I don't have any money. I can't pay you.

I don't need your money, Miss Brown. My mama left me enough of it when she took the dirt nap. How else could I run a café that no one ever goes to?

Sindano ran behind the counter and came back with an entire mousse torte, and a batch of still-warm buttercream cookies, and nougats whose recipe she had found in the copy of *The Jolly Housewife* still spread-eagled by the tray of confectionaries. Is this enough? she said.

Fuck-toad! Ayosa said. I will need to make two trips to bring all that home with me.

Don't be silly, I'll come with you, Sindano said.

They started across the street, Ayosa lugging the box of cookies and Sindano the biscuits and torte. They were out of breath by the time they burst into Ayosa's kitchen.

Poor woman! Sindano said when she saw Nabumbo Promise sitting at the table, watching the blank wall. She placed the things down. She moved closer to her, searched her neck for a pulse. She found it. Now she touched her damp forehead. Touched her stained cheeks.

Your mama is already halfway back here, she said.

When will she be all the way back?

Approximately fifteen minutes.

Ayosa watched Sindano in awe. She thought, There is something about Sindano. With her dead lovers, all ten of them. And her café that no one ever visits. And her midsection scarred by a hateful cow. She thought, If anyone is a wraith, it is *her*. Sindano.

Sindano, she said, are you a wraith?

Sindano was at the sink, filling a saucepan with water.

Do I look like one? she said, moving to the gas stove now and lighting the flame.

Somewhat.

What is somewhat? Either I look or I don't look like one. Make up your mind.

Ayosa said, Can we table this discussion?

You're afraid of hurting my feelings by telling me I look like a wraith?

No, madam. I just want to watch you some more. Try to figure you out. I will tell you when I've decided what you are.

That's reasonable, Sindano said, laughing. She opened the kitchen window and plucked a clump of lemongrass still wet with the dew. She wiped it against her Sunday dress and dumped it into the saucepan. She said, Hurry and switch the radio on. The poet is about to come on.

Ayosa leapt to the refrigerator. She climbed the footstool and reached for the transistor radio. She and Sindano stood side by side at the sink, listening. On the radio, Ms. Temperance said,

> *Where are they with their pitchforks and their coir*
> > *nooses*
> *that they carried in their patch pockets like polka*
> > *kerchiefs*

like pennies for wishing wells, like the blind beggar's
    harmonica?
The woman that met a haggard carpenter on the way
to Golgotha and brought back his message saying
    mercy for
all but damnation for the Jezebels? The man
    that wore
his own innards like a gold chain round his neck,
saying he had seen it all, so might as well
go dancing with his flesh necklace and his
    sandpapered boots?
The infants that sprouted tufts of hair on their gums
instead of milk teeth that entire year? Where are the
cows that walked on water? The fishes that leapt out
and foraged like rodents in the maize fields? The
    moon
we unstuck from the sky and stuffed in the underwires
of our brassieres?

Sindano stirred sugar and tea leaves into the saucepan of boiling lemongrass water. Ayosa watched her. She said, Sindano? One time I heard on the radio that the townspeople can't do without Ms. Temperance's poetry. They even threw a Molotov cocktail into the radio station. Is this true?

True as a malediction.

Because why can't the town do without her poetry?

Sindano turned off the heat. She searched about for a pair of clean mugs. She said, Something happened years ago. The whole town was involved.

Even my mama?

Especially your mama.

Was it bad?

Sindano furrowed her brows. She said, All I'll say is this: It's weighing heavy on the town's heart. That's why they need the poetry. It helps them to deal with what happened.

Just then, the house began to shake. A chair toppled out the open kitchen door. The window slammed shut. A great howl, like that of a bitter wind, swept by, making their ears ring.

What type of devil is that? Sindano yelled over the bedlam.

It's just the Fatumas.

That doesn't tell me a thing, Miss Brown.

They live in the attic. They listen to the death news. Sometimes they don't even listen to it, but just remember it. Then they get upset and throw themselves on the floor to weep, and the house does this. It's the Fatumas' grief.

Sindano shook her head. She said, I've got half a mind to go up there and shut them up.

How would you shut them up?

Oh, I've got my ways! she said darkly.

Immediately, the house stopped shaking. They heard you, Ayosa said.

I meant for them to hear me.

At the table, Nabumbo Promise grunted softly. Her fingers curled into claws on the table. She murmured unintelligibly under her breath, rocking back and forth in her chair.

Better I get going, Sindano said.

Ayosa walked Sindano out to the porch. Sindano?

Yes, my name?

I have a feeling about you.

Sindano turned, one hand raised to her forehead to shield her eyes from the sun. She said, Funny, because I have a feeling about you too.

Ayosa's toes curled. No one had ever had a feeling about her before. She waved her handkerchief at the disappearing Sindano. Then she picked up the chair that the Fatumas' grief had tossed outside. It had a wonky leg. She dug inside a drawer for a brush and some wood glue. She fixed the leg, set the chair out in the yard for the glue to dry, and made her way inside to drink a cup of water.

Got something for you, the girl at the window said with her eyes. She held out her hand. Inside her palm was a brooch in the shape of a bee that was hunched over, rubbing its antennae against its bristly forelimbs. Each of its eyes was a pigeon pea throbbing on either side of its hairy head. Its wings were fanned out, and were made of dainty white ribbon. The bee's thorax formed the pin with which to attach the brooch to one's lapel.

Ayosa gasped. So pretty, she said. Where did you find it?

Stole it from the tailor's stall, so mind, don't you wear it someplace you are likely to run into the tailor.

Ayosa laughed. She liked the brooch very much—its breathtaking delicacy, its complicated terms of use.

The girl at the window had another gift—two beefsteak tomatoes that she had stolen from someone's garden. Ayosa sliced them into quarters and salted them and peppered them. They ate facing each other—the girl outside on the veranda, standing by the open window, while Ayosa was inside at the kitchen sink. They said nothing to each other, neither with mouth nor with eye.

Your mama's back.

Uh-huh.

What's wrong with her?

She fell inside herself.

They watched each other in silence. Ayosa saw a dark shadow sweep over the girl, saw it cover her face like a low-lying rain cloud. She thought, Something happened. Must be the busboys and the preacher-men, must be that they did her dirty. Ayosa did not dare to ask the girl what bothered her. She did not want to make her cry, did not want to make her experience her misfortunes afresh by calling them out by name.

You got ice? the girl asked with her eyes.

Plenty, Ayosa said, and opened the refrigerator. She took out a tray and emptied it into a bowl. The girl at the window chewed the ice, cube by cube, like it was a mouthful of hazelnuts.

Fuck-toad, she said. These taste good. Real good.

After a while, the girl at the window turned to go.

Where are you going?

To watch people.

Because why do you watch people?

Because to see their lonesomeness. Some people wear theirs like a fine fur coat. Others poke at it and turn up their noses like it's a bag of mealworms. One lady, she invites her lonesomeness to lunch every Tuesday. She sets out her best porcelain and sits her lonesomeness at the head of the table and serves it pork ribs. I suppose that's really clever of her. If you wine and dine your lonesomeness, maybe it won't sneak up on you in the middle of the night and slit your throat.

Nabumbo Promise had climbed out of herself. She stood at the sink, scraping her hands beneath the tap. Her mama, her dazzling mama, pretty as a button. Her mama, with the eyes that crackled in the sunlight like embers, with the skin that shimmered like tinsel, with the cheekbones so sharp you could open soda bottles on them.

Her mama, who was soft as margarine but also hard as flint. The hairs on her legs were so long you could braid them. She stood barefoot on the terrazzo, her toes sprawled so wide you could fit apples between them. She pushed open the kitchen window, tugged at the heavy branches outside it, and plucked a handful of yellow loquat fruits. A fungus gnat darted onto the damp creases of her neck.

Her mama bit into a loquat. She leaned over the kitchen sink, her back hunched, her spine contorted. The skin of her neck and shoulders was spangled by scars that jutted out like hooks for hanging scarves and bags on.

You slept well? her mama said.

Ayosa dug her hand into the pocket of her frock. She found the dried core of a plum, and she poked at it with her fingernails. Well enough, she said.

She studied her mama, searching for . . . *what*?

Ah, she thought. New Oldness. Her mama always brought some back from the land down under. Each time she returned, she was physically adjusted. There it was—the swirl of gray on her mama's temple, the stack of creases on her forehead, the sun spots scattered on the back of her hands. Ayosa wrote these things down in her notebook. She had a page special where she kept a list of all her mama's symptoms of decay.

Her mama sucked on the puckered flesh of a loquat. She spat out a wet seed onto her palm. Buttercup, what are you writing?

Things.

Well, can you write a shopping list too? Carrots. Potato. Developer fluid. Coconut cream. Oh, and lentils. Don't forget the lentils.

Her mama spat another seed into her palm. She put the rest of the loquats on the window ledge. She took out a cigarette and bit it between her teeth. She reached for a box of matches and struck one. Looking over her shoulder, she noticed the table and said, Ayosa Ataraxis Brown, what's all that?

Ayosa shoved her notebook and pencil inside her pocket. You like it?

Her mama frowned. She said, Why are you so good to me?

Someone's got to be good to you, Mama. You're not very good to yourself.

Her mama let out a cloud of tobacco smoke. Sit, sit! Let me serve you some of the sweet lemongrass tea that you made.

It was Sindano that made it.

Sindano who?

Sindano from Mutheu Must Go Café.

Her mama lowered her cigarette from her mouth. She pointed it at Ayosa, spilling ash on the floor as she did so. She said, Now, now, don't start hobnobbing with those townspeople. I've told you how they are. Filthy and whatnot.

Sindano is not filthy.

Every single one of those people is, I am the one who's telling you!

Nabumbo Promise handed Ayosa a mug and sat across the table. She took drags from her cigarette in between sips of tea. She said, Don't trust anyone in this town. They will turn on you at the drop of a hat.

Ayosa stared at her mama, at the scar on her arm. This scar was shaped like a cashew nut. She had another on her neck. It was copper colored, like a skink sunning itself on a rock. Ayosa's fingers gnarled from the need to touch it. She tucked her hands beneath her armpits.

Her mama cut up the mousse torte. Ayosa bit into her piece, and its filling of cream cheese and fudge brownie melted on her tongue.

Fuck-toad! she whispered.

And her mama said, Lord have mercy!

They ate in silence for a long while—it was not possible for their tongues to speak words and taste such glory at the same time. For forty-five minutes, they were bound in a tight spell. They gorged their faces. Gulped tepid tea. Bit their tongues raw. And all the while, Ayosa thought, Sindano's a wraith, she's got to be. When the torte was gone, Ayosa and her mama emerged from their stupor. Their jaws hurt from relentless chewing. They undid their top buttons and held their ribs. They stared at each other, full of awe and full of shame.

Jesus, what just happened?

The cake *made* us eat it.

Her mama dabbed at some crumbs with a serviette. She said, Cakes are not sentient beings, they can't make one do a thing. *We* were gourmands.

Ayosa wiped her mouth with the back of her hand, and laughed, and said, It was real sinful how we ate.

Hmm, her mama said. She was silent for a while, thinking. Ayosa watched her, tried to unravel her thoughts. Her mama was thinking about things from years ago, when she was younger. Thinking of how Lola Freedom used to have her daughters write their sins down on a chalkboard in preparation for the priest's monthly confessional visits. Thinking of how Lola Freedom would examine her daughters' sins, berating them for intentionally leaving some out of the list. Their conceit? Their nihilistic lack of self-regard? Their vicious silence that they let swell like an ocean between them all? The murderous glimmer in their eyes?

Nabumbo Promise Brown, last week you were a stubborn little mule. Be sure to mention that to the priest. Tell him how you violate your mother with your impudence.

Her mama sighed. She took out a new cigarette and lit it. She said, How is school, Buttercup?

Good, Ayosa said, happy for the change of topic. She was silent for a moment, summoning all the details that Temerity—the shiny-eyed, snot-faced girl—had told her. She said, We have a new teacher. Her name is Miss Rahel Waiyaki Barnabas. She gives us Goody Goody if we can spell things right.

What happened to the old teacher?

No one knows. Maybe she just stopped being.

Being what? A teacher?

No. Just *being*. One day she was Miss Jalisa Shinobi and the next day she tired of it and stopped. She *became* someone else. And this someone else does not know anything about teaching and maybe doesn't even look like Miss Jalisa Shinobi at all.

Nabumbo Promise scrunched her eyebrows. Squashing her cigarette on the table, she said, I don't know what existentialist philosophers you've been reading, Ayosa Ataraxis Brown.

The telephone began to wail. Nabumbo Promise got up and walked to the nook in the wall. She paused to cough into her sleeve. She picked up the receiver and shooed Ayosa away. Go outside, she mouthed.

Ayosa left her mama and ran out into the sunshine. She found a pile of burning rubbish that her mama must have lit up in the early morning hours. Ayosa poked about it with a stick. The pile was mostly ash now, although a few things inside it had not burned at all, and other things had only half-burned.

With her stick, she picked up a thing that was burned beyond recognition. She raised it above her head, and it hissed furiously at her, as though it liked the burning, as though it resented being separated from the flames. Ayosa flung it through the air at the jolly annas.

The jolly annas were a type of bird that lived in Ayosa's yard. They had russet feathers and golden hackles. Their sickles were slick, glinting as though dipped in oil. Their wattles hung like scarves beneath their chins.

Ayosa had named them the jolly annas because that was the sound they made with their orange bills. They cawed jolly anna at you for no reason. The jolly annas were the most spiteful things she had ever known. They could make a person wither with shame just with one squawk. Sometimes they looked at you and you felt deep in your spirit that you were utter scum.

Ayosa threw the burned thing at the jolly annas but the jolly annas swerved away and the thing rushed back down at her like a frantic shadow and the jolly annas yelled jolly anna at her and laughed. Jolly anna, jolly anna, ha-ha-ha. And the burned thing landed on the back of her neck.

Ayosa thought that maybe that's how hunchbacks became hunchbacks—a thing coursed through the air and they did not duck on time so the thing landed on them and they had to carry it strapped to their backs or stuck to their necks like that.

She thought that maybe it was not a bad thing at all to be a hunchback. Your back bent from the weight of all the things that coursed through the air to find you. It meant that the thing that had made you a hunchback had wanted you very badly, that it did everything it could to find you and to crawl onto your body to be with you.

It was too hot out in the yard. Ayosa sat on the veranda, under the shade of the awning. She had a length of green string in her pocket. She played cat's cradle alone. Later, her mama came out, raffia basket slung over her shoulder. She said, Buttercup? Let's go to the market.

Ayosa jumped to her feet. She watched as her mama fussed with the keys, poking them in and out of the lock. Behind her, the house loomed high, the stone walls covered with ivy vines, the windowpanes broken, held together with tape and twine and newspaper. Ayosa's eyes sought out the attic. She saw the Fatumas standing in the window, their foreheads and noses and chins pressed to the windowpane, their breaths fogging up the glass.

What are you looking at?

Nothing.

Her mama grew suspicious. She raised her eyes.

The Fatumas vanished from sight. They were good at hiding, at shape-shifting. Right now, they let all their parts slacken, and they gathered themselves and scrunched themselves and split themselves and drew themselves out until their outsides were made of jagged spokes and their insides were made of sticky, bitter gel. It all happened quick as a gasp, and when Nabumbo Promise looked into the attic window, all she saw was an aloe plant in a seagrass pannier, sagging down a twine hanger.

Nabumbo Promise said, Is she watching?

She meant, was Lola Freedom watching? She believed that her dead mother was sometimes hovering up there. Whenever the Fatumas made the whole house shake, Nabumbo Promise thought that it was Lola Freedom throwing fits. She would stand at the bottom of the stairs, hands tight on the banister so as not to be swung down the corridor in either direction, and she would call, Grown woman that you are, you should be ashamed of yourself for causing such a ruckus!

And when the Fatumas were in a joyful mood, she heard their merry singing and humming and whirling, and she said, Well, damn, death must be a grand old party. Do you hear the dead woman dancing the chini kwa chini dance? Twisting her waist? Just *begging* for it?

Ayosa never told her mama the truth. Never told her that it was not Lola Freedom up there, but only two gaunt, forlorn creatures, halfway houses between girls and reveries. She never told because . . . because why?

For one, she liked knowing something that her mama did not. She liked having secrets to keep. And for two, she felt pity for her mama. Nabumbo Promise *needed* this one thing to believe in. This was what Nabumbo Promise believed, what Ayosa did not correct: Lola Freedom, who was dead and buried, sometimes returned, a phantasm, and dwelled in the attic, and threw fits, and shook the house, and gyrated wildly too. Nabumbo Promise believed that even in her long absences, Ayosa still had *someone* there in the house to watch over her. To tell her to eat her porridge and to wash the grime off her body and to go to bed before midnight. A governess of sorts.

When Ayosa was a child, all fussy and full of rage, her mama often carried her to the attic and left her there to weep herself hoarse. There, the Fatumas would soothe her, would sing lala kitoto to her in their soft echoey voices. Nabumbo Promise would hear all this from below and think that it was Lola Freedom comforting her grandbaby.

Ayosa shook her head. What a piteous thing to believe, she said to herself. Her mama, her hapless mama!

Back in the Yonder Days, Ayosa had seen Lola Freedom. She knew what the woman was like. Pungent hearted when drunk, which was almost always. Cold as a glacier. Besides, there was nothing that Lola Freedom had detested more than her daughters and more than her soulless home. Why would a woman like that then willingly return to either of those things? People had their ways; Ayosa knew as much. They did not suddenly change their habits, even in death.

Nabumbo Promise turned away from the attic window and reached for Ayosa's hand. Tugging at it, she said, We don't have all day to just stand here and stare.

The jalopy rocked over the rough murram road, metal parts clanging under the hood and in the dashboard. Out in the street, a stray dog barked, bewildered by the chickens that pecked in the bushes. A man wheeled his bicycle on the side of the road, the carrier laden with sacks of charcoal. A girl dipped her brush into a tin of wheat glue and pasted crusade posters onto lampposts.

You brought the shopping list?

Ayosa nodded.

You wrote down curry powder?

Ayosa took out her notebook. She riffled through the pages and studied the items her mama had made her write down. You didn't say any curry powder.

How is one supposed to make lentil curry without curry powder?

Can't read your mind, Nabumbo Promise. You didn't *say* it.

Nabumbo Promise raised her hand in mock defeat. She watched Ayosa scribble in her notebook.

Well, read for me I hear.

The shopping list?

No, the things you've been writing inside your notebook.

What part?

Whatever you like.

Ayosa turned back the pages. She read:

> *Hello milkman*
> *Sometimes*
> *That-cow-is-dead*

Her mama pushed a knob on the dashboard, waited a minute as the lighter heated, and then pulled it out. You're trying to be a poet these days?

I want to be like Ms. Temperance. I want people to throw Molotov cocktails because they can't bear to hear the sound of my silence.

Nabumbo Promise laughed. She said, That's some type of gluttony for sure. Lola Freedom would have made you write it down on the chalkboard.

Now Nabumbo Promise grimaced, as though she had not meant to remember, and had not meant to talk about the Chalkboard of Sins either. She said, Never mind that at all.

But Ayosa minded it very much. She reached her hand out and touched her mama on the elbow. She caressed her mama on the cashew nut scar. Her mama gave her a sidelong glance, smiling tenderly. Her mama, who was soft as margarine. Her flesh was supple between Ayosa's fingers. Ayosa was overcome by a sudden, desperate love for her mama. The type that made people drink Rat & Rat when jilted. She thought with wonder, This woman is all *mine*! She is my mama! And soon-soon, she will be my sister too!

Her mama took a cigarette from behind her ear and pressed its tip to the lighter. Her lips were gray and chapped—they looked like a pair of leopard slugs. She always smoked her cigarettes too close to the butt, and they charred her.

The jalopy hobbled over a pothole and the rearview mirror swung from side to side. Ayosa stared at the crack that slithered down the windshield. In the station wagon in front of them, a woman's shawl was trapped in the door, dragging about, fraying on the murram. On the roadside, a fish fryer dipped eels into ocher-colored oil. The fish fryer's eyes were bloodshot, her forehead furrowed, and her lips pinched into little crests on her mouth.

A flock of wild guinea fowl flew above, headed toward the river. In the street, a sack fell off the back of a bicycle. It broke, and the wind sifted the flour inside it into the coiffures of passersby. A Tabu Ley song poured out of the megaphones hanging on the roof of a fabric shop.

Mama?

Yes, Buttercup?

What was it like for you like when you were a girl?

You don't want to know!

I do want to know.

Her mama frowned. Maybe *I* don't want to know.

Her mama pursed her gray lips. She drummed against the steering wheel with her fingers. She adjusted the rearview mirror even though it was not lopsided to begin with. She rolled the window down and then up and then down again. She adjusted the side mirror too. She banged her fist on the horn, harder than necessary, and the driver of the matatu in front of them poked his head out and said, Madam, if you are in such a hurry why didn't you just leave yesterday?

Mama, stop. You don't have to Remember. You don't have to tell me a thing about your girlhood.

Her mama noticed her own agitation and was embarrassed by it. She ran a hand through her hair. She said, We will be sisters soon, you and me, and sisters ought to bare their souls to each other. She paused to think. She said, Let's see . . . When I was a girl, it was quiet. Mighty quiet. I remember that the most.

The quietude?

No, not quietude. Quietude would have been a great mercy. *Quiet.* Like a forest where something came and ate all the birds. That's what it felt like inside my head.

Ayosa turned to a fresh page in her notebook. She reached into her pocket for a pencil.

What are you writing?

What it's like for me as a girl. I reckon that one day, someone will want to know too.

Well, what is it like?

Lonely.

Every girl I ever knew was lonely. What's your specific lonely? Are there birds in it?

No, not birds. Memories.

It's true—memories are a lonely house to live in, Nabumbo Promise said. She tucked stray strands of hair behind her ear. She said, What sorts of memories?

Old ones. Sometimes, older than the seas and the mountains.

Like?

Like sometimes I remember what it felt like for the sun to warm up the frost that very first morning it ever crawled out into the sky.

Her mama furrowed her brow. Those memories sound awfully heavy.

They are. I can't bear them at all.

Her mama saw someone that she knew in the street. She raised her hand in greeting.

Mama? I remember you sometimes.

Me? What is there to remember about me?

That girl you used to be. The quiet one. The sad one.

Sad girls come a dime a dozen. Maybe in your memories you mistake someone else for me.

No, Mama. I could find you in a mob, even if my eyes were pecked out by crows.

Her mama looked dolefully at her. She said, I wish it were true.

You wish what were true?

That you could remember me as a girl. There are things I cannot tell you with my own mouth. I wish you could have been there to see them yourself.

Ayosa said nothing. In her notebook, she wrote, *I was there.*

Her mama gazed out the window. Do you want to see something?

Yes please, Mama.

Her mama turned away from the road that led to the marketplace. She took a littler road instead. A nonroad, really. For fifteen minutes, they wrangled their way through dense groves of she-oaks and junipers and cape chestnuts. Tree branches smacked against the windows. A boomslang snake did so too, which made them shriek with fright, and then cackle with delight. Nothing was funny, yet everything was. Ayosa and her mama guffawed hysterically.

Stop! Stop! her mama gasped. I'm going to pee myself.

Ayosa choked and coughed and got the hiccups.

Hold your breath, her mama said.

Ayosa gulped a mouthful of air and waited for the waves to stop crashing down on her diaphragm.

You okay?

Yes-yes.

Look, her mama said, pointing out the window. This is what I wanted to show you.

Sausage trees?

All this land belonged to my grandmother. Mabel Brown.

I heard about that on the radio one time.

Is that so?

Uh-huh. The radioman was talking about the history of the town. He said that Mabel Brown moved here from England in 1902.

That's right. She was the young wife of a missionary. They were brought here by the Church Missionary Society.

Your grandfather the missionary, what was his name?

Oh, I don't know. He wasn't my grandfather. Just a man that my grandmother married too young. In any case, the two of them defected from the church in 1916. They stayed on as settlers. As was the practice at the time, they petitioned the Crown and received a nine-hundred-ninety-nine-year title deed for all this land.

What did they do with it?

Grew coffee. Kept dairy cows. Fished. Hunted. Behaved badly. What else did the settlers do over here?

The radioman said that Mabel Brown founded the town. That there was no one here before she settled. That the land was unoccupied.

My dear, now, that's bollocks. There were people here, all right.

What happened after?

Well, in 1925, that sorry husband of my grandmother died. Liver cirrhosis. The fool drank like a kitchen sink. Afterward, all the land fell to Mabel Brown. She had a piece of paper that said it was *hers*. That's why they say she founded the town.

So, who was your grandfather, then?

Her mama clicked her tongue to the roof of her mouth. She said, Why do you keep asking about dreadful, no-good men? If you must know, Mabel Brown took on a lover after her husband's death. He worked for her, this lover. He was her gardener. They went at it for a year or so. Then Mabel Brown got pregnant, and the gardener bolted as soon as he found out. Just like my own father would do later, and yours too. One day, when it's your turn to choose, I hope you look elsewhere. This place is infested with dreadful, no-good men.

They drove in silence for a long while, through the shrubbery. Ayosa wished that her mama would tell her more about Mabel Brown. Ayosa had sometimes seen her in the Yonder Days. Severe-faced Mabel Brown. Angry-eyed Mabel Brown. Always with a musket against her shoulder. The type of woman whose mouth was filled with bile instead of saliva. Even as a wriggling thing, Ayosa had been afraid of her.

Her mama looked over at her. She said, The old lady has been good to you?

Her mama meant Lola Freedom, who she thought had watched Ayosa in her absence. Not more than usual, Ayosa said. It was not a lie.

Then she added, She's been asking about you. This part was a lie. Ayosa was not sure why she said it.

Asking for me? Why would she do that? All those years she didn't give a rat's tail about me. Why would she start *now*?

Her mama scratched her neck, scratched and scratched so hard it bled. Tomorrow, there would be a glistening scar, Ayosa was sure of it. She envied her mama this skin that was mottled and blotched, pockmarked, like a wondrous mosaic. This skin like an art gallery full of strange artifacts.

Lola Freedom wishes to have tea with you, Ayosa said.

Inside her mouth, where her mama could not hear, she said, Ayosa Ataraxis Brown, why are you lying to your mama?

Her mama flinched. She said, I would rather be tied to the back of a tractor and be dragged across a sisal plantation than have tea with that old lady. I would rather slit my tongue into pink ribbons using a box cutter. I would rather be mauled alive by a colony of bush rats. I would rather weld my eyes to the back of my skull.

That's an awful lot of trouble you would rather go to.

Her mama curled her lips and said, Tell that woman that I want her out of my house. I will fetch an exorcist to drive her away.

Exorcists only drive away ghosts that are trespassing. It was *her* house first before it was ever yours.

I will burn the damn thing down. Ghosts are very flammable.

Ayosa had not counted on this. The Fatumas! she thought, and a chilly wind swept down her spine. She needed to walk her mama off the ledge. She said, Mama, you'll no longer have a home if you burn it down.

Home? What home? That place has never been home to me. It was an English pauper's aristocratic fantasy.

Your *grandmother*.

A vulgar woman, who built a gaudy house. It deserves to be burned to the ground.

Ayosa began to panic. She imagined the Fatumas trapped in the smoky attic, writhing in anguish. She imagined the flames. Red as an orphan's sores. Ravenous as an orphan's belly. And the Fatumas would not even know that the fire was right there, that it was burning *them*. They would think that they were only listening to the radio, that it was only the harshness of the death news roaring in their ears, flaying their pudding-cloth skin, crushing their wire bones. And they would hurl themselves down with a grief so great that the whole house would crumble into the earth's crust.

Ayosa was livid. Crying and shaking, she grabbed her mama by the hair and tugged. Something ripped out, with the same alarming sensation of Velcro strips detaching. Her mama screeched and swerved sharply. The jalopy wobbled, almost toppling over.

Get out, her mama said.

She reached over Ayosa's lap and tugged at the latch in the door.

Out!

Ayosa stumbled into the woods. Her fist was folded. She unfurled it, saw a bunch of her mama's yellow hair inside it. There was enough of it to cover the scalps of two small children. Enough of it to tie to a stick and fashion a type of mop or a type of cobweb brush. What had she done? She was standing in a clump of sedge, disoriented, lips shaking, tears rolling down her face, soaking her frock. The jalopy screeched off.

Wait, she called. Nabumbo Promise Brown, WAIT!

Ayosa squatted in the shrubbery. Nabumbo Promise! she begged the trees. In the grass, she stretched her legs out so that the millipedes and earthworms and hornets that wanted her so bad could climb over her. The grass stung her, her calves ached where the hem of her frock ended, but she did not scratch the itch.

She gathered hornets and aphids and praying mantises, gathered driver ants and roaches and ladybugs, and she lined them on her thigh and watched as the wind fluttered their mandibles and antennae and forewings. She fondled their prickly faces and whispered warm, wet words to them.

She watched gadflies scurrying in dizzy circles above her face. A lark whistled at her. She sought it out in the branches, high up in a yellowwood tree. It turned its head away when it saw her looking. She studied its spotted feathers. It knew that she was watching, but it did not meet her gaze. It watched her from the corner of its eyes. When she turned away, it whistled at her.

They—Ayosa and the lark—did that all afternoon. They looked at each other and turned away and looked at each other again. Two beings that desired each other, not so badly that they could have torn themselves open so the other could crawl in and dwell inside them, but with a gentleness and a softness, with a contentment at being thought about if only for the moment.

They were both lonely, but it was a sweet loneliness that neither of them was willing to relinquish or interrupt. So they just watched each other and loved each other deeply, but both knew that their love could not be sustained. When the love was finished, they bade farewell to each other.

The lark flew west; she watched it join its own flock and drift toward the pink sunset.

Then her mouth wanted to say, Salamander.

So she said, Salamander.

The insects had all crawled away from her thigh. She found toadstools sprouting out of the mossy ground. She plucked one. Its head drooped. She thought that maybe it was the type of toadstool that would clog up your throat like a drain stopper. She wanted to see if this was true. So she tore off its stalk and bit into it.

But it was not the type of toadstool that did anything to a person. She spat it out. The shreds stuck to her feet. She scraped them off with her fingernail. She plucked a handful of lion's ears and shoved them into her mouth. The nectar made her throat itch. She sucked on her tongue until the itch went away.

She said to herself, Any minute now. And she looked about her to see if her mama's jalopy was wrestling and snapping the lianas. If her mama was returning in a cloud of tobacco smoke. It was not, and she was not. Ayosa let out a sigh—it came from somewhere deep inside her, so deep, somewhere *beyond* her. She was weary of herself. Weary of her girl-shaped body. She wanted to free herself of her anxieties and wriggle.

She thought of a poem that Ms. Temperance once read out on the radio. Ayosa had written the words down as Ms. Temperance said them, and she had memorized them. Now she recited it to herself, over and over again:

> *The red finch sick to its stomach with vertigo gave*
> *up flying and perched itself on a branch and wanted*
> *to be bird no more so it turned its claws to*
> *fibrous roots and its blood to sticky sap and its*
> *folded plumage to the wildflowers of a spiderwort*
> > *crawling and*
> *trailing and climbing wooded shambles stopping every*
> > *now and then to*
> *peer at the sun above and wonder, where was the*
> *tortoise going with its stuttering unsteady feet, and*
> > *would it*
> *perhaps walk much faster if unburdened of its heavy*
> > *brick house?*

Ayosa felt like the red finch in Ms. Temperance's poem. Except, for her, it was being a girl that gave her vertigo. Could she give up her feet and hands and neck? Could she give up her teeth that were yellow like marigolds or butter beans or washed-out fever dreams? Could she turn into something else too, just like the red finch that became a wandering plant?

Should have never listened to her, she said.

She was thinking of a time, back in the Yonder Days. Thinking of her mama's worn-out, bruised face, and her palms crinkled by the green river water, and her bloodied dress, and the sun dangling down from the sky, as though from a string, all loose and cold and gray. Her mama feeling her there, her mama having the wisdom of discernment, enough to know that Ayosa was not a wraith. That she was something benign, something bullish, something that could be coaxed to stay. *Please-please-please-I-need-you.*

Now Ayosa thought of how familiar this type of sitting was. This type of waiting. She had memories from the Yonder Days—memories of mama leaving daughter, and daughter sitting still with hands between knees, watching furtively, waiting until mama returned. Like, Mabel Brown off on a hunting trip, while at home, her daughter, Lola Freedom, swung on a tire in the yard, waiting, just waiting. Later, Lola Freedom gallivanting through the Rift Valley in her little piston-powered airplane—a Cessna C-165—while at home, her daughter Nabumbo Promise was on her own, huddling on the creaky steps, waiting. And now, Nabumbo Promise was doing all the leaving, and Ayosa all the sitting and waiting.

That was how it was. Mamas left. Daughters waited. Was that why mamas birthed daughters—so there would always be someone in the world devastated with desire for them? Someone in the world saying, Dear Lord, I would trade you my eyesight for my mama. Make me blind, but bring her back to me.

Ayosa fell asleep against a lichen-covered tree, with her cardigan wrapped around her for a blanket. All night, she dreamed of red finches and spiderworts. In the morning, when she awoke, she ate dandelions and wood sorrel, and then she found a crayfish by the nearby river and ate that too. She washed her face, broke a stick and scraped the grime off her teeth, and she looked around for signs of her mama's jalopy.

Wagtails and barbets flapped about, dizzy and joyful as gnats. The sky surged down, heavy with rain. Ayosa filled her pocket with primroses. She found a nest of shrikes. The birds were gone—they were across the river, impaling moths and grasshoppers on thorns. Their nests were full of pearls and silver bangles that they had stolen from women's purses. Ayosa adorned herself with these.

Her mouth wanted to say, Venus flytrap.

So she said, Venus flytrap.

She poked at the egg-laden husk of a bagworm that cleaved to a wattle tree. She drew a clock tower on the ground with a stick, drew large double-hung windows and bats hanging upside down in the rafters. A mosquito bit her on the ankle, and she slapped at it. Her canvas shoes were wet, their soles encased with mud. She kicked them off into the stream and the water carried them away on its back.

She sat on the ground and picked at her bunions. The inside of her arm stung and when she looked down at it, she saw that there was a skipper caterpillar crawling there. She did not flick it off, just let it creep up until it got fatigued and collapsed on the grass. Her arm had red welts where the caterpillar had touched her. She hoped that it would heal that way—in the shape of a crawling caterpillar, so that someday she would touch herself there and say to people, This is where something in the world missed me and came out to find me.

Still, her mama did not come.

She peeled off her frock and waded in the river. It shuddered beneath her. The water was colder than she had anticipated. Her teeth chattered. She saw a figure bob in the water, not far from her. It was a man, young-like, although she could not tell for certain for the water had bloated him up, made him oafish. She paddled out to him, stared into his gray, rubbery face. His name was Kalulu Musyoka. She knew this just by looking. The shape of his head—long and full of corners—looked as though it belonged to someone whose name was Kalulu Musyoka.

She poked at him with her index finger to see if his leg would move or if his eye would flicker, to see if he would say, You foolish child with the face of a hippopotamus, if you do that again you will cry mama yangu nisaidie!

But Kalulu Musyoka did nothing to her.

She pulled her hand away and watched him drift off.

She closed her eyes and now she was a jacaranda flower no a jasmine flower no-no-no a what do you call the long orange flowers that look like straws, the ones pregnant women pluck from strangers' fences and suck on, what do you call them—lion's ears? She was a lion's ear.

She was other things too—a jackfruit bulging on the side of a stranger's bicycle, and a tapeworm burrowing inside a person's gut, and coconut oil trickling down the soft vale of a stranger's belly.

She was—

You silly mongoose, did your mama never teach you how to swim?

Ayosa coughed and sputtered, green water bursting out of her throat.

She opened her eyes, saw that she was lying on the sandy shore, with rocks clawing into her face. A girl knelt over her, her palms pressed into Ayosa's chest, her wet tresses splattering water into Ayosa's nostrils and mouth.

What happened? Ayosa whispered.

Heh, let me just tell you! the girl said. You see now, the currents were taking you away and I saw them do that so I ran inside the river with a tree branch and I bashed them and I bashed them and I said,

Let-the-poor-girl-go-you-stinky-cane-rat, and the water let you go, so I pulled you out. That's what happened, I swear Bible-red!

Ayosa's stomach clenched. She turned to her side and retched. Her nose leaked into her mouth, and when she swallowed the salty fluid, it relieved the burning in her throat.

Who are you? Ayosa rasped at the girl.

Me? I am Mbiu. Everyone knows that. And you, you are Ayosa Ataraxis Brown. Everyone knows that too.

Ayosa sat up.

The river swayed back and forth. Flamingoes waded inside it, their pink feathers sopping wet, their skinny legs long and awkward beneath their bodies. She looked into the distance to see if her mama's jalopy was anywhere to be found.

She's not coming, Mbiu said. Your mama. I saw her dump you here like a corpse she was trying to get rid of.

You were here yesterday?

Uh-huh, Mbiu said. She pointed at a far-off parasol tree. I was up there. Didn't want to startle you. But I have a knife on me, so I kept guard while you slept. She paused to examine Ayosa. Do you know your color?

You mean what color I like most?

No. The color that a person likes most might not even be their color at all.

Then what is a person's color?

It's the color of their soul, Mbiu said. She reached into the pocket of her frock and took out a slab of jaggery. She bit into it, broke it between her teeth, and spat out the pieces. She held one out to Ayosa.

How do I find my color? Ayosa said, taking the jaggery that Mbiu offered.

You go to a color and you stroke it and you say jungu kuu jamani. If that's your color then you will know.

How?

Mbiu shrugged. You will just *know*.

Ayosa stared at Mbiu. She had pus-filled mosquito bites all over her arms. Her hair was pulled back so tight it tugged at the corners of her eyes, making her squint. She wore a length of string round her neck. She had stalks of dried grass lodged inside the tiny holes in her earlobes. She smelled of something softly, sweetly acerbic, and Ayosa imagined that ants often marched in spiral formation round her ankles and calves and knees, up her torso, to nestle in her armpits.

I know you, Ayosa gasped.

Of course you know me. I often come to your kitchen window.

Mbiu was the girl who sometimes stood on the veranda and peered in at Ayosa. The girl who gazed in and when she was done gazing, disappeared into the balmy air. She looked different out in the sunshine, here without her forehead pressed to a windowpane. She looked . . . *wholesomer*. And she talked too. Mbiu, this slip of a girl, with a sharp-edged body, with shimmering blue-black skin. Mbiu, with a loneliness, a disquiet inside her, and beyond that, a swirling presence, something at once strange and familiar. A sadness.

Did you follow me?

No! Mbiu said.

Say wallahi!

Mbiu shrugged and slumped her shoulders. Fine. I *did* follow you.

Because why do you watch me through the window? And why did you follow me here?

You're lonesome. Seems to me that someone ought to peer in the windows and look at you often. Make sure your heart is still beating inside your chest. Mbiu shook her head. She said, Look, I followed you because you drove off with a stranger. Thought maybe she was kidnapping you.

It was my mama.

A stranger to you, nonetheless. Mbiu paused. She stuck her little finger into her earhole and scraped at it. She said, I thought maybe she was a wraith. I've looked in your window sometimes and seen wraiths masquerading as your mama. I thought this time one must have really got you.

Ghosts can drive?

Can sail too!

And where would the wraiths take me, if they got me?

I heard there's a wraith town not far from here. I heard that sometimes when people go missing, that's where they've been taken. If you end up there, you're done for. There's no saving you! You had best watch out. If a wraith ever tells you to go somewhere with them, don't under any circumstances go.

I'm not planning to.

Good! Now tell me, why did your mama dump you out here like a corpse?

I tore her hair out. Ayosa reached into her pocket and then held out her hand to show Mbiu the yellow locks in it.

Holy green mamba! What did the woman do to deserve this—tell you that the milkman was your new daddy?

Ayosa grimaced. Spit out that dirty saliva!

Mbiu cackled.

She's not a bad mama, you know. Not always.

Didn't say that she was, Mbiu retorted, and shrugged. One must admit, though, that she isn't cut out for this. She hasn't got a shred of instinct about what to do with a daughter. I don't know whose clever idea it was to turn that poor woman into someone's mama.

Mine!

Even you now, what type of mud has your mouth started saying?

I was a wriggling thing and she felt me close by and asked me to stay, and I did. Went into her belly and she bore me as a baby. It's my fault, really. I knew how she was. I had seen it. And I stayed, even when I had seen all this.

Seen what?

My mama as a girl and my mama as a woman. When I was a wriggling thing, I followed her everywhere. I'm the one to blame for expecting a hyena to wash off its spots and sit at the table with a napkin in its collar.

Mbiu doubled over and laughed. She laughed so loud that birds took off from the tree branches, squawking. How odd that you remember all that, Mbiu said when she finally caught her breath again.

Don't you remember some of the things you did before you turned into a girl?

Not at all. People usually don't.

Oh, I know that. But I thought . . . if *I* remember, maybe I'm not the only one that does. Maybe there are other people out there who can too.

Mbiu crinkled her nose. It's a strange world, isn't it? Wraiths try to snatch people's bodies. I've seen preacher-men that walked into alleyways and turned into bush babies. I've seen vampires bite women's necks and drain them of blood. That's why I always have a knife on me. Mbiu gazed at Ayosa. She said, Anything is possible, my dear. And you, if your thing is remembering what you were like before you ever turned into a girl, that is the least peculiar of all the things that ever could be. What is remembering? Nothing, nothing at all! I'm sure there are others like you out there. That's not to say that you will ever find them.

Ayosa kneaded her shoulder, which was sore from her night's slumber upon a raised tree root. She said, What do you think you were like as a wriggling thing, before you ever turned into a girl?

Mbiu snorted. Awful. Setting fire to things, I bet. That's the type of spirit I have. A scorching one. But can I ask you something, my dear?

Ayosa's toes curled. She was Mbiu's *dear*? She picked up a rock and tossed it into the air, to stop herself from grinning like a fool. She said, Ask me something, please.

If you could do it again, would you?

What?

Choose Nabumbo Promise Brown.

Ayosa was silent for a moment, considering it. If she could do it all over again, she would not listen to the blathering pleas of a forlorn woman. *Please-please-please-I-need-you.* Better to be the daughter of a pied crow, or a featherfin squeaker, or a seaside caper. Better to be the daughter of a thunderclap.

She shook her head. Said, No, not at all.

Lies! Mbiu cried, staring incredulously at her. I know you, Ayosa Ataraxis Brown.

You don't know a thing about me!

I know that you would choose again and again and again, to make a mama out of that vagrant. That woman who would rather sleep with pigs in a trench than come home to you. I know that much about you!

Ayosa took in a sharp breath, and then she jerked away from Mbiu. Mbiu knelt, put her index finger to Ayosa's chin, and raised it. There now, she said softly. No need to be ashamed. We would all choose our mamas over again, wouldn't we? She tugged at Ayosa's hand, pulled her to her feet. Come and meet Bwana Matambara, she said.

Bwana Matambara was Mbiu's cat. He was short-haired and gray-eyed, with twitching ears and a colony of fleas burrowing through his fur.

He's a Korat, Ayosa said.

Because why is he a Korat?

Because that's the type of cat he is. I can tell by looking. Some cats are ragdolls and some cats are munchkins and others are Korats.

Okay, Mbiu said. She squatted down and let Bwana Matambara leap onto her shoulder. Come here, you Korat.

Then she straightened.

Ayosa Ataraxis Brown, let's go!

Where?

To find the color of your soul.

They stroked milk thistles and spiderworts and lichen. They stroked anthills that were big as palm trees. They stroked the rippled, bunched-up bark of a jacaranda tree. They stroked a stink bug and a blue skimmer and a lace bug. They stroked a giant slug, and it withered under their touch, becoming smaller and smaller, until in the end it was nothing but a piece of snot that someone had flicked from their nostril.

They found a stream and stroked it. It squirmed, and its gentle gurgling burst into breathless giggles. It was a little stream tangled round a rock. They set it free and it rushed to its mama, the wide, sprawling river that had tried so hard to keep Ayosa inside itself.

What's your mama like? Ayosa said. Does she sometimes go into the land down under?

Mbiu frowned at her. Do I look like the type of girl that has a mama?

Everyone has a mama.

Don't be silly. Everyone does *not*.

What happened to your mama?

Mbiu shrugged. Everyone knows what happened.

I don't.

Mbiu stopped walking. She stared at Ayosa, her mouth wide with shock. You don't know what happened to my mama? You never heard? No one ever told you? You didn't read about it in the newspapers?

Ayosa shook her head.

Mbiu squinted against the harsh sunlight. She said, A year ago, my mama robbed a bank. She had me in the front seat of her Volkswagen when she did it. She killed two security guards with her AK-47. Then she came back out with the sack of money and drove away. The police chased us. Look!

Mbiu lifted her frock to show Ayosa a spot on her thigh, right above her knee. Something protruded out. It looked like a wedge of amethyst stone.

Bullet, Mbiu said. It's still inside me. The police shot hundreds of them at us, but this is the only one that touched me.

And your mama?

You want to know about my mama? Heh! Let me just tell you! My mama, she looked like a carrot grater when they were done with her. Full of holes. Then the radioman refused to call her name out on the death news. He found her in-descent.

You mean indecent, Ayosa said. Then she thought about it further and decided that she liked in-descent better. She wished that she had a mama who was in-descent. A mama who robbed banks.

That was the best day of my life, Mbiu said.

Because why was it the best day of your life?

Because my mama went away laughing. She just held me and laughed until all the laughter inside her was finished.

Mbiu bit into a piece of jaggery. She cradled her cat close to her chest. She said, Bwana Matambara was there too.

Did he get hurt?

Just a bullet to his tail. That's why it's a little short. Look here! Mbiu paused and waved the cat's tail. She said, The bullet made the tail rot, and I hacked its tip off with my pocketknife.

Ayosa took out her notebook and scribbled down all the things that Mbiu had said. She did not want to ever forget this story. On the adjacent page, she sketched a picture of a carrot grater, and underneath it, wrote a caption: *Mbiu's mama when they were done with her.*

She said, What work did your mama do, before she robbed the bank?

She was a doctor.

A *whole* doctor, not even a half one?

Uh-huh, Mbiu said.

Ayosa quickly wrote that down.

There was no pay for eight months, Mbiu continued. Everyone was striking. Even the nurses and teachers and bus conductors. But my mama was not one to beg anyone for a damn thing. So she drew her gun and went out fighting.

Mbiu and Ayosa had wandered too far. They found themselves in a rice paddy, with their feet squelching in the flooded loam. The rice stalks were tall, they reached up to their shoulders. The sky met the earth in misty, slanted sheets. With their backs arched against the wind, they pressed their eyes tight and stood still until the rain passed.

After, they stroked a rock and they stroked the orange wind. They stroked the mud-lined nests of thrushes, and Ayosa felt something quiver inside her. It grew, this thing. It was a warm wind shifting down her gut, rippling through her midsection, twisting her legs together, as though they were made of hemp rope.

You found it! Mbiu squealed. You found the color of your soul! It is blue, like thrush eggs.

Ayosa wrote:

Blue.
Like thrush eggs.

It was almost dark now, and the sun was swiftly plunging down from the sky. Mbiu and Ayosa staggered back to Ayosa's lichen-covered tree, a Mexican cypress, where she had left her cardigan.

What now? Ayosa said, picking up her cardigan and plucking out dead leaves and caterpillars. She had long given up the notion that her mama was coming back to fetch her. She said, I suppose I will sleep here tonight too. Then tomorrow I will walk back home.

Mbiu shook her head. No-no-no, that won't do.

She stuck two fingers into her mouth and let out a whistle. Right then, a curious noise emerged from the trees. The clippity-clop of hooves, the crunch of tires, the snapping apart of aerial roots.

That's my car, Mbiu said.

Ayosa turned around. What she saw was not a car per se, but the shell of one, pockmarked with bullet holes, hitched by rope to a horse. The horse was now grazing in the grass, whipping its tail back and forth, swatting at flies.

My precious Magnolia, Mbiu said, petting the horse's head and offering it some jaggery to chew on. She hopped onto the bonnet of the car, with her cat, Bwana Matambara, on her shoulder.

Do you like it? she said. It's my mama's Volkswagen. My mama laughed her way out of this world inside it.

I like it very much, Ayosa said. She took a step closer and saw that the car had no windows. Mbiu had taped polyethylene bags into the gaping holes. In the backseat, a loft of pigeons sat. There were perhaps two hundred of them, all motionless, staring out with their blank, misty eyes.

I like pigeons, Mbiu said brightly. I let them live in my car with me. This is the nicest car I ever saw in my life!

Come on! I will drive you home.

So Mbiu drove Ayosa home. Or rather, they both sat inside Mbiu's car, eating wild berries and prickly pears that they had gathered, and throwing scraps at the cat and the pigeons, while Magnolia the horse drove Ayosa home.

Does your radio work? Ms. Temperance is about to come on. They usually repeat her noontime reading right about now.

Sure thing, Mbiu said. I figured out a way to twist the wires so the radio works even when the key is not in the ignition. Makes it so I listen to the radioman any time I want. Sometimes he will say there's a riot in this street, or a storm in that place, which helps me stay out of trouble.

Now Mbiu reached over and fumbled with the wires. She smoothed out the static, and they both listened to the sultry voice inside the radio:

> *My mother's child is a stranger whose neck I used to kiss*
> *back when we were a pair of black cats prowling*
> *in our mother's night terrors causing her to shriek*

in her sleep causing her to bend shirt hangers
trying to fish us out. We came twisted round each
other like tapeworms and my mother used that
same shirt hanger to pick us apart all the while
wondering why bad luck only doubled when you
prayed it away. Teeth black with old blood eyes
yellow with bilirubin of rage. At our christening
we received my mother's old Shirley Temple dolls.
We mutilated them with scalpels. Filled their
mouths with feces. And my mother wept. She
wondered, what did she do to deserve no ordinary
daughters? And why couldn't we just be the type of
darlings to sit on the mantelpiece so guests could
pet us when they came round for crumpets?

I don't like this poem, Mbiu stated emphatically.

You have bad taste, then.

Mbiu laughed. Well, what do you expect? I live with pigeons.

Mbiu looked smug and exceedingly pleased with herself, as though her bad taste was something she had nurtured carefully for years.

Ayosa said, You don't get it! Ms. Temperance, her words *ache*. Sometimes I feel as though she is telling a story that I know very well. Like she is writing for me.

For you, Ayosa Ataraxis Brown?

Yes-yes, for me.

Everyone probably thinks she is writing for *them*. That's why they threw the Molotov cocktail that one time.

Ayosa looked out the window. I wonder what she's like.

Prim. Very prim.

Ayosa's eyes widened. You know her?

Oh, I know all sorts of people. Mbiu shrugged, and added, Ms. Temperance eats an entire grapefruit every morning. She writes with her left hand. She makes celery soup for lunch each day. And she records all her poetry standing by the kitchen sink, then sends the cassette tape by post to the radio station.

Ayosa marveled at all these facts. She thought, This girl, Mbiu, she truly is my *dear*. Her toes curled. She scribbled in her notebook and said, I'm very thankful that you told me all this.

Well, I know even more things!

You do?

Mbiu nodded. Ms. Temperance has a child. A boy, almost eight years old. His name is Eusabius Pius M. He has a swing in the backyard. He likes to suck on soggy ice-cream cones and watch *Pop Made in Germany*. He always tucks his plaid shirts into his starched khakis. Every morning, he digs the earth with his grubby fingers, fills them with writhing worms, and goes out fishing for trout. His favorite things are the following: his gold-toe socks, his brass knuckles, his origami elephant, his pipe cutter, his can of bug spray. Ms. Temperance gives him a Cabbage Patch doll for his birthday each year.

How all *poetic*! Ayosa murmured.

And Mbiu laughed and said, I would rather have bad taste than get that glazed look on my face only because a poet *breathes*. She turned to the pigeons and the cat in the backseat and shook her head. Can you believe this?

The pigeons and the cat could not, and they cawed and meowed their dismay at Ayosa's hero worship of the poet.

Well, I've told you plenty. It's your turn now. You've got to tell me something.

What?

Anything. I mean, from the Yonder Days. Tell me a thing you once saw your mama do.

Ayosa chewed her prickly pear in silence. She leaned back against the worn leather of the headrest. She said, When Nabumbo Promise was eighteen, she ran away from the convent.

Your mama was a nun?

Not quite, Ayosa said. She never was any good at religious life. She smoked a pack of Marlboros each day in the toilets. Some afternoons, she left the convent to watch a film at the cinema. *Alien*, or *The Godfather*, or *The Deer Hunter*. She would return drunk on cheap whiskey, her clothing suspiciously rumpled, with red bruises trickling down her neck. She put very little effort into her discernment and knew that the mother superior tolerated her only as a favor to her mother. She left six months later, at the end of her postulancy.

You saw all this?

Uh-huh. I was only a wriggling thing back then, so my mama didn't see me. But I followed her everywhere just so she would not be alone. We hitchhiked for weeks on end. Slept in sheep pens and schoolyards and church pews. I would wriggle off on my own whenever Nabumbo Promise went into dirty motel rooms with sordid men that she met in bars. After her trysts in the motel rooms, she always had a little money tucked in her brassiere, and we took the next bus to a nowhere-town.

Tell me more!

One day, Nabumbo Promise found an isolated farmhouse and we squatted in it for four months. It had the comforts of the home she had grown up in: a phonograph, some records, a gas stove, a garden with carrots and leeks and potatoes. She found a point-and-shoot camera in a kitchen drawer and began to peddle herself as a portrait maker. It started off as a scheme to swindle strangers, but as the days went, her deceit turned into honest true-to-God toil.

And then what happened?

Well, the family that owned the farmhouse returned unexpectedly in the middle of a chilly July night. Nabumbo Promise and I escaped through an upstairs window. But she fell and busted her right knee open and dragged herself away like that. She bought a ticket to the farthest place the train could take us. She tried to mend that busted knee herself—tying the bones together with a handkerchief, waiting for them to stick.

Don't stop! Finish the story!

The bones did not stick. Nabumbo Promise was halfway dead with sepsis by the time a stranger carted her to the hospital in a wheelbarrow. She did not have any recollection of this, though. What she remembered was living many years in a vast desert city, where the clouds and the earth were the same dirty red color.

Monkey sweat! I've got to hear more!

In this city, her name was Shayla Mrisho, the daughter of Abdi Mrisho. Her father had been the royal drummer, but he blasphemed and got exiled into the sea on a raft. Shayla Mrisho had grown up in the high walls of the king's court. Now she was disgraced and was nothing but a beggar and a thief. She wore a tattered shroud and hovered in a cul-de-sac. She had a knife in her waistband and a lighter tucked in her matted hair. The knife was for gutting stray chickens, and for slitting the hamstrings of anyone that stared too long at her pasty face. The lighter was to build fires by the baobab tree hollow that she spent her nights in.

Uh-huh, uh-huh, uh-huh?

My mama, she plundered, she ravished, she belonged to no one but herself. Later, her sister, Rosette, told her that all those harsh decades she spent in the red city were just fragments of her lucid fever dreams. Eighty years in total, full of putrid breath, full of ghastly people, full of stark memory. My mama said, How can it be? She still remembered the ice-cold rain that soaked through her flesh, so that she always had to wring out her whole leg instead of just her skirts. She still remembered all the baskets that she filled with limes, which she then brought to the tannery to de-hair the animal skins. She still remembered the copper coins she would get in return, and the whiskey she downed straight from the bottle while squatting by her tree hollow. She still remembered all the times she was flogged in the town square for a thing she had stolen—a harmonica, a bag of onions, a tub of margarine.

That's not just bananas, it's mangoes too!

Yet, now she was back inside her old body, back to that busted knee. She struggled with grasping how eighty years—an entire lifetime—could be lived in just the week that she had lain comatose. It did not add up. Later, my mama discovered that she had a bizarre condition. That sometimes she just fell inside herself, and in there, she always found this other life in the red city. My mama has two lives—an inside one and an outside one.

Sick! Truly sick!

But that day, my mama lay in the hospital bed, with an IV tube in her arm. Beside her, her sister was slumped in an easy chair. Her sister had stayed on in the convent when my mama ran off. She was now a novitiate. She wore a horrible gray habit, with a crucifix round her neck. She snored softly. Invoked their mama's name under her breath. Lola Freedom, over and over. As though their mama's name was some type of devotion. And me, I lay next to my mama and said *her* name. Nabumbo Promise, over and over. And that was the day I knew that I would choose her a hundred times over to be my mama.

Mbiu exhaled. Phew, I can breathe again, she said. She reached into her pocket for some jaggery. She pointed out the window. Look! That's your stop.

They were parked in front of Ayosa's house. The sign that read *Manor Mabel Brown* shook in the wind.

This is it?

This is it.

Goodbye now.

Goodbye.

Ayosa did not know why, but she felt quite close to tears. She climbed out of Mbiu's car and stood at the rickety gate flanked by stone angels with severed heads. She watched Mbiu's horse, Magnolia, yank the pockmarked Volkswagen, dragging it away like a plow. Then she climbed over the gate and jumped down into the yard that was overgrown with tangled balls of thorn trees and wildflowers and barbed wire and stiff yellow grass.

Ayosa walked from room to room, searching for her mama. At last she found her mama in the bathroom, humming to herself as the shower ran. Ayosa lay down on the floor and looked through the rotten planks of wood in the door. She stared at her mama's nakedness. At the scars splattered all over her mama's body—a clam on the small of her back, an earwig in her underarm, a conch shell on her inner thigh, a pygmy mouse on her hip, a spiderling on the back of her ear.

Her mama's body was like flypaper—it was sweetly musky, and it drew little things to itself. Her mama was never truly alone. She was surrounded by objects. Something was always clinging on to her, stroking her, saying, I am here, Nabumbo Promise.

Some of her mama's scars were like ribbons and frills, wrapping and embellishing her mama. Some were like tarpaulins that cloaked entire swathes of flesh, hiding all the secrets inside her mama. Some could not be seen by the naked eye—they burrowed deep inside her mama, curled up into themselves, raw, shuddering, wet and cold and angry, like a wounded animal.

Ayosa reached for her notebook and took a record of her mama's body. She had a page special where she kept a list of all her mama's scars. When she was done writing, she put the notebook away and continued to watch her mama.

Her mama stood beneath the shower. She let the water run over her body. She scrubbed herself with a washcloth and then rinsed the soap off. She threw a towel down and stepped onto it so that her wet body would not drip all over the linoleum tiles. She rubbed the cloudy mirror with her palm. She shoved a toothbrush into her mouth and let it linger for a few moments. Then she spat out white foam and rinsed her mouth.

Ayosa ducked into a dark doorway. Her mama came out of the bathroom and walked past her, so close that Ayosa could have reached out and fondled all her scars. Her fingers ached. She curled them into fists and clenched them. Her mama disappeared into her bedroom, wet rubber slippers sloshing on the wood floor.

Ayosa followed her. She knelt outside her mama's door and peered through the keyhole. Her mama stood in the middle of the bedroom, staring at the dead gnats that floated in an old glass of burgundy wine on the window ledge. She lit a cigarette, took a deep puff of it, and flicked ash into a snake plant.

Then she opened the wardrobe, took out a handful of frocks, and dumped them on the bed. Some frocks had peacock feathers mounted upon their glorious wax fabrics. Some had sparkling safety pins biting into gossamer petticoats. Some had satin lining in them.

Her mama picked a plain cotton button-down, dull black and crinkled. She stuffed it inside her canvas bag. She picked a polyester frock in sienna tones. The front of the bodice was embellished with shell-edged tucks. The sleeves were short and scalloped. Near the hem of the skirt was a bouquet of lily of the Nile, embroidered in French knots. She stuffed it inside her canvas bag too. Then she pulled on a pair of high-waisted jeans and a cardigan.

Ayosa shifted from one foot to the other. A floorboard creaked beneath her. She stiffened. Her mama cocked her head. Buttercup?

Ayosa said nothing.

Buttercup, I know you're there. Come on in.

Ayosa pushed open her mama's door.

Hello, Buttercup.

Hello, Mama. Ayosa stared at the packed canvas bag on her mama's bed. Are you going somewhere?

Loitokitok.

Oh, Ayosa said, and the tears that had trembled in her eyes since Mbiu's departure now trickled down her cheeks.

What's wrong?

Nothing.

Are you sad?

Why would I be sad? I don't care enough to be sad!

It appears that you do.

Ayosa pursed her lips. It doesn't matter. I'm used to it.

Her mama threw away her cigarette. She said, If it upsets you so much to stay here by yourself, why don't you come with me?

Ayosa was stunned.

Come with me, her mama pressed.

Where shall we go?

Everywhere, Buttercup. We will take photographs. Travel the country in rickety old trains. We will hitchhike and we will eat questionable food in greasy, smoky diners. You're a big girl now, you ought to go see what the world is like.

What about school?

Her mama waved the question off. Oh, I know that you dropped out. Temerity told me.

Ayosa's heart clenched. Temerity, the shiny-eyed, snot-faced girl, had betrayed her after all.

Her mama walked toward her, her movement—the lightness, the softness of her feet—almost serpentine. *Please*, her mama begged. Let's leave right away.

Ayosa twisted the hem of her frock. You really want to bring me with you?

Wouldn't have suggested it otherwise, her mama said. She smiled her dimpled smile and picked up the canvas bag. Sidling past Ayosa, she said, Let's go!

Wait! Shouldn't I pack a few clothes?

Oh, you're almost as tall as I am. We will share whatever I've brought with me. What is mine is yours!

Ayosa could hardly believe her luck. She felt delirious. Her heart swelled in her chest, so large she thought it would surge out like a hot air balloon and break free of her rib cage and carry her out the window and into the sky. She hopped about from foot to foot, trying to contain her elation. She imagined all the places that she would go with her mama. Not small-small towns, but entire countries. São Tomé and Ivory Coast and Cape Verde. Stopping to make portraits of cripples and castaways and cretins. Ayosa would pick up a smoking habit. The cigarette smoke would age her. Make her look thirty-five.

People would stare at her and her mama and *think* that they were sisters.

Wasn't that what her mama wanted? Ayosa did not care one way or the other, as long as they were together. It would be just like in the Yonder Days, when Ayosa had been a wriggling thing and followed her mama everywhere. Back then, Nabumbo Promise had not known that Ayosa was there, accompanying her on all her journeys. This time, she would be unequivocally present. Doing everything she could for her mama. Blowing in her face so she would have enough air to breathe. Chewing her food for her if her jaws were tired of chewing for themselves. Punching in the teeth of anyone who said ng'we to her mama. Kneeing them in the crotch if they tried to swindle or deceive or be treacherous to her.

Nabumbo Promise hurried toward the stairs.

Wait, Mama! Ayosa said.

And she launched herself forward. Hurled herself at Nabumbo Promise. Grabbed at her neck. Except, there was nothing there to grab—no flesh, and underneath it, no ligament and no bone. Her mama let out a guttural scream, and then turned into a curly wisp of smoke.

Fuck-toad! Ayosa murmured in utter shock. I almost got snatched by a wraith!

The wraith was gone, but so too was Ayosa's *real* mama, and now here she was, Ayosa, facing that horrid Waiting. With a wraith's petrifying squall still ringing in her ears. There were Days that she could not bear—so frightful, so long and bright and empty. And then there were Nights like these, Nights when she just could not continue to *be*. Nights where her body unraveled from itself like yarn from a spool.

Her eyes unsaw, her ears unheard, her hands untouched, her tongue untasted. It was a repudiation of all her senses, as though something inside her were hastily closing shop, returning her back to Herself. Saying, Go on now and wriggle away. Saying, Isn't this what you wanted more than anything else in the world—to unburden yourself of your terrible mud suit?

And yet, in the moment of reckoning, when she stood at the door of her Self, she realized that she was not ready to abandon her feeble Girl-body. There were Questions that lingered, Questions that were worth sticking around to learn the answers to.

What schoolhouse tragedies would Temerity, the shiny-eyed, snot-faced girl, bring her the next time she came over? And, would an eleventh man ever come knocking on Sindano's door, asking for her hand in marriage? And, would Mbiu—her *dear* Mbiu—return to watch her through the kitchen window? And, most crucial of all, what would Ms. Temperance read on the radio tomorrow?

No-no-no, she said to her fragmenting body. *Stay.*

And then, Please-please-please-I-need-you.

She needed herself. Needed the resolute industriousness of her mouth to ruminate over bread and over idioms. And she needed the watchfulness of her eyes to untangle the enigmas of the world. And she needed her ears to listen for as long as there were poets left to speak. There now, she said to her heart, which beat, no, buzzed, fast as a hummingbird's hovering flutter.

She thought, This body of mine has its uses.

When she had been a wriggling thing, her experience of the world was somewhat muted, somewhat refracted. Everything she saw had felt distant and mediated, like watching a solar eclipse through darkened filters. Yet here and now, in this body of hers—this mud suit—things carried a certain sensuous quality. Birdsong, a poem, a cat's short raggedy tail—to her, it was all rapture, all obscene pleasure. It was something that her grandmother Lola Freedom would have made her write down on the Chalkboard of Sins. *Forgive me, Father, for I take immoral gratification in the aroma of oncoming rain.*

Oh! she thought. My mama!

She had plenty of Questions about her mama too. Questions that were worth sticking around to learn the answers to. Like, would Nabumbo Promise ever come home to stay? Would she ever make one promise and keep it? Would she ever telephone her sister, Rosette, and would the two of them get over their Stubborn Silence that had lasted almost two decades now?

They had done it once before. Gotten over the Stubborn Silence.

Ayosa hugged her knees. She thought of that time. Back in the Yonder Days. Back when Nabumbo Promise was still recovering from her injury. Back when she had screws affixed inside her busted knee and could not walk.

Her sister, Rosette, had stayed with her. Rosette had found a shabby flat for them to move into. She had cooked Nabumbo's gruel and washed her clothes. And all the while, they hardly said a thing to each other. It had been this way since they were six years old. This Stubborn Silence. Sometimes punctuated by a hollow hello-goodbye or pass-the-salt or please-and-thank-you.

Stubborn Silence was their mother tongue.

One evening, after a long day at work, Rosette stood at the window, smoking a cigarette, her nun's habit soaked with blood and stuck to her body. In those days, she wore her habit and veil daily, even though she no longer lived at the convent. She had found a job at a slaughterhouse. She wore her habit and veil even when she went out to hack animal carcasses.

Standing there at the window and smoking, Rosette had watched children chase after a football out in the street. Without warning, she had broken their Stubborn Silence. She said, Nabumbo Promise, do you miss home?

And Nabumbo Promise was taken aback by the sound of her sister's voice. She marveled at how different Rosette sounded when she was asking a *real* question, not only remarking about something perfunctory like the weather. She was surprised to learn how closely the cadence and timbre of Rosette's voice resembled their mother's.

She was also taken aback by the question itself, by its unceremonious announcement that their Stubborn Silence was over. That they were now free to reach into the recesses of each other's minds, the depths of each other's hearts. That they could touch whatever thing they found seething within the other. Shake it and turn it and examine it.

Nabumbo Promise was ecstatic. Stubborn Silence was their mother tongue, but it was a language of hot coals searing the teeth, a language that sent wildfire ravaging through the untended forests of the mouth. Nabumbo Promise could not wait to spit this language all out. To prattle on with her sister about things both profound and mundane.

Home? Nabumbo Promise said. Haven't thought about whether I miss it or not.

In the quiet that followed, Nabumbo Promise reflected on this. She thought of the house that they had been born in. She thought of the dust motes that swayed from side to side, like lace drapery. She thought of the odd-shaped rooms full of their grandmother Mabel Brown's daguerreotypes, full of colonies of fruit bats hanging from the ceiling. The shadows that skittered furtively. The sun rays that got trapped like mouse-birds when you left the window open. The creaking that one always heard—bed rails, or ceiling fans, or the whole house buckling under its own weight.

She said, I suppose I do miss it. Our mother's house.

And Rosette frowned. I never felt at home there.

Where, then?

Nowhere. Never found a place to lay down my head. To sing that song which my heart hums to itself inside my chest.

Maybe home isn't a place. Maybe it's a body.

Rosette looked down at her soiled clothes. She said, Today, while at the slaughterhouse, I thought about this very thing. I thought, I've got nowhere to sing the song of my heart, but at least this slaughter-house has some grace.

The slaughterhouse? Grace? You're speaking mud!!

The way the animal bodies fall apart. The way the flesh rots easy. The way the bones bleed. Did you know that, Nabumbo Promise? Your bones *bleed*.

Nabumbo Promise grimaced. She did know this. She had touched her own naked bones not too long ago, and found that they felt so alarmingly ordinary in her hands. Like an everyday object. A table leg. An umbrella shaft. The neck of a desk lamp.

The memory of her bones—her busted knee—clasped in her fist still repulsed her.

Rosette turned away from the window. She said, The grace was in seeing how quick I too shall degrade. Seeing that someday, I too shall leave myself. This carcass that I inhabit, and this flesh that rots, and these bones that bleed. The slaughterhouse made me think of my own body's impermanence. It was graceful. I felt at *home* in it.

Nabumbo Promise felt nauseated. She had hoped for another verdict. She had hoped to hear, *You* are my sister. *You* are flesh of my flesh. *You* are my home. Instead, Rosette was proclaiming that she belonged to herself. That she was her own flesh of her flesh. That she was her own home.

Nabumbo Promise blinked. Fought back tears. When she opened her eyes again, she noticed that the air stirred. That the drapes shook, even though the windows were all shut. Nabumbo Promise chewed on her knuckle. And she felt a thing—a presence—shift close to her. Touch her on the cheek with its soft cheesecloth touch. As though saying, *I* am your home.

And even though she could not see this thing, she knew that it was there all right. She had felt it follow her these past months. She did not know exactly what it was. A guardian angel? A restless spirit? A figment or a wish or an old undisclosed smell spilled over from the crannies of her mind? It did not matter. This thing was *hers*. She whispered to it, I am your home too.

That evening, Nabumbo Promise and Rosette drank beer and played rummy, and when they were drunk enough, they telephoned their mother's house. Their mother did not answer, and they wondered if she was off flying in her red Cessna, attending to some medical emergency, or if she had once again mixed Hennessy with painkillers and was unconscious in the blue farmhouse rocking chair in her bedroom.

Later, Rosette fried up some cow entrails that she had brought back from the slaughterhouse. For a long while, they stood silent in the kitchen, watching as steam rose from the pot, watching as it fogged up the window. And then Rosette asked, What are you thinking, Nabumbo Promise?

Nabumbo Promise smiled, glad that they had swallowed their

Stubborn Silence. Glad that they were talking to each other again, *really* talking. She said, I am thinking about Things That Happened.

Rosette frowned. She knew what that meant.

It meant that Nabumbo was thinking of Maxwell Truth.

He was their brother, whom they had drowned when they were six years old. Maxwell Truth, who was born on the eighth of August. Who had eyes the color of ocher, and a wry, effusive laugh. Who had loved warm toast with butter and sugar and cinnamon. Who had been afraid of turkeys.

She was thinking also of what happened after the drowning. How their mother sobbed inconsolably all night. How they laughed at her because her cries sounded like the shrieks of the crazy-birds out in the yard. *Jolly anna ha-ha-ha.* And the next morning, their mama had telephoned the police station.

Had said, My twins have drowned their three-year-old brother. Come quick-quick and take them.

How old are the twins? the policeman asked.

Six.

And the policeman said, Six? Sounds like an accident to me. Buy them ice lollies. Tell them not to go about drowning other children.

And that was that. The twins did not get arrested, as Lola Freedom had hoped. So she took matters into her own hands. She scooped them up into her jalopy and drove them to an orphanage.

The orphanage was called the Lola Freedom Brown Asylum for Abandoned Children, built from a donation that she had given to the Catholic diocese of the region.

Nabumbo Promise and Rosette lived at that orphanage for six years. In all that time, they hardly spoke a word to anyone, including to each other.

And they were certain that their mother had abandoned them

there just so she could go off and start another family. A *better* one. They were certain that their mother now had a husband, and different children. Sons, not daughters. Jolly ones, straight haired and pink lipped, who did not drown each other in wells.

At the orphanage, they wore frocks woven from rice sacks, and they ate soggy ugali and bean water, and every Sunday, they shaved each other's heads with razor blades. At the orphanage, they nursed their Stubborn Silence.

The other children there were afraid of them.

Evil twins, they whispered to each other.

Such wickedness, the nuns who ran the orphanage murmured, whenever one of the sisters was spotted. They had heard the story too—about the girls' drowning Maxwell Truth in the well.

Stop, Rosette wailed, her voice tremulous. Stop thinking about Things That Happened in the Past. Stop thinking about Things We Lost. I can't bear it!

Ayosa emerged from her reveries of the Yonder Days. She took out her notebook, and she wrote a letter to her mama.

Dear Nabumbo Promise Brown,

> *I wonder how many girls wandered off to God-knows-where following wraiths that sang their mama's foxy songs. Me, my wraith dressed herself in your body, she wore your scars like they were moonstones. She said, Buttercup, let's go away together. As though that were something you could ever say to me. As though your solitude isn't more precious*

to you than any gold or any daughter. Still, here I am,
Mama. I didn't follow the wraith and didn't close up shop.
If you forgive me for ripping your hair out, I will forgive
you for always saying you were Done Leaving when you
were not.

Ayosa tore off the page and put it in an envelope. She found a stamp in her mama's desk drawer. She addressed it to her mama's PO box, where she sent all her mama's letters. When her mama was lost in nowhere-towns, she usually left a forwarding address with the postmaster. Tomorrow morning, Ayosa would give the letter to the milkman, and he would drop it off for her. That's how she always did it.

Now she stood up, made her way to the bathroom. She took her mama's toothbrush from the tumbler by the soap dish. She sucked on the wet, minty bristles, wondered if this muskiness was what her mama's mouth really tasted like.

Her mama's bedroom door was ajar, the light in it still burning. Ayosa ambled in, went to the canopy bed, and stroked the lace that was draped over its four columns. She squatted on the sheepskin rug and sucked on her mama's toothbrush some more. She stared at the gallery wall, at the photographs that her mama had mounted there.

In one photograph, there was a stranger with a broomstick for a leg, and in the crook of his arm lay a bunch of wild carnations. In another photograph, there was a gas cooker abandoned in a street, its metal door hanging off the hinges, and inside its bare oven, a child squatted, peering out, eyes puny and bright.

In another photograph, Mabel Brown stared out contemptuously. She had a long chin, wide-set dirty-brown eyes, hollow cheeks, and hands so small and bony they could have belonged to a fowl. Gray ringlets tumbled down over her back.

Next to her on the wall was Lola Freedom, with a shrill, brooding countenance, but with heated, chirpy eyes. Ayosa could see the features she had received directly from her—the imperial jawline, the mouse's ears, the brows that grew wild as thickets, even the mole on the cheek, hairy, large as a ten-cent coin.

She turned away from the photographs. The moonlight trickled through slivers where the draperies did not touch the window. It slowly dripped down the walls, seeping into the white sheets, into the webs of her hands. The pillow smelled of her mama's hair—of the gooseberry and jasmine in it—and her heart wrenched with yearning. She fell asleep like that, curled up in her mama's bed, sucking on her mama's toothbrush.

9

The townspeople gargled salt water. They greased their elbows. They tucked a flower in their hair or pinned it on their lapel. They marched to Our Lady of Lourdes Church, where Father Jude Thaddeus thundered:

Service is anointed. You offer yourselves up to God when you offer yourselves up for your country. You are called to be faithful. How can you be faithful? By working hard. By obeying your superiors. By staying humble. By consecrating each moment of your service to the Lord. By following the footsteps laid before you. The Good Book says this: We work hard with our own hands. When we are cursed, we bless; when we are persecuted, we endure it.

Elsewhere, Mbiu and her cat, Bwana Matambara, walked past the marshes, past the boatyard, past the old cemetery, past the schoolhouse, past the clock tower, past the seer with a bowler hat at his feet. The seer raised a threadbare Bible in the air and said Jehovah-Jire-open-my-eyes, and then he knew all there was to know about everyone in the street.

He knew if they had once stolen pears from the neighbor's garden, or if they kept pagan idols hidden underneath their bed, or if they had ever lusted after their brother's wife. When Mbiu shuffled past him, he waved his Bible at her.

He said, Elohim–El Shaddai–Yahweh–Adonai! Father God, just see for yourself this heaven's little angel, white as snow, filled with the sweetness of Your Kingdom.

And Mbiu threw her head back and said, Ha-ha-ha.

White as snow, ha-ha-ha.

Filled with sweetness, ha-ha-ha.

Mbiu went to a row of tenement buildings, pushed the wooden gate of a nearby one, and entered the courtyard. The tenement was built in a U shape, with five houses on every side, fifteen in all. Each house was really one room the size of a milk crate. At the end of the courtyard was a communal bathroom.

This was where Mbiu and her mama used to live. Mbiu watched the ducks and goats and piglets that scrambled after scraps of gruel in the courtyard. Her house—her *former* house—was in the corner of the tenement. She stood on the veranda, her face pressed to the windowpane. A new family lived inside it. A man, a woman, a girl and boy. They sat at a table, eating their evening meal in silence. Chewing on cassava pieces and on smoked meat. They sat at the same table that Mbiu and her mama had sat at. They used the same plates and glasses that Mbiu and her mama had used. The same curtains, the same forks and knives and spoons, the same crate of Ladybird storybooks nailed to the wall.

Mbiu watched those people all morning, at first angry at them for taking over a life that had belonged so intimately to her and her mama, and then later, more sympathetic, for she began to wonder about the *before-time*. She thought, Me and my mama must have taken over from others too. Something unfortunate must have happened, and the family before had had to leave, had had to scatter. And one day, this family will be gone too. So Mbiu whispered a warning.

Children, fatten yourselves up now, the lean times are coming.

And her heart wrenched. She thought of those parents gone, say, minced to pulp beneath the rubble of a collapsed building, and that girl and that boy roaming the streets on their own. Stealing clothes to wear from strangers' yards. Wresting scraps to eat from the mouths of alley rats. She was lucky that she had her mama's car to curl up in when her feet could not bear any more standing, lucky that she did not have to crawl down into sewers to find shelter.

She whispered, Children, you've got to be limber, you see? And mind, you've got to keep the eyes at the back of your head peeled, for there is always some running to do. Look, you've got to run from those busboys and preacher-men, from those maize roasters and school-teachers, and, most of all, from those godforsaken policemen. Dilly-dally and you get knocked over and pinned down and you've got fists stuffed in your throats and you've got the dirty done to you. Let me just tell you, children, there's not a single man out there in those streets that you can trust.

Now Mbiu turned away. As she walked out of the tenement, she said to herself, Well, at least there's two of those children. Maybe if they have each other, things won't be so bad for them.

Up the hill, at Manor Mabel Brown, Ayosa and the Fatumas sat on the ledge of a bay window, and the breeze was cold even though the day was hot, and it slid inside their frocks, searching for parts of them to plunder. Outside, in the eaves, the jolly annas yelled, Jolly anna ha-ha-ha, at them, but Ayosa and the Fatumas paid their horrid cackling no mind at all.

The Fatumas tugged at Ayosa's sleeve. Do you know chakacha? they said.

What is chakacha? Ayosa said.

It's a dance.

I don't know how to dance any dances.

Have you ever tried?

No.

Then how do you know that you don't know how to dance any dances?

The Fatumas closed their eyes, tipped their heads to the side, and parted their lips. This is how you dance chakacha, they said, raising their arms in the air above their heads. They swayed, waists writhing round and round.

Jamani, Ayosa said. I could never dance like that!

Oh, but you could, my dear, they said to her.

Her toes curled because she was their dear.

Think of round things, okay? they said. Are you thinking of them?

Yes.

What round things are you thinking of?

The mouths of mugs. And hula hoops. And a person's palms when all the fingers have been cut off.

That is how to dance chakacha, the Fatumas said. You close your eyes and you think of round things. Then you draw those round things with your hips. Come, kipusa, dance chakacha with us.

Ayosa climbed down from the ledge, but she did it only because the Fatumas had called her such a sweet name.

Kipusa, like a pebble that fitted snugly in your nostril when you stuffed it in there. Or like cold cream dribbling out of a jar and onto the hollows of your collarbones. Or like strings of sunlight dancing on your bare back.

Kipusa-kipusa-kipusa.

Think of more round things, the Fatumas said.

Ayosa thought of dinner plates and cucumber slices and the faces of wristwatches. She thought of melon halves and split pumpkins and

Ferris wheels that she had once seen in magazines. She thought of gold bangles that jingled on the arms of Nubian women in the street. She thought of cereal bowls and the wheels of bicycles and the lids of margarine containers.

The insides of her eyelids were orange, and her tongue tasted cantaloupe on itself. Her chest heaved and her breath oozed out of her nose, hot and stinging, like candle wax. There, in the attic, she danced chakacha, writhing, turning herself inside out. Her mama was gone but it did not matter at all because she was the Fatumas' dear.

The windows were open and a gust of wind blew in, bringing them grit and blackjack needles and melodies from birds' throats. They clutched the things that the wind had brought them, and they thought of other round things: Marie tea biscuits, and shoe polish containers, and fifty-cent coins. They danced chakacha for all the missing mamas in the world, and they danced chakacha for all the daughters left at home waiting.

Later, she let all the parts inside her slacken, so that she became the very wriggling thing she once had been, back in the Yonder Days, the very wriggling thing that her mama had gazed out into the sky for and said, Please-please-please-I-need-you.

This wriggling thing slithered beneath the door and up the hinges and knobs and drifted to the ceiling. It spun on the fan and it was light as a gadfly. The Fatumas looked up at it and wanted it terribly and summoned it back down to them. So Ayosa returned, a girl again. She lay on the floor, breathless.

You want to know the color of my soul? she said.

What is it?

Blue, like thrush eggs.

That is a sweet color, the Fatumas said.

Ayosa watched as the Fatumas reached for the transistor radio. It was time for the death news. The radioman cleared his throat and said:

*The death is announced of Gogo Mkunga, who fell down
in a faint when the body of her brother, Shirima Mkunga,
was brought home from the mortuary. Shirima Mkunga
himself swallowed a biro pen cap while doing his math
homework. They are now both survived by no one.*

The Fatumas broke into howls, slamming their fists on the floor.
They sang Luwere-luwere-luwere for Gogo Mkunga. The whole house
shook. Ayosa dragged herself out of the attic. Fumbling into a pair of
clogs, she skipped out into the yard.

The milkman rode up the hill. He kept his eyes to the ground as
he stood his bicycle against the avocado tree. He kept his eyes to the
ground as he unstrapped a canister from the carrier and placed it on
the veranda step.

Hello, Mr. Milkman, Ayosa said.

The milkman said nothing.

Mr. Milkman, I said: Hello, Mr. Milkman. Look, I have a letter.
Would you drop it for me at the post office?

Wordlessly, the milkman took the letter, climbed onto his bicycle, jingled the bell, and rode away. Ayosa uncapped the milk canister,
raised it to her mouth, and gulped it all down. She did not care that it
tasted like the cow's rubbery udders.

The field outside was yellow, abundant with dandelions. She saw a figure move about. She squinted. It was the shiny-eyed, snot-faced girl,
Temerity, clipping flowers at the roots and throwing them into a rattan
basket.

Ayosa ran down the wooden steps of the porch.

Temerity! Temerity!

Temerity stopped clipping and waved her shears in the air.

What are you doing?

Fetching dandelions for my grandmother.

What does Jentrix want them for?

She will make soup with the leaves, and tincture with the florets.

Because why?

Because dandelions can glue broken bones back together.

Ayosa moved closer to her. Temerity, did you listen to the news this morning?

No, Temerity said, snipping away, her eyes scrunched with concentration. What did the news say?

It said a big airplane fell from the sky.

Where? Near here?

Not near here. In a place called Lockerbie, in Scotland. It happened last night. The airplane was going to New York City. Have you been to New York City?

Where is that?

In America. That's where Grace Jones lives.

Temerity placed her basket of dandelions on the ground. She said, Listen here, Miss Brown. Don't speak any mud to me about some type of Grace Jones and some type of New York City. What are those? If you want to ask me something, ask me about saffron and I will tell you how Jentrix makes a tonic with it to bring your mama back from the land down under. Or ask me about fever bark and I will tell you how it stops malaria from seeping to your head. Or ask me about sage and I will tell you how it treats bleeding gums. You hear?

I hear, Ayosa said, feeling chastised. She took out her notebook and wrote all those things down. She said, Temerity, Christmas is coming.

When is Christmas coming?

On Sunday. Do you have a Christmas dress?

This one, Temerity said, patting her gingham dress down. It's my work dress. I will go out to the fields on Christmas Day.

The *whole* day you will work in the fields?

No, just in the morning. In the afternoon, I will help my grandmother to make a lavender decoction.

Ayosa heard buzzing in a clump of dandelions near her feet. She squatted down, saw several honeybees foraging among the flower heads and bracts, searching for pollen and nectar. She straightened.

Temerity, I must go! she said.

Bye-bye, Temerity called out to her, waving her shears above her head.

Ayosa ran down the footpath, through the woods, past the cow barn that her mama had turned into a studio. She ran through the wattle trees and sycamores, to the place where, weeks ago, she had built a crude top-bar hive from PVC poles, discarded soda crates, plywood, rope, and steel nails.

Temerity had seen her do this and laughed at her. She had said, That's no beehive, Miss Brown. That's a nest for marsh rats!

Ayosa crept closer to the hive. She squatted, peered into one of the handle holes of the soda crate. An entire colony had swarmed in. She did not know when it had happened. She imagined it—a new virgin queen leaving her old home, taking with her as many workers as she could. The scouts going ahead, searching for a suitable crevice, and then finding this place that Ayosa had built for them.

She imagined all the bees crawling in, bellies distended because they had gorged themselves before they left. She imagined them frenzied, dancing with joy at finally arriving, staggering over each other to memorize all the places where the light clambered into the hive and all the places where the splinters in the wood could rip their guts out. She imagined their feeding their starved queen. Fattening her up again. Preparing her for her mating flight, for her first meeting with the drones.

She touched the chipped red paint of the bottom soda crate. She whispered to the bees, Hello, my name is Ayosa Ataraxis Brown. My soul is blue, like thrush eggs.

Later, she went to Mutheu Must Go Café, where Sindano was still in her church clothes, and eating blackberry pie straight out of a ceramic quiche pan.

You're just on time, Sindano said, and handed Ayosa a spoon for the pie, and a cup of milky masala tea. How's your mama?

Don't know.

Oh, Sindano said, studying Ayosa's face. She's gone, then? I'm sorry, my dear. Well, eat up.

Ayosa chewed the sickly-sweet pie. She glanced up at Sindano. She said, Sindano?

Yes, my name?

Why do wraiths try to snatch people?

Because they forgot what it's like to have a body. They want to remember.

I can understand that.

You can?

The way I see it, it's nice to have an itch on the arm to scratch. To eat raw mango, with salt and chili pepper. To pluck a honeysuckle flower and drink its nectar. It's even nice to get stung by a wasp. Really painful, of course, but nice nonetheless. Without a body, one couldn't possibly feel any of those things.

I wish that were true.

It *is* true. How would I know that this pie was delightfully sweet if I didn't have a mouth to taste it with?

Don't get me wrong. I agree with you on *this*. But you see, it is not so with the wraiths. The things they want to remember with their bodies are different. They have phantom pains deep inside the flesh they no longer possess, and they yearn to be filled inside with molten lava. They steal bodies in order to mutilate them with their twisted passions. Anger, bitterness, lasciviousness. They will wear a body and walk through fire just to feel the bones turn to ashes. They want bodies so they can molest and murder, so they can slit their own throats for the pleasure of it. It is a demented desire. Don't claim to understand it, Ayosa Ataraxis Brown.

Ayosa looked down at her tea. She dipped her finger in it and fished out a drowning ant. She felt Sindano's penetrating gaze on her face.

Seems to me that you've been getting some visitations.

Ayosa shrugged. Every so often, they come pretending to be my mama.

They always know the very thing that a person wants most in the world.

Did they ever try to snatch you?

Plenty of times. Well, only one wraith tried, but she tried it over and over again. She came here pretending to be men that wanted to marry me.

Is that the thing you want most in the world, for a man to marry you?

It used to be. All I wanted back then was to find a man to settle down and bear babies with. What lowly ambitions!

Sindano paused to fill her mouth with a forkful of pie. She stared out the window, her eyes rheumy. She said, The wraith, her name was Bessie. She came wearing a body that she had stolen. She pretended to be a man, all gruff, sleepy eyed, roughshod, smelling of cigarettes. Name of Balozi. She—he—seduced me. Brought me flowers and rubbed my back with fragrant oils and prayed with me and made love all night long. We had good days together. *Very* good days.

And then what happened?

She—he—asked me to marry him. On our wedding day, Bessie—er, Balozi—told me that we had to leave town together. He said that he had a house in Malindi, that he had made arrangements for us to leave right after the ceremony. I said, Balozi, what type of mud are you speaking now? Don't you see that I've got a whole café to run, not even a half one? And Balozi said he would die if I didn't come with him, and I said, Go ahead then, and he just took a machete and struck himself with it. The whole town was waiting for us at the church. I had to run there in my bloodied wedding dress, to say, Looks like there won't be a ceremony today.

So you lied the last time I asked? One man didn't swallow his tongue, and another didn't get struck by lightning, and another didn't have lockjaw, and another didn't swallow a mothball?

Sindano let out a dry laugh. All Bessie! she said. I can't believe a lick of it, looking back. But I swear on Mutheu the dead cow, I was the most desperate skank in the world in those days. Bessie disappeared for a year, and then she returned as a different man. The seduction began again, and the wedding preparations, and the vicious death when I would not follow him—her—to a nondescript town.

In the end, how did you get over Bessie the wraith?

To be honest, I just grew weary of it all. Being seduced had lost all its appeal for me—it was truly more trouble than it was worth. And *marriage*? Lord have mercy! I was no longer a naïve girl, but a woman who now lusted after her own solitude. A little like your mama, if I'm being honest. Next time Bessie came around, pretending to be a man called Balaclava, I said, Sod off, I'm going nowhere with you! Bessie was so enraged that she immediately took out a length of wire and strangled poor Balaclava with it. She emerged from his body, all feathery, like a cirrus cloud, and bellowing with fury. Saying, I am Bessie, and you are a dirty bitch. I suppose I really did a number on her—she was so sure that eventually I would leave everything behind and follow her.

But, Sindano, why was she so earnest with you?

She was after something. Something that I have.

What thing do you have, that a wraith would covet so deeply?

Sindano turned away from the window and dropped her spoon. You know what? I'm a little tired now. If you don't mind running off, I will go lie down. Take the pie with you.

10

Ayosa wandered out into the woods. The wind came chasing after her, uprooting plants, plucking pools of water from the ground, and hurling logs into the air. Rocks and tree branches and underbrush swirled about her, a turbid cyclone that went wherever she went. Her toes curled from being wanted like that.

But then, without warning, her Jinamizi struck. In the memories that it brought, she saw a great flood of water, and a great flood of fire, and the earth splitting down the middle, and the sea parting to swallow the stars that fell from the night sky, and then another great flood, of people driven through cobbled streets with wooden clubs tied to their necks as though they were oxen, and these people trampled on each other and bleated like sheep. Then there was an explosion, and those bleating people burst open, now no longer people but only bits of themselves—gravel shaped and shoelace shaped and belt buckle shaped. Later, the street sweepers came with their brooms and their pails of soapy water. Whistling jauntily. Singing, *My damsel ran off with the tinker-man*. And they scrubbed and they mopped, and when they were done, the cobblestones glimmered again, from the sun and from the pining music and from the spirits of the burst-open bleating people.

It was hot and clammy. Ayosa peeled off her skirt and blouse and hurled them away so that now she wore just her poplin petticoat. She plucked lion's ears from bushes that grew by the footpath. She sucked at them and drew out their nectar, and it was so sweet it made her eyes water. She found a rusted nail in the ground and she picked it up and made a tambourine-shaped cut on her thigh.

The world was desolate where her feet went. Or maybe her feet only knew how to go to lonesome places. But she no longer felt alone—she was surrounded by the screw pines and the bulbuls and the springs that bubbled so effusively out of the earth.

She had walked too far out and now could not find her way back. She wandered for hours, through marshes and groves and wastelands. The sun stayed with her for as long as it could, and then it tired of all her meandering, and it staggered off on its own.

Jackals bayed out in the distance, shrill and agitated. They had detected her scent—it wove into their soggy noses and tore them into a frenzy. She picked apart the tangle of their howls. There were at least fifteen of them, ribbing each other, working themselves up, their eyes rolling inside their heads.

She could not see them yet, so she imagined that they could not see her either. But when their howls died down, she knew that they were on the prowl already, that it would not be long before they found her and ripped her apart and dug their yellow fangs inside her. She would not even be dead when they did that. She would see it all with her own two eyes—see them tug at the strings of her intestines, see their muzzles and streaked fur soaked in her blood. She wondered what it would all be like—being devoured while she watched.

She imagined it—herself in the corner of herself, squatting, waiting for the moment when there would be nothing left of herself. Her toes curled from being wanted like that. She thought that maybe she should stand there and wait to be found. She thought that maybe she might enjoy watching herself being turned into nothing. But her feet would not let her—they moved of their own volition, shoving her forward, toward the river.

Her chest was bursting. She wrapped her arms beneath her rib cage and said, Please-please-please don't burst. Her chest clenched but did not burst.

The jackals were a few paces behind her now. She could feel their breaths on her heels and calves like hot rain pellets. She could see their orange eyes crackling like welding torches. She thought that there was no way at all she could make it to the stream. So she turned around, eager to yield to their need of her. But the river, which had never stopped needing her, broke out of its banks and yanked her.

There she was, falling inside it.

Ayosa Ataraxis Brown! someone called out to her.

Ayosa tried to hold still long enough to see who it was—the girl Mbiu was on the rocky shore, with her cat on her shoulder. Mbiu, her *dear* Mbiu.

Mbiu was sobbing.

She said, You're too far out!

She said, Fight the currents!

She said, Come back to me, please!

Ayosa's toes curled at the thought of being wanted like this. Still, she did not come out of the water. She descended into the brackishness. Inside it, she saw that she was not alone. She was surrounded by other objects that the river had yanked in too—a grandfather clock, an upright piano, a prosthetic leg, a porcelain doll with its eyes poked out. These things twirled together like a shoal of fish, and now she was one of them, twirling too.

Later, Ayosa went to the riverbank and watched the silver waters fizzling and frothing on the hot rocks. Lying there like that reminded her of the Yonder Days. In her memory, it was a week since Nabumbo Promise and her sister, Rosette, were returned home from the orphanage.

After abandoning them there for six long years, Lola Freedom had decided to fetch them. She must have thought that they had done their penance. That they were rehabilitated. She returned them home and had them wear bows in their hair and eat their Weetabix and study the piano as though nothing at all had happened.

On their second day at home, they sat out in the garden and watched the crazy-birds squealing and tearing at each other with their beaks. Screaming, Jolly anna ha-ha-ha. Mocking Nabumbo Promise and Rosette for their pathetic little lives. For the unspeakable evil inside them that had caused them to drown Maxwell Truth. For the dull silent years spent at the orphanage.

Jolly anna ha-ha-ha, said the jolly annas.

Your mama shall never love you. You are vermin. Riffraff.

Nabumbo Promise and Rosette turned away, tears trembling in their eyes.

There was a flurry in the rosebushes.

They got up to look. They saw bald-headed chickens fleeing from a bat-eared fox. They picked up rocks and hurled them at the fox. One of the rocks that Rosette picked up was elongated and smooth. It felt like a baton in her fingers.

Look at this rock! Rosette said to her sister.

Nabumbo Promise turned away from the crazy-birds and the chickens and the fox. It's not a rock. It's a bone, Nabumbo Promise said.

They both fell to their knees and started digging the earth. They discovered more bones: Skull. Vertebrae. Sternum. Carpals and femurs and tarsals.

Their mama had told them the story of their grandmother's blowing her head right off with a musket. How the crazy-birds tore her apart and ate her, and the bat-eared foxes fought over what was left.

Lola Freedom! they called to their mother. Lola Freedom! We found her! We found Mabel Brown!

And their mama ran out, shrieking, Christ, was that woman in the rosebushes all this time?

Now it was a few days after they had found their grandmother in the rosebushes. Their mother had gotten her bones cremated. Now she was holding a funeral service for her. The girls went with Lola Freedom to Our Lady of Lourdes Catholic Church.

The service was not really a service at all, just the priest standing over Mabel Brown's copper urn, saying, Eternal rest grant unto her, oh Lord, and let perpetual light shine.

Lola Freedom had bolted the church doors from the inside. She would not let any of the townspeople come in to pay their respects. A private service, she called it.

Nabumbo Promise and Rosette sat prim. Their white lace socks were pulled up to their thighs. Their taffeta dresses crackled with static. The ruffles on them were stiff, gouging out alleyways into their skin.

They sat in Stubborn Silence. Angry Silence. Disgusted Silence.

After the service, they trudged home in single file, with the townspeople standing by the roadside to watch, openmouthed, first because they had never seen a funeral like that, hush-hush and quick-quick, like a shotgun wedding, and second, because they had never seen the remains of the dead turned to ashes and then carried around in a jug, like lemonade. But then again, Mabel Brown was an Englishwoman, and the English people had shown themselves to be unspeakably violent and unconscionably odd.

At home, Lola Freedom wore her slippers and her silk slip. She downed half a bottle of vodka and went to bury her mother in an unmarked spot out in the garden. Nabumbo Promise and Rosette watched her dig about with an aluminum scoop.

They watched her in Pitying Silence. Sad Silence.

And the Sad Silence turned to Happy Silence when they realized something: Their mother did not have a husband, or different children. Did not have jolly sons who were straight haired and pink lipped.

Nabumbo Promise and Rosette had spent the past days waiting for a sedan to pull up front. For a man to come out, wearing starched khakis, smelling like cedarwood, carrying a briefcase, saying, Hello, girls, I am your new father.

And he would open the doors of the sedan and show the jolly, straight-haired, pink-lipped boys in the back, and say, Here is Matayo Brown, and here is Makai Brown.

Nabumbo Promise and Rosette were relieved. They had spent the six years of their sentence at the orphanage resenting Lola Freedom for her joy, and now they saw that she did not have any. She was just as drunk as always. Lonely too. No, drunker, and lonelier, than ever. She kicked rocks over Mabel Brown's grave and stumbled forward and fell facedown in the mud.

Then she shuffled to her feet and waddled down to the river. Nabumbo Promise took a towel, and she and Rosette followed their mother. They found her passed out on the sandy bank. They dragged her to the towel and laid her on her side. Nabumbo Promise and Rosette sat by her feet, swatting at the mosquitoes so they would not bite their mother's calves. Even though they did nothing at all for hours—just stared out at the far-off fishermen in their bobbing dinghies—that day remained their favorite one of their childhood.

It was the way their mother lay there between them, the way she let them care for her. It was the way the orange air was a softness, a deliriousness, simmering and crumbling. And they could sit with their mama, all three of them together, as though they were some sort of *family*. That day, at the edge of the river, they spent those long hours staring at their mama, reacquainting themselves with the shadows and the crests and the lines of her face.

Ayosa thought of that day because she was sitting at the very same spot as they had, under a date palm tree, being mauled by mosquitoes. She thought of Nabumbo Promise and Rosette. The Brown girls, with their Stubborn Silence, sharing a serene and tongue-tied conviviality. She envied that fellowship of their youth, easy, *beyond* language. Yet, what was easy in childhood became much too facile in adulthood. What was beyond language became beyond understanding. And in the end, it was the unspoken things, the *beyond* things, that soured their sistership, like creamy soup left to sit on the countertop too long.

Still, Ayosa envied them. She thought, My God, how I wish I had a sister here with me right now.

In the evening, Jentrix the apothecary sent Temerity over with a tiffin box. Temerity brought Ayosa a skull too—she had found it buried beneath some sunflowers by a stream. She thought it had once belonged to a bird of some kind, perhaps a kori bustard. Ayosa laughed when Temerity told her this.

The skull does not have a beak attached, therefore could not possibly have belonged to a bird, she said.

Temerity was flustered. I thought beaks were like a person's lips. That they just decayed when a bird died.

Not at all, Ayosa said. She showed Temerity pages from a book she had found in the library. It was an illustrated guide to animal anatomy. She showed her the bird section first, then the mammal section. Together, they tried to identify the skull that Temerity had brought. They concluded that, most likely, it had belonged to a cushioned gerbil.

The sun was quickly withering out of the sky. Temerity ran off to find some amaranth and ginger root that her grandmother needed, before it got too dark to see. Ayosa opened the tiffin box that Jentrix had sent. The first compartment had rice, the next compartment had curried lentils, and the third had pumpkin soup. Ayosa stood by the sink and ate, watching the jolly annas burrow among the dandelions. They said, Jolly anna ha-ha-ha. And she ate the blemished banana and punctured green apple that Jentrix had included in a brown bag. She ate the Goody Goody that Temerity had snuck her—Ayosa found it taped to the bottom of the tiffin box.

———

Ayosa wandered about in the woods, all the while thinking of the number six. She had just noticed that the momentous periods of her mama's life were bundled up in sixes.

Six years at home, before the drowning of Maxwell Truth.

And then six years carrying out their sentence at the orphanage.

And then six more years at home, before their mother scooped them up in her jalopy and carted them off to the convent.

When their mother had first returned them from the orphanage, Nabumbo Promise and Rosette were much too afraid of a khaki-clad man's coming to lay claim on them. Saying, I am your new father. The thing they had not anticipated was that this man might not be their new father, rather their *old* one.

It was six years after they were returned home from the orphanage. They were eighteen. Lola Freedom was gone off somewhere, and the girls were alone at home. There was a knock on the door. Rosette, who had come inside the house only briefly for a change of clothes, got up to open the door.

Before her was a man.

They knew that this man was their father, even before he opened his mouth and said a word about it. He was a schoolteacher, dressed in a pin-striped suit, with a biro pen clipped into his breast pocket. They knew it was their father because he wore those same spectacles that they did, with lenses so thick they made his eyes look like boiled eggs.

He sat at the kitchen table and studied the room—the dirty dishes in the sink, stacked so high some plates and bowls touched the ceiling;

the compost bin in the corner, with the flies buzzing so loud it sounded like the static of a transistor radio; the broken glass of the window-pane, held down by strips of packing tape. In the corridor, guinea fowls waddled back and forth.

He studied the two girls seated before him. Eyes bulbous behind their spectacles. Jaws clenched tight. They were dressed the same, in plaid pinafores, too hot for that time of year. They looked alike in every respect, except that one girl's body was full of keloids.

He saw their Stubborn Silence, and frowned.

He said, Sorry to come like this, unannounced. But your mother, she won't answer my letters.

They said nothing.

He said, The townspeople showed me where to find you. I didn't know there were two of you.

He looked from one to the other, confounded, as though trying to determine which one of the two was the original and which was the copy. Or, which was the girl he had thought of often all these years, and which was the one he still owed lots of thinking.

It's the one with the keloids. Don't you see, she came out all wrong! She's the copy. Copies sometimes come out dirty. These were Nabumbo's thoughts as she stared at him. She wished she was something worth looking at, so her father would go back and say to his people, Naam, my eyes have *seen*.

He said, My name is Celestial Ouma, from a far-off village called Namamali. I'm a teacher. Our school is named the Lola Freedom Brown Educational Center. It washed away in the rain once. We woke up and looked out the window, and we found that we had broken away to a new village in Koyonzo. We had lost twenty students to the mudslide. Your mother, the sky doctor, she came and sewed limbs into their limb holes, and she built our broken school back up for us.

My people still sing about the little red bird that came perching in our tree.

The girls said nothing.

He told them that he was here not as a father but as an emissary. He said, Please give your mother this message for me.

He said: Lola Freedom, the village wants its child returned. You must know that the child does not belong to you. She belongs to her people.

He said: Lola Freedom, you do not know what malignant spirits might have followed the child here. Unhappy kin, jealous clansmen, even night-runners upset because their names are not beseeched often enough. The child might see or remember things that she ought not to. This will not stop until you bring the child home for us to hold.

He said: Lola Freedom, if you ask your child, she will tell you how lost she feels. We understand why this sense of loss is so. There is a chasm inside the child. Bring her home so she can visit the graves of her grandparents. Bring her home so she can learn the faces of her ancestors. See, we make no new faces where we come from. Each face that you see is an old face; it has been here before; it returns again and again. Bring our child home so we can honor her forebearers accordingly.

Their father stood up to go. He paused. Added, The village shall now be informed that there are, in fact, two children.

Their mama heard about this visit from Jentrix the apothecary, who had been listening from the veranda.

Their mama said, I'll be damned if some dirty peasants try to take my children away!

So she scooped them into her jalopy. Drove drunk, drove slurring, to a convent called the Daughters of the Mystical Rose. There was a building there, by the main chapel, called the L. F. Brown Canonical Library. Their mama had donated the money to build it. Because of this, the nuns asked no questions. Took the girls right in. Gave them habits and veils to wear. Gave them rosaries and prayer books.

Ayosa Ataraxis Brown! someone called to her.

Ayosa got up from the kitchen table, where she had been drinking a cup of hot chocolate. She looked out the window, saw the girl on the veranda. Cat on shoulder. Dress tattered. Body caked with dirt.

Mbiu! she said, and ran out the door.

Mbiu was all leaking mosquito bites and gangly limbs and eyes as big and as gleaming as paper lanterns. She leaned against a pillar, sucking on the dangling cloth belt of her frock. She had shorn off all her hair. In her hand was a bouquet of canna lilies.

You brought me flowers?

I thought you were dead, Mbiu said. She tossed the bouquet at Ayosa.

Because why did you think I was dead?

Because I saw the river take you away and it looked like you drowned for sure. I thought the fishermen found your body and brought it to your mama to bury. So I came out here to put the flowers on your grave.

I am not dead at all, Ayosa said.

But *why*?

Because the river was good to me.

Mbiu spat out the cloth belt. She set the cat Bwana Matambara down, and he climbed into a nearby tree. Look, she said, that river is not a good river. People die inside it all the time. Do you know a boy called Dudu?

No, Ayosa said.

Well, his mama is a seamstress. And him, he drinks tamarind juice and sits on the veranda and listens to *The Daily Assortment of Astonishing Things* on his mama's radio. Or he just climbs a tree and makes spit bombs and throws them down at the people passing in the street below. Do you not know that boy? His mama has only one real eye and the other eye is a sheep's eye. How can you not know Dudu? Everyone knows Dudu. If you say to him, Dudu, how are you, he will say to you, Tell your mouth I don't feel like talking to it. That is just the type of boy he is. Well, Dudu, his father was a fisherman and he died in that very same river that you are calling good.

Kalulu Musyoka?

How did you know his name?

I saw him in the water.

You see? Mbiu said. That river is not good at all, let me just tell you that. Don't say any ng'we to it if you don't want to drown. It will whisper to you sweety-sweety but don't think you are its sweety at all. It just wants to drown you!

Ayosa shrugged. She raised the canna lilies up in the air. What am I to do with these now?

I don't know. Smell them maybe. People on the television are always smelling flowers.

Ayosa sniffed at them. They don't smell like anything. Where did you find them?

I stole them from the apothecary's place.

Because why?

Because you have to bring flowers when you visit dead people.

I am not dead.

So throw them away.

Ayosa hurled them across the yard. The bouquet slammed against the avocado tree. Yellow-red petals scattered all over the ground.

Ayosa studied Mbiu. What happened to your hair?

I shaved it.

Because why?

Because that's what you do when you visit a dead person.

But I am not dead!

Mbiu slapped at a mosquito on her arm. How was I supposed to know that?

Ayosa shrugged.

Mbiu was watching her with those large eyes that set fire to everything they looked at. Ayosa raised her gaze, and now the two of them stared at each other, brows scrunched and eyes pinched because of the bleary wind. They stood there, fingertips brushing lightly, and then fingers grasping at each other, clutching at each other. They matched each other thing for thing—wriggliness, loneliness, solitude.

Don't die on me, Mbiu said, eyes glittering with tears that she would not let fall.

I won't.

Ever since my mama died, I spend my days looking inside people's windows to make sure they are still there. That nothing happened to them. My dear, I can't bear the thought of someday looking in your window and not finding you there.

But who's looking in *your* window?

What do you mean?

Who's making sure nothing happened to you?

Mbiu shrugged and wiped the wetness of her eyes with the back of her arm. She said, Nothing ever happens to me.

Ayosa turned away. She opened the door that led into the kitchen. She rummaged in a drawer, found a butcher knife, and brought it to the bathroom. The mirror was cloudy, so she rubbed it with a length of toilet paper.

She splashed water onto her face and scrubbed it with a slab of soap. She did not rinse the soap off, instead letting all the suds slither onto her frock before she dried her face with the hand towel. Then she curtsied for no reason. Then she said to her reflection, How do you do, madam?

She gathered her hair to the side of her forehead, and now she looked like the type of girl who wore a mink coat that her mama had bought secondhand from the open-air market. The type of girl who hopped onto the roof of a stranger's car at a toll bridge and rode there, with her legs dangling down. The type of girl who wore a lace frock to Mass and did not care to cover her arms at all.

She sawed all her braids off with the butcher knife.

When Mbiu saw her, she said, What happened to your hair?

I cut it.

Because why?

Because you cut yours for me, so it's only fair that I cut mine for you.

Won't your mama be angry at you?

My mama doesn't care at all about me.

Mbiu stared over Ayosa's shoulder, at the double doors leaning weakly, buckling under the chokehold of knotweed. What is that? she said, pointing.

That's the drawing room.

You have a room special just for going in there when your fingers feel like drawing things?

No. It's just a place that we don't have any use for. Most of our house we don't have any use for. You want to see it?

Yes, my dear.

Ayosa led Mbiu into the house. They walked through the kitchen, down the corridor, to the part of the house where passages tangled into each other like necklaces in a trunk, where rooms were stacked one on top of the other, heaving, buckling into the earth. They went past the billiard room, the boudoir, the sun lounge.

This is the drawing room, Ayosa said, wrestling with a pair of louvered double doors until they gave way.

Above their heads, a sixty-light crystal chandelier dangled from the high-domed ceiling. The room was furnished with a glass table, two brown leather sofas, an ottoman, and a Persian rug. Built into one of the walls was a fireplace of red scrubbed brick. Inside this, a log rested on dead leaves that the wind had blown through the chimney. On the mantelpiece was a handcrafted ceramic lamp, a brass antique telephone, and a framed photograph of a woman waving from the cockpit of a small, red two-seater airplane.

Who is that? Mbiu said.

Lola Freedom. My mama's mama.

Ayosa walked across the room. A cloud of dust rose into the air when she moved. Cobwebs hung from the ceiling, dainty, and they cleaved on to her. An emperor moth shot through the air and slammed against the glass door. Something scurried across the room—a mole rat, or a ground squirrel—and disappeared inside a hole in the ottoman.

Mbiu nodded at one of the wood-paneled walls. What are those? she said, pointing at the heads mounted there—cheetah, rhinoceros, dik-dik, buffalo, impala, zebra, wildebeest—and at the hunting muskets that hung by threadbare sun-faded straps.

Those are Mabel Brown's things.

Who's that now?

Mabel Brown was my mama's grandmother. She was an English settler. She built this house.

Mbiu looked about her. It's an ugly house, if I ever saw one. She turned back to the muskets. Can they shoot?

THINGS THEY LOST

In the Yonder Days, Ayosa had seen Mabel Brown grabbing her muskets and roaming about the land. She had wriggled with her sometimes. Mabel Brown had liked to kill things for no reason at all. Oryxes and elands. Black panthers. Elephants and giraffes. She had led marauding expeditions, mostly of other English folks like herself, sometimes Yanks too.

One day, Ayosa was wriggling through the butterfly garden. Mabel Brown was on the patio, hunched over the carcass of a jolly anna, stuffing it with rags. A spool of thread sat at her feet. The other jolly annas flapped their wings about in the sycamores, screaming, Jolly anna ha-ha-ha. They thought that the jolly anna in Mabel Brown's hands looked comical with its gut pried open like that. They said, Jolly anna ha-ha-ha, as Mabel Brown picked thread out of the spool, as she fed it into a needle, as she stitched the jolly anna up again.

Mabel Brown was seventy-five years old, foul and bitter as could be. The village children sometimes poured pig's blood on her gates. They thought she was a witch. And so, between the jolly annas and the rowdy village children, Mabel Brown was at the end of her tether. She waved a musket about, at the jolly annas, and at the backs of fleeing, squealing children, and she swore that one of these days she would show them fire.

Can they shoot? Mbiu repeated her question.

Yes, Ayosa said. They sure can shoot.

Mbiu stepped forward and tore a musket off the wall. She let herself out the sliding glass door, into the butterfly garden that was overgrown with weeds. She climbed onto the tiered fountain and waved the musket about.

Come on, she called to Ayosa.

Ayosa followed her, stood on the patio. Above her head, a dozen wind chimes hung by string. They were made of copper and glass and crystal and bamboo.

Put the musket back, Ayosa said.

Mbiu ignored her. She raised the musket up and pointed it at the sycamores, where the jolly annas were rustling about.

What are you doing? Ayosa said, alarmed.

Nothing.

Don't, Ayosa yelled.

But Mbiu did.

She fired the musket.

There was a moment of absolute silence, of absolute stillness, during which Ayosa did not know exactly who she was. She thought she might no longer be Ayosa, or that she had never even been Ayosa, or that Ayosa was not the name of her Self but of a place she had only once visited.

She thought that she was a feather-soft thing drifting in the corner of someone's eye, or a ferocious hunger anchored deep inside the belly of a wild boar. She held herself, marveled that there was even a Self to hold on to, and she waited for her breath to return.

She met herself at the door of herself.

She said, Who are you, little girl?

She said, I am Ayosa Ataraxis Brown, who keeps chickens and bees and loneliness and old memories. She said, I am Ayosa Ataraxis Brown, whom the river wants with all its heart. She said, I am Ayosa Ataraxis Brown, who can't go too many days without listening to a poem.

She recognized herself now, and let herself in.

Jolly anna ha-ha-ha, the jolly annas screamed hysterically.

She opened her eyes. She touched her face, touched her torso. All of her was there, and all of her was whole.

Nearby, Mbiu was doubled over. Ayosa ran to her, grabbed her by the arm, lifted her up. Mbiu was bleeding in the hand.

I told you not to shoot, Ayosa admonished her.

I didn't! The thing just exploded by itself!

The musket was on the ground, in pieces.

My mama says these old muskets go off on their own sometimes, that they can shred you to bits with the shrapnel, so not to touch them.

Mbiu sulkily turned her face away.

Where is Bwana Matambara?

I don't know. He ran away.

Let me see that, Ayosa said.

Mbiu held out her hand. She had a gory wound in her palm, where something—the bullet perhaps—had gouged her. Ayosa spat onto it to clean it. She wiped the blood off with the cuff of her sweater, and now she saw that it was hardly a scrape, just a splinter lodged beneath the skin. Ayosa pulled it out.

Does it hurt?

No, Mbiu said. She clicked her tongue to the roof of her mouth.

Then what are you angry for?

It exploded by itself. I wanted to be the one to *explode* it.

Mbiu crossed her arms over her chest. The musket had sullied her mood so much that she was angry at everything she looked at.

Fuck-toad! she said, kicking at rocks. You know what?

What?

One day soon I will leave this stupid place. Me and Bwana Matambara.

Where will you go?

Mombasa.

Ayosa lowered her head. Tears sprung to her eyes. She watched the jolly annas in silence.

You want to come?

Ayosa looked up. Me? Ayosa Ataraxis Brown?

Only if you want to.

I want to! Ayosa gasped. What will we do in Mombasa?

We will climb the minaret and call people to prayer.

Ayosa's chest swelled. She doubled over, hands on her knees. She breathed slow breaths so that her chest would not burst.

We will live in a small house, Mbiu continued.

How small?

So small we could walk its breadth in two steps. In our house we will be the types of girls who know how to make flower vases out of mud. And Bwana Matambara will catch all our mice for us.

Ayosa imagined it. She and Mbiu would live by the seaside. They would eat mahamri and hold each other's hands and walk barefoot on the seafront, and if Mbiu stepped on a sea urchin, Ayosa would carry her home on her back and pluck the needles out with tweezers. They would smash overripe papayas beneath their feet, and they would roast maize on the charcoal grill and tell each other stories of jinnis that they once saw contorting themselves into soda bottles.

They would go to the marketplace and find matching sailor's uniforms, and they would pay five cents apiece for them, and every morning they would wash their faces and eat sweet scones and drink camel's milk and wear the sailors' uniforms and sit on the veranda to read the newspaper. In their small house, they would be the types of girls who kept a steam dryer beneath their bed. The types of girls who painted their nails wine red and who wore eau de parfum to sleep and who let the cat lie down on their pillow.

You swear?

Mbiu licked her finger and raised it high above her head. Bible-red, she said. You, me, and Bwana Matambara. We shall run away together.

11

Ayosa could hardly sleep because of the termites darting about in her belly. Finally, at five in the morning, she walked across the hallway and lay down on the cold floor, listening outside her mama's door. She heard no gentle sputter of breath from her mama's lips. No muddled words spat out with the drool onto her mama's cheeks. No whine of bed rails as her mama flopped about like a dying trout.

Ayosa listened hard. Silence was a mighty sound in its own right. If you paid attention, you could separate its warps and wefts. There was the calathea plant shifting its leaves. There were the silverfish crawling on the underside of the blue farmhouse rocking chair. There was the listless sigh of old shadows.

Ayosa knew about the shadows. It was like this: When people died, their shadows remained behind. Those shadows gathered like hair balls in the corners of things. They were light as mites, they scattered whenever the air swirled. That's why sometimes you saw things move in the corner of your eye. That's why sometimes you heard that terrible heaving, as though a great sadness sat in the room with you.

Ayosa opened her mama's door. She switched on the light.

She was right—her mama was still *gone*. But not for long. It was Christmas Day. Her mama always returned to her on Christmas Day.

She and her mama had a tradition. They built a fire and made breakfast on the hundred-year-old waffle iron that had once belonged to Mabel Brown. They did not use it often, and so they always had to spend a considerable amount of time scraping dead jumping spiders with a boar-bristle brush and washing it with vinegar and brine. Then they cooked eggs and strips of smoked bacon. They cooked plum pancakes with ginger syrup. They ate out in the garden, with the morning sun glistening in their brown eyes.

Afterward, they listened to her mama's records—Miriam Makeba, Fela Kuti, Nina Simone, Bob Marley and the Wailers. They soaked in the tub together. Her mama smoked cigarettes back to back, while Ayosa drank grape juice from a wineglass and read to her mama from a tattered, yellowed copy of *Their Eyes Were Watching God*. Then Jentrix the apothecary sent a lemon cake that she had made in the charcoal burner. Ayosa and her mama ate slices of this for dinner, with spicy masala tea.

On Christmas Day, Ayosa and her mama belonged to each other. They fell asleep together, breathing each other's curdled breaths, dreaming each other's bleached, yellow dreams.

Ayosa had a hen called Matasia that scavenged in the shrubbery with all ten of her babies. Matasia was flaxen colored, with a naked neck. A year ago, Ayosa had found her trapped in a manhole. It was after a rainstorm, and the hen had washed down a sewer. Ayosa had lifted the rusted grate, climbed down as far as she could, and grabbed hold of the terrified, shivering bird.

After, she borrowed an animal husbandry book from the library and learned how to build a coop. There was a pile of rotting timber by her mama's studio. Ayosa hardened the slabs she needed with varnish and then painted them over. Armed with Mabel Brown's old toolbox, a roll of wire mesh, and some tin, she constructed a home for Matasia. It took her three and a quarter days to finish it.

Her mama did not know that the coop was there in their vast, humming backyard. Her mama had seen the hen and its brood a few times already but did not know that it lived right there with them. That it gave them all the eggs they ate.

Now Ayosa wore rubber gumboots and pulled a rake out of the broom closet. She scraped droppings from the coop and changed the cloudy water in the trough. Matasia and her babies were foraging in the tall grass. Ayosa threw scraps of the olive sourdough bread that her mama had baked weeks ago, and they tussled over it, clucking. Matasia's babies were not really babies anymore. The pullets were already laying, and the one rooster of the clutch had a fine comb and tail and was learning to crow.

Ayosa walked through the yard, searching for eggs, gathering them in the scoop of her frock. There were twelve in total. She arranged them in a plastic tray and set them on top of the kitchen counter.

After, she went out to visit her bees. She peered through the handle hole of the crates. The worker bees had drawn out a comb. She lifted the plywood over the top crate. The worker bees swarmed around her, but none of them stung. She squatted, examined the frame of the comb. The queen was gone. Perhaps still out on her mating flight. She would soon return, exhausted, engorged with drone seed. Ayosa was glad there was a place for her to rest, to lay her eggs. She set down the plywood and watched the worker bees sidle back into the hive.

She sloshed in her gumboots to the edge of the property. The apothecary's house appeared through the trees. It was a little wood cottage with slanted walls and peeling orange paint. There was a papaya tree in the front yard. Behind the house, sugarcane grew on one side, and on the other, a field of flowers stretched down to the stream.

The house and the land it stood on belonged to Ayosa's mama. Jentrix and Temerity did not have much money. Yet, they often said that they were wealthy. It was not an outlandish or aggrandizing statement, just something that they truly, avidly believed. They said that the Earth Mother had been kind to them, that she had blessed them with plenty. For example, Jentrix was a midwife, and most of the younger townspeople had been born into her eager, waiting hands.

Isn't that something? Jentrix often said, shaking her head in disbelief. What a *great* gift.

She and Temerity ate only what the Earth Mother provided. They coaxed the ground until it broke itself open for them. They did not consume any flesh. Ayosa had once asked about it, and Jentrix told her this:

I know a thing or two about bodies, you see. Not many things, mind. Less than you'd hope, but more than you'd expect. So I know a little about their ailments and remedies. Let me tell you, animal flesh and human flesh are of the same matter. Maybe their essence is different. But they hunger the same, agonize the same, decay the same. They are lonesome in the same ways. They long to be touched in the same places. Don't you see? We are flesh of the same flesh. And me, I'm no cannibal, Ayosa Ataraxis Brown.

Nabumbo Promise called it bollocks.

Same as she called Jentrix's entire healing practice.

Quackery, her mama said.

Merry Christmas, madam apothecary, Ayosa murmured, curtsying at Jentrix.

Jentrix was sitting at her veranda, shelling peas. She looked up from her reed tray. We don't celebrate Christmas around here. Don't you know that?

Right, Ayosa said. She always forgot this fact. She made a note of it. Then she said, Because why?

Because we have better things to do.

Okay, Ayosa said. She supposed that that was as good a reason as any. She said, Is Temerity out in the fields, madam apothecary?

Yes, but she will be back soon. What do you want with the girl?

Oh, nothing. Nothing at all. Except maybe to see if Temerity fetched any flowers today. And to see if we will be getting a lemon cake today.

Affirmative for both, Jentrix said, picking a caterpillar from the peas and tossing it away. I will send her over as soon as it can be managed.

Thank you kindly, Ayosa said, curtsying. She started up the footpath. Then she stopped, turned. She said, Madam apothecary?

Yes, my name?

What do you celebrate, then? Instead of Christmas?

Many things. Flower Day, for one.

A day special for geraniums and begonias?

No, child. A day special for vulvas and uteruses.

Oh, Ayosa said, and scribbled that down. What else?

Water Day.

For fishes?

For babies journeying over. Swimming across from *beyond*.

Ayosa chewed on the tip of her pencil. She said, Madam apothecary, I remember those Yonder Days. Before I turned into a girl.

Jentrix tipped her head to the side. What do you remember?

Wriggling, mostly. Watching people do things. Mabel Brown.

Lola Freedom. Nabumbo Promise. They were lonesome, so I stayed with them sometimes. I saw you too. Saw that first time you came here, dressed all in rags, with bruises over your body. You said to Lola Freedom, Need a washerwoman? And she said, My girls wash quite well after themselves, thank you very much. And you fell to your knees and begged. You said, I heard you were a kind woman, Lola Freedom. I heard you were gracious. Please, for the love of the great Earth Mother, don't turn me out. Don't send me back to the horrors I just fled from.

A dark cloud came and dulled the shine of Jentrix's eyes. Ayosa paused. She bit her lower lip. She said to herself, Look at you, so full of mud! Are you really about to make this poor woman weep? She looked down at her feet in shame, afraid to see Jentrix's tears. She said, I've got to go.

Wait, Jentrix said. Tell me, what more did you see?

Ayosa shrugged. I stayed with my mama mostly. I could hear her thoughts sometimes. My mama, she started to feel me right there with her. It took a while for her to realize who I was. But eventually she did, and she asked me to stay. So I stayed. That's why I turned into a girl. That's why I'm here now.

Jentrix nodded gravely.

I was there the day you were born, Miss Brown. I could see it in your eyes. You had been here before. Such terror in your eyes. Such dread. And, I daresay, *regret*. You had made a rash decision to descend into this flesh and now you had to deal with the consequences. A *girl*? And worse, you had met your mama's indifference, and you did not know if this sort of life was livable. You wanted to leave right away.

And you begged me to stay, Ayosa said. She let out a sigh, and then raised her hand goodbye. She said, I really must go now. I've got to get things ready for my mama. She will be back soon, I expect.

———

The townspeople gargled salt water. They greased their elbows. They tucked a flower in their hair or pinned it on their lapel. They marched to Our Lady of Lourdes Church, where they sang "God Rest Ye Merry Gentlemen." They sang "Usiku Mtakatifu." They sang "The Little Drummer Boy."

Then the River-Lake Charismatic Dramatizing Society reenacted the scene of the three magi bringing gold, frankincense, and myrrh. They huddled by the manger next to the tabernacle, nodding serenely at the little Christ, not a sound to be heard, except for Father Jude Thaddeus's hem-hem-hem as he tried to dislodge the mangled scrap of something in the crevices of his throat.

After the service, the townspeople all filed down the aisles and into the blistering air, and then marched back to their tenements. Jokovu slaughtered a cow, and Solidarity slaughtered a goat. Chepeo and Martha slaughtered five cockerels each. Mama Chibwire dipped into her barrels and passed homebrew around. Sospeter Were brought out the PA system and radio cassette player.

They tied cardigans round their waists and stood in pairs and held each other's hips and did the chini kwa chini dance. Rocks crunching beneath their soles. Lithe bodies glistening, undulating. Fingers melting in other fingers. Laughter spilling from one mouth and frothing inside the next.

And Father Jude Thaddeus said, Hem-hem-hem. Not because anything was stuck inside his throat, but because he could not stand the carnal indignities taking place before him. The way the bodies desired and required and claimed each other during the chini kwa chini dance.

Hem-hem-hem, he said, and turned away.

He was—had always been—the guest of honor at the Christmas banquet. Each year he forgot that *this* happened. He forgot just how damned they all were. He grimaced with remembrance and disgust. He stuffed blood sausage in his limp mouth. He looked over his horn-rimmed trifocals, seeking out Dorcas Munyonyi.

There she was, his favorite faithful, stuffing blood sausage into her own limp mouth, seeking him out too. Experiencing his very same remembrance and disgust.

Hem-hem-hem, Dorcas Munyonyi said.

Father Jude Thaddeus wished he had touched her tongue a little as he had placed the communion wafer in her mouth. He raised an oil-stained hand. She raised an oil-stained hand too. They marveled at how they matched each other thing for thing. Remembrance. Disgust. Blood sausage. Oil-stained fingers. His mouth twitched fondly. Hers did too.

And the red wind, it swept past the cloud of blowflies hovering in a frenzy over animal carcasses, past the droves of townspeople staggering about with tinsel twined round their necks like nooses, past the fields of bristle grass and juniper bushes and sunflowers. And the river, it parted itself to let drunken townspeople through. It was a good river—it never drowned a soul on Christmas Day.

Ayosa dragged the kitchen table outside. She set it in the garden, where the sunlight streaked and dappled through the loquat branches. She covered it with a flowered cloth. She cleaned the heavy, long-handled waffle iron, built a fire, and made fried egg sandwiches on it. She took a jug out into the woods and returned with treacly blackberries and raw gashes all over her arms. She made pancakes with some of the blackberries, and a compote with the rest. She pulled things out from the pantry—a can of sugared pineapple, a can of baked beans, a can of corned beef, a can of button mushrooms. She brought out a jar of marmalade, a bag of scones, and a can of sausages that she roasted on the fire pit.

Later, Temerity brought a lemon cake and a bunch of yellow tulips. She gawked at Ayosa's table.

Holy Earth Mother! she gasped. Did you do all this, Miss Brown?

Yes-yes.

Is it a party?

Yes. A Christmas party, for my mama.

Where is she? Temerity said, looking about her.

Gone. But she will be back any moment now.

Temerity went away, chewing on a sandwich that Ayosa had offered her. Ayosa made her mama a card from an old cereal box lined with gift-wrap paper. She stapled in pages of rice paper. She wrote in it:

Merry Christmas to the World's Best Mama.

She wrote this although it was not true at all. Anybody could tell you that her mama was not the best type of mama there was. Her mama came and went like blackjack needles blowing where the breeze decided. She loved fiercely, but only just briefly, and then the effort of it tired her, and she forgot to love at all. She laughed effusively, but then, somewhere in the shade of herself, icicles tapered from above, waiting to decapitate you.

Still, you could not throw a person's faults at them on Christmas Day.

So Ayosa wrote:

I love you, Mama.

She wrote this even though it was not always true. This was one of Ayosa's faults—she was the type of daughter whose heart sometimes grew cold.

Ayosa sat on one end of the table, watching the empty place across from her. She was in her best outfit, a navy playsuit with frills and a lacy hem. She passed the time sketching in her notebook—the cirrus clouds tangled round the chimney and rain gutter, the wasps levitating over the rosebushes, the sprightly naked-necked rooster pecking at grasshoppers.

She listened to the transistor radio, to Anita Baker and Michael Jackson and Eartha Kitt. Then Ms. Temperance came on with a poem, and Ayosa held her breath.

> *The drunk woman teetering on a ledge with two*
> > *frost-chewed*
> *babies in her arms wondered which country those*
> > *babies would*
> *drift to if she surrendered them to the wind. Yesterday,*
> *the babies were bean seeds budging and splitting in*
> > *the soil. Cotyledons and hypocotyls and epicotyls*
> > *elongating.*
> *Bean sprouts. Now turned into blue-faced babies.*
> > *Snake-eyed*
> *babies. Squishy-boned babies. She loved them*
> > *sometimes,*
> *and despised them most times. Sallow-lipped babies.*
> *The drunk woman staggering at the edge of here and*
> *not-here, taught those babies how to pirouette with*
> > *shadows*
> *and how to stitch their tongues down to their teeth*
> > *and how*
> *to straddle the monsoon like a fisherman in a dhow.*

Ayosa said to herself, Ms. Temperance *knows*. She knows what it's like to want something with all your heart and not get it.

Just then, she heard a familiar sound—the clang of high-tensile iron chain against wood, and then the crunch of tires over gravel.

Nabumbo Promise! she gasped.

Heart racing, she put her notebook away. She gave the table a once-over, trying to see what she might have forgotten to set. She ran into the kitchen, brought out two candle stands, and lit the stubs in them.

The crunch of tires stopped. A car door opened and shut.

Ayosa Ataraxis Brown! a girl called.

Ayosa tossed away the matches. She ran across the yard, to the side of the manor. The car she found parked there was not her mama's shabby jalopy. It was not a car per se, but a shell of one, pockmarked with bullet holes, hitched by rope to a horse.

Mbiu stood beside the car, with Bwana Matambara on her shoulder. Merry Christmas, she said. I have a gift for you. For us both.

What?

Mbiu opened the car door and drew something out—two long-nosed Venetian masks, of twisted brass, embellished with crystals and peacock feathers.

Where did you find these?

Stole them.

She helped Ayosa put hers on, and then she too did the same. They looked at each other, and they threw their heads back and said, Ha-ha-ha.

You came to give me a Christmas gift?

No. I came to make you laugh. Knew your mama would *forget* to come home to you, and you would be sour about it.

Ayosa turned away. She walked back to the table and sidled into her chair. Mbiu sat across from her.

It's a feast for my mama, Ayosa said.

The woman truly does not deserve you.

Ayosa said, Listen here, I won't tolerate that kind of talk about my mama. If you have something bad to say, well, keep it to yourself!

Mbiu shook her head pitifully. Whatever. I'm *malnourished.*

She poked at a sausage, and when Ayosa said nothing in protest, Mbiu pulled it out of the plate. She bit into it. Said, Fuck-toad, it's very good.

So they both dug in, with grubby, mud-encrusted hands, which added to the joy of eating outside. There were wasps in their lemon cake slices, gnats in their grape juice, ants in their egg sandwiches. This added to the joy too.

After, Mbiu jumped to her feet. She grabbed the back of Ayosa's chair and shook it back and forth, as though trying to pour Ayosa out of it.

What are you doing? said the irritated Ayosa, her belly gargling.

Get up! We are going!

Where?

Follow me. I've got to show you something.

They walked through the woods, waving sticks before them to frighten off mongooses and snakes. The day crickets piped up—their song was louder, shriller, than that of the night crickets. Ayosa beat at the tall, stiff grass to quieten them, but they only grew more agitated, their cries swelling into obscenity. They sang:

> *You stupid girl with*
> *The face of a hyena,*
> *Your mama is a slut.*

My mama is not a slut, Ayosa shrieked.

Fuck-toad! Mbiu swore at the crickets. She took Ayosa's arm. Cover your ears, my dear!

Ayosa covered her ears. They ran until the cricket song was far off, the horrible words muffled. Now they were at the old cow barn that Nabumbo Promise had turned into a studio. It was a structure built of felled casuarinas, painted red like an engorged boil. It leaned on a fig tree, and the fig tree leaned on a hill, and the hill leaned on the sky. Ayosa pointed at it with a stick.

That's my mama's studio. Why did you bring me here?

Mbiu skipped toward it.

We can't go in! Ayosa called after her.

Because why?

Because my mama doesn't like people going into her studio.

Mbiu spat into the grass. Chelewa chelewa utakuta mwana si wako. You know that saying? It means tarry-tarry and you will find that the baby no longer belongs to you.

Stop speaking in riddles!

Ayosa Ataraxis Brown, I *need* to show you something.

She pushed the door open, let them in. The front room of the studio was mostly bare, furnished only with a rattan chair. A mug sat on the armrest of the chair. Fruit flies floated in the yellow liquid inside the mug. Rats scurried up the eaves. The wind blew, and the room heaved, leaning so far in that the window now became a door. Then the wind blew the other way, and the room stood upright again.

Mbiu led Ayosa to the next room, the workroom. The blue walls were filled with gilt-framed black-and-white photographs. In the corner was a table with rickety iron legs, and on it were a transistor radio, an ashtray, and a stack of *Popular Photography* magazines. Against another wall was a recliner, and on the floor beside it were a pair of dirty mugs, a grease-stained saucer, an Afro pick, and a can of air freshener.

Mbiu's eyes lingered on a wooden soda crate. She walked to it and began looking through a pile of photographs. She sat cross-legged on the floor and placed a handful of them in her lap. Ayosa crept next to her. They studied the images.

There was a child dazzled to tears by the strangers around her; a teenage girl whose hair had angular corners and a top shaped like a tea tray; an Indian woman with saffron smeared in the crack between her pigtails. There was the Indian woman again, a pea-sized bindi on her forehead, her blue sari dragging on dried leaves and broken avocado seeds and squirming caterpillars. The Indian woman picking one of the guavas scattered in her garden. The Indian woman rubbing the guava against her sari. The Indian woman biting into the guava. The Indian woman tossing the rest of the guava at the monkeys that hopped about the tree branches. The Indian woman bent over the tap in her garden, scrubbing sticky guava juice from her fingers.

Mbiu put the photographs back and took out another handful. There was a woman rummaging in her bag for a key. The woman sliding it inside the padlock on the door of her market stall. The padlock falling to the ground. The woman bending down to pick it up. The woman pushing in the wooden door. A cat that had been trapped inside the stall shooting out between the woman's legs. The woman staring after the cat, brow furrowed, lips parted. In another photograph, a girl was bent over a pan, frying fish.

I know that girl, Mbiu said. Her name is Nyaboke. On Wednesdays, she fries tortoises for people to eat. She cracks them out of their shells like eggs and lets them spin and spin inside the hot oil.

Where does she find the tortoises?

Me, I heard that sometimes if you are walking down the street and you find a stone, you should turn it over to see for yourself if it is really a stone. Sometimes it is just a tortoise hiding inside its shell.

In another photograph, dead flies were scattered on the ledge of a kiosk window. Ayosa counted them. There were thirteen whole flies and two crushed ones.

Your mama sure takes a lot of photographs, Mbiu said.

Yes, that's her job. She gets into her car and drives to places whose names you can't even pronounce, to take photographs for the newspaper.

Which newspaper?

The *Oracle Weekly*.

All these photographs here, your mama took them for the newspaper?

Not all of them. Sometimes she takes photographs for art.

What art?

I don't know what art. That's just what my mama says. She photographs beautiful things, or things which are ugly in a beautiful way, and then she develops the negatives and makes prints and sends them to hang in museums.

Where?

Dakar and Tokyo and Hanover.

Are those housing estates in Kisumu town?

No, they are cities far away from here.

I don't like photographs, Mbiu said.

Because why?

Because they give me a bad feeling. The people inside them always stare at you, and you can just tell that they are thinking awful things about you. It's like . . . they are looking past your face, seeing inside of you. Seeing what sorts of things you are made of.

Oh, Ayosa said. Me, I have a different feeling when I look at photographs.

What sort of feeling?

Pity, mostly. I feel bad for the people in the photographs. They look so sad, even when they are smiling. They look like they are imprisoned there inside the picture. They can't do anything to escape. And they are looking out with their sad eyes, pleading to you for help. But now what can a person do to help someone like that, except for throwing the photograph into the fire to put them out of their misery?

Mbiu tossed the photographs back into the crate.

What did you want to show me? Ayosa said.

Oh, Mbiu said, I got distracted and forgot to show you! Well, come with me.

Mbiu led Ayosa through another door, this time into the darkroom. They stared at the squares of ivory paper that hung on laundry pegs on the string above the worktable. In them, images congealed, foggy and frazzled, becoming a faint smile, the curve of an eyelid, secret lusts bitten onto lower lips.

There, Mbiu said, pointing at the end of the worktable.

Ayosa squinted in the red light. Was that . . . a person? Ayosa flipped the switch on the wall, and the overhead lamp flickered on. Now she saw that there was a woman hunched over the table, and not just any woman, but *her mama*.

Nabumbo Promise! she screamed. Nabumbo! Nabumbo Promise Brown!

12

Hello? she said into the telephone.

Miss Brown?

I just . . . I just found my mama . . . she's *dead*.

Miss Brown, you're hysterical. I can't understand a word!

Madam apothecary . . . My mama is dead!

Miss Brown, where are you?

At my mama's studio.

Is someone with you?

Mbiu.

Okay. Listen, Miss Brown, go sit with Mbiu. I'm on my way.

Ayosa and Mbiu sat on the porch steps. Ayosa was in tears, rocking back and forth, while Mbiu held her tight and whispered to her, Save your tears, my darling. There's nothing to cry about, my darling.

A few minutes later, Jentrix the apothecary came huffing through the woods, a corner of her heavy frock crumpled up in her hand.

Where is she? Jentrix heaved.

Darkroom, Mbiu said, pointing into the studio.

Jentrix bounded up the porch steps. She was gone for only a moment, before she came back out with Nabumbo Promise slung over her shoulder, like a sack of charcoal.

Is she dead? Ayosa said.

Jentrix said nothing at all. She ran back into the woods, toward the manor. Ayosa tore herself away from Mbiu and ran after Jentrix and her mama.

Ayosa spent the entire afternoon pacing up and down the kitchen. Jentrix would not let her upstairs to be with her mama.

Nabumbo Promise needs air, Jentrix had said. As though Ayosa would siphon it all off just by standing in the room.

My mama is *dead*-dead, Ayosa thought. That's why Jentrix is acting like this.

She took out her notebook and began to write a statement, something for the radioman to read on the death news.

> *Ayosa Ataraxis Brown is utterly heartbroken to announce the passing of her mother, Nabumbo Promise Brown. They loved each other irrevocably, although they often hated each other too. They had a murky love affair, as the late Nabumbo Promise Brown often put it. Still, Ayosa Ataraxis Brown is devastated. She spent most of her life waiting for her mama to come home to her. What does one do when all the Waiting is finished?*

She sat still and pitied herself. She was a mama-less girl. What a wretched thing to be. And yet, what a breathtaking thing to be. She marveled at this, at the fact that she was just like Mbiu. Her *dear* Mbiu.

She thought, I am sad but happy. Distraught but thrilled.

She wondered what it meant for a girl to feel like this. Tearful, yet, deep inside herself, full of brazen, manic laughter.

She heard footsteps on the stairs and looked up to see Jentrix the apothecary. Jentrix's face shimmered with sweat, and she smelled like a pit latrine. She said, You will be glad to know that your mama is not dead.

Ayosa opened the door and ran out into the yard.

Nabumbo Promise Brown is not dead, she shouted to the jolly annas.

Jolly anna, ha-ha-ha, the jolly annas said.

Ayosa doubled over, spat into the grass. Her whole body tingled. She watched as a Sodom apple jerked from a branch, milky sap oozing from its punctured flesh. She took out her notebook and crossed out the death announcement, glad not to have to use it. But also, oddly, crushed. Now she turned and saw the kitchen table that she had dragged out earlier in the day. She saw the feast that she had prepared for her mama.

She walked to the table. She sat down and ate—bacon, and canned fruit, and mushrooms, and sausage, and lemon cake. Her head reeled from the muddled emotions she felt. She was . . . *sad*! How could that be? She grimaced, disgusted at herself.

I'm *happy* that my mama did not die, she said forcefully. She said it to the guffawing jolly annas, but they only smirked and mocked her. They knew about her secret dejection. They said, Jolly anna ha-ha-ha, to her in the most loathsome way they could muster, and Ayosa recoiled with humiliation.

Of course you're happy that your mama didn't die, Jentrix said behind her. She hulked through the kitchen door, towering over everything, her long, heavy skirts sending chairs tumbling across the veranda.

How is she? Ayosa said, biting back tears.

Oh, child, Jentrix said soothingly. She walked up to her and patted her shoulders. She said, Everything will be all right, just you wait and see. Give her a week, she will be fit as a buffalo.

Ayosa looked down into her hands. She felt doubtful. Not about her mama recovering, but about everything being all right. It seemed to her that something delicate and salient had been breached. She had imagined being a mama-less girl, which was a violent act both to herself and to her mama. And worse, she had *liked* it. And anyway, what did all right look like? Continuing as things had always been? Sitting and Waiting, while her mama Went Away?

I'm going back upstairs to your mama, Jentrix said.

May I come with you? Please-please-please?

If you like.

She followed Jentrix back inside the kitchen, watched as Jentrix wiped her rumpled face with a tattered washcloth.

Jentrix fumbled by the stove, boiling a pot of water, infusing it with dried angelica and anise and sandalwood oil from her portmanteau. She added more things that Ayosa could not name. All the while, she whispered under her breath, weaving potent incantations into the remedy. After, Ayosa stood in the doorway of her mama's bedroom and watched as Jentrix worked. First, Jentrix soaked a muslin cloth in the fragrant infusion. She wiped her mama down, from scalp to sole, compressing the cloth to her skin, letting the remedy seep deep into her bones.

Then Jentrix lifted her mama off the rocking chair. She propped her up against the window, facing the waning sun. Nabumbo Promise recoiled, wriggling this way and that like a maggot, her eyes pressed tight. Jentrix was a large woman, more than six feet tall. She was wide and angular too, as though inside herself, she were full of brick houses rather than just flesh. With one arm, she immobilized the squirming mama. With the colossal fingers of her free hand, she yanked the squirming mama's eyelids open.

She said, Let the light return to you, Nabumbo Promise Brown.

Nabumbo Promise thrashed about. She screeched in anguish, the veins in her neck taut, her teeth red with blood.

Suddenly, everything stilled. The evening birds hopping about on the ledge fell into stunned silence. Ayosa watched the shadows—they twisted and groveled across the floor like monitor lizards.

Jentrix set Nabumbo Promise down on the bed.

Help me, she said to Ayosa. Together, they set the room right— stuffing drawers back into the vanity and armoire, putting away frocks and undergarments, scraping dried vomit off the rug. They washed and hung soiled clothing. They threw the windows open so that the light from the moon and stars could shimmer in.

Later, they sat outside the kitchen, on the wooden porch steps. They listened to cricket song and ate beans with coconut rice that Jentrix had swiftly whipped together.

Is my mama still in the land down under? Ayosa asked.

Not anymore. She's making her way up.

When will she arrive?

Jentrix shrugged. Who knows? A day. Maybe two.

Ayosa climbed up the stairs, jar in hand, the milk inside it trembling, dripping over her fingers. At her mama's door, she paused and pushed it open. It creaked loudly. She propped it with her leg and then wedged in the beanbag doll that her mama used as a stopper.

Her mama's bedroom was dark as a cavern. The canopy bed was unmade, the lace stripped off its four columns and bunched up on the sheepskin rug.

Her mama was in the corner, sitting in a blue farmhouse rocking chair, gazing out into the darkness. Mumbling under her breath. Her dress, once white, was now brown specked with orange. Blowflies and drain flies fluttered around her face, as though there were carrion decaying in her mouth.

Mama, Ayosa said, I brought you some milk.

Ayosa set the milk down. She tugged at the curtain to let in some light. Then she stood beside her mama and plaited her hair back in two neat cornrows. After, she picked up the jar and pressed it to her mama's mouth. Her mama tried to turn her head away, but Ayosa clenched her chin tight. She refused to let go until her mama unclamped her lips and gulped all the milk down.

Ayosa pulled at her frock, grabbing hold of the hem. She spat into it and wiped her mama's face, dislodging the dried snot on her nose and the tear tracks on her temples. She walked to the shelf and picked out a book at random.

Ayosa squatted down at her mama's feet. She turned the pages of the book. Slowly, she read out a passage to her mama. She read until her mama's incoherent murmurs died down, until her mama fell fast asleep, head bobbing against the cresting rail of the chair.

Now Ayosa stood on the veranda and watched the red wind rattle against the windowpane, upsetting pots of catchfly and lemongrass. The sky was a mint so deep it brought tears to her eyes. She wiped her face with the back of her hand. A pair of sandpipers flipped through the air, their plumage glistening with river water.

In the distance, she could see the shiny-eyed, snot-faced girl, Temerity, heading out into the woods.

Temerity! she called. Temerity! Temerity!

Temerity turned. She waved both hands above her head.

Where are you going?

My grandmother needs periwinkle flowers, so I'm going out to find some. She planted some in the forest.

Because why does she need it?

Because there is a pregnant woman distressed in our house. Jentrix says without the periwinkle, mother and baby won't make it at all. High blood pressure, like. Is your mama back from the land down under?

Not yet, but soon-soon.

Jentrix and me, we're praying for her to the Earth Mother.

Thank you, Ayosa said, and waved until Temerity disappeared in the woods.

Ayosa went up to the attic and sat with the Fatumas. They told her stories and sang her songs. She and the Fatumas taunted spiny orb weavers by dangling houseflies in their webs and then pulling them away before the spiders could catch them. They sucked on lantanas and peppergrass and winged bersama just to see if their throats would close up. They set traps for thrushes and red-chested cuckoos on the awning ledge.

Later, she got hungry, and went downstairs to eat a can of peas. She drank water straight from the tap. Outside the kitchen window, the tree branches shook, scratching the glass. Mbiu's cat, Bwana Matambara, purred on the window ledge. Ayosa let him in. He leapt onto the counter. He sniffed about, following a trail that led to a rumpled newspaper sheet. He licked the paper, licked the ink, licked the words that read:

> *There are 13 different Hansells essences, in 3 different sizes, 25 ml, 50 ml, and 100 ml. Yet we are thinking of adding more flavors to our range. If you would like to suggest a new flavor or two, fill in the coupon below.*

Bwana Matambara meowed.

What? Ayosa said. She peered out the window, searching for Mbiu. Where is she?

Bwana Matambara walked to the door, tail up, meowing. He seemed overwrought. Ayosa's heart slammed hard against her ribs. Did something happen to Mbiu? Did she send you out here to fetch me? Do you want me to follow you?

Ayosa fumbled into her clogs and opened the door. Bwana Matambara began across the veranda.

Wait, Bwana Matambara, she said. You're too fast. I will lose you.

The cat paused. She walked up to him and picked him up. Except, there was nothing at all to pick. Just wisps of smoke. The cat was not Bwana Matambara at all, but a wraith. Ayosa jumped back. She wiped her hands against her frock.

Fuck-toad! she murmured to herself.

Ayosa went out to the river, took off her frock, and swam in her camisole. After, she lay down on the rocks to dry off. She had brought a book with her—*One Thousand and One Nights*. She read until she tired of reading, and then she reached for her notebook and sketched some illustrations. Ali Baba in the cave of treasures. Aladdin rubbing his wonderful lamp. Periazade gazing at the talking bird in "The Two Sisters Who Envied Their Cadette."

She put the book and notebook aside and lay with her arms beneath her head, watching the birds drift lazily, contentedly, across the sky. She thought of her mama's sister, Rosette.

For a few days now, Ayosa had wrestled with herself about whether to take out the yellow pages and look up Rosette's contact details. She had practiced what to say.

Hello? Your sister had a terrible fall inside herself, perhaps it might be prudent of you to come and visit her.

Would Rosette come? Would Nabumbo Promise be offended to wake up and find Rosette there, wiping her snot and drool? Or would the two sisters stare at each other, tears of aching tenderness trickling down their faces?

One evening in the Yonder Days, Rosette brought home some bone soup after her shift at the slaughterhouse. She poured it into mugs, and she and Nabumbo Promise drank it together while listening to the transistor radio. They called their mother, and as had been the case for a while, their mother did not answer the telephone. It troubled them that their mother had been unreachable for so long.

Rosette got up and paced about the flat, reciting the rosary.

Nabumbo Promise watched her for a few moments. She said, Ask that Virgin of yours to watch over Lola Freedom. Make sure she did not crash her airplane somewhere.

And Rosette stopped mid–*Glory be to the Father*. She turned to her sister, brows raised in surprise. She said, You think I *believe* that there is a Virgin Mary?

Why else are you always asking for her intercession?

Rosette crumpled rosary beads in her palm. She said, I only recite the rosary because it soothes the tight ball in my chest. Mother takes diazepam. Well, this rosary is my diazepam.

You don't really believe any of it?

No, Rosette said, making a face.

But you wear that habit and veil, even when you're out massacring animals!

And so what?

Will you not take your vows next year?

I will take my temporary vows, yes. And after, I will take my perpetual vows too.

Why become a nun if you're a nonbeliever?

I don't think that a believer necessarily makes a good nun. Or that a nonbeliever directly makes a bad nun.

Nabumbo Promise shook her head. She wondered why Rosette always had to be needlessly complex and gratuitous.

I enjoy the regimented life, Rosette continued. I enjoy the beauty of the nun's habit, how it hangs over my body. All those years, down by the river on my own, there was never anyone to tell me what to do. No one to tell me what to wear. Now I take immense pleasure in it.

You're speaking mud! I know you, Rosette. The convent is not for you.

You don't know me! Rosette exclaimed. You don't know my thoughts or my fears. My desires or my motivations. You and me, we are strangers!

Nabumbo Promise was bewildered. They were twin sisters. Of course they *knew* each other.

Jesus! Rosette said. We spent six silent years at the orphanage. And later, after Mother returned us, we traded our silent childhoods for silent girlhoods. When did we get to *know* each other?

Nabumbo thought about it. She thought about the things that happened after they were returned.

Rosette had moved away from home when they were twelve. She lived like a tramp in a little shack of twigs and grass, washing in the river, eating birds that she caught with her slingshot, while Nabumbo Promise lived in the manor, eating eggs and ham, listening to Louis Armstrong records. On the days that their mother was home, Rosette crossed the woods and climbed the hill. Came back. Hung around the house and pretended that she lived in it like a normal girl. Pretended that she ate with a fork and knife. Pretended that every morning, she accompanied her sister to the schoolhouse for their lessons.

Pretended that she did not keep one of Mabel Brown's muskets for hunting snakes and polecats. That she did not fire into the air whenever she heard tree branches splitting near her shack in the night. That she was not a wild girl, a loner, who smelled of wet fleece, who spent her days skinning servals.

Their Stubborn Silence had made it so that they knew almost nothing about each other. Beyond biographical information about her sister, Nabumbo Promise drew blanks. She knew her sister's eye color, her preferences, her hobbies, all the places she had lived. But what did she know about her sister's greatest regret in life? About the things that her sister thought about the most? About the doubts that niggled at her sister's being? About the special gifts that she possessed as a person?

Rosette said, I think that I'll be a good nun because I'm obedient and also because I like to wear the same thing every day. It would be the same if I were in the armed forces.

And Nabumbo Promise said, You are right. We hardly know each other.

And Rosette laughed.

And Nabumbo Promise frowned. Tell me, she said.

Tell you what?

The things I need to know in order to know you.

I'm not interested in being known by *you*! Rosette said. She folded her brows. She said, People ask me what it feels like to have a twin sister. I tell them that it feels like nothing at all, since I never experienced anything but this. But it's a lie. The truth is that I never liked it. I never liked *you*. Having a stranger follow me everywhere I went since the day I was born? That's . . . *horrendous*!

Rosette shrugged and returned to her rosary.

Nabumbo Promise got up from her chair. She took her cane and wobbled into the nearby bedroom. She lay in her bed and stared at the ceiling for a long while, listening to her sister recite the Litany of the Blessed Virgin Mary.

She had a feeling in her chest, that she and Rosette were approaching a certain threshold beyond which their sistership would no longer be possible. Soon, they would no longer be an entity. No longer the Brown girls. Nothing had happened, yet everything had.

Whose fault was it—theirs, for drowning Maxwell Truth? Wasn't that when the chasm had first sprouted, back when they were six years old? Or was it the fault of their mother, who, in both her absence and her presence, had spurned them? They had resented Lola Freedom, and in turn, resented each other for being so hapless, so piteous.

Nabumbo Promise did not feel any sense of dread or loss. What she felt was a certain somberness, as though she had entered an empty cathedral. She closed her eyes and inspected all the sacred marble objects of their sistership.

The well in the woods, where they had done Maxwell Truth's drowning. The orphanage, where they had served their sentence. The river, where they had caught eels. The manor, where they had stored all their secrets. The convent, where they had tried to salvage the little good that was left within them. Their shabby, mold-infested flat, where they had come to know each other a little, or at least, come to know the limits of their knowing.

Here they were.

Nabumbo Promise felt a gladness in her heart. She was grateful for these slow, repetitive days together. Grateful that they could enact the final rites and rituals of sistership—talking to each other, eating together, offering each other their hands and their prayers and their truths.

Better not to find Rosette in the yellow pages, Ayosa thought to herself. It's out of respect for both Rosette and Nabumbo Promise. They chose this separation. This willful dissolution of all bonds they previously had. Like a divorce.

Ayosa made a note of it, just so she would not forget that the subject had been formally broached and analyzed and concluded. *Do NOT telephone Rosette Brown*, she wrote in her notebook.

Ayosa! someone called.

Ayosa sat up and squinted into the sunshine. She saw a girl nearby, with a cat on her shoulder. Mbiu?

Mbiu squatted down, so they were at eye level. She said, Are you angry at me?

For what?

For knowing that your mama was in the land down under, and not telling you right away?

That was not a nice thing to do. You should apologize for it, at the very least.

Sorry-sorry, Mbiu said.

Ayosa was silent for a moment. She watched Bwana Matambara, suspicious of his every movement. Your cat tried to snatch me, she said, scratching at a spot on her elbow.

When?

Earlier today.

Mbiu shook her head. Not true, my dear. Bwana Matambara was with me all day. We drove with Magnolia to another town, an hour and a half from here. I picked blackberries. I caught frogs with a butterfly net. I read in the encyclopedia that Indonesians eat frog legs. So I fried the frogs up in pig fat and me and Bwana Matambara ate them all.

What did they taste like?

Like grenada.

They tasted like an *island*?

No, my dear. That's just the taste that was in my mouth when I ate the frog legs. If that taste had a name, it would be called grenada. Mbiu paused and studied Ayosa. She said, So you're saying that a wraith tried to snatch you? That the wraith was pretending to be Bwana Matambara?

Uh-huh.

Mbiu burst into screeching laughter.

What's so funny?

It's me? I'm the thing you want most in the world? That's why the wraith tried to lure you, pretending she was my cat?

Ayosa stood up. She put on her frock. She picked up her notebook and storybook and stuffed them into her pocket. She said, Goodbye, Mbiu, and started across the rocks.

Listen! Mbiu called after her.

Ayosa paused. What?

Don't be sour at me. I didn't know for too long. I only looked in the studio windows minutes before I came to find you. I saw her and I wanted to say something immediately. But you had made that lovely feast, and it would have been a terrible shame to waste it.

Ayosa turned away and continued walking.

Where are you going?

None of your business!

13

When her mama returned from the land down under, she was as weak and unsteady as a newborn foal, and so physically adjusted that Ayosa could hardly bear to look at her. Her mama had a drawl, which spilled from her words and spattered into her mannerisms, so that her gestures seemed to have a stutter too.

How . . . how long . . . was . . . gone? she gasped, trying, and failing, to tear off the blankets. Fif . . . fiffy-teen years?

Jentrix the apothecary held her down to the bed and forced a spoonful of vegetable broth into her mouth. Two weeks, she said.

Nabumbo Promise swallowed the broth. She seemed to realize the futility of struggling against Jentrix, and she lay back down and closed her eyes. Ayosa, who was standing behind the curtains, twisted the hem of her frock. She watched as a tear, silver in the harsh afternoon light, trickled down her mama's temple and crawled into her earhole.

Where . . . my child?

Jentrix motioned at Ayosa. Ayosa let out the breath she had been holding. Her stomach was in tangles. She stepped forward, and when she was close enough to her mama, she bit her lip and kept her eyes to the ground. Her mama was only thirty-five, yet looked like a woman twice that age. Her face was rumpled and dirty, like a mechanic's oil-stained rag. The yellow in her hair was faded almost to white.

My . . . my lo-ve, her mama said.

Ayosa squeezed her eyes tight.

Look . . . look me, her mama said.

Ayosa opened her eyes. She gazed at her mama. Her mama watched her for a long moment, silent. She knows, Ayosa thought. She can see what I did. I was *gleeful* about her death.

But what her mama saw was the distress, and she touched Ayosa's hand and said, No . . . no cry, Butter-butter-cup. I am . . . well. Jentrix says . . . soon . . . fit as . . . buffah-lo.

Ayosa could not shake off her guilt. In the following weeks, she punished herself by attending to the tedium of her mama's care. Emptying her bedpans, brushing her teeth, clipping her toenails, giving her sponge baths. She learned to make noodle soup, and zucchini soup, and butternut squash soup, and she spent hours between these tasks and that of feeding.

The afternoons were for washing her mama's soiled linens and nightgowns. Ayosa did this in the yard, lathering detergent up in a bucket and then scrubbing each item between her knuckles and the heels of her palms. In the evenings, she tackled the dishes, the ironing and folding, and then another round of feeding before preparing her mama for sleep.

Each night, she went to bed aching all over. She listened to the Fatumas—sometimes their restless fidgeting, which caused the house to tremble, and sometimes their grief, which caused the house to shake.

She ate leftovers of her mama's soup while propped against a pillow in bed, so tired she sometimes fell asleep with her face pressed to the bowl.

Jentrix came by often, and also sent Temerity over whenever it could be managed. Jentrix and Temerity slashed the tall yellow grass, fixed the holes in the roof, pruned the trees that grew too close to the awnings. They set traps for mice, removed burlap bags of moth-infested cereal from the pantry, and tended to the overgrown hedges. They would help with her mama too, but this happened only occasionally, first because Nabumbo Promise wanted Ayosa to do all the caregiving, and second because Ayosa did so eagerly as atonement for her gleefulness.

Mbiu came by twice or thrice a week, and she stood in the kitchen window or in the yard, and she just watched and watched, all the while caressing Bwana Matambara. Each time she visited, Mbiu brought Ayosa wild berries that she had picked in her wanderings. She brought her library books, which she had stolen, no doubt. She brought her Goody Goody candy, blocks of jaggery, dandelion sprigs, and neon-colored Cutex for her toenails. She brought her the stamens of hibiscus flowers, and the shells of dung beetles, and snatches of poetry that she had torn off of strangers' newspapers. *When Susanna Jones wears red / Her face is like an ancient cameo / Turned brown by the ages.* She brought her stories of all the places she visited—the cannibals that she saw, the minstrels, the troubadours, the mimes, the ventriloquists. Then, always, she disappeared into the balmy air, leaving Ayosa yearning and empty and close to tears. Ayosa wanted badly to abandon her mama, to skip off with Mbiu. To sit in her car that was not a car per se, listening to Ms. Temperance on the radio, eating prickly pears with the cat and the pigeons.

One day, as Mbiu began her departure, she stopped on the veranda and said, I know you want to run away with me. Why don't you?

My mama.

The apothecary can care for her.

She can't. Not the way I can.

And *you* can't care for your mama the way the apothecary can. Makes no difference who cares for whom. Just let's go, okay?

You sound like a wraith trying to snatch me away.

Mbiu laughed. She moved closer to Ayosa and grabbed her hand. See? I'm Mbiu Dash all right.

Mbiu *Dash*? What sort of name is that?

I had a name, it belonged to my mama. But she died, and the name didn't fit right anymore. I think my mama took it away with her. So now I have a dash where a name should be. Well, are you coming or what? To Mombasa, I mean, with me. We will climb the minaret and call people to prayer. And we will live in a small house. Remember all that?

Ayosa looked up, and saw her mama standing at the window, watching. She pulled her hand away, like a child caught stealing from the cookie jar. Mbiu looked up too, saw Ayosa's mama, and took a step back.

Think about it, Mbiu whispered before disappearing into the woods.

Buttercup! her mama called.

Yes, Mama?

Who was that?

Friend.

Friend? You don't have any friends.

Ayosa pursed her lips. She detested her mama's bland, patronizing tone. She detested the all-knowing omniscience her mama assumed over her. What did Nabumbo Promise *know* about Ayosa? Nabumbo Promise, who was always gone for weeks and months on end? Who thought a child was like a painting, wholly unchanged by the passage of time, except perhaps by the alchemy of light and moisture? A child, like a painting, had no interior life, no complex thoughts or emotions, no memory of the past or aspirations for the future.

That's what Nabumbo Promise thought. It dumbfounded Ayosa. Even from her vantage point of twelve, almost thirteen, years old, she thought that her mama's age, thirty-five, was not great enough to justify her lack of sensitivity to the plight of childhood. Didn't she remember what it was like to be little, to be lorded over by adults?

You don't *know* me! Ayosa said under her breath.

What? her mama said, leaning out the window.

I said, Do you need something?

Tea.

A moment! I'm almost done here.

Ayosa went to the wash lines, her bucket filled with bedsheets. She pulled one up, letting water drip to the ground. She wrung it and hung it and held it down with pegs. She reached for another bedsheet and did the same. When she was done, she threw the leftover water in the grass. She stacked the buckets and tossed pegs into them.

In the kitchen, she held a handful of potatoes beneath the tap and turned the faucets. She rubbed the brown skin off the beets, crumbling earth into the plates and cups inside the sink. After peeling them, she placed the potatoes on a baking tray, sprinkled salt and rosemary on them, added some sunflower oil, and shoved them into the oven.

She boiled some water and poured it into two cups and added Earl Grey tea bags. Then she clambered up the stairs, slowly, so as not to spill any tea on the parquet floors that Jentrix had just waxed. Her mama was sitting in the blue farmhouse rocking chair, by the window, watching the jolly annas. When she heard Ayosa come in, she turned, and she said, You took your time with it, didn't you?

Ayosa set the tea down on the footstool. She pulled over a chair and sat next to her mama.

Cookies? her mama said.

Forgot, Ayosa said. She got up and went to fetch them.

Radio? her mama said.

Ayosa got up and fetched that too.

Now they sat sipping in silence for a long while, listening as the radioman read out the four p.m. news. Nabumbo Promise was growing stronger by the day. She could lift the weight of her own body and could even walk if she had the assistance of a cane. Ayosa was glad not to have to scrape out her bedpans anymore.

On the other hand, it meant that her mama slept less, and that she, Ayosa, had to spend more hours like this. Sitting with her. Both of them bumbling woefully, trying to find things to say that would be of interest to each other.

Did you know that bones bleed? her mama said to her one time.

Yes, she fought the urge to say. I was there when Rosette said this to you.

Listen to this! her mama said, and increased the volume on the radio.

The radioman had a segment called *Mapeli Today*, in which he callously shared gossip about the town's inhabitants. Right now, he was speaking about Ayosa's mama. He said, *Nabumbo Promise Brown, granddaughter of our founding mother, Mabel Eudoxia Brown, is critically ill and possibly dying. Her daughter, Ayosa Ataraxis Brown, confirmed this during a telephone call with our producers this morning.*

Ayosa, in her shock, knocked her teacup over and spilled hot tea all over her lap. I did *not*, she said, horrified.

Her mama laughed at her. Come on now, Buttercup. No need to pull teeth about it. The radioman is full of mud. Everyone knows that.

Just then, the house began to shake, so hard that rafters dislodged and swung about, almost pummeling Ayosa in the back of the skull. It was the Fatumas. They had heard the radioman's words. They were overcome with grief at the thought of Nabumbo Promise's dying.

Christ! her mama said, holding her chair arms tight.

Ayosa scrambled to her feet and ran out into the corridor. My mama is not dying, she called out. The radioman was just speaking mud!

And her mama howled with laughter, and she said, I think the old lady in the attic is only happy to hear that I might soon be joining her up there.

Mama, stop, Ayosa said. I really don't appreciate this kind of talk.

Her mama dismissed her with a wave of the hand. She said, You've changed a lot, Buttercup. You used to be . . . mellow, even-tempered. Now you are irascible. You remind me of myself, when the thing came and ate all the birds.

What birds?

Don't you remember? I once told you what it was like for me as a girl. There was quiet, not quietude. Like a forest where something came and ate all the birds.

Ayosa dabbed at her scalded lap with a towel. She did not tell her mama what she was thinking, that anyone would be irascible too if they had a mama even a little like *her*. She thought of Sindano's story—about her old desire to find a man to marry, and how that had ultimately cost her. *And* marriage? *Lord have mercy! I was no longer a naïve girl, but a woman who now lusted after her own solitude. A little like your mama, if I'm being honest.*

Ayosa thought to herself, I suppose I am growing too. I'm no longer that naïve girl anymore, who skipped about, whistling with childish abandon.

Ayosa wanted *more*, much more than she had. Much more than her mama was willing to offer. Did that make her irascible?

She put the towel away.

You like that? her mama said, and Ayosa realized that she had been staring at a photograph on the wall. Goats and sheep huddling in the cargo bed of a green Canter lorry. Her mama sipped on her tea and said, You want to hear about it?

Ayosa did not really, but she nodded anyway.

I watched a woman die that day. She was on the back of that livestock truck, giving birth with all those goats and sheep not even turning away. Surely, I told myself, I should put this camera down and help her. That woman was there, gasping, and later the doctor said she drowned from the fluid in her lungs. But when it was happening, all I could think of was: What a haunting photograph this will make!

Her mama stared at Ayosa, as though examining her, to see how *irascible* she would be at this confession. Was it a test? Ayosa kept her face blank.

Her mama continued speaking. You can't see her, but the woman is lying dead underneath all those goats and sheep. Doesn't the photograph then grow infinitely more powerful, once you're in possession of this knowledge?

Nabumbo Promise paused to slurp her tea.

She said, I often wonder why I constantly seek out death like this in my photographs. I mean, why do I want to capture death in the act, even prod it further so that it performs itself more dramatically for me? And why do people want to see these images?

Nabumbo Promise shook her head, as though stumped.

She said, Perhaps we are all trying to come to terms with our own mortality. You know, to overpower death. Maybe we consume these images of death because they soothe us. If you look long enough at a strange thing, it really does start to lose its strangeness. It becomes familiar, and a familiar thing is knowable. It cannot hurt you. Maybe we are seeking intimacy with our own deaths. Encountering it daily before that final encounter, so that by then, we shall be old friends, sweethearts even.

Ayosa looked at the photograph. The speckled goats with the tassels and horns and short shiny coats. The sheep with turbid eyes and dirty woolen coats. And beneath them, where no one could see, a lady who had drowned in a sea that swelled deep inside her own Self. Ayosa found it beautiful that there were no boats to save you from the water inside your own being. Just the moon outside you calling, and the tide inside you rising, and the waves crashing against your brittle bones. Filling your lungs. Drowning you.

Tears sprung to her eyes. She turned to her mama and said, You swore, Nabumbo Promise!

What are you talking about?

You swore never to leave me again. But you went away.

I didn't go away.

You did! I woke up and you were gone.

To my studio! I was only a stone's throw away from you. Developing old film.

And you didn't come back to me for Christmas.

Because I fell inside myself! Are you sour at me for *that*?

Ayosa glanced down into her hands. She said nothing.

How did you find me, anyway? her mama asked.

It was Mbiu that did.

The dirty throwaway girl?

She's not a throwaway girl!

Ayosa frowned. She lowered her head. She thought of Mbiu, and her heart smarted.

She thought of the two long-nosed Venetian masks that Mbiu had stolen for them on Christmas Day. And she thought of how they had sat outside her mama's studio door, their stomachs twisted up. How they had looked out of those impish crystal-studded masks, the peacock feathers fluttering in the breeze.

Ayosa sighed. How she wished to be with Mbiu right this moment. Digging through the dirt, searching for gold coins that the Vikings might have dropped out of their pockets if they ever had walked through this way. Or sticking their feet into the river, hoping their toes got chewed up by angry tiger fish.

Mbiu, her *dear* Mbiu.

Ayosa thought of the day Mbiu's mama robbed the bank. She thought of Mbiu and her cat, Bwana Matambara, sitting in the Volkswagen, waiting while Mbiu's mama held an AK-47 to a security guard's head. She thought of the mama in-descent, the mama laughing her way out of this world.

She thought of how much Nabumbo Promise would have loved to be there to capture the moment with her camera. *Documenting*. But really, only just sullying things.

It was like this: if Nabumbo Promise had been there with her camera, then Mbiu's mama would not have laughed her way out of the world the way she did. The laughter was important, she thought. Its defiance and its triumph. It was about the mama's having the *last* laugh. Maybe that's what it meant to be in-descent.

And documenting it would have stolen that moment away, from Mbiu and from her mama and from her cat. And Mbiu would not have had that memory left behind, to bring with her everywhere she went. Ayosa wanted to tell her mama this. To say, Mama, maybe you should stop bothering people with that camera of yours. But her mama would say to her, Stay out of grown folks' business. So Ayosa said nothing at all to her mama. Silently, she sketched in her notebook, a picture of Mbiu with Bwana Matambara on her shoulder, his tail hooked around her neck.

Later, she sat on the veranda, playing checkers by herself. Sindano came running up the hill, across the yard. I heard on the radio, she said, breathless. Your mama is dying?

My mama is not dying. She's only a little worn out from her journey in the land down under. The radioman was only speaking mud.

Where is she now?

Ayosa pointed at the awning above her.

Sindano walked past Ayosa and into the kitchen. She took the stairs two at a time. She was gone for a long moment. She returned with several dirty plates and mugs, as many as she could fit in her arms, and washed them in the sink.

Your mama's asleep.

Ayosa shrugged.

She looks so frail.

Ayosa gave up playing and pushed the checkerboard away.

Did you eat today?

I'm not hungry.

Atse! Sindano said. Look at the type of mud your mouth has started speaking.

Sindano opened the refrigerator. She was taken aback by its yawning yellow emptiness. Why do you keep this thing running, if there's nothing inside it?

Don't know.

Sindano began for the door.

Where are you going?

I'll be back soon.

An hour later, Sindano returned with a pot of chicken soup, pork stew, and a mincemeat casserole. She brought Ayosa a bag of glazed doughnuts. She made her eat two of them, and then she said, Follow me, Ayosa!

Where are we going?

For a walk. You ought to stretch those bones of yours. You're looking almost as frail as your mama. A bag of kindling sticks, that's what you are.

Sindano began for the door.

Wait, Ayosa said. Are you a wraith? You sound like a wraith trying to convince me to get up and follow it. Trying to snatch me.

Why would I—oh, I see what you mean. No, I'm not a wraith.

Give me your hand.

Sindano held out her hand for Ayosa to touch. It was solid. Ayosa nodded. Okay, let's go, she said. She wore a pair of rubber shoes and walked with Sindano into the woods.

It's not your fault, Sindano said.

What?

I know that you're blaming yourself for what happened to your mama. But how could you have known that she was in the studio? That she had fallen inside herself?

I'm not feeling guilty about *that*.

What then?

About the gleefulness.

What gleefulness?

It's what I felt when I thought my mama might die. I wanted to be rid of the burden of being her daughter.

Oh, Sindano said, crossing her arms over her chest.

I am abominable, aren't I?

No, Sindano said. Your mama, she's the one that's abominable.

Ayosa did not like the direction this conversation was going. She did not like it when people spoke ill of her mama. Stop this talk, she said.

And Sindano stopped that talk. They walked in silence to the edge of the water. Then Ayosa and Sindano took off their frocks. Now in their petticoats, they waded into the river. The water came out to meet them, overjoyed at seeing them, gushing and leaping up their ankles and knees, like a dog that had dearly missed its masters. Ayosa dove in, and she swam with a shoal of fish, a stranger's grinning dentures, a shelf of leather-bound books, a kitchen table with a candle stuck by its own wax to the middle. Ayosa was still inside the river when the Jinamizi struck. She writhed, and the water twisted her about like a piece of manila rope. The Jinamizi brought memories that were heavy as boulders—she fought against them, scratching, kicking, biting, but they subdued her, buried her deep in the brackish water.

She saw a woman led to the guillotine, saw a priest anoint her head with oil, saw the crowd gasp and then cheer as her decapitated head rolled off the precipice. She saw three little girls huddled together inside a poor farmer's dark cellar. Their papa was gone for a day now, or was it two, three? In search of bread. The kind but destitute farmer had given them bean water and a fish head to eat. A humbug candy too. The children were malnourished, their bones feeble as grass stalks, their faces hollowed out. Their voice boxes were empty, which was a small mercy, because they could not cry out when the soldiers came searching for them.

In another memory, a boy staggered home to his mama, bleeding out of the stumps where his arms used to be. He had not slashed enough rubber, and the FP lined up the tappers in a clearing and then severed their limbs. The boy's name was Bokali. He did not make it home to his mama.

Ayosa! Ayosa!

Ayosa coughed and sputtered.

Sindano turned her over to her side, so she would not swallow the green water rising from her lungs.

Easy now, Sindano said, trying to soothe her.

The Jinamizi came for me.

I know, I know.

Ayosa lifted herself, sat on the rocks, sniffling, sobbing for the boy who did not make it home to his mama. Bokali.

Bokali is all right, Sindano whispered. He is no longer in pain. What you saw happened a long time ago.

Ayosa looked at Sindano in awe. How did you *know*?

I can see things, Sindano said. She sat down next to Ayosa. She said, Long ago, when I wanted a man to marry me, I thought that that kind of domesticity would numb my . . . er . . . *gift*. I wanted to be ordinary.

If you can see things, then why did you not see that it was Bessie the wraith and not ten men wanting to marry you?

Good question. The answer is simply that it doesn't work like that. My gift is useful to everyone but me.

What can you see anyway?

All sorts of things. For example, I see people's most awful afflictions.

Can you help them? Can you relieve them of their pain?

No.

What good is it to see, then?

Oh, plenty good. Doesn't it comfort you to know that I saw your Bokali? It is a heavy load for a young girl to have to carry on her own.

Sometimes it's good just to know that someone else saw too. That you're not lonesome in your carrying.

Ayosa nodded. It was true, she felt better already about the Jinamizi's terrible visit. Tell me more, please, she said. About the things that you can see.

Sindano raised her head, stared out into the trees. She said, Ayosa Ataraxis Brown, what do you see when you watch the air?

Nothing.

Really? Nothing?

Nothingness.

Me, I see a three-dimensional arena, full of objects and people. She pointed toward a nearby casuarina tree. Over there, I see a pair of wraiths watching us. Scheming. She turned, pointed right in front of them. Over there, I see some Sufi poets of yore, burning the midnight oil, composing epics about the Prophet's ascension to Isra and Miraj. And over there, I see you and your sister.

Sister? You must be mistaken. I don't have a sister.

The girl with a cat on her shoulder.

Ayosa's eyes widened. What are we doing?

Fishing. Catching blue marlin in the ocean. The horse and the pigeons and the cat, they are all foraging on the beach, waiting for you to come back.

Ayosa swallowed. She thought, No-no-no, that can't be right. It was too sweet a fantasy, it could never come true. What use was there in indulging it? So she abandoned the thought. She said, What else do you see?

Over there, I see your mama.

My mama? Ayosa asked, surprised once more. What would Sindano tell her? That her mama was in a field somewhere, photographing a dying mother and child, refusing to help?

I don't know if she is still your mama when she's the woman in the red city. That is where she is as I'm looking at her right now. She has stolen a barrel of figs. She's kicking it over, rolling it down a hill. She's . . . She's smothering a baby with the barrel of figs. My God, the baby is *dead*.

Ayosa's heart flew into her mouth. Was her mama stuck in the land down under again? She jumped up. Got to go, she announced.

She did not bother to put her frock on. She ran through the wattle trees and sycamores.

Nabumbo Promise Brown! she called, sprinting up the stairs, bursting into her mama's bedroom. Her mama was sitting in the blue rocking chair, nodding in her sleep, while the radioman talked about an armyworm infestation in the wheat crop.

Nabumbo Promise, Ayosa said, and her mama's eyes flew open.

What? Is there a fire?

No, Ayosa said.

And now she let out a sigh of relief. For one, her mama was fine, perfectly fine. And for two, she, Ayosa, had felt concern for the well-being of her mama. *Not* gleeful at all about her misfortunes. What a relief it was, to feel normal feelings. Appropriate feelings. Sadness for sad things, and joy for joyful things.

She crawled to her mama's feet. She and her mama listened to the transistor radio together, and her mama tut-tutted and sucked her teeth bitterly when the radioman talked about the hostile protests against African students in Nanjing, China. Her mama said, Now, tell me, Buttercup, where can we go in this world where we won't be downtrodden like mules?

14

On New Year's Eve, her mama awoke feeling good. She said that she felt better than she ever had felt in her whole entire life. She said that the thing that once came and ate all the birds in her forest had now spat them out. That the birds were everywhere, singing their little hearts out. Flycatchers and canaries and cuckoo finches. Even dodos, which were supposed to be fossils, had been resurrected, and were hopping about in her marula trees, whistling with ecstasy.

Her mama could walk without a cane, and could run too, which she did, up and down the stairs, dizzyingly, calling, Buttercup, time waits for no fool! And, Buttercup, for God's *sakes*!

Coming! Ayosa said. She was cleaning herself up. She'd spent the whole morning making candied plantains and frying green gram and potato sambusas. She wore a clean dress and went downstairs, and she and her mama ate breakfast outside on the porch, watching the bees flutter in the frangipanis and jasmines.

Afterward, she and her mama brushed their teeth, spitting suds into the kitchen sink. They gargled salt water. They greased their elbows. They tucked poinsettias in their hair. They curtsied for each other. Said, How do you do, madam? And then they said, I do just fine. And then they giggled.

Nabumbo Promise grabbed Ayosa's hand and tugged. They ran out of the house, past the awnings and chimneys, past the yard full of tangled balls of thorn trees and wildflowers and barbed wire and stiff yellow grass, past the stone angels with severed heads, past the rusted sign that read *Manor Mabel Brown*. They arrived at Our Lady of Lourdes just as Father Jude Thaddeus was giving his homily.

He said, Again I say to you, as is written in—

And he paused, and raised his head, and watched as Ayosa and her mama sidled into a whimpering pew.

Sorry-sorry, they whispered, brushing past townspeople's knees. All the faithful turned, eyes wet with old devotion and new derision. Akh! they hissed their disgust.

Father Jude Thaddeus cleared his throat. Hem-hem-hem, he said, and the faithful remembered that they ought to be focusing their attentions on *him*. He said, Again I say to you, as is written in Ephesians: Let all bitterness, and wrath, and anger, and clamor, and evil speaking, be put away from you, with all malice. And be kind to one another, tenderhearted, forgiving one another, even as God for Christ's sake has forgiven you.

He said, If this year has taught us anything at all, it is that turning the other cheek in radical forgiveness—which is what we know the Christlike love to be—has the power to save our broken world. Where haven't we seen it? From East to West, people are choosing to honor the two greatest commandments as inscribed in the Gospel of Mark: Love thy God, and love thy neighbor. We have seen it with South Africa, Cuba, and Angola putting their hands together to what? To free Namibia. We have seen it with Yasser Arafat saying what? Saying no to terrorism and yes to the state of Israel. We have seen the superpowers doing what? Destroying their nuclear weapons. We have seen cease-fires where? In Iran and Iraq.

Next to Ayosa, her mama fidgeted. Made the bench whimper and then squeak and then cry out like an enraged toddler.

The birds inside me, they are really loud, she said to Ayosa.

Hush! a woman said. She was sitting at the front pew, dressed in a purple suit, with a bunch of sticky black currants pinned to her straw hat, caramelizing in the heat.

That's Dorcas Munyonyi, Nabumbo Promise said to Ayosa.

Ayosa gawked at the woman. At her stub of a nose, which looked like she once leaned too close to a candle and melted the tip of it off. Her beady, chameleon's eyes seemed to grow out of her temples. They rolled about, observing all that took place behind her and in front of her and above her and below her.

You heard me? Nabumbo Promise said. That woman there, she is Dorcas Munyonyi. She and the priest are lovers!

The entire church fell silent. Nabumbo Promise had spoken louder than she had intended, and everyone in the church had heard. The priest tripped on his words and then fell mum, his eyes growing large as mugs. Nabumbo Promise cupped her mouth with her hand. Ayosa wished she could shrink into the pew. There were sniggers among the faithful, and then laughter suppressed in mouths, that then grew and grew and then burst, like excess air in latex balloons. Dorcas Munyonyi's yellow face took on a tinge of maroon, as though it were suddenly, viciously rusting. She stood up, marched down the aisle, her pumps going kong-kong-kong on the granite floor, her fruit hat leaving violet splotches on townspeople's faces.

She stopped at the pew where Ayosa and her mama sat. She was foaming at the corners of her lips, like an enraged bull.

She said, The Brown girls! Always up to here with their gobble-dygook.

She pointed at her own neck, to show the amount of gobbledy-gook that the Brown girls were full of, and also, intentionally or not, conveying a more sinister message. Her index finger slid over her neck in a motion that suggested that jugulars would soon get slit.

Nabumbo Promise took Ayosa's hand and squeezed it tight.

It's okay, her hand was saying.

Dorcas Munyonyi said, Nabumbo Promise Brown, this town has had enough of your conniving and philandering and murdering. We should have hung you fifteen years ago, when we had the chance. We should have tied you to a tree in front of your mother's house. And no one would have cut you down all those years. You would still have been hanging there, until today. And you would never have spawned that—she looked at Ayosa now, mouth curled in utter disgust—that . . . that aphid of a child, that arachnid, that sorry red louse.

Buttercup, let's go!

Ayosa and her mama brushed past townspeople's knees. They hurried to the door, cheeks stinging as though Dorcas Munyonyi had smacked them right across the face. She walked closely behind them, chasing. They thought she would follow them out to the churchyard, where she would grind them right into the ground with a tree branch. But Dorcas Munyonyi stopped at the wooden double doors and crushed them shut. They heard her bolt the doors from the inside.

Jesus Christ! Nabumbo Promise said. What came over that woman?

You! Ayosa said. You came over that woman.

Her mama looked at Ayosa, mouth hanging open, as though she was truly gobsmacked. Me? What did I do?

You goaded her. Why did you have to talk that type of talk inside the church? It was disrespectful to everyone.

Even to you?

Yes, Mama. Even to me.

See, I don't really understand that. I mean, put aside the fact that the woman has been goading *me* for far longer than you've been alive. And put aside the fact that nothing I said in there was a lie. What I want to know is this: What's it to you, personally? We don't go to church but once a year, on New Year's Eve. Tell me why you care about any type of disrespect to the priest and the faithful and that godforsaken woman.

Because . . . As you said, we go just once a year. I was really looking forward to eating the body of Christ. And drinking the blood of Christ.

You mean that awfully dry communion wafer? And you mean that cheap red wine?

Don't patronize me, Nabumbo Promise Brown!

Her mama took a step forward. She slapped Ayosa across the jaw. Ayosa, in turn, pushed her mama so hard that her mama slammed into a tree. Her mama launched herself forward, plucked Ayosa off the ground, and lifting her to her shoulders, carried her bodily out of the churchyard.

Put me down! Ayosa screamed.

Not until you apologize, her mama said. There was a cheerful note in her voice, so Ayosa knew that she did not mean it at all, and that all the tension between them was suddenly gone. Her mama said, You're lucky I've got all those birds singing inside of me. Means I can't stay sour at you for too long.

She put Ayosa down, and grabbed her sweaty hand, and the two of them skipped away from Our Lady of Lourdes. Nabumbo Promise took Ayosa to a diner run by an Indian woman called

Bhavna. The lunch special was chicken makhani with kachumbari. They sat down by the window, and the ceiling fan cast shadows in their lassi glasses. A man moved between the tables, hawking a cure for syphilis.

Little Miss, he said, holding out his wares, do your unmentionables pain you?

No, sir, they do not.

The man turned to Nabumbo Promise and asked the same.

Nabumbo Promise rolled her eyes. Get out of my face, she said.

The man moved to the next table.

The irony is, her mama continued, Father Jude Thaddeus was just preaching about forgiveness. Turn the other cheek. Christlike love. Her mama laughed. She said, I will tell you *this*. There is nothing Christlike about the way the priest and Dorcas Munyonyi love each other.

Bhavna stood at the counter, ladling fried rice into takeaway boxes.

Ayosa stared at the port-wine stain on the tip of Bhavna's nose. Please-please-please-I-need-you, Ayosa whispered to the port-wine stain. She hoped that it would come to her, maybe onto her forehead, so that it would be the first thing that people saw when they looked at her. Like a doorbell for her face, which people could press if they wanted to.

Are you listening? her mama said.

Ayosa tore her eyes away from Bhavna. She said, Seems to me the townspeople haven't forgiven you.

Her mama raised her brows. Forgiven me? For what?

For the things that happened.

What do you know about any of that?

Plenty, Ayosa said. I know plenty, Mama.

———

It was the middle of July. Nabumbo Promise and Rosette were terribly concerned that their mother had not answered any of their telephone calls. At first, they thought that Lola Freedom was on an unusually long journey. They figured that she was in her red Cessna, attending to an emergency somewhere.

Lola Freedom was a flying doctor. Whenever the telephone rang, she would drop everything she was doing, and she would jump into her airplane and head out to the backwater village where she was being summoned. She loved the dying. She loved to coax them back, loved to caress spirit, to reacquaint it with body. Sometimes the spirit was bent on leaving, and she loved this too. She loved the resoluteness of its departure. The vacant body that remained behind.

Lola Freedom loved flying, and she loved being a doctor. It was a great wonder that she had managed to weld the two professions together. She ran a nonprofit called Wings of Freedom, which solicited funding from donors abroad. She used this money to maintain the Cessna and to buy medical supplies. She also used it to make significant donations to public offices that might someday be useful to her: the police and the church and the magistrate and the provincial administration. Lola Freedom believed in preventative medicine. She paid bribes and called it philanthropy. She created a long roster of favors that she could call in at the drop of a hat.

And so, between the maintenance work for the Cessna, and her duties as a physician, and her schemes as a philanthropist, Lola Freedom was immensely busy. She was hardly ever at home. That's why it took a while for Nabumbo Promise and Rosette to grow apprehensive over their unanswered telephone calls.

Still, after three months straight of radio silence, they decided to go home and visit. They thought that maybe their mother had fallen and broken her hip. That she was writhing by the staircase, saying,

Lord, I know I don't deserve it, but send those girls back home to me. Nabumbo Promise hoped that this was true. She wanted to see her mother's humiliation when they found her sitting in a pool of her own excrement.

Rosette had Lola Freedom's jalopy with her. When she'd received the news about Nabumbo's sepsis, she had returned home briefly from the convent. She had borrowed their mother's jalopy and driven off to the comatose Nabumbo Promise. Their mother hardly drove anymore. She was never sober for long enough. She was never even sober when she flew her little plane across the sky.

Now they hopped into the jalopy, with Nabumbo Promise at the wheel, and began the journey back home to see their mother. Four hours into the trip, at a place near the halfway point to their mother's house, Nabumbo Promise started to grow drowsy. Rosette was fast asleep beside her, head bobbing against the window, her nun's veil covering her face.

Nabumbo Promise lit a cigarette. She switched on the radio. The station was closed for the night, and there was nothing but static. She switched off the radio. She drove in silence for several kilometers, hoping to God that their mother had some painkillers nearby. She still remembered her busted knee, remembered that anguish deep inside the bone. It was not the sort of suffering she wished on anyone, not even her mother.

Suddenly, the jalopy swung. Nabumbo Promise startled. She saw that she had fallen asleep and veered off to the side of the road. She steered it back to the left lane. Then she lowered the window so that cold air could smack the sleep out of her eyes.

She began to hum. She bent down, tried to reach the bucket bag at her feet. To retrieve another cigarette. She could not find her pack of Sportsman.

Shit! she whispered.

And she bent even further, digging among the kerchiefs and coins and condoms and prescription medications and hair ties at the bottom of her bag. She tossed aside her spare pair of spectacles.

There it was!

Her fingers grabbed the cigarettes. She took one out and stuck it between her teeth. Now she dug around inside her pocket for the matches. She let go of the steering wheel, and she struck a match and brought it to the tip of the cigarette. She closed her eyes. Inhaled. Exhaled. Sighed.

And then.

A scream.

Edging out as though from a beast ensnared in a hunter's trap.

She tore her eyes open.

And she saw two women. They looked like spirits. They looked like the undead. Like the unburied. They wore white tunics and yellow turbans. They carried goatskin drums, which they beat as the jalopy careened toward them. They beat those drums and sang a dirge.

> *Luwere-luwere-luwere.*
> *It is finished.*
> *Hand yourself back to your maker.*

Nabumbo Promise stepped on the brakes, and the momentum threw her and Rosette forward. The next few moments were a blur of dust and burned rubber and guttural howls. Nabumbo Promise and Rosette were rattled about like clay dolls as the jalopy soared above, crashed back down, and shuddered to a stop.

First, Nabumbo Promise looked over at her sister. Rosette was shell-shocked but otherwise unharmed. Next, Nabumbo Promise stuck her head out the window. The two women lay facedown in the road, their goatskin drums beside them in the dirt.

Nabumbo Promise pulled at the latch, started to scramble out. Before her feet could touch the ground, Rosette grabbed her arm, gripping it hard with her cold fingers. She did not say a thing.

Nabumbo Promise paused. She wiped her stinging nose with the back of her hand. She let her head fall forward, onto the steering wheel. Rosette climbed out. She walked round the hood to the driver's side. Nabumbo Promise inched away. Now, with Rosette driving, they started moving away from those motionless women. Their dirge still rang in Nabumbo's ears. She wondered if, through some instinct, the women had known of what was waiting on the road. If they had been singing the dirge for themselves.

Nabumbo Promise poured her some lassi. Ayosa drank it. She ate the chicken makhani and red rice that Bhavna brought. Then she ate a plum sorbet. Then she ate a nut haluwa. She could taste some rosewater and ghee in it, as well as another potent flavor that she could not quite put her finger on, and that slightly repulsed her.

She and her mama did not say a word to each other through the meal. They were both thinking of things that had happened. Thinking of the Yonder Days.

Nabumbo Promise and Rosette said nothing to each other the rest of the way. They said nothing to each other even after. As soon as they pulled beside their mama's house, Rosette ran off to her little shack by the river.

Nabumbo Promise got out. She stood still for a long while, relishing the crisp morning air, the far-off smell of donkey dung, the cackle of geese in the valley. She sat on the wooden porch steps, the gentle sun shining in her eyes. She thought of years gone by. Thought of the time after their mama returned them from the orphanage. Thought of how she and Rosette sometimes sat like this on the porch steps, next to each other, saying nothing at all.

Just watching the crazy-birds that made that jolly anna ha-ha-ha sound. Watching those russet feathers and golden hackles. Those slick sickles and heavy wattles. Wondering where these birds could possibly have come from. Wondering how many women the birds had eaten whole. She'd seen those birds nowhere else but here, in this yard, under these sycamores. They were nasty, mocking birds. They knew all your secrets and laughed because of how pathetic you were.

And she thought of how sometimes Rosette would go to the woods and catch a wild fowl. This was the year before Jentrix the apothecary came and squatted on their land, so there was no one watching over them, no one bringing them soups or bread still warm from the oven. Rosette would carry back the fowl by its wings, and Nabumbo Promise would press her palms over her ears so as not to hear the terrible squalling as Rosette broke its neck. Rosette plucked the feathers and boiled the fowl, and they ate salted meat for supper, still sitting on the porch steps. Then Rosette would grab her musket and return to her little shack down by the river.

Now Nabumbo Promise looked at her mama's house. The screen over the kitchen window was ripped, flapping about in the breeze. She stared at the trees surging with fruit, at the wasps scurrying under the awning. She got up and entered the house. Her mama never locked the doors. No one ever came this way.

Nabumbo Promise walked through the kitchen, to the corridor. She swept her eyes up and down the stairs. Nothing was amiss. Her mama was off in her Cessna for sure, which Nabumbo Promise was glad for. Although she had entertained it briefly, she did not particularly enjoy the thought of being her mama's caregiver. She also did not wish to argue with her mother about the fact that she had run away from the convent.

She made herself some bitter coffee in the moka pot. She drank it out of an empty jam jar because she could not find a single clean mug in the cabinet. She thought of what to do with the day. Clean, for one. Her mother's house was a pigsty. Nabumbo Promise marveled at how something that had felt ordinary to her growing up could seem so bizarre now.

Had they really lived like *this*? With the dishes in the sink stacked all the way up to the ceiling? With empty glass bottles on the curtain boxes and window ledges, crammed under the kitchen table? With trash in the corner, which, judging from its state of decay, had been there for months on end? With dirty dishes stored in the cabinets, because there was no more space for them in the sink?

But first, she would nap for a while. They had driven all night. Her knee throbbed where she had once busted it. She placed her coffee jar back in the cabinet. She took her bucket bag and climbed up the stairs. Shuffled down the corridor. She had to walk past her mother's bedroom to get to hers.

Her mother's bedroom door was ajar. Nabumbo Promise stopped in the corridor and stared in. Saw that her mother was right there, sitting in the blue farmhouse rocking chair, facing the window, as though watching the rumpled sky, as though listening to birdsong. Her yellow hair, which she bleached on the last Sunday of each month, was stiff as fodder.

Lola Freedom? Nabumbo Promise said.

Her mother was silent.

Nabumbo Promise stood still for a few moments, half expecting her mother to turn and hurl the nearest object at her for interrupting her quiet time. That is what she always called those hours spent in her rocking chair, with a bottle of cognac in her lap. She would hurl a lampshade or flashlight or watering can. Anything she could reach. One time, their mother had to give Rosette stitches in the middle of the night after the water jug that she threw split Rosette's bottom lip. Their mother sewed it back crooked, and the next day, jumped in horror when she saw the lip. She said, Did Jentrix the apothecary practice her whipstitch on your face?

Nabumbo Promise stepped into the room and gagged. She reached for her handkerchief and pressed it to her face. She ambled closer to the rocking chair, touched her mother's shoulder, and leapt back when her mother fell apart like a pile of wooden blocks. The crazy-birds watched from the window. Jolly anna ha-ha-ha, they guffawed.

It began to rain the type of bitter rain that seeped into houses and drowned drunkards and sleeping babies. Nabumbo Promise went down to the kitchen. She stood at the window, eyes submerged in hot tears. She saw Rosette emerge through the woods. Probably the river had swollen up and the water was knee-high in her shack. Rosette struggled against the gray gale, periodically stopping to hold on to sycamores and wattle trees so the terrible swirling currents would not fling her down the hill. She finally reached the veranda, sopping wet, her habit and veil completely soaked, her spindly limbs askew like the mangled spokes of an umbrella.

Rosette patted herself down to make sure she was all there—a rain like that sometimes pilfered body parts. She hunched over, palms on the wall, and kicked off her sodden clogs. Then she let herself in, shrugged off her coat, and hung it on the nail behind the door. Rosette looked at Nabumbo Promise, and even though Nabumbo Promise said nothing at all, Rosette immediately *knew*. They had spent years next to each other, sitting in Stubborn Silence. They knew the different textures of each other's quiet. They knew which one was bare and which one was bursting at the seams.

Rosette brushed past Nabumbo Promise. She ran down the corridor. Bounded up the stairs. She returned five minutes later, breathing slow, breathing heavy. Wordlessly, Rosette filled the steel kettle with water and set it on the stovetop. She was singing that awful dirge.

> *Luwere-luwere-luwere.*
> *It is finished.*
> *Hand yourself back to your maker.*

Nabumbo Promise froze.

It was for their mother, the dirge.

The women with the goatskin drums, the ones whom she had knocked over with the jalopy, they were singing that dirge for Lola Freedom.

Buttercup, come back to me!

Ayosa blinked. Her mama leaned forward and touched her hand. What were you thinking?

About Lola Freedom. How you found her dead.

Her mama frowned. I suppose there is still talk all over the town about that. Do you believe that I did it? Murdered her? That's what some townspeople think. That's what Dorcas Munyonyi was yelling at me about in the church.

No, Ayosa said. I know you didn't do it.

How do you know?

You're all kinds of awful, Nabumbo Promise. Just not the kind to kill her own mama.

Nabumbo Promise frowned. I've killed other people, though.

I know.

You know? What do you know about that?

You killed your brother, Maxwell Truth.

Her mama furrowed her brow.

The two priestesses with the goatskin drums, singing the horrible dirge, you killed them too.

Her mama hung her head, half in shame, half in confoundment. How did you know?

I remember things.

You can't remember things that happened before you were born.

Can too.

Her mama sucked her teeth. Look, I'm not about to argue with a—

Aphid of a child? Arachnid? Sorry red louse?

I was going to say a silly little girl.

Nabumbo Promise could no longer stand Ayosa. She got up, walked to the counter, and paid Bhavna for their meal. Then, without looking back to motion at Ayosa, she made her way out the door. Ayosa jumped to her feet and followed. They walked home in silence. When they arrived, Nabumbo Promise changed from her church dress. She wore a red chiffon blouse, with brown high-waist Levi's jeans. A shamrock dangled between her clavicles. She sat barefoot on the stoop, drinking an espresso and reading *Being and Nothingness*.

Ayosa watched her mama for a long moment. She wished she had not upset her. Wished she had not said to her things about remembering the past. What good did it do, anyway? Now she wanted desperately to diffuse their crossed wires, to restore their good spirits, so that she and her mama were laughing with each other again. Were they always at loggerheads like this? It seemed to her that they were having much more discord than accord these days. She said to herself, I've got to stop provoking her.

She crawled next to her mama. Said, Mama?

Huh?

What's the color of your soul?

Her mama set down the dainty china cup. If I were to guess, then green.

Like pickles?

Not at all. More like seafoam.

That's a nice color, Mama.

Why, thank you, Buttercup.

Mama, you want to know what color my soul is?

Yes, I'm dying to know.

It's blue, like thrush eggs.

Not bad! her mama said. She placed aside her hefty book. She closed her eyes, took in a deep breath.

I'm feeling fit as a buffalo, she said, over and over again. She marveled at it, at this newfound wellness, and she skipped about and did cartwheels in the grass to illustrate it.

I am all *fine*, she said, laughing so loud that she scared the jolly annas. She said, The birds singing inside me, they sound marvelous!

Now she closed her eyes once more, and she tipped her head to listen to the birdsong. She hummed it, her voice rich as the church organ at Our Lady of Lourdes.

I'm going to the studio, she announced. I've got a few crates of old film, with several thousand rolls inside. Got to start developing them.

She poured herself more espresso.

Then she said, I've been so afraid to look at those photographs, Buttercup.

Because why?

Because I took them in the seventies. I wasn't yet a reporter for the *Oracle Weekly* in those days. I was only a girl who didn't speak much, yet had lots to say. Those photographs were my voice, and Christ, did I yell! The critics called me gifted. They called me East Africa's Diane Arbus. They said, Better watch out, Nabumbo Promise is coming for you! But look at me: I never went for anyone.

She shook her head sadly.

She said, I've been afraid to look at those photographs because they will indict me. They will speak the type of truth that I'm not ready to hear.

What will the photographs say?

That I squandered my gift. That I fumbled my hand and lost all the things. They will say, Look at you now: You are only a photo-journalist for a scrappy tabloid that the butcher uses to wrap meat in. You are no one. You are a mound of ripe, steaming shit.

Nabumbo Promise laughed dryly.

Ayosa frowned. She said, You are *someone*, Mama. Your photographs hang in Dakar and Tokyo and Hanover. A no one could never do that.

They don't hang, my dear. They *hung* there, briefly. In the mid-seventies. Back when the critics could not get enough of me in the *New Yorker* and *Der Spiegel*. Now I send letters to curators in those same museums. You know what they do? They write me back, asking, Nabumbo *Who*?

Nabumbo Promise picked up her empty espresso cup and hurled it at a stone pillar. It shattered into a dozen glittering shards.

She cackled and said, Nabumbo *Who*? Nabumbo No One.

Nabumbo Promise stood up, dusted her jeans, and hopped down the porch steps. She said, At least the birds in my forest are singing again, and I am fit as a buffalo, so see you later, Buttercup! I'm running off to face my demons.

Ayosa watched her mama make her way down the path, toward the studio in the middle of the woods. She thought of her mama alone out there. She thought of Christmas Day. How she had found her hunched over the long table in the darkroom.

Ayosa's guts tangled up.

Mama! she called. Mama, don't!

Don't what?

Don't go out there. To the studio, I mean. Stay here with me.

Her mama laughed at her. I'm not a child, Buttercup. You don't need to watch me.

Mama, please, Ayosa said, her voice tremulous, desperate.

Her mama walked faster. Tell you what, she said over her shoulder. Come by and visit me at four o'clock, okay? You will see that I am all right. We'll have tea together, okay?

15

A honeybee drifted through the window, hovering near her finger, landing on her knee. Ayosa watched it buzz for a few moments. Then she jumped to her feet and ran out into the sunshine. On and on she went. Beyond the fields of bristle grass and juniper bushes and sunflowers bobbing drowsily. Beyond the wattle trees and sycamores, to the place where her beehive was.

Mbote? she said to the bees. Sango nini? Bolingo na ngai!

These were all words that she had heard in Lingala songs. She thought that if bees could understand a language, it would have to be this one. Lingala. Something about it felt sticky and warm and golden, like honey.

She stroked the outer edge of the crooked wooden crate. Some bees emerged, wrathful, eager to attack the intruder. She whispered, It's just me, Ayosa Ataraxis Brown. Look!

She took a glazed doughnut from her pocket and offered it to the bees. They hovered near her finger too, just as the first bee had done. They recognized her from the salt embedded in her skin. They knew it was the same person who had built this home for them. The same person who had been leaving pans of sugar water out in the yard for them.

See? she said. I mean no harm at all.

The queen was back from her journey. Ayosa could tell because the worker bees were more agitated than usual. They would not let Ayosa close to the hive, no matter how softly and sweetly she cajoled. The queen was heavy with seeds that her drones had left inside her before they all fell down and died. She was vulnerable—entire colonies crawled in her belly, depending on her to usher them over from *beyond*.

Ayosa marveled at this thought. Of the queen bee looking up and saying, Please-please-please-I-need-you, and summoning thousands of eager little bees to herself. The thought filled her with joy and wonder. She did not mind at all that the worker bees did not want her close to the hive. Respectfully, she turned away. She refilled the pans of sugar water, hoping it would help the worker bees with their honey making.

At half three, she made her way back to the house. She took off her shoes and stood on the veranda, drinking a jar of ice water. She waited for the milkman to come up the hill on his bicycle.

The jolly annas above her said, Jolly anna ha-ha-ha. She shielded her eyes from the sun and watched as the milkman carried the canister to the door. Milk spilled over the mouth of the canister. Condensation dribbled onto the milkman's work boots.

Hello, Mr. Milkman. What a nice shirt you've got there.

The milkman looked down at himself, patting the shirt as though discovering its presence for the first time. It was a Kaunda shirt, sprinkled with a bougainvillea print, with pockets large enough to stow entire watermelons in.

It's my New Year's shirt, the milkman said, beaming.

Ayosa was taken aback. She had tried for years to speak to him, but he had never humored her. Now she stared at him, thinking of how his voice did not match his body at all. He was a dainty man. With veins embroidered in green silk onto his neck and temples. A gleaming face that was waxed and buffed each morning. Teeth like sequins sewn into his mouth. But his voice, it emerged as though from a sky god or a thing like a sky god. Ragged and profound, dancing in the air long after he had finished speaking.

It startled Ayosa. She looked up into his face. It was the first time she had really seen it. His eyes like a calf's. His weak, quivering chin. She had heard that voice before.

Are you the radioman? Your voice, it sounds like the radioman's.

His weak chin steadied under a coy smile. I sure am, he said, pleased to be recognized in this manner.

Ayosa hesitated. If you're the radioman, then say something I hear.

What type of thing?

A death news thing.

The milkman sat down on the stoop beside Ayosa.

Hem-hem-hem, he said, dislodging all the debris in his throat. He waited for it to settle down in the corner of his voice box. He would sweep it up later.

Well? Ayosa asked.

Patience, my dear, he said, and she winced because she was not his *dear*.

Well, here we go now, he said. The death is announced of Nunu Okoth, who ate aflatoxin by accident in her roast maize. Nunu is survived by her sister-in-law, Janet Okatch. The cortege will leave Coast General Hospital on—

She was convinced. She dropped her hands from her lap and onto the hot stone of the stoop. What is aflatoxin? she said.

Something you should never eat in your roast maize.

Because why?

Because it will make your heart stop.

Ayosa looked up brightly. Can I jingle your bell?

You sure can!

She skipped to the avocado tree where his bicycle leaned. She jingled the bell. Then she fell to her knees and spun the pedal round and round, watched as the spokes of the wheels glinted in the sunshine. There was a sticker on the mudguard. It read, *Don't Bring Friendship to Business.*

She said, You have any resolutions? For the New Year I mean.

To find myself a wife, the milkman said.

What sort of wife?

Oh, beggars cannot be choosers. I will marry quick-quick the first woman that looks my way, before she has a chance to come to her senses.

Ayosa jingled the bell some more. She said, What happened there? She was pointing at a scar on the milkman's forearm.

A spider bit me.

What kind?

A rain spider.

Oh, Ayosa said, frowning. I wish a black widow had bitten you instead.

Because why?

Because you would be dead by now. Then everyone would have to sing for you Luwere-luwere-luwere. She fell silent for a moment, considering it. Wait, she said. If you die, who will announce your death for you on the radio? Your mama?

No, not my mama. She doesn't have the type of voice for saying things on the radio. And besides, she would be all choked up from the crying.

Then who?

Me, I suppose. I've been making a list of all the ways I think I might go. I have thirty-seven so far. So I am making thirty-seven different recordings of thirty-seven different scenarios. Then one day, when I'm gone, people will just have to find the appropriate recording and play it on the radio. That is how I plan for it to happen, my dear.

Ayosa winced again. I am not your dear, she said. She walked back to the stoop. She said, It's good that you are here. There is something I've been meaning to talk to you about.

What's that?

I was listening to the radio with my mama the other day. I heard you say something very offensive.

Oh, you mean that time I lied? When I said you had spoken with our producers and confirmed that your mother was terribly ill and possibly dying?

Yes-yes, that's it. That was an awful thing to do. Why did you lie?

Oh, lying is nothing. I do it all the time.

My mama said as much. She said that you're full of mud.

The milkman laughed. That's true. I am full of mud. But your mama is one to speak! Pot calling the kettle black . . . ?

Doesn't make it right, though. What you did, I mean.

The milkman raised his hands in defeat. He said, I'm sorry that you got offended.

What type of apology is that?

I'm sorry. Plain and simple. It's just show business. It's the way things are.

That apology is no good, either!

The milkman stood up. I am no good at this.

Ayosa huffed.

He pointed out his bicycle. How about we go downtown? I will buy you strawberry and vanilla ice cream. You eat it, and we call it even?

Ayosa giggled with glee. Deal, she said, and hopped down the porch steps. Then something clenched in her belly. Hold on! she said to herself.

The milkman was loading an empty milk canister onto his front carrier. He did not see Ayosa walk up to him. She grabbed his elbow.

It was an empty elbow. He was an empty milkman. Only his bicycle was solid. He must have nicked it from somewhere.

Fuck-toad, Ayosa said.

It was now a little past four o'clock. Ayosa turned away from the avocado tree where the wraith pretending to be the milkman had tried to snatch her. She took a box of Marie biscuits from the pantry and ran to her mama's studio. Her mama was waiting at the door, leaning on the jamb, smoking a cigarette.

Thought you were going to stand me up, her mama said.

No, not at all, Ayosa said. She did not admit to trying to run off to eat ice cream with the milkman. She said nothing about nearly getting snatched by the wraith.

Good that you brought tea biscuits. The kettle is already heating.

Sometime in the middle of January, her Mama remembered that they had not had much of a Christmas together, and felt remorseful about it. The birds were still singing loudly inside her forest, and she was indefatigable—working long hours in the studio, developing photographs, and then later, working even more hours in the sewing room, making them matching ball gowns. Christmas dresses.

She used velvet fabric that had once belonged to Mabel Brown. She fashioned off-the-shoulder dresses decadently trimmed with pearls and copper coins, with bell sleeves so big you could fit newborn infants in them. Their ersatz Christmas Day fell on the twentieth of January. Ayosa and her mama built a fire and made breakfast on the hundred-year-old waffle iron that had once belonged to Mabel Brown. They cooked eggs and strips of smoked salami. They cooked flambéed crepes, and when the fire burst out of the pan, they pretended to be medieval witches chanting incantations over a cauldron. They ate, and then they wore their ball gowns and roamed through the streets. They went past the smoke-filled hair salons and fish fryer's stalls and brew houses. The world throbbed in their ears, a tangled ball of sound. They isolated each of those sounds, said to each other, This one belongs to that ugly baby of the maize roaster, and this one belongs to that tractor that reaps napier grass for the grade cows, and this one here, this is what it sounds like when a person has saved all their sorrows for you. They threw their heads back and said, Ha-ha-ha, said it so loud that their throats hurt, and they imagined that somewhere out there were a girl and woman just like them, a mama and daughter, who scribbled things inside notebooks for no reason, who hated raisins, who had done a whole lot of Leaving and Waiting, and who, at that very moment, were also walking barefoot on another road, listening as the world throbbed inside their ears.

They said, Ha-ha-ha for that mama and daughter. They said it so that the mama and daughter would hear the sounds of this sweet laughter among the rhythms tangled inside their own ears. A tourniquet for their bleeding hearts. They would say to each other, Jamani, this is what it sounds like when someone thinks of you!

In the late afternoon, they cooked together—pishori rice, and then mutton, fried with garlic, ginger, onion, tomato, and green peppers, seasoned with freshly crushed pilau masala, and then tenderized with yogurt and papaya. They brought the food down to the river and sat on a picnic blanket. They ate from a shared platter, fingers caressing as they reached for tamarind chutney and mutton-soaked rice. As they ate, they watched the birds swaying in the sky. They watched as dandelions and blackjack needles and black-eyed Susans coursed through the air, searching for something to cleave on to. The dung beetles and the praying mantises and the dragonflies hovered near the water, dipping in and out. The wind was yellow as curry powder. It came after them, and it rested at their feet, like a destitute dog.

Nabumbo Promise and Rosette wrapped Lola Freedom in a white bedsheet. At sundown, they buried her in the woods, beneath the casuarinas. After, they sat by the grave with the shovel between them, swatting at mosquitoes, unsure of what to do. In the end, Rosette went to her shack to sleep, and Nabumbo Promise went to the brew house. She drank moonshine. She went home with a stranger, to his one-room tin house three hours by road from Mapeli Town. She drove her mama's jalopy there, drunk and slurring like her mama used to do. She slept on a mattress on the floor, entangled round the stranger's long, bony limbs. He was a logger-man. He smelled like a eucalyptus forest.

In the morning, he went out with his axe, and she gathered herself together, retched in the gutter, and drove back the way she had come. At her mama's house, she made an omelet, and she ate it alone because Rosette did not come out of her shack. She listened to old Louis Armstrong records on the phonograph, and then Jentrix the apothecary passed by, a child tied to her back. Jentrix brought a bouquet of white daisies, wrapped in newspaper, the stems bound together with sisal string. Nabumbo Promise took the daisies, tore the newspaper and string off, and stood them in a vase of cold water.

Jentrix said, Are you back from the convent? Your mother said you two are nuns now.

Nabumbo Promise said nothing. She stared at the child on Jentrix's back. At its dirty face, at the string of beans in its mouth.

Jentrix saw her looking. She said, That's my granddaughter, Temerity. Her father—my son—ran off with another woman. Her mother said to me: I swear to God if you don't bring that man's spawn away with you, I will take a butcher knife and decapitate it.

Temerity whimpered, as though she understood her grandmother's words. As though they petrified her.

Jentrix rocked the baby. She said, Nabumbo Promise, your mama wanted me to come by and clean the windows one of these days. The child has kept me awfully busy, but I think I can do it today.

My mother's gone, Nabumbo Promise said.

Jentrix looked at her for a long moment. She had never heard that voice. She had not even thought that the girl could speak.

Gone? she asked.

Gone, Nabumbo Promise said.

There was something eerie about the way Nabumbo Promise inflected the word.

Jentrix the apothecary turned. She looked about the yard. She saw Lola Freedom's jalopy out by the avocado tree. She saw the crinkle in its bonnet. The broken headlights. The crack in its windscreen. She said to herself, Gone?

Never mind, she said out loud to Nabumbo Promise, and started back to her cottage. She walked fast, and when she got home, she locked her doors, shut her windows. She took out a vial of sandalwood oil and rosewater, smeared some on her forehead and on the snot-faced child's forehead too. Earth Mother, she whispered. Earth Mother, do not forsake us.

For days, Nabumbo Promise sat on the porch steps. She played checkers on her own. She took naps on a reed mat. She walked through Mapeli Town, camera hanging down her hip. She photographed the townspeople: the man who hawked mousetraps at the marketplace, the woman who fried termites on the street corner, the boy who went door to door and sharpened people's knives. She drank Stoney Tangawizi at the Coca-Cola kiosk. She visited the logger-man's tin house and returned home smelling like a eucalyptus forest. She cleaned her mother's house, scrubbing the dishes, burning trash in the corner of the yard, driving empty bottles out to the glassworks factory.

She waited to feel something—anger, pain, sorrow, grief. She sobbed because she felt nothing at all, and the crazy-birds laughed at her. And she thought of how her grandmother Mabel Brown had become a taxidermist just to trap these birds and skin them and hack at their body cavities and gut them. To stop that terrible cackling of theirs. But the jolly annas, as it turned out, could not die. They gritted their proud little beaks and puffed their sewn-up chests. They flew right back into the sycamores, even when their insides were nothing but galvanized wire and polyester resin. Screeching, Jolly anna ha-ha-ha.

Nabumbo Promise felt scraped out, hollow inside. She felt like her body cavity was filled with galvanized wire and polyester resin too. Like she had been sewn all the way up. She wished that Rosette would emerge from the woods, with a guinea fowl in her hands. She wished that they would sit next to each other, saying nothing, just chewing on salted meat and watching the crazy-birds together.

Ayosa gazed at her mama. Nabumbo Promise looked like a hibiscus flower, so delicate, so tender, so radiant. Tears sprung to Ayosa's eyes. Tears of joy. Tears of sheer, unbridled affection. She loved her mama deeply. She wished that she could break her open and be ensconced inside her like her organs and blood vessels and muscles and ligaments. She wanted to hear the birds screeching in her mama's forest, hear her heartbeat roar like a savage beast, hear her moon rising and beckoning to the tides that washed her bones clean. She wanted to possess her mama, like a soft thought, like an oil-slicked thought, like a dainty firefly thought.

Her mama looked at her, eyes sloped, smile crooked, plum-colored lipstick smeared over Cupid's bow, and she said, Ayosa Ataraxis Brown, you want to be more than just a daughter to me, don't you? You want to be sisters too. You want the priest to come right this instant and perform a sister-making ceremony. I can see it in your eyes—that's what you are thinking.

Yes, Nabumbo Promise Brown. That's exactly what I'm thinking.

And her mama gathered her like a precious little creature, a bunny perhaps, and held her to her bosom, matching their faces, so that now the two of them were twins, eye of the same eye, and nose of the same nose, and mouth of the same mouth, except that one twin had sprung from the depths of the other. Ayosa could finally hear those birds inside her mama—larks and indigobirds and shrikes. Jolly annas too, cackling that mean-spirited cackle of theirs, all sharp, like glass shards. Jolly anna ha-ha-ha. It was a terrible cacophony inside her mama.

Nabumbo Promise was working in the studio.

Ayosa was supposed to be at school, therefore she could not possibly spend the entire day hanging about the house, lest her mama see her and grow suspicious. So she left. Went to Mutheu Must Go Café. She found Sindano worked up, pacing up and down between the plastic chairs.

What happened? Ayosa said.

Sindano stood at the window and looked out into the street. Got visited today.

By whom?

Sindano pointed. Ayosa walked up to her and looked. Two men were walking away, pastel blue suits sparkling in the sunshine. They rounded the bend and disappeared into thin air. Sindano walked to the counter and grabbed a mug from a stack. She placed the mug down in front of Ayosa.

Who were they? Ayosa said.

They said they were from the Department of Health and Sanitation. They wanted to make sure that the portrait of the president hanging on my wall was not dusty. Then they wanted to make sure that I fried maandazi with sunflower oil and not hydraulic fluid. And then they wanted to make sure that my fingernails were not rimmed with dirt. Well, they are. Look at them! I am rolling greasy dough all day. What can one expect? So they said I had violated the food preparation codes, and that they had no choice but to arrest me. Said I had to follow them to the police station. So I said to them, Wait a minute! I'm following you nowhere. How do I know you are what you say you are? That got them all panicky. They ran out of here like their bloomers were full of termites. Saying to me, Madam, we forgot to bring the search warrant . . . And so I knew right then that they were just a pair of wraiths trying to snatch me.

The bell in the window tinkled. Sindano crossed herself. Wajamani-that-cow-is-dead, she said.

You should have touched them, Ayosa said.

Now, how would that help?

You would have seen that they don't have any flesh at all. That their body is made of smoke. All empty. That's what I do whenever I get suspicious that someone's not a real person.

Sindano shook her head vigorously. Remember how Bessie managed to fool me ten times? Pretending she was a man? That was no smoke lying down with me all those nights. That was a man, a *rock-hard* man. I reckon it's because I *see* things. My eye looks at the pretense flesh, and my mind's eye fills that flesh out. It's a collaboration of sorts, between seeing and believing. See, when *you* touch a wraith and know with all certainty that there's nothing there, just wisps of smoke, me, I touch her and I feel all her tendons and ligaments, all her veins and arteries. The two that came here today even took my hands in theirs in order to inspect my fingernails. I didn't detect a thing *then*. What gave them away was my own intuition. I thought, No one's been here to eat for more than a decade. Why would anyone care about my dusty photographs? My cooking oil? My fingernails? So I said, Gentlemen, I've got to see a search warrant and an arrest warrant too before I let you take me anywhere. That took them off guard. I suppose they get no law enforcement training. They are really foolish, the wraiths. Conniving, but dumb as footstools.

Sindano?

Yes, my name?

Maybe the wraiths are growing desperate by the day. Maybe they aren't finding enough bodies to steal.

Sindano turned to Ayosa. No, that's not it at all. Open any newspaper, and you will see reports of missing persons in the back, next to the obituaries. They have bodies in abundance.

Ayosa shivered at the thought. She said, Maybe we should talk about something else.

Sindano had a tea towel slung over her shoulder. She grabbed it and waved it at Ayosa as she spoke. She said, Ayosa Ataraxis Brown, we've got to discuss this. It will do you no good to bury your head in the sand.

Sindano took out a knife and halved some lemons. She squeezed them into a bowl. She grated their skins, made syrup with brown sugar and the zest of the lemons. Then she mixed it all up in a jug and added a handful of ice cubes.

You like lemonade? I suppose I should have asked before I made it. But if you don't like it, I can make you something else too. Maybe pineapple juice?

Lemonade's okay, Ayosa said, and accepted the glass that Sindano offered.

Listen, Sindano said. You got some new visitations recently? By wraiths, I mean.

The other day, one tried to snatch me. Pretended to be the milkman.

Sindano nodded gravely.

I don't understand, Ayosa continued. You told me that wraiths come to you masquerading as the very thing you want most in the world. But see, I don't want the milkman in any type of way.

Well, it's not the milkman that you want, just what he represents. Someone loving you enough to bring you milk to nourish your bones. You want the care. The attention. That's what the wraith came to you pretending to be.

Oh, Ayosa said. Are they usually so persistent? Coming often?

No. That's unusual. That's why we ought to pay attention. Me, I haven't been visited since that time Bessie tried to snatch me. But they came in just now, which makes me think that maybe it has something to do with you.

Ayosa's eyes widened. Me? Ayosa Ataraxis Brown?

Sindano sipped from her own glass. Look, she said. They want something from me, and they want something from you too. She sipped again, then wiped her top lip with her wrist. She said, You know that I *see* things. I think maybe they want to snatch this vision. It would make them mighty dangerous to *see* a person's deepest afflictions. They would prey on them so terribly. I'm thinking that with my vision, they could catch *you* more easily. It's you that they want.

Why do they want me so bad?

Guess it's something to do with your memories from the Yonder Days. It's what interests them.

Ayosa pursed her lips. What do they want with them?

Oh, my dear, you saw a whole lot of things. A whole lot more than you remember. You have intimate knowledge of most of the townspeople, even though you try your best not to let your mind wander there.

But this knowledge would be invaluable to the wraiths, if they snatched it from you. Catastrophic for everyone else. They could decimate the entire town. That's why you've got to be careful. You understand?

Ayosa nodded.

I know you do, Sindano said. She gave Ayosa a warm smile. She said, Now tell me, how's your mama? I was there in the church the other day when she let her mouth run like a broken sewer. Dorcas Munyonyi started a petition after that. Tried to get all the townspeople to sign an eviction order. Wants you and your mama kicked out of the town for *endangering the townspeople's moral compass*. No one but Dorcas and that priest of hers signed the petition. Must have done it while he was lying on top of her in the sacristy after Mass.

Ayosa giggled. Sindano frowned. She said, Sorry, child. I should not speak such mud to you. It's inappropriate. She finished her lemonade. Then she said, Tell you what, I've got a surprise for you.

Really? Let me guess—a potato gratin with pork belly and lots of cheese and broccoli inside it?

Sindano laughed. Apologies for having to disappoint you. It's not that at all.

Sindano brought her thumb and index finger to her mouth. She whistled. Right then, a thing, all black and furry, like a giant pompom, barreled through the open doors, yapping. It ran straight for Ayosa and leapt into her lap, slobbering all over her arms and neck.

That's Hurulaini, Sindano said. Found him tied inside a burlap bag, floating downriver. Someone was trying to drown him. Thought you might like the company of a sprightly pup.

Ayosa giggled because Hurulaini had his head in her belly, trying to bore in, like a mole digging itself into the ground. Stop, she said, breathless. Stop, stop! Hurulaini, you're smothering me.

She got up and ran across the café, in between the chairs, and

Hurulaini followed, floppy ears turned inside out, tongue lolling, eyes rolling like a pair of dice. He was making a fool of himself on purpose, like those clowns in the marketplace, the ones who wore women's frocks and stuffed their brassieres and underpants with newspapers in order to exaggerate the sizes of their bosoms and rumps. The ones who made tasteless jokes at their own expense. Clenched their throats so that their voices came out high and squeaky. Picked a man from the crowd and hit him with their fists and said, Look at me, I'm a *feminist*. It seemed like that was what the puppy dog was doing right now. Putting on a show for them. Waddling about like an old woman. Demeaning himself. Saying, Look at me, I'm a *bourgeois poodle*.

Sindano laughed and slapped her knees. She said, Is this a puppy dog or a comedian?

Ayosa curled her lips. That's enough, Hurulaini!

She did not like those street performers. They always made her ears burn. Fremdschämen—that was the name of this type of feeling. Shame on behalf of another person. She had read about it in the encyclopedia.

Ayosa did not want a dog that desecrated itself just so it could be petted. Just so it could get scraps of food.

Hurulaini, that's not funny.

Oh, it is, Sindano said.

Hurulaini snapped out of it. He studied Ayosa's face. Searched inside her eyes. And right then, there was a gentle tug in her gut. A pleasant warmth radiated from her navel, as though someone were drawing patterns up her belly with the stringy feathers of a peafowl. She recognized the sensation. It was Hurulaini's sweet Please-please-please-I-need-you. Begging her to take him home with her and *keep* him.

I'll be good, his eyes were saying. Real good.

The Jinamizi knocked Ayosa down on the veranda, and she fell, with Hurulaini yelping madly and tugging at her clothes, and when she did not wake up, he lay down between her feet and licked her toes.

The Jinamizi brought her memories of women burned at the stake for being witches. Of girls taken apart limb by limb, like Barbie dolls. Of men lined up on a parapet, and shot, one by one, each crumpling down like an origami frog. Of death marches—to mountains and seas and deserts.

Now she was watching one of those death marches. Children trudging on in single file, under the unforgiving sun, all of them wizened by hardship, wrinkled like dried figs. The smell of urine burned their nostrils. One girl wore a dead comrade over her shoulders, like a rain poncho. She and the others, they were all ten years old or younger.

Calves, the soldiers called them.

Now the soldiers noticed her, noticed the girl with the rain poncho. They pried it off and tossed it by the roadside.

Lord have mercy! the girl gasped.

She watched how the white-rumped vultures roared as they descended from the threadbare trees. She watched how voraciously they dug into the rain poncho, tearing it into shreds.

You, move! a soldier called.

The girl wavered, and the butt of a Kalashnikov rammed into her skull.

The Jinamizi left Ayosa. She leaned against a tree, disoriented. She sat there, trying to slow her careening heart, trying to right her wayward breath. She wondered why the Jinamizi never brought her happy memories. Was it because joy got passed down through generations, in songs and legends and tales, while pain got stuffed away, buried in unmarked graves? Was it because not all ghosts stayed down, and some got spat up, and they needed for someone to light candles, pour libations, sing dirges, bloody their scalp, look them right in the eye and say, I *see* you?

As soon as Ayosa was steady on her feet, she thought of round things, and she twisted her waist. She danced chakacha for all the dead whom no one had mourned. Chakacha for the ones who got worn over shoulders, like rain ponchos. Chakacha for the children with the smell of urine burning their nostrils. Chakacha for the ghosts that got spat up, that were lurking in the trees. Chakacha for the calves wizened by hardship, wrinkled like dried figs.

Ayosa went out to the woods, walking through the weeping ferns and morning glories, her shoes sloshing in the wet earth. It was past four o'clock, which meant that school was out, that she could present herself to her mama, no questions asked.

She knocked on the door of her mama's studio.

Come in, we're open, her mama called in a cheerful voice.

Ayosa poked her head in.

Oh, it's just you, her mama said.

Nabumbo Promise was hunched over a wooden crate, arranging receipts inside a plastic folder.

You sound disappointed that it's me, Ayosa said, kicking off her muddy shoes.

What's *that*?

Dog.

Whose?

Mine.

Since when did you get a dog?

Since today. Sindano gave him to me.

Her mama curled her lips, smashed her cigarette against the glass ashtray, and turned away. She said, What is it with you these days? Sindano this, Sindano that. Who is this Sindano, your new mama?

Ayosa crossed her arms over her chest. Her mama's jealousy was a thing entirely new to her. She did not know how to deal with it. Should she gloat? Should she stoke it like kindling, make it crackle? Or should she recoil from it, as though it were a mangled mouse that a cat had vomited onto her shoe?

She frowned. She thought, Poor Nabumbo Promise Brown, so used to doing all the Leaving, so used to seeing me stay put at home, doing all the Waiting. Nabumbo Promise is supposed to know people, and I'm supposed to know only myself.

No dogs allowed in here, her mama said.

There's no sign saying that, Ayosa said. She set Hurulaini down. She said, He's a good dog, Mama. He won't ruin anything.

She watched her mama work. It used to be that she needed her mama in a desperate, anguished, forlorn way, the way a sunflower needed a sunbeam, the way parched earth needed the heavens to break open and quench it. When had things changed? The day she had violated her mama with her *gleefulness*? In any case, her need for her mama was all different. She needed her like a hungry mouth needs a glob of something to chew. Could be anything—peppermint gum, clam chowder, the cat's mangled mouse, a spool of thread. She needed *people*. Could have been anyone, really.

They were in the front room of the studio.

Help me clean this place, her mama said.

Ayosa wet a rag and wiped the table in the corner. She emptied the ashtray. She moved the stack of *Popular Photography*, aligning it with the edge of the table. She picked up the dirty mugs and saucers by the recliner. She folded the afghan and slung it neatly over a chair.

Her mama dragged out a metal box from the next room.

What's that? Ayosa said.

Prints that I have been meaning to frame for a long time. Seydou Keïta. Rotimi Fani-Kayode. Samuel Fosso. Jean Depara. Malick Sidibé. Many others too.

Her mama paused to catch her breath. She knelt, unhooked the keys from the carabiner on her waistband, and poked each into the padlock in turn.

Oh no! None of these keys work.

She stood up and stared at the box, as though willing it to open itself up. It did not.

Fuck-toad! Ayosa said on her behalf.

Potty mouth! her mama admonished.

Ha-ha-ha, Ayosa said.

Her mama frowned. Buttercup, please remind me to check the kitchen drawers later. The key must be there somewhere.

There was a knock on the door. Ayosa and her mama looked up. Come in, we're open, her mama called out in a cheerful voice. To Ayosa she whispered, It's open house today. People are coming to get their portraits taken.

A woman clambered up the front steps, handbag clutched tight beneath her arm. The woman's face was taut, like tanned leather. Her lips were stained a deep red, as though she had spent the morning up some branches in her yard, sucking at tree tomatoes. Her kitenge headgear was so elaborate that it touched the four corners of the ceiling. Her perfume, a mixture of jasmine and citrus, was cloying.

Nabumbo Promise pulled out the tripod and mono light stand from their storage corner in the darkroom. The woman placed her bag down. She sat grandly on the recliner, her legs crossed, a small mirror in her hand. She puckered her lips at the mirror. Satisfied with the condition of the lipstick, she snapped the mirror shut and stowed it away inside her bag.

Nabumbo Promise showed her where to stand. The woman held her arms akimbo. Her smile stretched out, treacly and unnerving, crawling across the apples of her cheeks. Nabumbo Promise peered into the viewfinder of her Minolta Hi-Matic. She frowned. For the next few minutes, she haggled with the woman. She told her that her headgear could not fit in the frame of the photograph, and the woman retorted, You if you do not know how to photograph people just say so instead of crying headgear, headgear.

Nabumbo Promise breathed in. Okay, she said. Whatever you wish, madam.

Ayosa switched on the radio. In the news, a man had been shot dead outside Club Dakar at Rustic Kiambogo Trading Center in Gilgil. He had been arguing with a soldier over a waitress that they both fancied.

Me this world, where is it going now? the woman murmured, shaking her head. A man will kill another man over a waitress! If it were a secretary or a teacher I would understand. But a *waitress*?

Nabumbo Promise glanced up at the woman. Madam, if you are ready, on the count of three . . . One . . . two . . . three!

When the woman left, Nabumbo Promise threw the windows open to let out her lingering perfume. Then she filled a kettle and switched it on. While the water boiled, she jotted notes down in her daily planner.

———

Ayosa studied the framed photographs that hung on the wall. A boy in a polo shirt, collar fastened with a shoelace, a Band-Aid over a gash on his forehead. A woman in a batik dress and wide-brimmed hat, hair short and silver, falling over her jaw. A girl on a seesaw, her face twisted in glee. Her shirt read *United Colors of Benetton*. Boys in pin-striped suits standing in a queue, their trousers hardly touching their ankles, a priest before them, about to give them their first Holy Communion. A child in a woolen sweater, sitting in an armchair, eyes bleary.

The kettle whistled. Her mama poured hot water into a mug, dunked a tea bag inside it, and sipped. She walked to the window and lit a cigarette. She took a drag from the cigarette and then exhaled out into the veranda. She said, You know, I was thinking about you today.

You were thinking about *me*, Ayosa Ataraxis Brown?

Her mama chortled. Is that a thing so difficult to believe, that a mother would sometimes think of her own daughter?

Ayosa said nothing. She did not feel like debating her mama. Saying, Let's be honest now, you only ever think about yourself. Instead, she said, What did you think about when you thought about me?

Her mama was silent for a long moment, staring out into the sunshine. Then she said, About the thing you said the other day. That you *remember*.

There was a knock on the door.

Come in, we're open!

A couple walked into the studio, fresh from their marriage ceremony. The bride had one main face onto which was drawn a dozen other faces, each layered haphazardly over the last, and all the faces were heaped so high over each other that they become mounds, appendages, vestigial brides fresh from their own marriage ceremonies.

The bride sat on the recliner, and the recliner hobbled, and her stringy legs got tangled inside the lace of her wedding dress. The bridegroom fell to his knees and worked at the lace, separating leg from dress. The groom's name was Chrispin. He did not say so—it was just a thing that one saw when one looked into his face. He had two Bic biro pens in his shirt pocket. A black one and a blue one. A dense forest of hair climbed over his topmost shirt button. He carried a jerry can of kerosene with which the bride would soon cook their wedding meal. Some of the kerosene had seeped out and left an oily square on the leg of his trousers.

It took ten minutes for Nabumbo Promise to set up a suitable background for them—a large canvas onto which was painted a picture of a rain forest. All the while, the groom stroked the bride's hand and told her about the stone house he would build for them behind the airport at Embakasi. He told her that their house would have a Sony television caged in the corner of the sitting room. No one would watch that television, though, because in their stone house they would be rich and rich people had no use for the things that they owned. In their stone house, they would have a red, east-facing window on whose iron grille the bride could hang her brassieres to dry. He stroked her hair and told her that every evening, they would sit on their sun-baked veranda and drink bone soup and watch as airplanes jumped from the ground and went to America.

They stood before the canvas, and the bride held her hand up and her toe out so that later, when the photograph came out, there would be an illusion of her clutching at a liana, of her wriggling her white shoe inside the clear waters of a creek. Her new husband stood behind her, arm draped chastely round her shoulder. When they left, Nabumbo Promise got two sodas from the next room. She pried them open with the base of her cigarette lighter and handed Ayosa one.

Tell me what you remember, her mama said.

Hurulaini licked the salt off the soles of Ayosa's feet. She bent down to rub his furry neck, and her mama grimaced.

Look, her mama said. Suppose I believe you . . . which I don't . . . But in a hypothetical sense, what do you *remember*?

The Yonder Days.

You mean the old days? Before you were my baby girl?

Yes, Mama.

A fly buzzed about the mouth of her mama's soda bottle. The fly lingered, and then was sucked into the sweet, sticky vortex. It clung on to the surface of the Stoney Tangawizi, flailing its arms. Nabumbo Promise pushed the bottle away, harder than she meant to. It toppled over, the soda spilling onto the floor. She crumpled up a newspaper sheet and wiped the floor with it. She tossed the newspaper away.

Nabumbo Promise got up. She walked through the studio, flipping off all the lights. Ayosa grabbed her puppy dog, and they started for the door. As they made their way to the big house, Ayosa stopped every so often to pick up flowers. In the end she had a bouquet of peach-colored bougainvillea in her hands.

For you, my lady, she said to her mama.

Her mama stooped so that Ayosa could place the flowers in her hair and in her buttonholes and in the backs of her ears. Are you courting me, miss? she said.

Yes, Mama! Ayosa giggled.

When they got home, they sat on the porch steps, and they ate butterscotch gelato and blackberry slushies. After, her mama got a pot started, with chicken feet and cow's tongue and pig's eye in it. The milkman brought them a wheelbarrow of manure from his cattle, and Ayosa and her mama repotted their plants, transferring catchfly and cross berry and adenium from plastic bags to terra-cotta pots. Later, her mama took out infusions that Jentrix the apothecary had given her—cloves and deadly nightshade and saffron. She ran a bath, and she and Ayosa sat steeping inside it.

Won't you answer me? her mama said. I asked you something earlier. At the studio. I asked you: What do you remember?

Plenty, Mama. You've got to be more specific if you want to know.

Hurulaini lay in the corner of the bathroom, snuggled on Ayosa's shoe. Ayosa wished her mama were gone—off to a nowhere-town, or sunken inside herself, lost in the red city. She wished that it was just she and the puppy dog sitting inside the tub. She wanted to pick through his fur with an Afro comb. Rid him of fleas. She wanted to work coconut oil through his coat. And after, to rub his belly, find that spot that made dogs lose their minds, that spot that made their hind legs get the shakes. She wanted to spend the evening with Hurulaini snoring in her lap. They would sit at the kitchen table, both their bellies distended with chicken feet, and they would listen to the death news, listen to the Fatumas' shuddering grief.

Her mama said, Do you remember Maxwell Truth?

Ayosa nodded.

What do you remember about him?

He had dirty-brown hair.

He had fidgety hands.

He had a birthmark, a strawberry hemangioma on his forehead.

Nabumbo Promise and Rosette would often fight over who ought to hold Maxwell Truth. They were three years older than him. Their mother was gone a lot, and so they carried Maxwell Truth on their backs and brought him everywhere with them. They chased rock hyraxes and flamingoes and banded mongooses. They caught stink bugs and June beetles and water scorpions in their palms. They cut Maxwell Truth's hair with paper scissors. They bathed him on the sandy bank, and let him float out as far as he wanted because the river was a good river and always brought him back.

One day, Maxwell Truth choked on a potato wedge, and Rosette grabbed him by the diaphragm and performed abdominal thrusts on him. Their mother had taught them the Heimlich maneuver when they were quite little. She figured that they ought to keep an eye out for each other. And that's what they did. And Maxwell Truth spat out the potato wedge and laughed.

Another day, Nabumbo Promise and Maxwell Truth were walking through the bramble, plucking berries, staining their fingers purple with the juice, when a snake bit Maxwell Truth on the arm. Nabumbo Promise rushed him to the river. Set him down on the rocks. His face was turning a bluish-gray color. He was gone for sure, she thought, because he neither stirred nor made a squeak of a noise. Still, she ripped a strip of fabric from her frock, and she wrapped it above the bite. Then she brought her mouth down to his arm. She sucked on the venom and spat it out. Sucked and spat out.

Maxwell Truth returned to her, laughing. She tugged at his little ear. Why is dying so funny to you? she said.

———

Stop, Nabumbo Promise said.

Ayosa stopped. Now she studied her mama.

Nabumbo Promise, who was slender as a cypress needle, with hip-bones that poked out like antlers. Ayosa memorized all the scars that she could see, so that later, she would open her notebook and add them to the place where she kept a record of her mama's body. *Shrew on right shoulder blade. Field cricket between breasts. Koi fish near elbow.*

Her mama reached for the cigarette and lighter on the window ledge. She ignited the flame and took a puff. She rested her head on the soap dish. Rinds of smoke curled above her head. Ayosa slunk back so that now she was lying inside the tub, watching bubbles dance, watching shreds of things float on the skin of the water above her.

Don't stop, her mama said. Telling, I mean. About Maxwell Truth.

What do you want to know?

About the day he drowned.

Lola Freedom was at home, sitting in that blue farmhouse rocking chair. Gazing out. Watching as the crazy-birds cried, Jolly anna ha-ha-ha! Lola Freedom had been away in her red Cessna for weeks, and Maxwell Truth had missed her. He clambered up the stairs. Stumbled through Lola Freedom's door.

Mama? he said, holding out his arms, begging to be picked up. He was too young to understand that Lola Freedom was not to be bothered when she sat in that rocking chair like that.

Lola Freedom turned around, furious at the interruption. She grabbed the first thing she could find. A side table of heavy teakwood.

She flung it at him.

At Maxwell Truth.

And they both fell.

Lola Freedom into her blue rocking chair, and Maxwell Truth down to the floor.

Nabumbo Promise and Rosette were in the kitchen when this happened. Eating canned artichokes that their mother had brought with her from God-knows-where. They heard the crash above and leapt up. Ran after Maxwell Truth. Found him on the floor.

They fell to their knees and lifted the table off of Maxwell Truth.

He lay still. His eyes were open. He was blinking. His lips moved. He let out soft mewls. Nabumbo Promise and Rosette lifted him up, but he could not stand. Something was wrong with his body. As though the bones inside him were now zigzag instead of straight. They pulled off his sweater and saw that his neck was floppy. His head could not stay up on its own.

Nabumbo Promise and Rosette took Maxwell Truth away. Carried him swinging between the two of them. Down the stairs. Out into the cold night air. Through the sycamores, with the crazy-birds following.

Their mother had once told them that it was cruel to let a creature suffer when it was gravely injured. That sometimes the kindest thing to do was to put it out of its misery. So, they dragged Maxwell Truth out to the old well in the middle of the woods, in the middle of their mother's property.

They did it quick as they could, so as not to prolong his suffering. They lifted the tin sheet covering the mouth of the well. And they dropped him in. They heard the gentle splash as Maxwell Truth hit the water.

Then they covered the mouth of the well once more, pinning the sheet down with rocks so that the crazy-birds would not go in and eat

Maxwell Truth. After, they walked away, sobbing with anger at their mother.

How *dare* she?

Maxwell Truth was a sweet little boy. He laughed often. He wore pepper grass in his buttonholes. He brought them earthworms and leopard orchids and shards of mirror glass that he had found in the dirt. He brought them owl flies and screw pines and paper planes.

They were angry at their mother, not for hurting him per se, but for her making it so that *they* no longer had a Maxwell Truth. No one to wade through green, frog-infested ponds with. No one to put on a cardboard sled and push down the hill. No one to run through the bad-smell melons with. Their anger was at being denied a plaything.

The next morning, their mama awoke from her stupor, and asked where Maxwell Truth was, and they went and showed her. She did not fish him out, just covered the well back. And she spent that whole day drinking. And that whole night weeping. And the next morning, she telephoned the police, and they would not take the twins away. So she took matters into her own hands. She scooped them up into her jalopy and drove them out to the orphanage.

Nabumbo Promise was silent for a long time.

Studying Ayosa's face.

Then she reached for another cigarette and lit it. She lowered her head, exhaled, kneaded her right shoulder blade.

She said, Who told you all these things?

No one told me. I was there. I saw it all for myself.

Nabumbo Promise shook her head vigorously.

I can't, she said. I just *can't*.

And she got up from the tub, abrupt and graceless, making pools of water gather on the terrazzo floor. Wordlessly, she took a towel from its hook on the back of the door, wrapped herself with it, and disappeared into the dark corridor.

Hurulaini the puppy dog looked at Ayosa with his worshipful eyes, yellow as mustard in the evening light, and he leapt to his feet and ran up to the hand that she held out to him. He licked her fingers, and she stroked his ears, and then he buckled down and sat in the pooled water on the floor as though he were a dumpling in a saucepan of stock.

I can, he was saying with his eyes. I just *can*.

17

On Saturday, Ayosa did not need to pretend that she was off at school all day. She awoke at six and spent the early hours of the morning reading *Charlotte's Web*. Then she took coins from the cookie jar on top of the refrigerator and went to the market. She bought a bagful of oranges, haggling with the market women for the thrill of it, receiving their steely insults for the pleasure of it too. They called her names. Kettle-hand for being so miserly, and mongrel for being so bastardly, and deranged for being one of the Brown girls.

That's how it always was when one went to the marketplace. The vendors were ruthless. They cackled like maniacs and ganged up on you to show you all the ways you were nothing, nothing at all to them.

We don't need your coins, they said. We are doing *you* a favor, offering you our wares for next to nothing.

And then they laughed, and they called her an aphid of a child, an arachnid, a sorry red louse, just as the enraged woman—Dorcas Munyonyi—had done at the Catholic church on New Year's Eve.

Ayosa laughed with them so as not to cry. What else could one do? She threw her head back and said, Ha-ha-ha.

And they said to her, Now hurry along to that cunt mama of yours.

Her mama was still asleep when Ayosa returned home. She made marmalade—separating piths and pips, chopping up rinds, boiling the oranges with a half kilo of sugar. She sterilized some jam jars in the oven, and then she filled them with marmalade, and she stood them upside down on a kitchen towel to vacuum-seal them.

Later, she beat an egg into a glass mixing bowl, and she added milk, added cinnamon powder, added sugar and vanilla essence and baking powder and all-purpose flour. She whisked the mixture, switched on the stove, and prepared a stack of pancakes. At eleven o'clock, her mama came down the stairs, her bathrobe tight over her naked body. Her eyes were puffy, the bags underneath them like air-filled half cakes. She said nothing at all as she brushed past Ayosa, as she filled the moka pot with coffee grounds and water, as she set it on one of the stove plates and waited.

You slept well? Ayosa asked, even though she knew the answer already. Her mama looked like a mob had waylaid her in the middle of the night, like it had assaulted her with crowbars and baseball bats. She shrugged off the question, and when the moka pot whistled, she poured her coffee into a mug and went out onto the veranda.

I made pancakes, Ayosa called after her mama.

Her mama lit a cigarette.

Ayosa carried the pancakes out. She brought a jar of marmalade, still warm, the sugar not yet congealed. She took a pancake, spooned golden marmalade onto it, and held it out to her mama. Her mama took the pancake, and she looked at it as though it were something exceedingly strange, like a woman's foot roasted and salted and buttered up. Her mama tossed it onto the ground.

Hurulaini the puppy ran up to lap it all up. Tail wagging. Eyes rolling with ecstasy.

Why do you got to behave like a big old child? Ayosa said.

Her mama slapped her so hard her teeth shifted, and she tasted blood in her mouth, sour as rain from a tarnished tin roof.

Then it happened by reflex, like a sneeze rippling through her nose. She slapped her mama back. Her mama's coffee mug fell, splattering coffee all over the veranda. Ayosa and her mama stared at each other, eyes raging red, and dynamite shards detonating and then smoldering beneath the mounds of their tongues. And Ayosa thought, I *hate* her. And she thought, If there was a well right here in front of us, I would push her into it.

Ayosa could not bear to be near her mama. Could not bear to be near the heat radiating from their hatred of each other. She grabbed the puppy dog and the transistor radio, and she ran through the yard that was not a yard but a tangled ball of thorn trees and wildflowers and barbed wire and stiff yellow grass. She meant to go down to the river, but then she got distracted when she saw the hen Matasia and her babies who were now not babies at all.

She noticed that they were pecking rabidly at their feathers.

She took ahold of one of the pullets and, sure enough, saw the wretched critters scuttling in the down feathers. Red mites.

Ayosa had read in an animal husbandry book that chickens that were infested with red mites could soon die of anemia. In a panic, she made her way to their coop, and she raked off the grass bedding and burned it, and then hosed down the whole coop.

The book said to wash the chickens in pyrethrin. She had change in her pockets. She went to the hardware shop, and she found fertilizers and insecticides next to locks and paints and toilet plungers. She spent the next hours bathing her chickens.

Temerity, the shiny-eyed, snot-faced girl, saw her doing this and laughed. People say there's crazy in all the Brown girls, she said. Maybe they are right. I mean, why are you washing those hens as though they are little suckling babes?

Ayosa was in a sour mood because of her mama and because she thought her flock of chickens was dying. She said, Look, Temerity, I say nothing about your periwinkle and your decoctions and your litanies to the Earth Mother, even though people call it *deranged*!

Temerity looked down, ashamed. She said, What's the matter with the chickens?

Mites.

Need help?

Ayosa shrugged. Do as you please.

Temerity moved closer. She helped Ayosa bring in a new grass bed and lay it down in the chicken coop. She said, Miss Brown, look! Killer bees!

Ayosa lifted her head. Saw a ball of bees hurtling in the air toward her. Temerity dropped her armful of dried grass and ran off.

Ayosa waved her hands, said, Hello there! Mbote?

She let the bees climb all over her, buzzing in excitement. They crawled in her nose, in her throat. They tried to wedge into the spaces beneath her toenails.

She said, What is it? Do you need me to come with you?

She followed them through the trees, to the clearing where she had built their home for them. The bees sidled away. She lifted the top crates of the hive, studied the frames inside it. She found several wax moth larvae, which she squished dead with her chisel. She found gunk building up in the bottom of the crates and knew that this would only attract hive beetles. The animal husbandry book said that hive beetles could cause hive collapse, that prevention was certainly better than cure.

Ayosa busied herself with scraping the gunk off with her chisel. Then she inspected the crates for wood lice and termites. Glad to find none, she changed the water that she always kept close by for the bees.

Ayosa whistled, and Hurulaini the puppy dog came running to her. She lifted him into her arms. Down the hill she went, and then through the fields of bristle grass and juniper bushes. The puppy dog stuck his tongue out like a flag hanging at half-mast, and he panted, and his foul breath made Ayosa gag. She set the dog down, and he followed from a distance, stopping to sniff at tree trunks swollen from strangers' urine.

Ayosa walked to the river, and she roamed about the rocky shore, searching for things that people had lost, and then picking them up into the scoop of her frock. She found a pack of playing cards with the king of hearts missing. She found a yard of fabric with the warp yarns frayed. She found a poster of a pinup girl with holes poked into her eyes and nose, and with her teeth colored with red ink. She found safety pins hooked together into a necklace. She found a lightbulb that flickered and sparked when you rubbed it against your arm. She found a braid plucked out of someone's scalp. She found a mannequin that wore a loose-fitting gingham dress. She found a jar of formalin, and a can of garden peas, and a tube of skin that a snake had shrugged out of. She found a canoe and a child's bootie and the frame of someone's monocles. She found a pair of firestones that clinked in your pocket and set fire to your frock when you walked.

She dug a hole in the wet sand and stuffed all these things inside it and covered it again and marked the place with a two-pronged stick. There were a dozen two-pronged sticks down the shore, where she had once dug into the sand and buried other things inside. In her note-book, she kept a roster of which hole had what things inside it.

Then the river rushed out to meet her, overjoyed at the sight of her. She took off her frock and wrapped the transistor radio inside its skirt. She yielded to the river, let its currents take her deep inside the water. Arms outstretched, she stroked things as they drifted by: An azolla fern. A steel tape measure, stiff and crimson with rust. A heart-shaped glow stick. A raffia hat with a violet pinned on its side. A shoal of fishes swimming in spiral formation, like a corkscrew. A girl's locket with a chicken beak inside it. A bandana wrapped in twine. A wig made from purple merino yarn.

Later, when she emerged from the water, she found Hurulaini the puppy dog curled up on her frock, whimpering with sorrow. He saw her coming, and leapt up, and launched himself at her knees, tail wag-ging wildly, and that pink slimy tongue of his still hanging at half-mast.

You left me, he said to her with his russet eyes. You said you would not leave, and then you did.

I said no such thing, Ayosa retorted. Look, you can't *need* me. It will do you no good. I needed my mama and see how that went.

She reached for the transistor radio and switched it on. She lis-tened to the four o'clock news, and then Ms. Temperance came on with one of her poems. She said:

> *I think of the girl with the ants in her socks*
> *who gave her mama French toast for breakfast*
> *and coconut rice for lunch and a skinned cat in her*
> *soup for supper. The girl watched her mama eat*
> *the soup watched her pick the bones clean saying*
> *mama it's a cockerel that I caught for you in the*
> *yard. Cooked it special in the lard. And after her*

mama chewed on those soft feline bones, this
girl that I knew went down to the creek and
counted the stars and thought, How lucky is it that
skunks and butterfly cods and lonesome girls
have the great undulating sky all to themselves?

Ayosa looked at Hurulaini, with tears standing in her eyes, and she said, Ms. Temperance knows me. She *knows* me. How does she know me?

Woof! Hurulaini said.

He was barking at a tree. She looked up the branches, saw Mbiu with Bwana Matambara on her neck.

That dog wants to eat us up, Mbiu said.

No, he doesn't.

How do you know? Feral dogs always want to eat something up. Always stirring trouble. Starting things.

He's no feral dog, Ayosa said, and picked up Hurulaini in her arms.

He's *yours*? Mbiu asked, eyes wide with surprise.

Sindano gave him to me.

Mbiu climbed down the tree. Didn't mark you for a dog person, Ayosa Ataraxis Brown. Rats maybe, or mongooses, or bush babies, because you're sort of strange. Dogs are so . . . *ordinary*.

Ayosa laughed.

Mbiu said, I've got something.

What?

It's in my car. Wait here.

Mbiu walked out into the trees. She returned with an axe head, some firewood, and a catfish.

You like catfish?

I suppose, Ayosa said. Did you steal it from the fishmonger's stall?

I'm an orphan. People should *feed* me. I should not have to steal.

She built a fire. Then she took a switch knife out of her sock. She slit the belly of the fish, used a stick to scrape out its entrails, and then set it down over the fire.

We need sugar-names, Mbiu said.

What's a sugar-name?

Something sweet that you call a person you like.

Ayosa scratched her head. She said, What about . . . er . . . "Potpourri"?

Mbiu looked up from the fish, eyes gleaming. I don't like "Pot-pourri."

What do you like, then?

"Tetanus." What about you, Ayosa Ataraxis Brown? What do you like?

Ayosa contemplated it for a little while. "Apple-crust," she said.

Mbiu spat into her hands and rubbed the saliva over the grime on her legs. I wish I had kwashiorkor.

Because why do you wish that?

Because how terrible can a disease be if it goes by such a pretty name?

Bilharzia is the disease that I would like to have. It sounds so nice.

Rinderpest too, said Mbiu. It's a cow disease, but I would like very much to have it.

They spent the rest of the day like that, roasting fish, eating it, talking about different diseases that must feel nice to have. Then their mouths yearned for mustard seeds and for ginger roots and for fruits that they called rheumatoids and that leaked sticky pink juice when you bit into them. They looked for these rheumatoids, found them in the bramble, and sucked on them. The sun went down and the evening breeze was warm.

We should dance, Mbiu said.

What type of dance should we dance? Ayosa asked.

What type of dance do you know?

I know chakacha.

What's chakacha?

Well, you close your eyes and think of all the round things you have ever seen, then you try and draw those round things with your waist. Look!

Ayosa thought of vinyl records. She thought of glazed doughnuts and Tylenol tablets and the lids of mason jars. She thought of her mama's hoop earrings. She thought of colanders and the holes of pencil sharpeners and glass ashtrays.

When she opened her eyes, she saw tears streaming down Mbiu's cheeks. Lord have mercy, Mbiu said. Apple-crust, that was the most beautiful dance I ever saw.

Ayosa drove home in Mbiu's car, tugged by Magnolia the horse. She jumped over the gate and stood waving until Mbiu disappeared down the dirt road and into the grove of jacarandas and casuarinas.

Come on, Hurulaini, she said, and walked toward the house. The kitchen light was on. She kicked off her shoes at the porch steps, pushed open the door, and went in. Her mama was sitting at the kitchen table, fiddling with an old camera.

Sit, Nabumbo Promise said, and Ayosa sat down across from her.

Ayosa's hatred for her mama from earlier in the day was gone. In its place was bewilderment. She was not used to this at all. She was not used to her mama's being *there* after a fight. She was used to her mama's storming off when angry. Being gone for so long that Ayosa could not remember what they had fought about in the first place. Sometimes her mama picked a fight with her for no real reason at all. She only needed a pretext to jump into her jalopy and drive off. So she quarreled with Ayosa over untied laces, or wrinkly hankies, or the obnoxious sound of her sneezes. And her mama screamed, I can't stand you! Problem child! See, this is why I always leave you!

Other times, her mama said nothing. No goodbye given. No excuse offered. She just left. And Ayosa sat out in the yard and watched the jolly annas and nursed her wounds. Promising herself that soon, very soon, she would be the one who did the Leaving.

She stood staring at her mama.

You're still here, Ayosa said.

Told you I was done leaving you on your own, Nabumbo Promise said.

That doesn't make a lick of sense. You always go. What made you be done this time?

Her mama frowned but said nothing. Ayosa watched her. She could see it clear as spring water, there in her mama's eyes. *Fear.*

What are you afraid of?

The red city. Been falling into it more often than I care to admit. I reckon it's no longer safe to go traipsing about far from home.

Ayosa let out a wry laugh. Ha! There had to be a *good* reason. You weren't done leaving me on my own. You just couldn't any longer.

Po-tay-to, po-tah-to! her mama snapped.

Ayosa took a deep breath. Bit her lip. Tried not to be riled up by her mama's flippant attitude. She said, Where did you go, anyway? Every time you got sour at me, and you jumped into your pickup and left me alone, where did you go?

Work, Nabumbo Promise replied, shrugging. I took on assignments. Went out to the field with my camera and covered stories for the newspaper.

For months at a time?

No. Usually for weeks at a time. After, I would just drive on, from bar to bar, and city to city, and lover to lover. On the road, I was someone else. I got seduced, I got wasted, I got lost, I got found, I got imprisoned, I got scammed, I got so high that I could see my mama flying her red airplane up in the clouds, and I got so low that I could see her bones thrashing in the earth's crust. Which is to say that I went away and I was full of passion out there. I lived life like my petticoat was on fire. And every night, I dreamed of you, Ayosa. You came to me wearing rumpled linens and tap-dancing shoes. With that indignant snarl on your mouth. With those wrathful eyes rolling like millstones in your skull. Sometimes in my dreams you had a shiv between your teeth and you spat it out and slashed my throat. Sometimes you had a jerry can of battery acid and you poured it over me and burned my face.

Ayosa's toes curled. Hearing her mama admit all this was oddly cathartic. Her mama was baring herself. Not denying and not apologizing and not searching for any pity or forgiveness. Ayosa had asked for a fingernail and received the whole arm and the whole torso too. Her mama was conceding. Handing Ayosa all the weapons that she possessed.

Are you afraid of me, Mama? Ayosa asked.

A little.

You think I could kill you?

I think that if you did kill me, I would certainly deserve it.

Ayosa laughed. She peered into her mama's hands and saw that her mama was holding the first camera that she had ever truly owned. It was a Pentax 35 mm that her sister Rosette had gifted her years ago, right after her stint with sepsis. Ayosa remembered it all.

———

After the busted knee mended, Nabumbo Promise started standing on street corners. Then someone—a kid on a BMX, or a man with a chipped front tooth, or a woman with a naked baby on her hip—came to fetch her. Said, Picha-Woman, you are needed quick-quick. And Nabumbo Promise would follow whoever had come to seek her. She photographed day-old infants, or two-headed goats, or brides-to-be in their unyago kitchen parties, their faces twisted in dismay as elderly aunts demonstrated to them how to touch a man in a way that would finish him.

One day, a nine-year-old girl came to fetch her. She said that it was her first Holy Communion. That her papa had thrown her a party, and she was to have her first taste of red wine. Her papa wanted a photo of the girl as the wine touched the back of her throat. As the blood of Jesus Our Lord and Savior filled her inside.

The girl said, Picha-Woman, hurry up, my papa is waiting.

Nabumbo Promise eagerly followed, camera dangling over her shoulder. The girl led her off. Into an alleyway. Her papa was waiting there all right. Chewing on mswak and listening to a football match on the radio. No party. Just a knife, which he drew and pressed to Nabumbo's neck. The girl and her papa robbed Nabumbo clean of everything that she had, even the clothes on her back.

She walked home covered by nothing, nothing at all. It was the middle of the day. Everyone turned away from her nakedness as she dashed through the streets. They shook their heads sorrowfully. One woman offered her a head scarf that she had unwrapped from her own hair, but Nabumbo Promise was too prideful to accept it. One man went to the telephone box on the street corner. He called the mental hospital. Told them that one of their inmates had escaped.

After this incident, Nabumbo Promise moped for weeks, refusing to get up from bed, neglecting all personal hygiene, recoiling from the memory of her humiliation. When Rosette could stand neither her moaning nor her revolting smell, she went out and spent her entire salary on the Pentax. She came home and threw it at Nabumbo Promise. She said to her, You had better get your life together, Nabumbo Promise Brown.

Nabumbo Promise saw Ayosa looking at the camera. She said, Fifteen years ago, it truly confounded me.

What did?

Nabumbo pulled at her earlobe and then leaned forward in her chair. She said, How everyone acted as though photographs were something ordinary, how no one ever gawked at them. Of course I knew how cameras worked—pinholes, lightproof boxes, prisms, and so on. Still, I always imagined the photographer to be a kind of sorcerer. All these years later, and it still confounds me. Each time I see a photograph, I am gobsmacked. It's as though I am part of a primitive tribe, as though I am seeing the sorcery of pinning people onto squares of paper for the very first time.

They sat in silence for a long moment. Then Nabumbo Promise said, Do you remember when you were younger, how you stood in the yard and chased after the dried leaves drifting down from the trees? You said that catching them brought you luck. You said it with such conviction that I joined you too, because I needed all the luck that I could get. We spent entire afternoons chasing after the golden leaves. Catching them. Counting them in our laps to see how much luck we were bringing home with us.

One day, we were outside waiting for the leaves to fall. This time, it was the dandelions that came visiting. We didn't know where they were traveling from. There were millions of them, bobbing together, swirling above us in a great cloud. You said, Quick, Mama. All the luck in the world is contained in that cloud! And again, you said it with such conviction that I thought we would die if we did not catch some dandelions. So we spent what felt like hours out in the yard, you and me, jumping up and down, trying to catch some dandelions in our fists. And we did. But we could not make them stay with us. We could not keep them whole. The florets were fragile and they broke apart in our fingers. That made you cry. You said it meant that we only had shredded-up half-luck, and that half-luck was worse than no luck at all. Holy tripe! It scared me to hear you say those words. It felt like I had handed a fortune-teller my palm to read. Do you remember?

Ayosa nodded. She was eight years old back then, and long used to her mama's lengthy absences. She would come home from school, drop her satchel on the veranda, and climb a tree. She crawled to the very top branches, there where the sky's underskirts sometimes got snagged, and she hummed and swallowed the gnats that flew into her mouth. She tried to recall the words to Ms. Temperance's poems that she'd once heard on the radio. *I don't have no soul swirling inside me like fog over boggy marshes just ask my mama she made me this way dogged beast that I am all bite but no bark.* And she looked over the camphor trees, watching out for wandering spirits, watching out for the marabou storks and honey badgers that sometimes ate lonesome children, watching out for her mama's wobbly jalopy. Sometimes her mama came. Most times she did not.

When Nabumbo Promise did come, Ayosa made up silly games for them to play. Catching those dried leaves was one of the games that she made up. She had not really believed that the leaves brought any luck. All she had wanted was to keep her mama right there in the yard with her for as long as possible. To occupy her with leaves and sticks and dirt so that her mama would not go away so soon.

Nabumbo Promise studied the camera in her hands. She said, Didn't mean to pick at old scabs. I was only thinking, you see. I was only searching for a good metaphor. Those dandelion florets that broke apart in our fingers, I was thinking to myself that memory does the same. It's so thin. So fragile. It comes drifting and we jump up and down to catch it. But it breaks apart. When we photograph, we ask the camera to catch the dandelions of our memories. To keep them whole for us. Photographs help us to remember. I've been thinking about this all day. About the camera lens as an appendage of sorts, an external eye to which we delegate the task of memory. Remembering. Re-membering parts that fell apart. Reconstituting them.

Okay, Ayosa said. She wished that her mama would release her from the obligation of sitting there and listening. She wondered how much longer she had to wait until it was appropriate to say, I have seen you, we have talked, I will go to sleep now. She looked up to find that her mama was staring at her.

What?

I've been thinking about you, Ayosa Ataraxis Brown.

There's nothing to think about me.

There's plenty to think about you. Such a curiosity you are! You claim to remember. To re-member, just like a photograph. Looking at you, I start to understand why those primitive tribes could not bear to see images of themselves in the photographs. I start to ask questions which those primitive tribes must have asked the photographer: What gives you the right to re-member? What gives you the right to access the archival material stowed away in our subconscious? To excavate and unbury memories that do not belong to you? That's what I want to know. I want to ask you: Do you realize how violent your re-membering is, Ayosa?

I don't care, Ayosa said.

You don't *care*?

I can't help that there's violence. There was always violence, Mama. I didn't cause it. I found it there. As to your other question . . . I give myself the right to re-member. The memories are mine. Mine! *You* never have to constantly look at the violence. *You* forget it easy. *You* close your eyes and turn the other way and receive the mercy of forgetting. For me, there's never any mercy. Never any forgetting. If I forget for a moment, then the Jinamizi comes chasing me and makes me remember. So, if I have to see the violence, and wear it under the skin of my eyes, then it belongs to me too and I have the right. So there!

Jesus! her mama breathed. She rubbed her temple. She said, What shall I do with you, child? You're more than I can handle. You're more than I deserve.

Ayosa frowned. This sounded like pretext. It sounded like her mama preparing to leave. It sounded like her mama preparing to say, You are too good for me and I always ruin good things so I had better go before I ruin you all the way through.

Ayosa lowered her gaze and waited for the other shoe to drop.

Her mama let out a long sigh. They sat in silence, listening to Hurulaini's soft snores. After a long while, Nabumbo Promise said, I could not remember all those things about Maxwell Truth. But then the other day, you said them to me, and suddenly the memories came gushing forth like a sewer that burst. Just like it happens when I look into a photograph. I could not sleep the last nights, for all the remembering that you made me do.

Nabumbo Promise lit a cigarette.

She said, Lord! I need a whiskey sour!

She got up. She fetched a glass and poured herself some bourbon. She fumbled about at the kitchen counter, cutting and squeezing lemon, stirring sugar, separating egg white from yolk. She took a sip from her drink, then she closed her eyes to relish its flavor.

In a half whisper, she said, How do you do it, Ayosa?

Do what?

Remember.

I don't know, Mama. I don't do anything. It's just the way it is. The memory unwinds in my head like a roll of film.

Her mama frowned. I think there is an explanation. You found their journals, didn't you?

Whose?

My mother's. My grandmother's. I know that you taught yourself to read at a very young age. Let me tell you, I was astounded and frightened and horrified when I caught you reading the newspaper out loud. You were just three years old, Ayosa! What business did you have breaking that kind of code? I took you to the doctor, begged her to cure you. I said, Mrs. Doc, there's got to be some syrup that can fix her. She's broken. She's *reading*, and no one taught her how. The doctor only laughed at me. She said not to look a gift horse in the mouth, even though I could see clear as anything that that was no gift, only a curse!

Nabumbo Promise shook her head, as though outraged afresh by the ordeal.

I have a theory, she continued. You found their journals. You read them. And you adopted their memories as your own. You didn't mean to. You didn't even know that you did it. Memory can be quite fickle. Sometimes we take on other people's memories as our own.

Nabumbo Promise finished the rest of her drink in one gulp and made herself another.

I have a second theory, she said. It's my mother's ghost. Up in the attic. My mother is the one that's telling you these things!

Ayosa shook her head in disbelief. Nabumbo Promise had no problem believing that the ghost of her own mother lived up in the attic. She had no problem leaving her daughter behind to be cared for by that ghost. Yet she drew the line at *this*? At believing that Ayosa could have these memories?

I don't care what you think, Ayosa said. I was a wriggling thing before I turned into a girl. I was there! I saw what I saw. And I *remember*!

Were you there the day my mother took Rosette and me to the orphanage?

Ayosa nodded.

What do you "remember" about that day? Nabumbo said, using air quotes to emphasize her skepticism.

I remember Lola Freedom's swollen eyes, from weeping all night for Maxwell Truth. I remember your dry eyes, from not-weeping. Rosette's dry eyes too. I remember that you and Rosette sat pressed to each other. You wore matching denim dresses, red bows in your hair, spectacles so scratched up they were almost opaque. You wore safety pins in your earlobes, for earrings. Your mother wore dark sunglasses, a wide-brimmed sun hat, a silk smock. Her hands trembled on the steering wheel—she really needed some Hennessy.

I'm taking you to Girl Guides camp, your mother said to you, her voice hoarse. You will have lots of friends there.

You and Rosette flinched. You had never been the type of girls who needed to have any friends. You were not even friends with each other.

Your mother said, You will learn how to gut fish, and how to rub sticks together to make fire, and how to know which berries are safe to eat.

You and Rosette silently chewed on sugar-coated peanuts.

I'll pick you up in a week, your mother said. In that moment, she truly believed this. She thought that a week was enough time to grieve for a boy and forget him. But grief does not work like that. You can't hurl lamps and vases at it, can't tell it to hurry itself up or else you will hurry it with your own two hands. Your mother did not take the boy out of the well. She sat in her rocking chair and cried for him. Then she climbed into the red airplane and went off. She could not stand to be near you, or near the house, or near the town, which was aghast at the news of the drowning.

She hated us.

She didn't hate you. Matter of fact, she understood what you must have felt.

What do you mean with that?

Ayosa chewed on her lip. She jiggled her feet. Hurulaini whimpered. She picked him up and laid him in her lap. She stroked his curly black fur.

Ayosa, what did you mean?

Ayosa shrugged. She said nothing. She was already regretting this entire exchange with her mama. She could tell that it was headed nowhere good.

Please, Buttercup, I'm begging you to tell me.

You won't like what I tell you. You won't believe it either. So, let's drop it. Me, I am tired. I will go to bed now, Mama.

She began for the door. Her mama moved to block the doorway.

Sit! Nabumbo said, pointing at the table.

Ayosa froze. Slowly, she walked back and slid into her chair.

Now tell me!

Well, okay, since you really want to know. Lola Freedom understood what it was like to kill a person. She had killed her own mother. She had killed Mabel Brown.

That's not true. That's simply not true.

It is too.

No! her mama said, slamming her hand on the table. I know what *happened*. Don't lie to me, Ayosa Ataraxis Brown. The crazy-birds making that jolly anna ha-ha-ha sound, they drove my grandmother mad. So she blew her head right off with a musket. Everyone in the town heard the shot ring out, and they knew, they just knew, that it was the old hag doing everyone a favor by ending herself. Later, they searched everywhere for her. No one could find her, so they thought that the crazy-birds ate her flesh and her bones too. This happened before we were born. But we found her, my sister and me. When we returned from the orphanage, we found her bones in the garden.

Ayosa shook her head. She said, That's the version of the story that Lola Freedom told you. It's the one she wanted you to believe. The one she wanted everyone to believe.

Her mama raised her eyebrows. You're trying to tell me that . . . that . . . God! My mama killed her own mother?

Ayosa pursed her lips. She said nothing.

Answer me, damn it!

Ayosa stood up. She set Hurulaini down on the chair. She walked to the sink and poured herself a glass of water. Looking over her shoulder, she said, Your mama was a bitter woman. Sometimes I still hear her screaming inside the earth, and I rush quickly on by because you taught me to not be compassionate to her suffering. But she wasn't *all* bitter. That's what we must remember about people. That no one is all good, and no one is all bad either.

Nabumbo Promise sucked her teeth. Quit with the speechmaking. Are you Martin Luther King now? I just need you to tell me what happened.

No story is complete unless it's fair, don't you see? I've got to be fair to Lola Freedom if I am to invoke her name with my mouth. She's been dead so long I sometimes forget that she was a real woman. But maybe that's what we've got to do. We've got to shroud flesh over her bones first, make her a person again, so we can *understand*.

Nabumbo Promise rolled her eyes.

Your mother had the nicest hands I ever saw. Her fingers were long and smooth as bamboo flutes. She had an arresting laugh, something that fell out of her mouth and startled strangers right in their tracks. It sounded all wrong. Mismatched. How could a face so severe have a laugh so feathery?

Nabumbo Promise nodded. She said, That woman, she taught me and my sister how to perform CPR and how to make mint chutney and how not to drown in the roiling currents of the river. She taught us how to sit still even when there were flames licking at the soles of our feet. She taught us how to break ground and how to build walled cities inside ourselves. She taught us that prideful silence, that way of caging our tongues behind our teeth. She taught us to move like shadows— gliding in and out, there beside you one moment, and not-there in the twinkle of an eye. She taught us to love but not to dote. To feel but not to break open with feeling. She taught us that there wasn't a hurt in the world deep enough to kill us. She taught us that we might die, yes, but even death itself couldn't kill us.

Ayosa placed her glass down.

And she taught you to be scornful rather than afraid. To be kind, but just enough to have others beholden to you. To belong to no one but yourselves. She taught you that daughters can be loved well enough from a distance.

Nabumbo Promise grimaced. She said, Are you going to tell me or not? What's with the suspense? You think you're Alfred Hitchcock?

Ayosa walked back to her chair. She picked Hurulaini up. She said, When Lola Freedom was fourteen years old, she saw her mother kill a child.

Doesn't surprise me!

Lola Freedom was standing at an upstairs window, watching as children poured pig's blood onto Mabel Brown's front door. Taunting her. Calling her the White Witch. And she saw her mother fire into the air with her musket, as Mabel Brown always did when the children offended her. Except that this time, the shot hit one of the fleeing boys. Lola Freedom saw what her mother did next. She saw her mother stuff that boy's body in an oak coffer and shove it away in the billiard room.

Shit!

The radioman beseeched the town for many months. He said, Has anyone seen Dickson Were, fifteen years old, gap-toothed, with one leg shorter than the other? Dickson Were writes with his left hand and eats with his right. He was last seen wearing a Mickey Mouse crewneck shirt. But in the end, the town forgot about him. They thought that he must have got himself snatched by the wraiths.

Uh-huh?

Your mother, she never turned Mabel Brown in to the police. But she never forgave her either. And she never forgot that boy Dickson. She never forgot his crooked smile, or his caramel teeth, or the way he straddled over cows and rode their backs like he was a surfer boy riding waves.

Really?

Twenty years later, Lola Freedom took her mother's musket and shot her mother in the head with it. It was Dickson's caramel teeth that she thought of when Mabel Brown's brains splattered all over her shoes. It was his litter of savanna hares she thought of too, and his lisp, and the notes he always passed to her in class, saying, *L. F. Brown, I saw a ghost on my way home last night.*

Stop now! I don't know why I even asked. Stop, please.

Ayosa did not stop. She said, Lola Freedom buried her mother in the night. This was right before you and Rosette were born. Lola Freedom killed her mother and then reported her missing. Years later, the rains and the chickens scraping at the earth brought the remains back up like something undigested. Like a cow's cud, still needful of chewing. You and Rosette found the bones. And you kicked her skull about like a football. Then Lola Freedom ran out, shrieking, Christ, was that woman lying in the rosebushes all these years?

Stop!

Your mother couldn't take any chances this time. She had Mabel Brown cremated. Carried her in an urn to the church for her sham funeral. Then she buried her in the rosebushes once again, and after, you all went to the river together.

Nabumbo Promise took a deep breath. She closed her eyes and leaned back in her chair. In a half whisper, she said, That boy, Dickson Were, are his remains still in the billiard room?

Yes, they are. No one ever took them out.

Her mama stood up, chair legs scraping against the floor. The chair toppled over. Crashed against the refrigerator. Liar! Nabumbo screamed. You filthy swine. You blathering ninnyhammer. You foul-smelling ferret. You *con*!

And she leapt over to where Ayosa sat and, in one swift flick of her fingers, grabbed Hurulaini the puppy dog. She raised him high above her head. Before Ayosa could say a word, before she could even compute what was happening, her mama tossed the dog hard at the floor. Hurulaini squeaked like a rubber toy, and startled awake, just in time to catch himself passing away. He thought that he was in the burlap bag, tied by rope, swimming downriver. The waves soothed him. He curled into himself and mewled quietly. Ayosa watched, wide-eyed, openmouthed, teeth chattering, hands trembling. She fell to her knees next to the puppy dog. Touched his wet unbreathing nose. His fat unmoving belly. His open unseeing eyes. She said, Nabumbo Promise Brown, what have you done?

18

The townspeople gargled salt water. They greased their elbows. They tucked flowers in their hair or pinned them on their lapels. They marched to Our Lady of Lourdes, where they sang,

> *Bind us together, Lord,*
> *Bind us together,*
> *With cords that cannot be broken.*

Father Jude Thaddeus swung his gold thurible in the air, and the chains clanged, clouds of incense swirling above his head. He gazed at Dorcas Munyonyi, his favorite faithful. There she was, Dorcas Munyonyi, rising, no longer herself but the Handmaid of the Lord, gliding all the way to the lectern, squinting, turning the pages of the lectionary.

Hem-hem-hem, she said. To the faithful, this was an innocuous clearing of the throat. But it was meant for *him*. A greeting.

Hem-hem-hem, he responded.

How he longed to take her Someplace Else. He would sit her sideways on the back of his Black Mamba bicycle and off they would go.

They would both wear cassocks and white collars, with glass rosaries tucked into their waistbands. They would ride until their knees ached. Then he would give her a sip of holy water, and he would touch the wetness of her tongue with his finger.

He turned away. He never could look at her for too long. His Adam's apple squirmed in his throat like a foraging gecko. His eyes filled up. He bent down, pretended to tie his shoelaces, and squeezed his tears onto the marble floor.

In another part of the town, Mbiu was roaming about with her cat, Bwana Matambara, upon her neck, when she made a disconcerting discovery. Ayosa, her *dear* Ayosa. Her Apple-crust, whose soul was blue like thrush eggs. Who had that sharp jawline, the mouse's ears, the brows that grew wild as thickets, the mole on the cheek, hairy, large as a soda cap. Ayosa, whose mama was full of mud. Ayosa, the loneliest girl she ever saw. Except, it was not her Ayosa at all, but the remains of her. A girl-shaped boulder.

The boulder lay on its back, the yellow-red sun streaming into its granite eyes, making granite tears trickle down its granite cheeks.

Mbiu squatted next to her. Fuck-toad, the wraiths finally got to her!

She touched the rigid stone face. Fanned it with her fingers. Flicked its stone ears.

She said, Please-please-please-I-need-you.

Above her, the jolly annas watched, beaks open, eyes gleaming with dread. Jolly anna ha-ha-ha? they gasped, a question that Mbiu knew not how to answer.

She stood up. HELP! she yelled. HELP! HELP!

Temerity, the shiny-eyed, snot-faced girl, was just passing by, on her way to search for blister beetles for an ointment that her grand-mother the apothecary needed to make. She was chewing on a dirty carrot that she had pulled out of the ground. She saw Mbiu and stopped. She said, You're that girl who peers inside people's windows.

Mbiu said, I need help. Will you help me?

Temerity lowered her gaze and saw Ayosa sprawled there. You *murdered* her?

No. I think a wraith did.

Temerity moved closer. She bent down over Ayosa and examined her for a moment. Maybe she's not dead. Maybe she's got the falling disease, just like her mama. We ought to bring her to my grandmother. She's the apothecary. She will know what to do.

They bumbled through the underbrush, the girl-shaped boulder dragging between them. They each held an arm, but the rough texture of its granite chafed their palms, so they let go, and the girl-shaped boulder fell. It lay facedown in the earth.

She's too heavy, Temerity said, scratching her elbow at the spot where a lacewing had brushed her skin.

What if we roll her?

Mbiu and Temerity tried first with their hands and then with their feet, pushing until the girl-shaped boulder budged. And then, because they were on a steep incline and also because the hill was shift-ing about, the girl-shaped boulder picked up speed, and it rolled down by itself, so fast it became a blur. Mbiu and Temerity ran after it, the stiff yellow grass and the thorns pricking them, tearing gashes into their legs and thighs.

The girl-shaped boulder came to a rest near the apothecary's little wood cottage with the slanted walls and the peeling orange paint. Te-merity called out to her grandmother. Jentrix! Jentrix! The Brown girl turned into a stone!

Jentrix came out of the kitchen. She had been stirring a pot of pigeon peas, and the steam had rumpled her entire face. She wiped herself with the hem of her skirt and squinted in the harsh light. She saw the two girls, and between them, what looked like a corpse. Skin gray and pallid. Lips blue-black. Body stiff with rigor mortis.

Earth Mother, have mercy! What did you do, Temerity?

Didn't do a thing.

That better be true, or I will kill you dead myself.

Ayosa found herself standing at the edge of a jagged cliff. She leaned forward to peer over its side, and immediately vomited into her mouth. There were waters below, she could hear them roaring with fury and spite, yet could not see them due to the curtain of clouds drawn just beneath her. The cliff was so high it touched the hems of the sky.

There was wailing around her, sharp, baleful, echoing wildly. It came from the birds. Sandpipers and sooty gulls, moaning, flapping their wings, and launching themselves like darts, into the clouds below, into the waters underneath them.

Ayosa shuddered, and when she tried to step away from the edge, found that her feet were all cotton wool inside, that they no longer worked. She spat out the bile in her mouth, and then crawled on her hands and knees away from the cliff edge. Now she turned, and saw that she was in front of a gate, made of scrollwork wrought iron, high as a skyscraper. She picked up a rock and began to bang on the gate.

Let me in! she cried. Someone, let me in!

Soon, she realized that her efforts were useless. That the rods of the gate were too hefty, the stone in her hand too puny, and her arm too feeble. Besides, the roar of the water and the wail of the birds below swallowed all sound lesser than a thunderclap.

Please-please-please-I-need-you, she heard.

The voice was Mbiu's. It was garbled. It seemed to come from the gray heavens.

Mbiu! Mbiu! I'm over here! Where are you? Mbiu, can you hear me?

Mbiu said, She's dead, isn't she? A wraith did it. Deaded her.

Now Ayosa heard the apothecary's stern voice, admonishing. Spit out that dirty saliva! Ayosa is not dead.

Then why won't she come back to me even though I'm saying please-please-please-I-need-you?

Because she fell inside herself, Temerity said.

No, Jentrix the apothecary said. She didn't fall inside herself, either. That only happens to her mama.

Then what?

She saw something that pushed her over the edge.

What sort of thing?

Can't tell you that for sure.

And the thing pushed her over the edge of what?

Of fury.

She got so furious she turned into a stone?

She's just having a fever dream. The fury brought it on. Now enough with the questions.

Maybe she did not eat enough sugar. Maybe she needs some jaggery!

Take your filthy hands away from her mouth! You want to be useful? Go to my portmanteau and fetch me a few sprigs of chickweed and lungwort. That ought to make the swelling go down.

Don't know what chickweed and lungwort look like.

Jentrix the apothecary let out an exasperated sigh. Temerity, fetch them for me!

Ayosa was furious.

But about what? She racked her brain, and she remembered what Nabumbo Promise did to the puppy dog. She slunk down against the high gates. Her head reeled. Her teeth chattered. Her toes burned.

She closed her eyes, and now something else joined her, something wet and frigid, something *wrong*.

Her Jinamizi.

It had followed her here. Over the edge of her fury. Inside her fever dream.

She fought against it, gnashing, writhing, biting, but as it always happened, the Jinamizi subdued her.

Now it was a stereoscope, mounted over her head, and she had no choice but to look at the grisly images it brought her.

Men hanging down from tree limbs. And then, women getting their eyes gouged out with teaspoons, their skins scraped off with scalpels. And then, girls abducted, tied up, violated, and after, unclothed of their own flesh, until the bones underneath them were stark naked too. And then, villagers marched into the desert to die of heatstroke. And then, children cleaving on to each other in a gas chamber. And then, a man and two prepubescent children, wearing white hoods, throwing a firebomb into a Plymouth, and eating a picnic of Spam sandwiches and pigs-in-blankets while watching the car and its occupants burn.

Make it stop! Ayosa screamed. Make it stop, I'm begging, please!

When she awoke, she was lying on a divan in the apothecary's cottage. Jentrix was patting her face with a wet cloth.

There you are, Jentrix said. You've come back from your fury.

Ayosa blinked, disoriented.

What happened to cause the fury? Was it your mama? Did she leave you again?

She . . . the puppy dog . . .

Ayosa fell back against the pillow. She could not breathe. Could not see or hear. She felt Jentrix's hands work ointment into the creases behind her ears, and the moist flesh inside her bottom lip, and the webbed skin between her toes. Slowly, her heart slowed. She gulped sweet-tasting air. She focused her eyes on the avocado print of the curtains.

Jentrix said, You almost went over the edge again. Try not to think about what happened with your mama.

Ayosa clenched her teeth.

Jentrix shifted her weight from the edge of the divan. She reached for a bowl on the side table. You must be hungry, she said.

Not at all.

Well, you're going to eat anyway. I'll be damned if you starve under my watch. Open your mouth.

Jentrix settled on the divan next to Ayosa and fed her spoonfuls of rich, creamy spinach soup. The sun shining through the open shutters burned Ayosa's eyes. The apothecary stood and adjusted the shutters.

Temerity went to fetch your mama, Jentrix said.

I don't want to see her.

It's not up to you.

Just then, Temerity came in, shiny eyed and snot faced as ever, except she looked crestfallen, and her lips shook.

What's with you? Jentrix asked.

Ms. Brown said that no thanks, she has little interest in coming here to see her daughter.

And that got you looking like you saw a wraith?

No, madam. I saw *bones*. Ms. Brown has them laid out on the kitchen table. Said she found them hidden in her grandmother's coffer. She said to me, Well, I'll be damned! Ayosa wasn't speaking any mud, after all. Still, doesn't make me want to go see her. And she said to me, Temerity, go tell Jentrix I'm not coming. Got a lot on my mind. Tell her to do what she must with Ayosa.

Ayosa pushed the bowl of soup away. The apothecary looked at her with sad eyes. She shooed Temerity away. Said, Go upstairs and clean your room, Temerity. It's fit for pigs and rats, not a decent girl like yourself.

Temerity went away. Jentrix handed Ayosa a glass of water.

She said, Your mama doesn't mean to hurt you.

Didn't want her here anyway.

Jentrix said, Oh, you did. Look at you, you're hurt. But your mama doesn't mean it.

She *means* it. All my life I made excuses for her. I said, She is just Nabumbo Promise Brown, she does these sorts of things. No harm intended. But fuck-toad! I'm so sick of acting like my mama doesn't mean to be mean. If she didn't mean it, then she wouldn't be it.

Jentrix grimaced. Ayosa could not tell which part had offended her—her foul language, or her obstinate lack of compassion for her mama.

I've waited so long, she said.

For what?

For my mama to say, Buttercup, here is a plate of food that I cooked for you. Eat, my child, so you may grow big and strong. Is that so hard a thing for a mama to say?

It's not as easy as you think.

Why not?

You're a child, you don't understand.

People should stop treating children like some fools. We are not morons, only young.

Jentrix grimaced once more. Do you mind? I don't like to hear that type of language in my house. Jentrix looked down into her hands. She said, I squatted on this land twenty years ago. Your grandmother Lola Freedom, she said I could stay here as long as I kept an eye out on her daughters. They were young girls, only fifteen back then. Broken already when I found them. And quiet as mice—I thought they'd been born mute. Those poor children, I came to love them like my own. Didn't matter to me what the townspeople said. So they drowned their brother, Maxwell Truth? That couldn't be all there was to the story. I knew there were missing pieces to it. Something buried or something forgotten. And knowing that mother of theirs, that Lola Freedom, knowing the way she spent entire days blacked out after a drinking spree, it was quite likely that *she* was the one that hurt Maxwell Truth. That she just could not remember doing it. The girls were so little when all this happened. Only six! Still, they were punished for it. Cast away by their mama, shunned by everyone else. You think that's an easy thing for anyone to get over? It cost them *everything*. It cost them each other. They can't bear to look in each other's faces. Strangers, that's what they've become to each other. Your mama has been running from herself for so long. She falls inside herself too for the same reason. To forget, to be another person for a spell. Now, I'm asking you to bear all this in mind and be a little kinder, Ayosa Ataraxis Brown. Your mama doesn't mean to be mean. She's just so broken up. She's all rubble inside.

Ayosa bit her lip. Tears trembled in her eyes. She wiped them with her arm. No, she said. I *won't* be kinder.

Jentrix placed her bowl down. She said, You always were a head-strong child. I could see it the very day you were born. I held you in my arms, and I saw clear as anything that you were so bent on leaving. You made me beg and beg and beg for you to stay. That type of begging is disgraceful. You made me grovel for your life, Ayosa.

Should never have listened to you.

Jentrix pursed her lips. She stood up, took the soup bowl in her hand, and began for the door. Try to get some sleep, she said.

Ayosa lay down on the divan, head against the pillow that was stuffed with black beans and scraps of sewing cloth. She watched as beads of sunlight dappled on the wall. She thought about what Jentrix had told her. She thought about that day, almost thirteen years ago, when Nabumbo Promise had thrown her away in the water, and Jentrix had come and fished her out.

Jentrix burst into the back room, pot of water and muslin cloths in hand. Nabumbo Promise was on her side, staring at the slats of the wall. Her new baby lay beside her on the divan, swaddled in a fleece blanket.

Are you feeling better?

Nabumbo Promise did not respond.

Jentrix set the pot down on the table. She placed a hand on Nabumbo's forehead. She said, I'm mighty glad your fever is no more.

Lord knows, you were hallucinating when you burst in here in the night.

Jentrix unwrapped the baby from its blanket. She dipped a muslin cloth in the warm water in the pot, wrung it out, and began to wipe the baby down. It squirmed but did not slip from her firm grip. Jentrix lifted the baby closer to the light.

You birthed your mama! Even the mole, on the exact spot on the cheek as your mama's used to be. All that time you spent running from your mama, only to bring her back like this!

Jentrix let out a chuckle.

Nabumbo Promise pulled the coverlet up to her chin.

Her eyes are a little yellow, though, Jentrix said. You should latch her on more frequently.

She pressed her finger down on the baby's arm to see the severity of the jaundice, and then sighed with relief. It's not all that bad, she said. I will watch out for it, so don't you worry yourself, Nabumbo Promise.

She dressed the baby up and swaddled it in its blanket once more. Then she sat at the foot of the bed, with the baby's forehead pressed lightly against her chin. She began to rock back and forth, humming softly, even though the baby was not fussy. Jentrix was troubled by its stillness. It was alive, yes. Breathing, yes. Open-eyed, yes. But this terrible stillness turned something in the pit of Jentrix's stomach. The baby did not like it here. It was deciding for itself whether to leave or to stay. Stay, she pleaded.

Jentrix sat on her stoop, watching the chickens and ducks in her yard. In the distance, she saw the milkman on his bicycle, riding up the hill.

She raised a hand in greeting. Then she stood up and walked round to the back. Nabumbo's jalopy was parked over the roses. Jentrix sucked her teeth.

The soil here was much too wet and much too heavy for the flowers, but she had cajoled them for months on end, knelt for them like a jilted lover, stroked them, made libations to them, until, in the end, they sprouted for her. Now they were all ruined, crushed beneath the jalopy's weathered tires. Jentrix set her tea down on the window ledge and moved closer to the jalopy. She peered inside it.

This was where Nabumbo Promise had tried to bleed herself in the middle of the night. She had driven out into the woods and waited for her baby to cross the threshold to her. It came and she laid it down and hoped that they would slip into the darkness together. Then Nabumbo Promise caught a fever. It brought with it an instinct that was steelier than Nabumbo's greatest resolve. And so, without her own knowledge, and without her own consent, Nabumbo Promise had driven madly to the apothecary's place. She had staggered out of the jalopy, the baby now blue in her arms, still attached by string to her body.

Jentrix was stoking the hearth, stirring tomorrow's lentils, when Nabumbo stumbled in. Please-please-please-I-need-you, Nabumbo said.

And Jentrix knew, she just knew, that these words were not Nabumbo's. Something beyond Nabumbo was calling out.

Now Jentrix searched for the rubber pipe, found it coiled inside the lemongrass thickets, and stuck it to the mouth of the garden tap. She opened the doors of Nabumbo's pickup and let the stream of water crash inside it. She hosed the seats and the floor mats.

She hosed the dashboard and the windscreen. She hosed the gear lever and the steering wheel. She hosed the headrests, hosed the glove compartment, hosed the pedals.

———

Later, Jentrix melted vegetable fat in a pot. She fried onions and garlic and ginger. She chopped up two ripe tomatoes and let them sizzle in the fat. She added cubes of sweet potato, coconut milk, and split yellow lentils that she had slow-cooked overnight. She seasoned this with salt, curry powder, bouillon, and some hot pepper. She let it simmer, then ladled the stew into a bowl and sprinkled over it a sprig of fresh coriander from her herb garden. She went to the back room. The door was ajar.

Nabumbo Promise, you must be hungry now, she said, poking her head in.

Nabumbo Promise was not in the room. Jentrix put the bowl on the side table, next to Nabumbo's cloudy spectacles. She drew back the drapes and opened the windows to let the sour air out. The sheets were soiled. She stripped the bed and tucked in new ones. She stuck her hand through the open window and plucked a bunch of crimson bougainvillea. She placed this on top of the coverlet.

Nabumbo was probably out back, sitting with her baby in a wicker chair, assessing the damage she had caused to the roses when she drove over them. Jentrix let herself onto the veranda. Never mind the flowers, she said.

But Nabumbo Promise was not there, either.

Nabumbo! Nabumbo Promise Brown! Jentrix said, scrambling into a pair of gumboots. The wood of the veranda creaked beneath her feet. A spiderweb clung to her face. She ran out into the grass, wiping the silky thread of the spiderweb off her cheek. The sun blinded her with its orange-yellow light. She raised her hand to her forehead and peered out. There was no one in the dirt road that led up the hill to the crumbling mansion that Mabel Brown had built.

There was no one by the blackberry bushes. There was no one by the wattle trees.

Jentrix took the footpath that meandered through a clump of timber. Above her, wagtails and barbets flapped about, delirious. She quickened her pace. The timber turned into tufts of grass. The grass rolled and turned into sand. The sand turned into mangrove stalks and hyacinth and the carcasses of crayfish. Beyond this was the river, trembling as though it were cold deep inside its bones. Jentrix swept her eyes across the riverbank. She saw a figure lying on the rocks.

Nabumbo Promise!

Jentrix broke into a run, her frantic movement frightening the flamingoes and the shrikes and the Egyptian geese. The figure was Nabumbo Promise all right, curled up in the sand, eyes squeezed shut. Her sleepshirt was soaked with river water. She had baobab seeds and stork feathers in her hair.

Where is the baby? Jentrix said. Goddamn it, Nabumbo, answer me!

The river lapped at the baby, yearning to crawl into her, to enter her and fill her inside. It held her tight and whispered, Stay here with me. It coaxed and coaxed, until she yielded to it, and now all the things inside it—the pebbles and jetsam and fishes—clambered over her, tugging, wanting so bad for her to stay down there with them too.

The baby sank inside the water. She spun about in a shoal of things that people had lost. Ceramic flower vases. The stoppers of earrings. The chimes of a grandfather clock. Newspaper cuttings with crossword puzzles on them. The scent of primrose on the back of a stranger's ear. A night-woman's hair strands stuck to the teeth of a comb. An eyelash here, a whistle there, and laughter everywhere, deep and garish.

The baby was a thing that someone had lost too. But it was not lost for very long. Someone came to find it. There was sloshing, splashing, large hands dragging it out. A voice drawing it back into the sunshine. Saying, Your name is Ayosa Ataraxis Brown, and you are wanted here. And the voice began to plead. Please, it said. Please, I'm begging you, you've got to stay, you've got to forgive her, she didn't mean to throw you away in the water, please, Ayosa, please, she's been through so much, her mind isn't right, please, look I'm down on my knees, look I'll tear my clothes off, look I'll cut off my tongue, look I'll burn my eyes out, please, is that what will get you to stay?

A yosa gave up on sleep. She climbed the steep, narrow stairs to the attic room that belonged to Temerity. Temerity called it a turret, as though she lived in a sprawling castle rather than a shabby wood cottage. Jentrix the apothecary had built it herself, with her own two hands. She had felled the trees, debarked the timber, and dried it and hewed it. Then she had cut out the windows with a saw, had traded some of her sugarcane crop for windowpanes and roofing bricks, had fashioned out a floor from flattened bamboo stalks.

Temerity's bedroom was trapezoidal in shape, with walls that she had plastered with yellowing newspapers. Temerity was rummaging through the old reed cupboard where she stored her clothing.

What are you looking for?

A fifty-cent coin. I had it in my pocket yesterday, but now I don't anymore. Think it might have fallen in here. I want to buy an ice lolly from the corner shop.

Temerity continued searching for a few more minutes.

Jentrix says I can help you clean.

It's clean enough, Temerity said. She gave up on her coin.

Now she dug around for her bucket, found it beneath her bed. Her implements—knife, clippers, trowel, sickle—clanged inside it. She tucked them inside the large front pocket of her frock. She and Ayosa ran down the stairs and out into the sunshine.

Temerity, what's the color of your soul?

Manganese.

What color is that?

Something close to maroon, but with some green in it.

Sounds like vomit, Ayosa said.

What's the color of *yours*, Miss Brown? Temerity said.

Blue. Like thrush eggs.

Temerity and Ayosa walked through the flower garden, among the neat rows that Jentrix had planted. Temerity inspected each bloom, gently feeling its stem for any slime.

The canna lilies won't make it, she said.

Because why?

Because the nights are too cold nowadays, she said. Then she squatted and began to peel off mushy foliage. The roses won't make it either, she added.

They don't look sickly at all.

My grandmother says that the river is moving closer and closer to us. Roses can't grow with so much water near them, Jentrix says.

They walked slowly through the rows, plucking dead leaves and petals and insects from around the stems. They snipped the ones that were good enough for Temerity to bring over to the flower-monger's shop. They were walking back to the cottage when they heard a curious noise—the clippity-clop of hooves, the crunch of tires over the gravel of the narrow path, and then twigs and tree branches noisily breaking apart. A horse neighed.

Holy Earth Mother! Temerity exclaimed. When she saw Magnolia, she dropped her bucket and ran off.

Apple-crust! Mbiu called, sticking her head out of the window. Quick, get in, before the apothecary comes and forbids you from leaving with me.

Where are we going?

Don't know. An adventure.

Ayosa jumped into the passenger seat of Mbiu's car, and Magnolia steered them away. Mbiu leaned forward, grabbed Ayosa, and held her tight. They sat there, gazing at each other, fingertips brushing lightly, and then fingers grasping at each other, clutching at each other.

They matched each other thing for thing—wriggliness, loneliness, solitude, even the constant state of waiting for their mamas to return to them. They matched each other thing for thing—the aching that gnawed at them, the yearning that filled them inside, the fear that consumed them. The fear of being all alone in the world. Their hearts slammed in unison.

Don't you ever do that to me again.

Do what?

Try to die on me. You turned into a stone!

Didn't do it on purpose.

Mbiu leaned back into her seat. She took out a slab of jaggery and chewed on it. She tossed morsels of old bread at her cat and pigeons in the backseat.

What happened? Ayosa asked.

Mbiu gave her a sidelong glance. Don't you remember? I found you. I screamed and Temerity heard and came too. We brought you to Jentrix. I thought that you were dead-*dead*. That a wraith finally got you.

Where did you find me?

On the hill, halfway between your mama's house and the apothecary's cottage. Figured you were headed to see Jentrix when you turned into a stone. Do you remember any of it? Do you remember running? Do you remember turning into a stone?

Ayosa shook her head.

But your thing is remembering. Why can't you *remember*?

I only remember my mama. I remember that she . . . she . . .

She what?

Killed my puppy dog.

How did she kill the puppy dog? Fed him Rat & Rat?

I don't wish to go over the details of what happened. Bottom line is the dog is dead and my mama did it.

I want to cuss out your mama, but I know you'll get all fizzy mouthed if I do it.

Oh, I don't care about protecting her honor anymore. She doesn't have *any*. Matter of fact, I don't care about her at all.

So, if I call her a nasty hag, you won't care?

No.

And if I call her a bloody trollop, you won't care either?

No.

And an old twat?

The vein in Ayosa's forehead twitched. She had the urge to smack Mbiu's teeth. Make her bite the tip of her tongue. But for what? Her mama sure didn't deserve Ayosa's loyalty. And besides, Mbiu was only provoking her to prove a point.

Mbiu looked at Ayosa. Doesn't matter! she said. Mamas are full of mud, anyways. Nothing anyone can do about that.

Yours wasn't full of mud.

She was too, I'm telling you.

Because why?

Because she should have thought of me before she went and got herself all shot up. She left me alone. *Alone.* I'm never ever going to forgive her for that.

Ayosa stared blankly out the window. She watched the trees darting by, swift and green-blue and blurry. They were hurtling past the clock tower when Magnolia the horse saw a barrel of water and stopped to take a drink. He dozed off, fell asleep while standing right there in the dank corner, with his chin on the lip of the barrel. They did not want to rouse him, so they climbed out of the car and stood barefoot on the ground.

Got to pee, Mbiu said. She disappeared behind some bushes. Ayosa waited by the car, and when Mbiu returned, they walked together into the clock tower. Ayosa stood at the door and stared at the bats thwacking the high roof, and at the rats scurrying about at their feet. She thought to herself, I've been to this here place before.

Mbiu watched her, scraping earwax out of her ear hole with the tip of her index finger. You're remembering something, aren't you?

Ayosa nodded.

What?

My mama, when she first got with my father. He brought her here one time.

Ayosa thought of that day. Thought of the song—Miles Davis's "Freddie Freeloader"—playing on Nabumbo's pocket radio, the chords echoing against the musty brick walls. She thought of the smudges of drawing charcoal on Nabumbo's frock. She thought of her mama's hair, how crinkly it was from having been fastened in the same bun for weeks. She thought of how her father, the logger-man, had put a dried flower in Nabumbo's hair. It was a peony. He had found it in the pocket of a used leather jacket that he had bought from the open-air market. He did not know how many oceans that peony had crossed to find its way to them. It seemed emblematic of their affection for each other—peonies did not grow in these parts, were wrong here, and yet, here it was. Nabumbo stood still while he pinned the flower down with a barrette. She watched him with large, kohl-rimmed eyes.

Did you ever ride in your mama's airplane? the logger-man said.

Nabumbo Promise shrugged. Even though it had been four years since her mother's death, Nabumbo Promise was still raw inside. She said, You know I don't like to talk about my mama.

She patted her wet, sweaty hands against her frock. She had sewn it herself from a linen curtain. She had mixed dye from turmeric and water, and then block-printed tangerines all over the fabric.

Nice tunic, the logger-man said. Pretty, like. Brings me home to my mama's orchard. And he laughed, and he added, I never had a mama, and if I did, she would never have owned an orchard. Orchards and things like orchards, those are for *your* mama to have owned.

Nabumbo Promise frowned. Speak one more word about my mama and I swear to God you'll never see me again.

The logger-man raised his hands. An unspoken apology. He punctuated the apology by reaching into the back pocket of his corduroys and taking out sachets of rum that he had bought from the corner shop. He handed Nabumbo Promise one, and they tore them open with their teeth and sucked on the liquor. What's that? he said.

Nabumbo Promise had an envelope beneath her arm. She opened it, showed him a handful of photographs. She had developed the film herself, turning the closet in her bedroom into a darkroom, fumbling her way between tubs of developer fluid, spilling some, ruining her best coat. The photographs were of dead things—housefly on a windowsill, rabbit in a stranger's coop, toenail on a beggar's foot, ox head in an earthen pot, and then, last of all, a shoulder, slender, bony inside a nun's white habit. The shoulder was not really dead, but it belonged to someone who was dead to her.

Pretty, real pretty, the logger-man said. How come everything you touch comes out golden? Is your middle name Midas?

Nabumbo Promise rolled her eyes.

The logger-man frowned. Everything is dead, he said, leaning forward. Why is everything dead? Is that how you feel inside your head?

Earth to Ayosa, Mbiu called.

Ayosa blinked. The memory of her mama and the logger-man dissipated. She watched as Mbiu sprung forward in the clock tower. There was a coir rope hanging down from the rafters. Mbiu grabbed ahold of it and launched her body off the ground, swinging across the tower, from side to side.

Your mama and papa, did they do the dirty in here? Mbiu asked.

No. I mean, I don't know. I always went away when I thought my mama needed privacy. Didn't want to see *all* the things.

Mbiu climbed higher up the rope, up, up, until she was close to the rafters. She pulled herself onto a narrow ledge and tossed the rope at Ayosa. Join me! she said.

Ayosa took the rope. Climbing it was not as easy as Mbiu made it look, but slowly, clumsily, she too made it onto the ledge. She stepped beside Mbiu and squatted next to her.

What are you doing?

Making spit bombs, Mbiu said.

How does a person make a spit bomb?

Watch, Mbiu said. This is my spit bomb machine.

She had the tube of a biro pen in her hand. She chewed on a piece of paper and then she pushed it into the tube and waited for someone to walk in the street beneath the guava tree. She put the tube to her lips and blew, sending a wet bullet down to the bottom. It seemed to take a minute or so for the spit bomb to arrive. It made Ayosa's stomach turn. She was reminded of going over the edge of her fury. Reminded of that jagged cliff high above the clouds, and the enraged waters below, and how she had banged on those twisted gates of herself. How stingingly cold it had been. She shuddered.

What? Mbiu asked.

Nothing, Ayosa said.

Mbiu threw aside her spit bomb machine. She stood up straight. She leaned forward and grabbed ahold of the swinging rope.

Mbiu took out a cigarette lighter from her pocket. It clicked loudly as she tried to ignite it. Once, twice, thrice.

What are you doing? Ayosa asked.

The lighter ignited, the fire rushing from it, eager and lustful. Mbiu held the fire to the rope, and it started to burn, the fire twisting round the coir fibers like a lithe contortionist.

Ayosa's eyes widened. Mbiu, you're burning the rope?

The fire traveled up, and it traveled down too, smoldering, spitting. Soon, the rope's charred remains broke off from the rafter above, and the rope tumbled free, its ashes scattering everywhere.

Mbiu, how will we get back down from here, without the rope?

We won't be getting back down from here.

Ayosa's heart slammed madly inside her throat. This girl before her, this was no Mbiu. Mbiu was still out in the bushes peeing. Someone else, a wraith, had come out pretending to be *her*.

Fuck-toad! she said.

The wraith burst into clucking laughter. She sounded like a vexed turkey. She said, I am the great Besinaliakatumagongo. But they call me Bessie for short. And you, my dear, you are Ayosa Ataraxis Brown.

Ayosa winced. I'm not your dear.

Bessie snickered. Oh, you are my dear. You are *our* dear, all of us. She paused, studied Ayosa's face. She said, Many before me have tried and failed to bring you home to us. I come to you as our last hope. My beloveds, they are weeping. They are afraid. They are waiting with bated breaths for news that I've got you. Oh, how long our hearts have bled. But at last, we've got you. At *last*!

Bring me where? And who is waiting?

Bessie ignored the question. She spun around, her feet no longer on the ledge but in the air itself. She levitated. She said, You know, I used to be a girl too, once. Long ago. All of us were.

You mean you and the other wraiths?

Bessie rode the air, round and round, as though it were a plastic mule on a carousel. Me and the other *wraiths*, as you call us. Yes, we were once like you. Jaunty young things. Spry. Agile as monkeys. We laughed with our siblings and got loved on by our mamas. Learned to write words on slates. Got our buttocks thrashed at the mission schools. But we learned the names of the planets and the bones of the body. We were going to be doctors someday. Engineers. Economists. We were the future of this country, we were told. But the future never came, and we are stuck in something worse than yesterday.

What happened?

Bessie shrugged. Died. Real ghastly, too, how we died.

How did you die?

Bessie continued to ride the air. A gust of wind blew. Her dress puffed up. She said, Damned if I know. That's why we're stuck here, waiting.

And snatching bodies!

Oh, don't judge us too harshly for that. We did it only to make others *feel* what it was like for us. Doesn't make us feel better, but then, you know, we've got to while the time away somehow. Bessie let out a long sigh. She said, A decade or so ago, we tried to snatch the woman that runs the café.

Sindano told me all about that. She told me that it was you, Bessie. You're the one that tried to do it. Ten times. Came pretending to be a man that wanted to marry her.

Bessie laughed. Lord, she said, that woman, she was so desperate! Almost as desperate as *we* are.

Desperate to be loved. That's nothing like desperate to snatch a person's body. Don't you dare compare her to yourselves!

Bessie shook her head. Call it whatever you like, she said. Desperate is desperate. Just like angry is angry, and mean is mean. Let me tell you, that woman hungered the same as we did. No, no, that woman did not just hunger. She *lusted*. That's how I was able to fool her over and over again. She needed a man to touch her so bad.

Because why did you do it? She's a good person. You should have left her alone.

Because, like I said, we are desperate. *She* can see things. Thought if we got her, we could take her vision and use it. But in the end, we figured that it was hopeless.

You mean she wouldn't let you snatch her.

Yes, she was a difficult nut to crack.

Impossible, actually.

Yes, impossible. But it did not matter. We analyzed all I had learned from my time with her, and we saw that her vision isn't half as good as we need it to be. She can't *see* what happened to us. She can't help us get into the sky. That's why me and the others didn't pay her too much mind in the years after.

Ayosa contemplated jumping down. She looked over the ledge, and her breath caught in her throat. She would break her neck for sure, she thought.

Don't bother, Bessie said. And don't bother screaming either, else I will snatch your friend too. I know you don't want her to suffer.

Ayosa chewed her lip. Well, what do you *want*?

You, Ayosa Ataraxis Brown. I already told you.

Because why do you want me?

Because you're the only one that can help us. You know how we died.

How would I know how you died?

You were there. You saw it.

Ayosa shook her head. No, no, you've got me mistaken for someone else.

Bessie turned away. Me and the others, we got the best grades in the country for our primary exams. We got sent to secondary school together. We were in form two at St. Theresa of Avila Girls' Secondary. Traveling by bus to a netball game at our brother school. But something happened on that trip. Did we get kidnapped? Did the bus plunge into a valley? Did robbers attack and shoot us? Don't you remember?

Ayosa closed her eyes and racked her brain. No, she said. I'm sorry. I don't remember a thing.

Bessie stood before Ayosa. She pointed at her with her index finger. She said, Sometimes a thing comes over you. Takes over your body. Brings you bad memories.

The Jinamizi?

Don't know what you call it. All I know is it makes you remember lots of awful things. Things you would rather forget. That's where you need to look. The memory of us dying is stuck in there.

I can't *go* to the Jinamizi, it comes to me whenever it wants. Besides, the memories it brings me are not mine at all. They belong to other people. The Jinamizi only makes me look at them. Then it goes away, and it takes those memories back to wherever it stole them from.

Bessie burst out into her dreadful turkey laugh. She said, Ayosa Ataraxis Brown, for a sharp girl, you are alarmingly dense sometimes! Those memories that the Jinamizi brings you are yours all right. You were there, a wriggling thing. You repress those memories because they are awful. That's why they keep returning to you—they are *yours*. You were there, and you saw us die. And we saw *you* as we passed into the air. Now we are stuck here hovering. Waiting to be relinquished to the sky. But the sky won't open up and take us in unless we come knowing. The buzzards and the shoebills and the pelicans, they are standing guard, asking us, Who killed you, and, Did they use a mallet or a sickle to do it, and, What's the last thing you laughed about before you died? The sky won't open up and let us in if we don't come knowing these things, and there's no knowing these things unless we split your head open with an axe and take what you've got inside it. My apologies, Ayosa Ataraxis Brown, but you've got to die a real ghastly death too.

Ayosa leaned against the brick wall and rubbed her arms. For all it was worth, she felt glad. Afraid, yes, but glad too. Glad because Sindano was wrong. The wraiths did not intend to use her memories as a weapon to decimate the entire town. They only wished to save themselves. That was a great comfort to her.

Where's the axe? The one you've got to split my head with? I suppose we should get on with it. I need to pee soon, and you would save me the discomfort of holding it all in my bladder.

Bessie snorted. You've got some way about you, Ayosa Ataraxis Brown. Pity we've got to end you. But if it's any consolation, I won't open your head with an axe just yet. That's for later. Me and the others, we will do it together. We will go through your memories together. For now, I will just break your neck.

Bessie stopped spinning around. She inched closer and stared into Ayosa's face. It unnerved Ayosa to see a wraith leering at her with Mbiu's delightful face, all sticky with jaggery. With Mbiu's slender body. Mbiu's large eyes that set fire to everything they looked at. Mbiu's tiny flaring nose. Mbiu's pink lotus lips. All she wanted to do was throw herself at her, at Mbiu, her *dear* Mbiu. Hold her tight, and sob into her neck.

It won't hurt at all, Bessie said. I will snap your neck, but it will feel just like a little bee sting, that's all. I can sing to you too. There's a song my mama sang to me when I was a child. Hear:

> *Take me to the river*
> *Where the water is warm*
> *And the memories are soft*
> *And the dreams are caramel.*

Ayosa watched Bessie's hands slide up her body. They touched her arms and stroked slowly, higher and higher, up her elbows. Ayosa knew that the wraith's hands were stroking her because she saw them do that, but she felt none of their movement. Wisps of smoke, which was what Bessie was made of, felt like nothing at all as they brushed up her shoulders, and then as they curled round her neck.

> *Take me to the river*
> *Where the ghosts await*
> *Gnarly-backed and shrewd*
> *And vicious and good.*

Ayosa felt a tightening in her throat, the walls in them collapsing, the bones crushing, the esophagus burning and twisting in on itself like a chicken's innards on a charcoal grill. She closed her eyes and thought of a sky so blue it blinded anyone who looked at it. Blue as thrush eggs. She thought of the jolly annas fluttering about in the sycamores, laughing that diabolic laugh of theirs, that loathsome laugh of theirs. She thought of the Fatumas, their grief so mighty that it made the whole house shake. She thought of Mbiu, her *dear* Mbiu, up in a minaret, silhouetted against the merry blue sky, calling people to prayer. She thought of the river— thought of a mist rising up from it, hunching from the weight of all the fishes caught in its vapory frills, and shimmering from the noonday light. This mist did not drift heavenward like all other mists—it did not carry inside it the souls of drowned drunkards or the bitter desires of vengeful spirit children. It was a hollow mist, except for the fishes it carried inside itself. It was light enough and free enough to go wherever it pleased.

And, on the other side, where the mist was hurrying, scrambling to reach, there was a shady grove, and inside it, people waiting. Maxwell Truth, still sopping wet from his drowning in the well. And Dickson Were, standing on his head, relishing his newfound litheness after spending decades stuffed inside Mabel Brown's coffer. Even Hurulaini the puppy dog, leaping up and down, rolling on the ground, desecrating himself so that someone—anyone—would toss him a cow's tongue. And next to the puppy dog, two women stood, wearing white tunics and yellow turbans, beating goatskin drums, singing a dirge for her, for Ayosa Ataraxis Brown, who kept chickens and bees and loneliness and old memories, whom the river wanted with all its heart, who couldn't go too many days without listening to a poem. Saying,

> *Luwere-luwere-luwere.*
> *It is finished.*
> *Hand yourself back to your maker.*

They saw her, this eclectic group of beings waiting in the shady grove, and they waved at her, calling, Climb into the mist. The water inside it is a bridge. It will cross you over to us.

A scream pierced the damp air, loud as a passing train, and shrill, so shrill it jolted Ayosa out of her dying reveries. What was it? She opened her eyes. Blinked to focus them. Then she saw that Mbiu— that Bessie—was still hovering before her. But her mouth was open, and blood, or something like it, stained her teeth and splattered out in gummy strings. Bessie had a knife in her back—it had pierced right through her midsection, poked right through her belly. Her frock was soaked in the gummy blood.

Are you all right? a girl called from below.

Ayosa peered over the ledge. She saw Mbiu, the real Mbiu, her *dear* Mbiu, tiny as a ragdoll from that distance.

What happened? Ayosa rasped. Her throat hurt when she spoke.

Hold on a second, Mbiu said, and went away.

Ayosa heard the slam of car doors. Or was it the trunk of Mbiu's car opening and closing? Mbiu returned, Bwana Matambara perched on her shoulder, and a roll of manila rope in her hands. She placed the rope on the ground and prodded it, searching for the two ends of it. When she found them, she took one, and then she straightened.

Catch! Mbiu called.

It took a few tries for Ayosa to catch it.

Lucky for you, my mama always kept rope in her car. She always said, you never know when you might drive into a mudslide and need to be pulled out. I laughed at her for it. Said, Mama, why would you drive into a mudslide? Won't you *see* it coming, and swerve, take another fork in the road? But now I see that my mama wasn't speaking only about flooded streets. She meant, life comes at you fast sometimes. She meant, keep those eyes at the back of your head peeled.

Now Mbiu examined the musty brick wall. She pointed at a

rusted hook. She said, Think that's supposed to be for propping up string lights or megaphones when there is a party of some kind in here. Looks good for a knot, what do you reckon?

Ayosa touched it. I suppose.

Tie one, then.

Ayosa knelt down, rope in hand, and did as instructed. Mbiu tugged on the dangling end of the rope to test it. Looks good, she said. Now you've got to shimmy back down. But first, grab my knife from that wraith's back. It was my mama's. I threw it at the wraith. Killed it dead. There's no way some dead wraith's getting to keep my mama's knife.

Wait here, okay? Mbiu said, and then crossed the street. She leapt over a hedge, into a stranger's yard. She walked to the stranger's clothesline, unhooked a frock, tossed its pegs to the ground, and ran off with it. A lady came out, waving a broomstick, yelling, Mwizi! Mwizi! Mwizi!

Mbiu and Ayosa took off running, chased by a handful of little boys and one wayward goat. Over here! Mbiu called, and they leapt into the bramble, inside of which the river was waiting. It washed them away from the squawking boys and bleating goat and rocks snapping at their ankles. They emerged, ten miles away, coughing, sputtering, giggling.

Why did you do that?

What?

Steal the dress.

Mbiu wiped her face. Because the one I'm wearing is tattered and I need another one. Figured I should change into a new one.

You've got only one dress?

Uh-huh. I don't like to have more than one dress. Or more than one handkerchief. Or more than one cardigan. When one thing gets tattered, I get another thing. But if not, then I don't do a thing about it.

Because why?

Because, my dear, that's how it all starts! If you have more than one dress, then you are going to need a cupboard to put them inside. If you have a cupboard, then you are going to need a room to put that cupboard inside. If you have a room, then you are going to need a house to put that room inside. If you have a house, then you are going to need a town to put that house inside. Now, see, if you have none of those things, then you can wake up in the morning and wash your face and just say, Me, this place is so full of mud, I can't stand it anymore. And then you can go away just the way you are because everything you need is right there with you already.

Fair enough, Tetanus.

Mbiu grinned. She reached over for Ayosa's hand, and they walked with their palms clasped tight, and dung beetles and the broken wings of rain termites and even the stiff sprigs of burnt sage darted through the air after them, wanting desperately to land in their hair or on their shoulder blades or elbows. When their fingers ached to do bad things for no reason, they stopped beneath a banyan tree and sat on their fingers until the urge to blind people or to snip off the ears of babies with paper scissors passed. Then Mbiu took jaggery out of her pocket and broke it with her teeth, and they sucked on it and the sweetness made their eyes water.

Tetanus, I've been wondering something.

What, Apple-crust?

How did you manage to kill the wraith? I didn't know that wraiths could be killed.

I didn't know, either, Mbiu said. She reached into her pocket and showed Ayosa an amber glass bottle, full of sticky liquid. Firewater, she said.

What's firewater?

Jentrix the apothecary has a lightning catcher in the forest. It's a device that she made, bit like a rain gutter, and she drove it through a tall banyan tree and into the ground, where there is a septic tank of sorts. When lightning strikes this banyan tree, the lightning catcher gathers the fire inside it, and it stores it in the septic tank. Then Jentrix comes by and collects it. She mixes it with homemade whiskey and mulls it with star anise, cinnamon, and cardamom. Most potent poison in the land, she says. Earth Mother showed it to her in a dream, she says.

You stole it?

Jentrix gave it to me with her own two hands. Me and Temerity, we brought you over to her thinking you were dead-*dead*. And she took you away and nursed you to bring you back from the land down under. After, she gave me potato soup to eat and offered me a bottle of this. She said that I'm a lonely, throwaway girl, meaning that wraiths will try to snatch me for sure, and that if I was gone, no one would notice my absence for some months, maybe even for some years. That's what Jentrix said.

I would notice! I would notice *immediately*!

Mbiu shrugged. Doesn't matter.

It *does*! See, it means that there's someone else loving you, not just your cat and your horse and your pigeons and your dead mama. It means that someone would be left nursing a Mbiu-shaped hole if something happened to you. Someone would be completely devastated.

Mbiu snorted. Stop speaking mud. No one loves a throwaway girl. No one gets devastated over girls like me. In any case, Jentrix said if I got snatched, then I am to sprinkle some drops of this on the wraith and then PUFF! Wraith gone! That's what I did. Doused my mother's knife with it and threw it into the wraith's back. But you didn't see any of it on account of your eyes were closed. Dying, even though you promised me that you wouldn't ever die on me.

Ayosa looked down sorrowfully. Didn't do it on purpose.

You say that a lot!

Ayosa chewed on her lips. She could not decipher Mbiu's current mood. Her moroseness. Her relentless lack of cheer. Tetanus, what's the matter with you?

Nothing.

Please, Tetanus! You've got to tell me. Why are you all sour?

Because I'm sick of it! Being a throwaway girl. I want to mean something to someone. And don't you say I mean something to *you*! You have that big house up the hill. That mama who loves you in her own botched-up way. You think that you're a throwaway girl too, but you're not. You just play make-believe at it. Then darkness falls and you run off to your *real* life. The warm soup and cozy bed. The mama that gives you botched-up kisses.

I . . . I . . . Ayosa started, her eyes filling up. She wiped them with her wrist.

Hush, Ayosa Ataraxis Brown. What are you crying for? Because I won't coddle you? Because I won't speak soft and tender to you? But who speaks soft and tender to *me*? I've got the busboys and the preacher-men doing me the dirty, and no one ever says to me, Mbiu Dash, close your eyes now, both sets of eyes, the ones at the front of your head and the ones at the back of your head too. Mbiu Dash, you are safe here, lay down your knife, unhunch your shoulders, there's no more running to do. Mbiu Dash, I've got you, old girl, I've got *all* of you.

Mbiu put the amber bottle full of firewater in her pocket. I came out to say goodbye to you, she continued.

You are going somewhere?

Mombasa. I'm leaving tonight.

They walked in silence, and Ayosa imagined how things would be like for Mbiu in Mombasa. What Mbiu's little house would look like. The sour cream that she would slather on the windowpanes instead of covering them with drapes, and the brass doorknobs that would be shaped like fingers so that when Mbiu opened the door it felt like a person who loved her was squeezing her hand. In Mbiu's house, she would put fifteen sugars in her tea, and she would chew on pieces of reed or string if that's what her mouth felt like chewing, and she would spend her mornings telephoning strangers whose names she had found in the yellow pages. To say to the strangers, I bet your mouth ulcers are purple-red in color, and big as radishes. Or, There's always an asteroid coming, Mr. Katana Matu.

Ayosa stopped walking. Doubled over. Clutched at her ribs and spat foam into the earth. She turned the spit over with her big toe and saw that it was blue, like thrush eggs. I've got to go, she said.

Where do you got to go?

Don't know. Wait for me right here, Ayosa said, and ran off on her own.

She stole a prayer book from Father Jude Thaddeus's sacristy, and she knelt on the wet rocks by the river and said,

> *Mystical rose,*
> *Tower of David,*
> *Tower of ivory,*
> *House of gold.*

And she danced chakacha for all the girls sitting alone at kitchen tables, waiting for their mamas to return. Chakacha for the throwaway children roaming the streets alone. Chakacha for the gaunt, grief-stricken creatures stuck in attic rooms. Chakacha for the wraiths who had died real ghastly deaths. Chakacha for the boys who had drowned in wells and the boys who got folded away in oak coffers. Chakacha for the puppy dogs that desecrated themselves for tatters of deli meat.

She swam in the river and swallowed mouthfuls of muddy water and when leeches sucked on her insides, she threw her head back and said, Ha-ha-ha. She found vipers' nests and crushed the eggs with sticks. She lay in the sunflower fields and wasps stung her, and her ears rang, and her nose bled. She walked by the rocky shore of the river and collected objects—a bottle full of pink, sugar-coated pills, a Q-tip that was brown-red on one end, a crowbar, a catalog of different types of wax-print fabrics. She found a paring knife in the mud and chiseled out a grotto in the bark of a teak. She stuffed all the things that people had lost inside this grotto. She touched the objects and then she touched herself in the hair and on the elbow and wrist and knee.

She touched the gossamer things that hung above her head— those things that fell from the birds' throats as they sang their melodies, or which spiders spun to trap stone flies and tiger moths. She found rubber bands and paper lamps and butterfly wings and tortoise shells. She carried these things in the wet scoop of her frock, and she buried them in the grotto of lost things that she had chiseled out in the teak. And she looked up at the gentle aquamarine sky with the paper kites fluttering in its lace pockets and the buzzards and the shoebills and the pelicans soaring about, watching out for wraiths who died their real ghastly deaths. She looked away, and with arms folded beneath her rib cage, chin hung against her chest, she thought, I would rather be tied to the back of a tractor and be dragged across a sisal plantation than go back home to my mama. I would rather slit my tongue into pink ribbons using a box cutter. I would rather be mauled alive by a colony of bush rats. I would rather weld my eyes to the back of my skull.

Later, she found Mbiu leaning against a lamppost, waiting for her. Mbiu chewed on jaggery and stroked Bwana Matambara's shiny gray coat.

Where did you go? Mbiu asked.

I needed a moment.

Your stomach had the runs?

My soul did.

Happens sometimes. Mbiu shrugged. Then she took Ayosa by the elbow and edged her away from the footpath.

Where are we going?

Got to show you something. Look!

In the valley below them was a procession of wailing women. These women wore petticoats that they had darned with their fragrant fingers. They sobbed as they trudged, the creases on their foreheads stacked high, like folded laundry. They drank water from cups and chewed on strings of offal. They whispered to each other, Mwenda tezi na omo marejeo ni ngamani.

What's happening? Ayosa said. Is it a funeral?

No, nothing like that. They just come out of their commune every Sunday.

A commune? Like for nuns?

No, Apple-crust. That's a convent.

A convent is a type of commune.

Well, these women are not Dominican or Camel Light or Sisters of the Bloody Mary. They are just Sisters of the Broken Heart.

What's that mean?

Means someone hurt them so bad that they can't bear this world anymore. They moved away and now they live in the hills all by themselves. On Sundays they come out here. Weeping is their worship. Look at that one!

Which one?

Mbiu pointed at a woman who was whipping her bare back with a cat-o'-nine-tails. Mbiu and Ayosa squatted in the grass and watched in openmouthed wonderment.

The sun scorched. The Sisters of the Broken Heart crawled beneath the shade of a baobab tree. There, they sat the way their mothers had taught them, with their legs crossed tight so that the awful things inside them would not trickle down and sear the grass. The women covered their heads with their arms. They rocked back and forth. They kneaded their petticoats. They wrung their hands. They watched the sky darken with the promise of rain, but they did not gather themselves up to go home. The rain came and drenched them and they pulled each other close and wiped each other's tears with the lace of their camisoles.

The muezzin called from a distant minaret, his song a plaintive accompaniment to the women's simmering grief. Hail Mary full of grace, the women mumbled. It was the only prayer they knew how to say. Not the whole prayer, or even half. Just a shred of it. Yet it was wholesome, this shred, and it was a soothing balm to their scorched throats.

Mbiu scratched the roof of her mouth with her index finger. She said, You reckon that's a real cat-o'-nine, or it's only made of cardboard?

Ayosa did not respond, because she was no longer there beside Mbiu. She was running, running, closing the distance between herself and the Sisters of the Broken Heart. A yearning came over her, for stone walls with passionfruit vines crawling across them. For blisters in her palm, which she could pop with a pin, like bubble wrap. For flower petals—to bite them between her teeth, to feel sticky nectar and ant pincers and gossamer spiderwebs on her tongue. For her father the logger-man, who was born on an island called Lamu. Who had grown up swimming in the mangroves. Who came from a long line of dhow makers. Who ate a blood orange each morning. Who once found a peony in the pocket of a coat he bought in the open-air market. Who had left with just his milky-eyed dog and his crate of warm beer, swearing at the gnats and at her mama, saying, Lord knows, there's something *wrong* with you Brown girls.

Ayosa was there among the wailing women, but she was not all *there*. She was shuffling on her feet, her eyes glazed over, unseeing. She wove through the weeping women, feeling with her hands, until she found the one with the cat-o'-nine-tails, and she grabbed it, and took off her own frock, and began to whip herself. Cracked open her own back, like a coconut. And her Jinamizi came along with her and cracked her open too. It snapped her in two like a sugarcane twig. Ayosa held still. She gnashed her teeth. Bit her tongue bloody. And waited for the horrific memories to come.

It was two weeks after Rosette and Nabumbo Promise had buried their mother. Nabumbo Promise made five trips down to the timber yard to fetch building poles. After, she drove to the hardware shop and picked up two bags of cement, as well as a tub of masonry nails. She meant to work on her mother's old cow barn, to transform it into a studio. She meant to enclose the cow barn completely with wooden shutters, glass windows, a door. To separate it into three functional spaces—a front room where she would photograph people, a back room where she would balance all her books, and a darkroom where she would develop the photographs that she took. She also needed to dig a trench out into the sewer system, to fit the new studio with a WC and shower cubicle.

Nabumbo Promise brought out a measuring tape. She used a pencil to mark the poles in the spots she planned to drill into. This is what she was doing when a Peugeot 504 pulled up behind her. She straightened. Took off the carpenter's gloves that she wore to protect her hands from the splinters. She watched as four uniformed policemen jumped out of the Peugeot, AK-47s hanging at their sides. She thought that maybe there had been an incident down in the town. Sometimes chaotic things happened—cattle rustlers passed through, or neighbors knifed each other in the groin, or Mama Chibwire served moonshine that blinded fifteen people in the brew house.

Where is the doctor? the policeman said.

Ah, she thought. They wanted her mother. Probably there was an accident out in the highway. It surprised her—she had imagined that, through some sort of instinct, people would know not to come here seeking Lola Freedom anymore. She thought of all those years she had spent hating her mother for offering to everyone else an abundance of something she could never bring home to her daughters. Now she drew immense comfort from the fact that they too could not have any bit of her mother. Lola Freedom had taken everything with her when she had keeled inside herself.

Your mother, the first policeman said. Where is she?

A second policeman nudged the first one. She does not always speak. The apothecary said so.

Nabumbo Promise recoiled as realization hit her. The policemen were here because Jentrix had called them. Nabumbo Promise took a step back. Then she broke into a run. She needed to get to Rosette. To warn her. To protect her. Rosette with her musket in her shack by the river, she would shoot first and ask questions later. Maim or kill a policeman. And then what? Nabumbo Promise quickened her pace. Branches gouged at her face. Then a gunshot rang out.

The jolly annas fled from the trees, screeched into the skies. Jolly anna ha-ha-ha. Nabumbo Promise fell to the mushy ground. She patted herself down and was relieved to find that she had not been hit. She heard footsteps approaching, boots squelching wet leaves. Then she heard a thump, saw flashes of light, and after, nothing at all.

When she came to, Jentrix the apothecary was fussing over her. Forcing something down her throat. It tasted like quinine. She clamped her teeth, bit down hard, and Jentrix yelped. Jentrix said, Now, look, I didn't expect that they would do this to you. The Earth Mother knows my intentions were not to hurt you. Just wanted them to make a wellness check. Make sure your mother is all right.

Nabumbo Promise squinted to focus her eyes. She saw that she was sitting on the porch steps, next to her sister. She saw that her left wrist was cuffed to Rosette's right one. She saw that Rosette wore her habit and veil, her crucifix. Rosette stared glumly out into the distance, at a pair of black-billed turacos hopping on a tree stump.

Didn't think they would break your skull, Jentrix continued.

With her free hand, Nabumbo Promise touched the side of her head. She found a knot the size of a cannonball. She winced at the scathing pain that radiated where the butt of the gun had collided with her face. Jentrix had brought them a jug of milk, with a loaf of sweet bread. They did not touch it. They did not even look at it.

Jentrix said, Now, don't be prideful. Your mother lets me stay here on the understanding that I will watch out for you.

Jentrix switched on the transistor radio and set it up on the windowsill behind them. She made a broom out of twigs and went about sweeping dead foliage from the yard. She whistled as though no part of this were strange at all—the policemen poking through the property, searching for their mother's remains.

It was on the lunchtime news too, the unfolding story of the missing sky doctor and her dubious twin daughters. After reading out this news piece, the radioman added his own commentary. He said, *Let me just tell you, dear listener, twins are never up to any good!*

He said that he had twin children too. That lucky for him, he had known to separate them at birth. That he had given one twin to an Irish missionary to bring to Papua New Guinea with him, and had kept the other for himself. His twins were boys, which was a little better, but not by too much.

Nabumbo Promise wondered which of his twins the radioman had kept for himself. The original or the copy? And had the copy come out dirty when it was born? His body full of keloids, like a field of toadstools? She had never met another set of twins and did not know for certain if this was how it always happened. A clean twin, and a dirty one.

Jentrix stopped her sweeping. The shiny-eyed, snot-faced baby, Temerity, was crying in her Moses basket in the grass. Jentrix picked her up and pressed her to her bosom, whispering, Hush, child, before they come and break your skull too.

It was just like the time when their mother drove them to the orphanage that bore her own name, and the orphanage had no choice but to take them in. Or just like the time when their mother brought them to the convent whose library bore her name too, and the convent had no choice but to take them in. They figured that their mother had done something or other for the police commissioner. Given him money, or cut his wife open to take out a cluster of fibroids. In any case, the police commissioner owed their mother some sort of favor. They were riding in the backseat of the police car, on their way to a remand cell, when word came through the two-way radio that Nabumbo Promise Brown and Rosette Temperance Brown were to be kept under house arrest. The Peugeot stopped, turned around, and immediately returned them to their mother's house.

When she saw them, Jentrix the apothecary fell to her knees and kissed the ground. She praised the Earth Mother. Said, Remand cells are no place for sweet girls like you.

And they thought to themselves, This woman has truly lost her mind. What about us is *sweet*?

They remained cuffed to each other, with Rosette's right hand to Nabumbo's left one. They had an officer assigned to watch over them, meaning that he sat in a wicker chair and ate rice and green gram and read every single word in the newspaper. He let Temerity sit on his knees while Jentrix the apothecary scrubbed the windows or pruned the rosebushes.

Jentrix implored the officer on their behalf. She said, Let them walk about. They won't run off, and if they do, they couldn't possibly get very far.

The officer allowed it, as long as they did not get near the train tracks or wander beyond the valley.

Nabumbo Promise and Rosette began to spend most days out in the woods, walking through the trees, waving sticks before themselves to ward off mongooses and boomslangs. Sometimes the crickets sang in the daytime, and Rosette beat at the tall, stiff grass to quieten their shrill cries, and the crickets only grew more agitated, their song swelling, making their ears ring.

They started to collect objects during their walks. Things that people had lost. A ballpoint pen whose ink had dried out. A broken heel of someone's oxfords. A moldy crumpet. A handful of foreign change in an embroidered purse. A page torn from a hymnbook.

They walked with their hands shielding their eyes from the glare of the sun. Stinging nettles tugged at the corners of their frocks, making their shins bleed. They watched the flamingoes and pelicans and seagulls fly across the sky. They plucked handfuls of clovers, held them close to their eyes, searching in vain for the ones that might bring them luck.

Sometimes they brought the transistor radio with them, and they listened to the death news as they walked.

The radioman said:

> *The death is announced of Burudani Mzigo, who plastered people's walls for a living. Burudani Mzigo no longer wanted to live, so he refused to come out of bed and just lay there until the end. Burudani Mzigo is survived by his wife, Joanna, his mistress, Rehema, and his bicycle, Kitumbua.*

They watched as the crazy-birds flocked about a bat-eared fox, taunting it. The fox raised its tiny head and stuck its tail between its legs, offering a gentle yet profuse apology for trespassing. But the crazy-birds, they were unrelenting. They bore down on it, and each crazy-bird grabbed a part with its beak—large ear, wet stub of a nose, eyes like zambarau fruits, the squishy ombré tail. The crazy-birds tugged the fox apart. Jolly anna ha-ha-ha, the crazy-birds cackled.

The radioman said:

> *The death is announced of Father Moses Otieno Bosibori, who had a thing growing inside his skull. Father Moses is survived by the entire parish of Molo, which does not know how to have Mass without him.*

They found a tattered briefcase. A standing lamp. A stack of post-cards with loopy handwriting on them. A doll's head with ruddy cheeks and a rat-tail comb stuck in its hemp hair. A broken planter box. A plastic magpie staring at itself in a mirror. Someone's mud-encrusted boot. A glass bottle with a string of sunlight trapped inside it. A fanny pack with a crooked rubber finger in its pocket. A sign that read *Road Works Ahead*.

The radioman said:

> *The death is announced of Raymond Shabiki, who got fallen on by an oak tree. Raymond was a metal welder at Kariakoo Market. He is survived by his brothers Jackson Shabiki and Matthew Shabiki, as well as the entire Metal Welder Association of Kariakoo.*

In the evenings, when they returned from their walks, their stomachs growled indignantly, yet, obstinate as they were, they would not admit to such a thing as hunger. They spoke no word at all, not to anyone else, and especially not to each other. They ate only because Jentrix threatened to have them thrown in the jailhouse for being on a hunger strike. She served them red lentils with rice; bitter vegetables with ugali and kachumbari; bread with spicy beans and avocado slices. She served them sugared buttermilk, which she had made by curdling fresh milk with lemon, or which she had leftover in her jugs after churning butter. Every second day, they took a sponge bath. One girl would stand with her back turned away and her eyes pressed tight, still cuffed to her sister, while the other undressed, dipped a washcloth in water, and wiped herself down. They reeled from the humiliation of it, but Jentrix would hand them fresh towels, with clean frocks and underwear folded inside, and she would soothe them, saying, No need for that long face, the Earth Mother has got you—she's got your navel and your toenails, she's got your spleen and your liver too. She helped them dress, sucking her teeth when their clothes did not hang right because of the cuffs on their wrists.

They followed the investigation on the transistor radio. Learned that the police had found their mother's grave, that they had exhumed their mother's body and taken it to the forensic pathologist. Ah, baye! Jentrix murmured when she heard all this. She was combing Rosette's hair, spreading pomade on her scalp.

They thought that she would grab the shiny-eyed, snot-faced child and run off to whatever backwater village she had come from. Instead, Jentrix sobbed softly into her sleeve, and then she continued to do things for them—scared off the townschildren who came to pour pig's blood in the yard; baked unleavened bread because yeast bungled their bowels; brought them garden umbrellas, fly swatters, ice water, banana pudding, and a heap of Asterix and Obelix comics that she had found thrown on a street corner.

They accepted her kindness only because it was owed to them. Their mama used to say that there were no kind people in this world, only conniving ones, only people keeping score. And so they ate Jentrix's pea patties and her marrow cakes, and they drank her wild berry cordials, because it was nothing but the return of credit, a mortgage payment of sorts. Jentrix had squatted on their land, and this care that she offered them was but a small payment for the home their mother had given her.

Jentrix saw that they thought all this, and even though in a manner of speaking it was true that she owed them this kindness, it still hurt her to see how badly their mama had twisted them up inside. How she had made a mess of them, taught them to think of loving and caring only as currency, to think that they could accept it only if they could exchange it for value. Their mama had taught them that nothing about them was truly, deeply, genuinely lovable. What a pity, Jentrix murmured to herself, and any thoughts she had of returning to her own backwater village disappeared. I am needed right here, she said to herself. I ought to give some loving to these hapless girls, to this wretched town.

One afternoon, Jentrix wanted to cheer them up, and so she took them out to eat. It was at Bhavna's diner, and they ordered the lunch special, chicken biriani, which they ate while ignoring the wild whispers at the tables around them. They drank glasses of passion juice. They ate plum sorbets. They ate nut haluwa, relishing the aftertaste of ghee and rosewater on their tongues. Bhavna came to take their plates away, and Nabumbo Promise handed her a money note from her pocket. Bhavna eyed it, shook her head, and said that she could not touch their blood money. This riled Jentrix. She stood up, shoulders squared, saying, You've got some nerve to talk like this when their mama cured your child of cerebral meningitis for no pay at all!

No pay? Look, just *look*! Does this look like no pay at all? Lola

Freedom knew what she was doing. Knew that one day her daughters would come to collect. See, now I've got to *feed* them.

Jentrix left in a huff, returned to her shiny-eyed, snot-faced grand-baby, whom she had left bouncing on the policeman's knees. Nabumbo Promise and Rosette walked to the river, and they sat with a transistor radio between them. They learned on the news that the police had gone to their old orphanage to investigate their conduct there as young girls. That they heard of what terrors Nabumbo Promise and Rosette had been—it was not due to anything specific that the girls did there, rather, because of the dark air that clung to them, as though they were constantly on the verge of a great darkness, a great wickedness. The police learned that the girls had been kept there for six years as punish-ment for throwing their brother into a well. Afterward, the police re-turned to the manor and searched for that old well in the middle of the woods. When they found it, they climbed down, retrieved the young boy's bones, and took them to the coroner's office.

Now the radioman sucked his teeth.

Tch! Tch! Tch!

And he said, *What did I tell you, dear listener? I said, twins are never up to any good! See, the Brown girls! See how they started murdering when they were six years old. Six. Before they even knew to tell their own faces apart when they looked in the mirror!*

Mbiu gathered her up like a handful of scattered beads. She said, Apple-crust, come back to me.

And Ayosa roused. She saw that the Jinamizi was gone. She saw that she was no longer in the valley, no longer surrounded by the Sisters of the Broken Heart. She saw that two faces stared down at her. Sindano's one, dewy with sweat, and Mbiu's one, sticky with jaggery and crinkly with worry.

Where did you go? Mbiu said.

Never mind where she went, Sindano said, and propped Ayosa up against a chair. I think your blood sugar fell, Ayosa. You need a glazed doughnut.

Sindano trudged away. Ayosa and Mbiu stared at each other, their eyes pinched from the brassy light.

Listen . . . I . . . , Mbiu began, but then fell silent when Sindano returned with a tray of confectionaries.

Thank you, Sindano.

Oh, it's nothing. Eat up.

And they ate up. And after, Ayosa asked to use the telephone. She dialed the apothecary's number and listened to the singsong tone.

After a long moment, Jentrix answered. Hello?

Hello, madam. It's me, Ayosa Ataraxis Brown. I am calling to apologize for the way I left. You asked me to go to sleep, but I really wasn't feeling drowsy, so I followed Temerity to the flower fields, and then—

The throwaway girl fetched you. Temerity told me already. She came back here startled half to death. A horse tried to eat her. That's what Temerity said.

Ayosa curled her lips. Mbiu's not a throwaway girl.

Jentrix paused. Let out a long breath. Said, Listen, Miss Brown. You've got to return to my cottage.

Because why?

Because I've got your mama.

Why do you got my mama?

Nabumbo Promise fell into the land down under. I fished her out, but she's not looking too good. She keeps asking for you.

Ayosa was standing behind the café counter, where the telephone was stationed. She twirled its string round her finger. She looked at Mbiu seated at a table a few paces away, her head rested against her palm. The breeze slid in. It tinkled the brass bell. Mbiu crossed herself. Said, Wajamani-that-cow-is-dead. Mbiu, with a wedge of amethyst stone on her knee. Mbiu, with her forehead a little flattened from all the strangers' windowpanes that she had leaned against and stared into. Mbiu, whom the busboys and preacher-men did the dirty to.

Ayosa wanted to hold her. She wanted to cradle Mbiu's head, to caress her temples, to say, Mbiu Dash, lay down your knife on me. Unhunch your shoulders on me. Close your eyes on me. Weep your salty tears on me. Curl up and be a small sniffling suckling baby on me.

Laugh your head off on me. Kill your wraiths on me. Eat your jaggery on me. Mbiu Dash, I've got you, old girl, I've got *all* of you.

I'm not coming, she said to the apothecary. I'm never coming back. I will be a throwaway girl too.

You don't understand. I've never seen your mama like this. With one foot here and the other foot at the Earth Mother's doorstep. My dear child, I'm begging you to have some sympathy.

I *won't* have some sympathy, Ayosa said, and set the telephone down.

Mbiu looked up at her, blinking a few times because she had nodded off to sleep by accident, and was now a little disoriented. She said, If you're looking for Sindano, she went outside to gather the laundry.

I'm not, Ayosa said, slowly walking up to Mbiu.

You've got a look on your face, Apple-crust. Something feral.

I had an epiphany.

What epiphany?

About botched-up mamas, and their botched-up love. See, botched-up love isn't any kind of love at all.

You're speaking mud. Did you get bit by a stray mutt?

Take me with you to Mombasa. I'm never returning to her. To my mama. I've decided to be a throwaway girl too.

Mbiu stood up. She grabbed her cardigan from the back of the chair and stomped toward the door.

Where are you going, Tetanus?

I can't do this.

What?

Loving you, okay? I loved my mama, and she left me. She was my mama, and she still left me. You? What are you to me? Just some lonesome girl that I watched through the window. I can't love you—you'll leave me quicker than my mama did.

Mbiu pushed the door open and marched outside.

Ayosa ran after her. Mbiu, please. I hate my mama. I'm done with her. All the way *done*.

Mbiu shook her head and continued walking. That's the problem with you. You're not listening to a word I'm saying. This isn't about your mama. It's about *you*. I'm not a plaything you can pick up and toss off at will. If you want to come with me, you've got to be something more to me. Not just a girl I looked at through the window.

Ayosa stopped short. Thinking fast. Heart pounding in her ears, loud as a nipple gong. She had another epiphany, and laughed at its absurdity, and then gasped, saying to herself, But . . . what if? Ayosa looked over the café. At its tin eaves trembling pitifully in the breeze, its door hanging on one rusted hinge, its flea-chewed walls, its white tassels and hedgerow. She was searching for Sindano. She saw her form a little ways off, stuffing a handful of starched table linens into a woven basket.

Sindano? she called.

Sindano looked over her shoulder. Yes, my name?

I've got a question for you.

Well, ask away.

Do you know someone who can turn girls into sisters?

No, Sindano said, and stuffed the last of her table linens into her basket. She straightened, hoisted her basket onto her hip, and began for the café door.

Goodbye, Ayosa Ataraxis Brown, Mbiu said.

Ayosa watched as Mbiu crossed the street with her cat, Bwana Matambara, perched upon her right shoulder. Watched as Mbiu chewed on jaggery. Watched as she stopped to spit onto a patch of napier grass, and to swear at some decaying roadkill that was covered in blowflies.

Goodbye, Mbiu Dash, Ayosa said, her throat wriggling. She closed her eyes and swallowed something that felt like a hot branding iron.

Inside the café, the telephone was ringing. Sindano quickened her pace, bounded out of sight.

Hello? Ayosa heard her say. Hello? Yes, yes, hold on . . .

Sindano came back outside. She peered into the distance. She brought her fingers to her lips and let out a shrill whistle. She said, Hey! Throwaway girl! Come back right this instant!

Mbiu slowed her walking. She turned. *Me?*

Yes, you! Do you see another throwaway girl over here?

A minute ago Ayosa was talking about becoming a throwaway girl herself.

Stop being contrary and come back. There's a woman on the telephone. She wants to speak to you.

Tell her to go suck on a hemorrhoid.

Why is your mouth so full of vinegar?

Why is your mouth so full of mud?

Mbiu, I'm only trying to help you. You've got to come back. The woman on the telephone, she really needs to talk to you. She says it's urgent.

Mbiu crossed her arms over her chest. Is it a Jehovah's Witness? Because I've seen the Truth already.

Yeah? And what's that?

The Truth is that *this* is Armageddon. We are living in it. At least I've got my horse and my pigeons to keep me company in the lonesome nights. You, what have you got? You call me a throwaway girl, but don't you see that you're a throwaway woman yourself? That's the Truth too.

Sindano blinked a few times, stunned.

Goodbye, Sindano! Mbiu called.

Wait a minute . . . Wait! Wait! Please, *wait*! The woman on the telephone, she says her name is the Sister-Maker of Ramani. She says she will do it. Turn you and Ayosa into sisters. She will do it tonight.

Here it comes! Ayosa said.

The ground beneath their feet shook. A warning horn blared. They were near the railway crossing, where the cargo train always stopped for a few minutes before winding on into the next towns. It came slithering toward them like a giant millipede with jerking legs. The three lights of its locomotive shone in their eyes, blinding them for a moment. Then the wagons slid by. The writing on the wagons read: *Danger Petroleum*, or *Radioactive Material*, or *Grade II Scrap Metal*, or *Produce of Mursik Cereal Growers*. The last of the wagons pulled up to a stop a few paces ahead of them.

Mbiu and Bwana Matambara hopped in, then Mbiu held a hand out for Ayosa and helped her embark. They found a stable place to stand, and they pushed the window there as far as it would go, and then they leaned out, the waxy branches of camphor trees whipping their faces. The sky above them was crinkled, it jerked the birds, made them woozy with vertigo, so that some of them lost their balance and tumbled on the tracks and were immediately crushed. Mbiu and Ayosa tried to guess which of the birds would die this way. It was never the geese, which were much too hefty to be tossed about like that. It was never the jolly annas either, which were much too sly to ever be waylaid like that. It was the swallows and the honeyguides and the woodpeckers.

Hand in hand, Mbiu and Ayosa wobbled through gangway connectors and hopped over buckeye couplers, from wagon to wagon, until they found the last train car. They sat on the roof with their legs dangling, kicking at neem trees and at marabou storks and at rotten jackfruit as they rode past. Mbiu had grabbed a jar of marmalade from Mutheu Must Go Café. They took turns scooping it out onto their index fingers and sucking on it. Mbiu fed some to her cat, who, as always, was sitting on her shoulder, his tail curled around her neck.

Ayosa Ataraxis Brown?

Yes, my name?

You really want to be sisters with me?

I really do.

Because you hate your mama?

No.

Why then?

Because I never had a friend as true as you.

Mbiu let out a half laugh. The sun hitting her face made her eyes glow russet. Ayosa touched her there, where she glowed.

What are you thinking, Tetanus?

About my mama.

What about your mama?

About how I would get out of school and she would be there waiting by the gates, with a lollipop for me. She was a tooth doctor, which was funny, because she fed me all the sugar she could find. She said, Goat, you have my permission to ruin your teeth because I will fix them for you.

Goat?

That was the name she liked to call me. She said that when I was born, I got stuck inside her pelvis. The doctor pulled me out with forceps. Dented my head quite a bit, so I came out looking like a desert goat.

Ayosa laughed. Mbiu smiled, and then laughed too. Don't you dare call me Goat, though, she said.

We'll see about that, Ayosa said. Then she added, Tell me more about your mama.

Mbiu stared out into the distance. She said, My mama and me, we ate molasses and caramel toffees for lunch on most days. But on Sundays, we ate proper because the good Lord was watching. Spinach and brown rice and black beans. Mbiu paused. Fiddled with the wedge of amethyst stone jutting out of her knee. She said, She wasn't always appropriate, my mama. She often told me things I didn't want to hear. Like whom she was doing the dirty with. And which of the two Jeremiahs on our street was better at sticking a finger up a woman's secret place. And how once, when I was inside her belly, she tried everything she could to get rid of me—ate handfuls of parsley, and sticks of cinnamon, and entire papayas. She drank nutmeg and aloe and eucalyptus teas to coax her monthlies back to her. But nothing worked. I refused to come out, so she was stuck with me. That's why we were mama and daughter. When she told me all this, I said to her, Dottie Nyairo, you had best watch your mouth, you can't go speaking just fwa into your daughter's ears. And she said to me, Goat, Lord knows you're more than a daughter.

What were you, if more than a daughter?

A friend of her heart, that's what she said to me.

Ayosa put her arm around Mbiu. Drew her closer. Kissed her head at the place she thought her goat horn had once stuck out. Mbiu laid her head in the cranny of Ayosa's neck, and they rode like that, on the roof of the train, watching the swallows and the honeyguides and the woodpeckers, petting the cat. Just the two of them. Mbiu and Ayosa. Goat and Buttercup. Tetanus and Apple-crust. Ayosa's toes curled. She thought, I would do anything for this girl. I would scoop the river out of its rocky bed to find a hairpin that she dropped in the water. I would go rogue for her, if that's what she wants. Ayosa imagined it—the two of them in braids that went down to their ankles, with bamboo beads sewn into them. Wearing velvet gowns with necklines that plunged down to their navels, where tiny jewels gleamed. Wearing gold armlets, and below them, bangles piled from their wrists to their elbows. And they would accost strangers in alleyways. Raise the hems of their gowns, show gold-plated daggers in their jodhpur boots. Say, We mean no trouble, but we are not afraid to cause it. Now hand over your wallet.

The cargo train slithered into a new town, where the trees and shop windows and streetlamps were draped over with tea lights. The people in this town stood on their terraces, fanning themselves with banana leaves.

This is the town, Ayosa said.

They slid down from the roof of their wagon even before the train came to a complete stop. They walked away from the station, running their hot fingers over cobblestones and planter boxes and telephone wires. They climbed over strangers' roofs and ladders and shingles, climbed over festering cisterns and the wrinkled bonnets of abandoned taxicabs. Their tongues yearned for the stringy pulp of Kilifi mangoes and the buttery flesh of Maseno avocadoes. Their mouths wanted to say, Pilipili hoho. So they said, Pilipili hoho.

They found a chapati on a street bench. They tore it into three strips and each girl and the cat got a piece. Then they walked through the paved streets of the town. The houses were baby blue in color and stood on stilts. People lived in the rooms upstairs and grew golden carnations in the rooms downstairs.

The girls then saw a house standing off on its own, a lonely thing surrounded by a scraggly picket fence, overgrown with pepper grass and knotweed. It looked like the type of house where a shunned person lived. They walked up to the house. Took off their shoes at the picket fence because the soles of their feet wanted to feel the wild undergrowth. They stood at the window, their hands cupped over their faces. Inside the house was a woman. She wore a rayon apron-dress.

The woman raised her eyes and saw them there. She opened the door. Her face broke apart to reveal a wide, yellow grin. Well, hello there! she said. You must be Mbiu, and you must be Ayosa.

You're the Sister-Maker of Ramani?

Of course I am! Who else would I be?

How did you know?

Know what?

To telephone Sindano right at the instant that you telephoned her.

That's my question too, Ayosa said. We were at a crossroads. We were saying goodbye to each other.

Then you telephoned Sindano talking about how you could turn us into sisters . . . how did you *know*?

I always know when I'm needed, the Sister-Maker said, smiling mysteriously. She held the door open, let them into a room whose ceiling and walls and floor were covered with red, handwoven tapestries. There was a banana tree in the corner, tilted forward, buckling under the weight of its own lavish yield. In another corner was an instrument, large as the bough of a flame tree, covered with taut wire strings that seemed to be plucking themselves and playing a dejected tune.

What's that? Mbiu asked.

That's a valiha, the Sister-Maker said. I once turned three Malagasy women into sisters. They gave me this in gratitude.

Does it ever shut up?

It's a special valiha. It plays an unending song.

I bet that gives you an earache.

324

Oh no, it doesn't! After a hundred and fifty years of listening to it, I hardly notice its song anymore.

A hundred and fifty years? How old are you, Madam Sister-Maker?

Two hundred two next month.

You look twenty-eight!

What's a twenty-eight-year-old look like?

Plucky. A little young, but a little ripe around the edges.

The Sister-Maker laughed.

The oldest person I ever heard of was one oh six, Ayosa said. They wrote about her in the newspaper. Her name was Changu Malumbano. She was a Dawida woman from the Taita Hills. Her house was full of skulls, from all the relatives who had died before her. I didn't think it was possible to live until two oh two. Will they write about you in the newspaper too?

No, I don't think so.

Are there many of you? People who turned two oh two years old, I mean.

I know that there are many people like me in this world, but they won't come out and tell you about it.

Because why?

Because when you've lived this long, you learn that certain things don't matter. Why should I be proud of my age? It's *my* special gift. But having a special gift is nothing special. Others have special gifts too. You, for example, you *remember* things. Why should anyone write about that in the newspaper? Our gifts were freely given. We did nothing at all to deserve them. So why should we *gloat* about them in the newspaper? They are not achievements.

What's *my* gift? Mbiu asked.

You talk to animals, don't you?

I certainly do not. I'm not cuckoo!

I meant that in a manner of speaking. You have a way with horses and pigeons and cats, don't you?

That's true!

Sit! Sit! the Sister-Maker of Ramani said.

She gave them fermented millet porridge in clay mugs. She inserted a Sam Fan Thomas cassette into the radio, and they listened to "African Typic Collection." When the town bell knelled, they stood on the veranda and watched as the sunset parade wound its way down the street. They watched as clowns, acrobats, jugglers, dancing puppets, even minstrels and masqueraders, all drunken, staggered to someplace that no one knew. The Sister-Maker told them that the sunset parade passed by each evening. She told them that you could only watch it from a safe distance like this. That they were not real people. They were *creatures*.

Where do they come from? Mbiu asked.

A hole in the ground, the Sister-Maker said.

Like the hole that Alice fell into? Ayosa said. She was thinking of other creatures. The white rabbit with the pocket watch. The caterpillar with the hookah. The grinning Cheshire cat.

Not like that, the Sister-Maker said. These creatures in the sunset parade are sinister. They are what you see when you have night paralysis. They stand right there over you, leering. They want to take your breath away.

The parade disappeared from sight. Or rather, dissipated into the ragged hem of the sky. And there was nothing left of the creatures but a rubber snake squirming in the dirt, hissing. Darting its forked rubber tongue in and out of its mouth. Squeaking like a dog's toy. They watched it undulate into the underbrush.

Then they turned away from the street.

Mbiu said, Madam, why are you called the Sister-Maker of Ramani?

Because this town is called Ramani. I live here and I turn girls into sisters. If I'm ever in another town, then I'm called the Sister-Maker of Such-and-Such Town.

Ayosa took out her notebook and wrote that down. She said, How do you turn them into sisters?

Through a sister-making ceremony.

You turn them into *real* sisters?

I never heard of sisters that weren't real sisters.

The Sister-Maker brought out bowls of soup.

I cooked some soup for you, she said.

I'm not hungry.

Me neither.

Don't matter if you're hungry or not, you've got to eat to preserve your energy. We have a long journey ahead of us.

When the day eased into night, the sky hung low, and the stars danced before their eyes like fireflies. The Sister-Maker had given them white seamless gowns to wear, with laurels of knotweed and baby's breath for their heads. The Sister-Maker wore a gown like theirs and a mask of heavy gold that covered her entire face. The glow from the mask fell before them like a moonbeam, illuminating their path. They had been walking so long that it did not feel like the same country anymore.

Madam Sister-Maker, where are we? Ayosa asked.

Almost there, the Sister-Maker said. As though Almost There were another town on the map.

They had passed many towns on the way here. Towns full of just cows, spotted and long horned, staring serenely into the distance. Towns full of just beady-eyed throwaway children, weaving cornrows in the waist-high grass. Towns full of just mud huts with cups and loaves of bread and newspapers on the tables, but no one—no one at all—who lived there.

They walked in great silence. Ayosa's mind wandered off on its own. It brought her back to the Yonder Days. To Nabumbo Promise and Rosette hunched over the radio. Hearing that the police had visited their old convent—the Daughters of the Mystical Rose. During his broadcast, the radioman telephoned the mother superior. He asked her if she could speak to his listeners, if she could tell them what it was like to have the Brown girls there in her convent.

To be frank with you, the mother superior said, I always knew that no good could ever come of those Brown twins. One girl whored herself flagrantly. Thought that because we were cloistered nuns, we had no clue as to where those bruises on her neck came from. And the other girl, at least *she* tried. By God, she tried. Still, there is no way of shining light inside a black hole, is there? If you stand too close, it swallows you whole! But see, I pity those girls. Of course I hope that they will get their just deserts, and be hung for what they did to their kindly mother. At the same time, I hope that they will find peace and redemption first. That theirs will be a merciful death.

In those days, Jentrix the apothecary was having trouble keeping throngs away from their yard. It was not just children carrying buckets of pig's blood. All the townspeople who had time to spare came to look at the murderous twins with the wrists that were shackled together. The preacher-man came, placed his bowler hat in the grass, raised a worn Bible in the air, and said, Jehovah-Jire-open-my-eyes. And then he slid into a trance, spoke in tongues for hours on end.

The fish fryer set up her three stones in front of the house, and she lit a fire and fried tilapia and mbuta and mgongo wazi so no one would go hungry while watching the murderous girls. Sospeter Were brought out his PA system, so that everyone could listen to the news through a megaphone. Mama Chibwire brought out her barrels of brew so that no one would go thirsty either. They sat there and listened to the radioman and watched the shackled girls' faces.

On the three consecutive Sundays that the investigation continued, Father Jude Thaddeus moved the Mass from Our Lady of Lourdes and into the Brown yard. He did this because he knew that no one would be coming to the church—that they would all be here gawking at those murderous girls.

On those three Sundays, he gave sermons about repentance. About confessing to the faithful and the just Lord, about receiving His purity from all unrighteousness. One time, after the Mass, he went to Nabumbo Promise and Rosette, touched their shackle, and said to them, There is no sin too great for the Lord to forgive. I urge you to confess and return to His grace.

He stared directly at Nabumbo Promise as he said this. Rosette wore her convent's habit and veil, an act that seemed to speak favorably for her character, to exonerate her of any wrongdoing. In contrast, Nabumbo Promise had that sweetheart collar plunging between her breasts. She had those prominent clavicles at the base of her long, slender neck. She had those thin arms extending out of her butterfly sleeves. She looked like Jezebel. Like Delilah. Like Bathsheba. A filthy temptress, and worse, a *murderer*.

Nabumbo Promise stared over the priest's shoulder. Behind him, that woman, Dorcas Munyonyi, with the grapes hanging off her pillbox hat, spat angrily at the ground. She came over to them after the priest had departed. She slapped Nabumbo Promise across the face. Said, You harlot! Did you have to throw yourself at him like *that*?

And Jentrix came running out of the kitchen, with a frying pan in her hand. She waved it at Dorcas Munyonyi. She said, Lay a finger on my girls again and I will knock those buckteeth off your face!

Dorcas Munyonyi turned around to see if anyone had heard this. Everyone averted their eyes, pretended to be preoccupied with other things. Dorcas Munyonyi ran to the policeman who always kept guard in the corner of the yard. He was sitting in a ladderback chair, bouncing the shiny-eyed, snot-faced baby on his knees.

Officer! Dorcas Munyonyi cried. Officer! The apothecary threatened to murder me. She is in cahoots with the Brown girls. Don't just sit here, arrest her too.

The policeman took a sip of the sweet tea that Jentrix had made for him. He slurped on it slowly. He said, I saw what you did back there, Dorcas Munyonyi. If you don't shut your beak, I will arrest *you* for assault.

Humph! Dorcas Munyonyi cried. She left in a huff, running down the hill to catch up with her beloved priest.

Mbiu's words broke into Ayosa's memory.

How much further? she asked, stroking her cat's tail.

Not far at all, the Sister-Maker said.

The Sister-Maker fed them something that she called hosanna cake. It was a bread made of salt and flour and crushed clay and molasses, bound together with water, baked under a noontime sun. It parched their throats, and the Sister-Maker gave them lemongrass tea to drink. She carried all this in a burlap sack slung over her shoulder.

They walked on rocks as smooth and round as human skulls, stumbling over themselves and over each other. The Sister-Maker feared that they would break their chins, so she plucked tree branches and gave each girl a staff to balance herself with.

They were silent once more, and Ayosa's thoughts returned to the Yonder Days. To Nabumbo Promise and Rosette going on long walks to avoid the crowds clamoring in their yard. Fumbling through the thorn trees and wildflowers and barbed wire and stiff yellow grass, tearing their dresses or scratching their faces in the raspberry bushes and the jacaranda branches. They walked through the fields of gloriosa lilies and fever trees and lantanas. One time, they found the Sisters of the

Broken Heart, and they sat with the wailing women and ate strings of offal and rocked back and forth and kneaded their petticoats and whipped themselves raw with the cat-o'-nine-tails.

Later, they went to the edge of the property, to the apothecary's cottage, where Jentrix was soothing the baby to sleep. She gave them boiled yams to eat, and an orangeade to drink. She saw the welts in their arms where they had whipped themselves. She sat them at her kitchen table, which was so old that the grains of the wood warped and curled into themselves like millipedes. She had the baby tied to her back with a khanga, and she held their heads to her bosom, stroking their faces, saying, No one ought to feel this unloved inside. Before them was a stack of melamine plates, a soggy onion, a box of matches. Jentrix ransacked behind these things until she found a jar of honey, melted and separated in the heat. She fed them spoonfuls of the honey, and sang to them, and said, I don't know what really happened, but I am certain you never murdered your own mother.

The shiny-eyed, snot-faced baby was restless. Jentrix unstrapped her from her back and started to coo at her. Nabumbo Promise watched. She thought, If we don't get hung at the gallows, I ought to start over. Get a little girl of my own. A daughter. And I will give her all the loving I never got.

Ayosa chewed her lips. I should have never listened, she said to herself. I should have never gone to her when she begged.

In the darkness, Mbiu reached out for her hand and held it. She squeezed, as though saying, There there, my sweet potato, there there, my jam tart!

The Sister-Maker brought them to a place called Mount Try Me Not. They walked through the brush, past rodents and brutes and critters whose eyes gleamed with phosphorescence. They hopped over rumbling steam vents. They walked on to the caldera at the very top.

From there they could see the entire Rift Valley. It was dark but it did not matter. The valley was luminous with the heat and the light of old suns. The crests of far-off mountains rose, their craters swirled, and their flanks shook from the hooves of hidden beasts.

Mount Try Me Not was too much. Its beauty was not soft and gentle. Its beauty was savage and frenzied. It struck you in the gut with its radiance. Ayosa fought the urge to vomit.

They stopped walking. Then the Sister-Maker set down her burlap bag. She started to hum, so soft it could have been the gentle howl of the wind. Her voice gathered water from the bedrock beneath their feet, and the water gushed out to them, a murky stream that got entangled round their ankles.

The Sister-Maker hummed louder, and now a mist descended from the sky, over the juniper bushes and bristle grass and sunflowers. And the grebes and albatrosses chased after the mist, tangling in its vapory frills, pecking at, and gripping in their wet beaks, all the little fishes that the mist carried inside itself. Over the flame of the woods and the parasol trees it came. Casting iridescent light on the flower chafers and the blister beetles scuttling in the earth. It spun around them, a whirlwind full of objects that it had found along the way—pebbles and sodden feathers and twigs and tadpoles. Swans and rotting arrowroots and wristwatches and pen caps.

Ayosa marveled at the sight. She said, Madam Sister-Maker, are you Mami Watta?

The Sister-Maker said, I have some of that blood in me. That's why the water comes to me so easy. But worry not, I will not steal your soul.

Could your mama? Mbiu asked.

Who knows? Mamas don't say how many souls they stole.

Two, Mbiu said. That's how many my mama stole. I saw her do it.

The Sister-Maker touched Mbiu on the cheek. Child, that type of seeing can blind a person.

My mama was in-descent, Mbiu continued.

We all are, the Sister-Maker said.

The water was now up to their necks.

Madam Sister-Maker? Mbiu said.

Yes, my name?

Why do you wear a mask?

A mask? What do you think this is, a masquerade party? This is no *mask*, it's a talisman.

She told them how she had come from a long line of Sister-Makers, how each had caressed and charmed and blessed the talisman during her time, and then handed it down to her descendant. They, the Sister-Makers, were from nowhere and everywhere. They had started off somewhere in the Berber mountains, roamed across the Sahel, lived a few centuries in the Kordofan region, and then moved on eastward through the Horn.

So how come you are here?

I've been in Ramani Town for five years, waiting for you two to come to me.

Us? the girls shrieked, discomfited.

Yes, you. Mbiu Dash and Ayosa Ataraxis Brown.

How did you know we would come to you?

The talisman always knows where it's needed.

Where is it needed next? Ayosa asked.

Down south. In Mozambique, if you must know.

You have a passport?

The Sister-Maker burst into cackling laughter that ricocheted across the lake. She said, Let me tell you something! Us Sister-Makers have been walking this land since long before the white man drew any lines on it. It's ours—from the Maghreb down to the Cape Peninsula. Let them try and stop me with their borders. *Let* them.

She started to hum again, and they sank deeper into the lake, until their feet touched the boggy ground. Eels and liverworts brushed against their elbows. The Sister-Maker fell silent, but her song continued. There were a thousand voices chanting around them. They belonged to the Sister-Makers of yore, who had also worn the moon upon their faces, whose feet had also been unbound. They were the shape-shifters, the gold-smelters. And they were here in the turbid currents, unseen but not unheard.

The Sister-Maker held out her hands. She took Mbiu's, took Ayosa's, and held their fingertips to the talisman. She said, This language that we speak is far too unsophisticated for the things I mean to convey. She was silent for a long while, listening to the sultry song of the Sister-Makers of yore. She said, Your ears cannot hear my prayer. You must *hear* it with your souls. Yours that is pink like the inside of an eyelid. And yours that is blue like thrush eggs.

And right then, inside Ayosa, a key turned, its teeth and notches biting down, wriggling for a few seconds, before finding its cavity. Filling it. Locking it. The click from this locking reverberated, loud as an excavator's barreling. Ayosa held tight to her staff and to the Sister-Maker. She looked over at Mbiu and, when she saw the panic in her face, knew that she had felt that locking mechanism too.

Close your eyes, the Sister-Maker said.

And they closed their eyes.

Ayosa tumbled and fell. She leapt to her feet, so fast and so sudden that her head spun. She stumbled. Fell back down in a faint. There was darkness everywhere. And she was raging, crawling, kicking, tearing against this darkness, until it turned to light again. And she saw that she was no longer a girl—that she was only a speck of a thing now, squatting in the corner of a beetle-shaped room. She held her Self tight, felt her heart of hearts throb somewhere in her middle. The beetle-shaped room darted through the air, and she, encapsulated within it, toppled over.

Please-please-please-I-need-you, she heard someone call.

And then she was changing. It was not a neat transformation—something had shifted, and now she could not fit all of herself inside herself. Some of her spilled outside of her, so that now she was two selves. A girl, and a leftover girl. So she dismantled herself and tried again. This time, she came back together the right way.

She stood up straight. Where was she? Ah, she said. She was inside herself. She recognized the shape of her being. That shuddering softness of her throat. That parched ground of her feet. That emptiness where her Jinamizi sometimes nestled. She was alone. Shaking. Feeling that icy wind from the jagged cliff top. Hearing those spiteful waters below. Hearing the baleful cries of the sandpipers and sooty gulls. And the voice that said, Please-please-please-I-need-you.

She went out in search of that voice. Burrowing further within herself. Making Ayosa-shaped motifs. A girl crawling into her own body, standing in a corner of herself. And then, that same girl crawling into another cavity, standing there. Crawling further, crawling deeper, girl inside girl. Searching. Until she had a hundred girl-shaped rooms standing over her.

And she found her. Mbiu, her *dear* Mbiu! She threw her arms around her, crying with anguish and relief. Now there were two girls—two sisters—crouched together. Knees up. Heads tucked in the crannies of each other's necks. And at their feet was the cat Bwana Matambara. Honeybees fluttered about them. Chickens clucked. The jolly annas said, Jolly anna ha-ha-ha.

The Sister-Maker showed them the way that would bring them back home.

Follow the shrikes, she said, pointing at the salmon-colored morning sky.

It took them no time at all. Five steps away from Mount Try Me Not, and then the shrikes descended, as though turning on them, as though reaching to seize them and impale them on stalagmites. The two sisters squealed and yelped and flailed about, but the shrikes only showed them the way to the river.

Their river was here, sprawled out as far as the eye could see. It had traveled a great distance to find them. With its grebes and albatrosses wading in the roiling mud of the riverbank. With its papyrus reeds and the skeletons of sycamores and wattle trees wading in the water. With its lungfishes writhing between their toes. With its music of the larks, and its devil wind full of orange ladybirds, and its frenetic call of the jacanas.

Holding hands, they sank deep inside the river and it felt them in its currents and riptides. They opened their mouths and it rushed inside them and they swallowed the water that had held the fishes and that had held the words of old prayers and the bodies of hopeless drunkards. The river brought them away from the dried brush and the rodents and the brutes and the critters. Away from the steam vents and the caldera. Away from that pompous, nauseating beauty of the mountain.

Now they were home, which was to say, sitting in Mbiu's car, eating jaggery, throwing scraps of moldy bread at the cat and the pigeons in the backseat. They had decided to rest up for a few hours. At noontime, they would hitch up Magnolia, and they would begin their journey to Mombasa. To their new life together.

The radio was switched on, and they listened to an old recording of the poet. Ms. Temperance, she said:

> Hail Mary full of grit, the Lord's not with you on
> account he's too busy holding court with less
> dowdy girls, their White Diamond perfumes
> and netted hats and butterscotch skin
> entrapping him in their honeypots. Still, dear
> girl, you are blessed among them all. You're
> an old woman with milk teeth in her mouth.
> Old woman with tender youthful flesh. Old
> woman with breasts not yet budded. Old
> woman whose moon has yet to rise inside her.
> Griot basket-weaver soothsayer memory-keeper.
> Sweet Virgin whose wrists smell of saffron.
> Sweet Virgin haunted by sleepless spirits.
> Sweet Virgin with cobwebs hanging inside
> her eye holes. Our Lady of the stray limping
> maimed dirty beasts. Our Lady who is that
> stray limping maimed beast herself. Our Lady
> of pealing laughter. Our Lady of gawking
> wonder. Our Lady of aching solitude. Our
> Lady of impertinence and talking back and
> talking smack. Our Lady of catching fireflies
> in lard jars. Our Lady of lucid fever dreams
> and curled-up toes and singing folk songs that
> the wind whispered in her ear—glory, glory,
> Aminata of the creek returned to heaven on a
> termite wing.

Mbiu yawned. She leaned back in her seat and fell asleep, her breath drifting out candied and curdled, clouding up the window glass that she lay against. Ayosa switched off the radio. Bwana Matambara leapt into her lap. She stroked him, and then she closed her eyes too.

Ayosa tried hard to sleep. She counted sheep and goats and piglets. She sang herself a lullaby. She thought of the most boring story in the world, where a boy sat in a maize field by himself and did nothing at all. He just stared at the sun so long he went blind.

Ayosa could not sleep. She was full of butterflies and ants and wasps scurrying and hopping and darting about inside her belly. She felt like scurrying and hopping and darting about too. She felt like jumping onto the roof of her sister's car and proclaiming to the whole world, We are leaving. *Leaving.* To Mombasa. To our minaret.

They would set out in a few hours. Once they had both slept. Once they had stolen a couple of things that they needed. Some cuts of meat from the butcher, some cans of beans from the supermarket, some coins from the barbershop. They would follow the river as it roamed through the valleys and plains and hills, and it would bring them to the ocean.

To Mombasa. To their minaret.

Ayosa's breath caught in her chest. She could hardly believe that all of this was real and all of this was hers. She touched Mbiu on the foot, to make sure that she was really Mbiu and not a wraith. And to make sure that all of this was really true and not just a dream that was cruelly sweet.

Mbiu's foot was solid as could be.

The butterflies and ants and wasps in Ayosa's belly went hysterical with joy. She doubled over, laughing and crying and spitting all at once. She wiped snot off her cheek. And she laughed so hard she thought she'd broken her ribs.

Then, something unexpectedly grabbed at her joy and ripped it. And the laughter fell clean off her mouth, leaving it wide ajar and empty. She was filled with despair. And she searched herself, until she found it, that thing that ripped all her joy apart. The thing that brought the despair.

It was Jentrix the apothecary's words to her:

Your mama has been running from herself for so long. She falls inside herself too for the same reason. To forget, to be another person for a spell. Now, I'm asking you to bear all this in mind and be a little kinder, Ayosa Ataraxis Brown. Your mama doesn't mean to be mean. She's just so broken up. She's all rubble inside.

It was the fourth week that Nabumbo Promise and Rosette had been shackled to each other, but now the investigation had finally reached its conclusion. It was a Tuesday. The radioman said that there would be an announcement at half past three in the afternoon. He said, *Let's hope that those murderous girls will be put away forever.*

That day, everyone left work early. Shops closed. Buses stopped running. Schools sent children home to their parents.

The townspeople gargled salt water. They greased their elbows. They tucked a flower in their hair or pinned it on their lapel. They marched out to the Brown yard to listen to the verdict. The entire town gathered there. They brought umbrellas for shade against the harsh sun. They brought bananas to shove into the mouths of whining babies. They brought smelling salts to revive those who would tumble down in a faint. Even Father Jude Thaddeus came to listen, with

Dorcas Munyonyi following closely at his heels, hissing at any woman who dared raise her eyes to the priest's face.

Jentrix had gone to the open-air market and bought chiffon blouses and pleated skirts. She had laundered them and given them to Nabumbo Promise and Rosette to wear, so they would look half-decent for the occasion of the announcement. Nabumbo Promise and Rosette were barefoot, toes digging into the soft earth, hands folded in their laps.

Dorcas Munyonyi found the chiffon blouses obscene. She thought that they wore them purposefully, in order to seduce the priest. She curled her lips at them. She said to the person beside her, a fruit vendor, that she could not wait to attend their hanging.

When the clock struck half three, the townspeople held their breaths. The music on the radio stopped playing, and the policeman in charge of the investigation spoke. He said:

Lola Freedom Brown was the daughter of the conservationist Mabel Eudoxia Brown. She was beloved of many. She flew her little red airplane across the plains and escarpments of the Great Lakes region. Her fingers restored, her touch was healing. She had a full heart and steadfast faith. Her generosity was unmatched, and her kindness inspired us all.

Nabumbo Promise tipped her head to the side. The woman being described could not possibly be her mother. She looked over at Rosette, to see if she was equally befuddled by the eulogy. Rosette stared unflinchingly at the sky, avoiding Nabumbo Promise, avoiding everyone.

The investigator in chief continued: As you all know, we have been searching tirelessly for answers. What happened to our dear sky doctor? My team has left no stone unturned in its quest for the truth. I'm here today to present our findings. To establish whether there are sufficient grounds for the Brown girls to be tried for murder.

The crowd grumbled. They yelled at the PA system, We know all of this already! Just tell us when and where they are to be hung!

Jentrix the apothecary came out of the kitchen with bottles of cold soda. She handed one to each girl. The crowd grumbled about this too. They yelled, Pampering the murderers makes you a murderer too.

Jentrix waved her frying pan at them and said, Shut your dirty mouths before I shut them for you. She sat down next to Nabumbo Promise and Rosette, bouncing the shiny-eyed, snot-faced baby in her lap. Nabumbo Promise closed her eyes. Took herself away from that blistering yard.

Nabumbo went away to her red city. Sat next to her tree hollow. She had a wound. Once, a fight had broken out after a street fair. A stranger rammed a pike through her thigh. She had spent weeks pouring whiskey into the red hole to stop it from festering. Now she lifted her skirts. Saw that there were things living in the hole. Maggots. Squirming into and out of her flesh. She reached into her matted hair for the lighter she always kept in it. She reached into her waistband for her knife. She held the lighter to the knife's edge, until the blade glowed. Now she brought the knife to the wound, prepared to sear the flesh and the maggots.

The ground shook. There was loud yelling. Nabumbo Promise felt arms on her shoulders, shaking her. She opened her eyes. Saw Jentrix the apothecary jumping to her feet. She was laughing, throwing that shiny-eyed, snot-faced baby high into the air and catching it again. The townspeople were trudging off, singing, Solidarity forever, as though they were at a trade union protest.

What happened? Nabumbo Promise asked.

You're free to go! the policeman said, removing their shackle.

What happened? Nabumbo Promise repeated, for she had heard none of the broadcast on the radio.

Jentrix grinned at her. She said, The police can't do anything about the bones at the bottom of the well. They said that six-year-olds can't be held responsible for murder. As for your mama . . . Well, they listened to the cassette tape in her answering machine. They heard your frantic inquiries over the telephone. *Mother, where are you? Mother, we are worrying. Mother, this silence is cruel.* The police visited the meat processing plant where Rosette worked. They visited the landlord at the flat where you both lived. In the end, they constructed an accurate timeline of when you came home searching for your mother. Your time of return is not congruent with the degree of decomposition of your mother's remains. That's what they said. Lola Freedom was already dead when you found her, that's what they said. She'd been dead a long time already. The case is now closed.

Jentrix whooped. She laughed. She threw that shiny-eyed, snot-faced baby high into the air and caught it again.

Wordlessly, Rosette stood up. She beat dead grass off the hem of her skirt. She walked across the yard, in the opposite direction of the singing crowd. Past the weeping ferns and frangipanis. She took the dirt path that led to her little mud and thistle shack by the river.

Nabumbo Promise watched, openmouthed.

Rosette! she called. Rosette! Rosette Temperance Brown, come back to me!

But Rosette did not come back to her. Did not even turn her head sideways to give her a weary smile or raise her hand above her shoulder in crestfallen farewell. She kept walking, steadfast, and disappeared into the wattle trees.

Nabumbo Promise did not run after her. She knew, she just knew, that this was it for them. The end of the road. The threshold beyond which their sistership was no longer possible. They were no longer an entity. No longer the Brown girls. Nothing had happened, yet everything had.

Ayosa opened her eyes. She set the cat down and shoved the car door open. Mbiu startled awake. Apple-crust? Where are you going?

To Nabumbo Promise, Ayosa said. I've got to say goodbye to her.

23

She found Nabumbo Promise in one of the flower fields near the apothecary's cottage. The apothecary was with her. They stood watching as grass snakes jostled over mice. Then the apothecary walked to the fruit trees to tug at the deadwood in the branches, and Nabumbo Promise checked the raised beds where romaine lettuce grew. She had set traps for slugs inside the raised beds, cutting grapefruits in half and laying them facedown in the wet earth. Now she used her fingers to poke the slugs out, throwing them into a bucket of salt water.

Jentrix was the first to spot Ayosa. She lowered her shears. Nabumbo Promise, your girl is here to see you.

Nabumbo Promise straightened. She turned, and Ayosa almost screeched in horror. Her mama had changed completely. It seemed that all her youth had packed up and gone. Abandoned her. Her face was all withered, like a mushroom left out too long on a windowsill. Ayosa's heart flipped over. How harrowing had her mama's journey in the land down under been?

Ayosa felt some pangs rise up her throat. Of agony, of regret. And she clamped her teeth and bit them down. No, she thought. I won't feel sorry for *her*.

Her mama said nothing, did nothing, and so Jentrix ambled over and made chitchat to fill the silence. She pointed at shrubs and bushes, gave Ayosa tidbits about the flowers.

She said, I was just telling Nabumbo Promise that we ought to cut up the chrysanthemums. If not, they will grow too tall and fumble on their stems and fall over. The pyrethrum has been propagating in that spot too long, five years now. This week, Nabumbo and I will move it right over there. Did you know that you could squeeze the petals in your fingers and rub them on yourself to repel mosquitoes? Look there, see those regal beauties where the golden butterflies and the honeybees are flocking? Those are delphiniums. They usually prefer high ground and cooler air, but I threw myself down and begged them to stay with me, much like I did with you when you were a newborn, Ayosa. Just see them, they heard my prayer and stayed, and they are blooming. We better watch out, though, they're getting real comfortable now, and could turn invasive.

Ayosa nodded. She said, I'm sorry to interrupt you, madam apothecary, but I've got to speak to my mama.

Jentrix carried her shears over her shoulder and began toward the footpath.

Wait, Nabumbo Promise said. Jentrix, don't go. Please.

I'll be back in a moment. I will just fetch you both some cold Coca-Cola.

Jentrix left. Nabumbo Promise looked about her in panic. Searching for *what*? She found it, a long, girthy stick, and held it to her bosom, placing a barrier between herself and Ayosa.

You're afraid of me? Ayosa said.

No.

Looks like you are. Looks like you picked that stick up because you need protection.

No, Buttercup. I'm afraid of myself. I just need something to hold, else I might float away.

You're really thin too. Looks like you *will* float away.

Nabumbo Promise frowned. She said, Follow me. And yank up the hem of your frock, you've got slugs hanging on for dear life.

Where are we going? Ayosa asked.

Her mama said nothing. She led them away from the flower garden, led them to the river, using a path that tore through fields of sunflower and bristle grass. She stopped at the old pier that Jentrix had built with her own hands twenty years ago. Tethered to it was a dinghy. Nabumbo Promise worked at the rope, forehead twisted from the effort it took to unknot it.

Bought this a few days ago from a fisherman.

Because why?

Because I've got a lot of time on my hands these days. Got to fill it up with something.

Fishing?

Gardening too. I'm learning all sorts of things from Jentrix.

Nabumbo Promise slid into the dinghy. She grabbed its oar and held it in her lap. She gazed out at Ayosa.

Coming? she said.

Ayosa bit her lip, scratched her elbow. Where are we going? she repeated.

Are you afraid of *me*?

No, of course not, she said. She dropped her hands, let them hang at her sides. She *was* afraid—of the structural integrity of that dinghy, and of the oar sitting in Nabumbo Promise's lap, and of the little space they would have between them. She did not want to *touch* Nabumbo Promise.

We'll ride quick-quick and talk. You want to talk, don't you?

Uh-huh, Ayosa said. She waded into the water and climbed into the dinghy. She squeezed water off the hem of her gown. They sat knee to knee, which made Ayosa uncomfortable. When had this happened? When had she stopped craving Nabumbo Promise's skin and begun to be repulsed by it?

She shifted, tucked her legs closer to herself. Then she raised her head to watch the sky. The sun was high, but only just. Its heat was mild, which Ayosa was thankful for. She felt a bit run down after journeying all night with the Sister-Maker of Ramani.

Nabumbo Promise dug the oar into the water, and they bobbed gently, edging slowly away from the riverbank.

Buttercup?

Yes, Nabumbo?

You never came. I asked for you and you never came.

Now you know what that feels like, Ayosa thought. All those weeks and months and years that you left me on my own, I asked for you too and you never came.

Nabumbo Promise stabbed the water with the oar. Why didn't you come? she asked.

Ayosa lowered her head and stared into her hands. I'm here now, she said.

Something tells me you're not.

Ayosa folded her arms. She thought, But why does *she* get to do this? To act all wounded, when she's the one that did the wounding?

Nabumbo Promise Brown! someone called.

They both turned, saw a figure on the riverbank. It was Jentrix the apothecary. She was waving. Saying, Don't go too far out in that boat. I don't trust the fisherman that sold it to you. I bet it has holes in the hull somewhere.

Nabumbo Promise smiled, her eyes soft and moist. She said, Jentrix has been caring for me. She's the closest thing to a mother I ever had.

And me? Ayosa thought. What's the closest thing to a mother that I got to have? The Fatumas and their grief? The jolly annas and their cackling? The manor that Mabel Brown built and then filled with sadness and Waiting and the bones of fleeing boys? She thought, No, no, none of that. It's me. All those years, I raised myself. I wiped my own shit when I soiled myself. I hugged myself right back to sleep when I was afraid. I spoke kindly to myself if I had been dastardly, and I scolded myself harshly if I had been too wide-eyed. Everything I know, I taught myself. I was my own closest thing to a mother.

I should have never listened, she said.

To what?

To you. You said that you needed me. I remember it like it happened this very morning. Your bruised face, your palms crinkled by the green river water, your bloodied dress. My papa the logger-man held a knife to your throat, tearing it open. And, you, in turn, drove after him and ran him over. Broke his legs. And he crawled away with just his milky-eyed dog and his crate of warm beer. And he swore, Lord knows, there's something *wrong* with you Brown girls. And later, you came to the river and you felt me wriggling close by, and you said that you needed me. But you didn't need me. You only needed a thing to hold tight so you wouldn't float away. Like that stick in the flower garden, and like that oar in your lap, and like Jentrix waiting for you on the riverbank.

Nabumbo Promise lowered her head. She hunched forward, chin and nose to knee, and stayed like that, so long that Ayosa thought she had fallen asleep. Or worse, fallen into the land down under. Ayosa grew panicked. She looked about the dinghy. She was glad to see Jentrix still waiting on the riverbank. Watching.

Ayosa made a quick contingency plan, in case of emergency. She would tear off the white gown that the Sister-Maker had given her. Tie it on a stick. Wave it above her head. Jentrix would be sure to see the SOS sign. She would run off to fetch a nearby fisherman, and the fisherman would come and haul Nabumbo Promise out.

Ayosa was not afraid for herself, just for Nabumbo Promise. She, Ayosa, could swim. And if she could not swim—perhaps due to exhaustion from the long night with the Sister-Maker—she knew the river quite well. It had always been good to her. It would take her to the rocky shore, no problem.

Tell me, Nabumbo Promise said.

Ayosa let out a breath that she didn't know she had been holding. Tell you what? she said.

The thing you came here to tell me.

Ayosa looked down into her hands. Where to start? Should she just blurt it out? Say: I decided not to be your daughter anymore? I'm leaving this place today? You and I will likely never see each other again?

Nabumbo Promise raised herself. Sat straight, hugging the oar. You could start by telling me about your frock. It's all white. Like you were at a special occasion.

Ayosa said nothing. This riled up Nabumbo Promise, made her smash the water with the oar. The river splashed into the boat, splashed into their faces.

Damn it, Nabumbo Promise said, and dropped the oar into the dinghy. She wiped her raggedy face with her sleeve. She said, Least you can do is tell me the truth, Ayosa Ataraxis Brown.

Ayosa stood up abruptly. Made the dinghy wobble. Shut up, Nabumbo Promise, she said.

Nabumbo Promise stood up too. They were exactly the same

height now. Equal amounts of tall. When had it happened? They used to dream about this moment. How they would scream with delight when they discovered it. How this fact would change them forever, make them irrevocably tied to each other. No longer just mama and daughter, but an enduring pair. The Brown girls. And they would braid hemp and tinsel and strings of sunlight into each other's hair. Saying, Bas now, I've got you, dear girl. I've got your back and your shoulders. I've got your neck too and your hands and your feet. All of you fits on me, see?

Nabumbo Promise spoke, her voice low, almost a whisper. You're all grown now, huh? You're going to talk to me just anyhowly now, huh?

I don't want to fight, Ayosa said.

Well, what do you want? Nabumbo Promise said, poking Ayosa in the chest with both index fingers. Tell me, Buttercup. What do you want, strutting down here with a chip on your shoulder, acting all high and mighty? Acting all infallible? Well, who appointed you Pope, Ayosa Ataraxis Brown?

I'm sorry, Ayosa murmured. She took Nabumbo Promise's hands from her chest, where they were boring holes. She squeezed them. Brought them to her lips and kissed Nabumbo Promise's knuckles. And she said, I'm sorry, Nabumbo Promise Brown. I'm very sorry. Didn't mean to hurt you. Didn't mean any of that. I just . . . I just . . . Look, I've been on a journey.

Where?

Everywhere. I just . . . you see . . . I can't keep staying at home waiting and forgiving and hoping that you will come back to me and be my mama.

Softly, Nabumbo Promise said, I *am* your mama.

Ayosa shook her head. She had snot pooled over her top lip. She blew her nose into her robe. She said, I'm not sour at you, Mama. I was for a long time. I was just a few moments ago. But I'm not anymore. I . . . See, you don't have to be my mama anymore. I release you from those duties, Nabumbo Promise Brown. No need to trouble yourself any longer. See, it's *you* that needs looking after. It's *you* that needs caring for. You can't be anyone's mama if you're all rubble inside. You can't be anyone's mama if you need to be mothered yourself.

No, Nabumbo Promise said. I know what you're doing, Ayosa. And the answer is no. Categorically, no-no-no! I'm not letting you do it. I'm not letting you say goodbye to me.

You've got to.

Nabumbo Promise burst into silent tears. They bobbed in the water for a long while, further and further from the shore. Now Jentrix was tiny as a kitten on the sandy rocks. But someone else had joined her, and was waving and yelling too. Saying, Apple-crust, I'll be here when you get back. Me and Bwana Matambara and Magnolia and the pigeons. We will leave for Mombasa immediately.

Who's that?

Mbiu Dash. My sister.

Ayosa watched Nabumbo Promise, to see if she would wince or quiver or recoil. She did not. Instead, she shivered, even though she could not possibly have been cold. The sun was climbing higher and higher into the sky.

Come here, Nabumbo Promise said, and swept Ayosa into her arms. Nabumbo Promise leaned over, bent her head, so that their foreheads touched and their faces matched. Eye of the same eye. Nose of the same nose. Mouth of the same mouth. And above them, the jolly annas shrieked, Jolly anna ha-ha-ha. Following them closely, watching them sharply, as though they too knew what was happening. Knew that this was it for mama and daughter, a threshold beyond which they could no longer be an entity. They would never be the enduring pair. They would never be the Brown girls.

Is she good to you, your sister?

Yes, very good.

At least that's something, Nabumbo Promise said. She paused, and added, It's mighty nice to hold you again, Buttercup. Even if it be for the last time.

Nabumbo Promise kissed Ayosa behind the ear, stroked her on the temple. She said, This is so familiar, you know? This type of leaving. At least with you, I get to say a proper goodbye. My sister, she never gave me that chance. She just up and left.

You should call her, Ayosa said.

Nabumbo Promise laughed. Call her? Call the poet, Ms. Temperance? That's *your* sister?

Yes. That's my Rosette. My Rosette Temperance Brown. The first person I ever loved. The first person I ever truly lost. But Lord knows, my sister, she was gone long before she ever left me. She was gone that very day we walked out into the woods and drowned Maxwell Truth.

Nabumbo Promise slid her arms around Ayosa's waist. She held tight, so tight that Ayosa could not breathe. Ayosa made to pull away, but Nabumbo Promise only tightened her grip. She kissed Ayosa slowly on the forehead, and down the bridge of her nose, and on her Cupid's bow. Hush, she said, speaking sour-tasting words into Ayosa's lips. Hush, my darling, she said.

And now she pressed Ayosa's head to her bosom. Ayosa listened to the white noise inside Nabumbo's chest.

You hear that?

I don't hear a thing.

That's right. There's nothing in there. No birdsong in my rib cage. The birds inside my forest, they got ate up again.

Let go, Nabumbo Promise. I can't . . . breathe.

Nabumbo Promise did not let go. She tipped her head to the side, and she closed her eyes, her brows pinched, as though she were listening intently to something that the wind whispered in her ears. She started to hum, and then to sing her song out loud. To sing words that were not words but lumps of dirt and grit and earthworms.

And now, with Ayosa still pressed against her, Nabumbo Promise darted off the dinghy. They were falling, falling, the both of them, and the river was lapping at them, yearning to crawl into them, to enter them and fill them inside. It held them tight, and they yielded to it, and now all the things inside it—the pebbles and jetsam and fishes—clambered over them, tugging, wanting so bad for them to stay down there with them.

Ayosa had never been wanted with such earnestness. Her toes curled. Tadpoles and mosquito pupae and stork feathers gushed into her throat. The water heaved and spun her round and the twigs and seaweed inside it smacked at her back and thighs. She watched the things floating inside the water—a leather boot, a pair of horn-rimmed sunglasses, a messenger's satchel, a jar of marmalade, a lopsided candle. And then she saw Nabumbo Promise Brown, arms and legs outstretched, eyes and mouth open wide, and she was drifting away.

Nabumbo Promise Brown! Ayosa cried. Nabumbo Promise Brown!

She tried to move, but her body was bloated, at once light as a gnat and heavy as a grand piano. Then the darkness came, and the next thing she knew, she was being dragged out onto the rocky shore, and she was coughing and sputtering, and Mbiu knelt over her, saying, Wallahi, my sister, will it always be like this—you constantly trying to die, and me saving you?

ACKNOWLEDGMENTS

I am indebted to the proverbial village that supported me in countless profound ways. Thank you: MacDowell for the little cabin in the woods for that dreary winter. Art Omi for welcoming me so wholeheartedly to Ghent. Lizzy Attree and Ellah Allfrey for your care. Mavhu Hargrove and family for that time you took me in when I was in Maryland. Grace Ngugi and Tope Folarin for your generosity of heart and spirit. Lan Samantha Chang for seeing something in me. The Iowa Writers' Workshop for pushing me to grow as a writer. Eric Wohlstadter, Tameka Cage Conley, Lila Savage, and Ryan Tucker for being such dear, dependable companions and careful readers. My parents, Austin and Florah, and my entire family in Nairobi. Ndinda Kioko and Wanjiku Mwaurah for your undying love the last decade. Moritz Kasper, Ralf Kasper, and Jeanette Student in Munich for your kindness and encouragement. Clarissa Vierke and Katharina Fink for your support these last years in Bayreuth. Novuyo Rosa Tshuma for being an early reader and beloved friend. Alba Ziegler-Bailey for meeting me in London and accompanying me on this journey. Jacqueline Ko in the US, and Jessica Bullock in the UK, for seeing to it that the

ACKNOWLEDGMENTS

manuscript didn't end up forgotten in an attic, just like the Fatumas were. Robin and Aya for being the ones I go home to. And last but certainly not least, my editor, Sally Howe, for your patience, attentiveness, and good counsel, without which this novel could not have been possible. Asanteni sana!